# WHAT ROSIE DID NEXT

Nina Dufort

Hodder & Stoughton

First published in 2000 Hodder and Stoughton
A division of Hodder Headline

10 9 8 7 6 5 4 3 2 1

A CIP catalogue record for this book is available from the British Library.

ISBN 0 340 76717 0

Typeset by Palimpsest Book Production Limited,
Polmont, Stirlingshire
Printed and bound in Great Britain by
Mackays of Chatham, plc Chatham, Kent

Hodder and Stoughton
A division of Hodder Headline
338 Euston Road
London NW1 3BH

For Hamish

# Chapter One

# Chapter One

Ben Hooke died on Wednesday night, unmourned, except by his ferrets and his sister Janice. Concussed by the abruptness of her release, Rosie Hooke watched the undertakers leaving the Jack Cade Inn and cried, with relief. Unable to stomach the idea of her husband being buried alongside her own family in Middhaze parish churchyard, Rosie had arranged for him to be posted back to Hythe, from whence he came.

She floated incoherently for a short while, isolated in a fretting fog after the issuing of the death certificate, but during the spasmodic activity of the next day or two, her emotions see-sawed from unnecessary guilt to unseemly hilarity. Curiously, she also seemed to alternate between feeling very small then very large but by Saturday morning, although still physically unstable, she was calmer and less inclined to moping or inane giggling. Enveloped in a companionable silence, she paced up and down the inn's long, low-ceilinged front room, arms folded protectively across her chest.

The past was omnipresent but Rosie imagined herself insulated from the prods of its knobbly, judgmental finger. The walls were thick and the silence reassuringly opaque after the fury of the last few years. Even the March gales had faltered, unable to compete, as Ben had roared and blustered his way to a fatal heart attack, the escape of a favourite ferret having been the cause of his final whisky-sodden rage.

The sensation of peace did not last for long and overcome by fidgeting, she went behind the panelled bar and pushed bottles into line, shifted a pile of papers, set out ashtrays and straightened beer mats which were already straight.

The dog, Trash, yawned and whined a little by the fire. Rosie's commands no longer flowed straight from brain to fingers but clotted on their journey and a wine glass shrank back from her hand, shattering on the floor. Cursing, she swept up the shards and retreated to the kitchen to lean against the sink and stare blankly at the familiar bare branches of the mulberry tree and the mounds and hummocks of the untended vegetable garden.

Her hair needed washing, as did the windows and the kitchen floor. There were a lot of things she was noticing now that Ben was safely nailed down in the chapel of rest. It was time to take stock, before the funeral on Tuesday afternoon. She would open the bar again at twelve o'clock, since she could now make the decision, alone, to shut or to open, even if it were doubtful that there would be any customers.

'Widow,' she said, rolling the word round in her mouth with her tongue, like a cherrystone, ready to spit it out as far as possible. 'Widow. Widow's mite. Widow's weeds, Widow Twanky, widdershins, Widow Hooke ... Widow Hooke and only forty-one. Alone, except for Aylwin, poor darling. He's taking a long time with the shopping. Perhaps Elvira had some things to buy; she didn't bring much with her when she came. All her belongings in one suitcase and a bin-liner. Elvira the elf, not at all the sort I would have expected Aylwin to have as a girlfriend, but why should I have expected someone more substantial? It must be awkward for her, coming into the middle of all this, whatever "this" is. I must make her feel welcome.'

Rosie stood up straight and stretched her arms, an elbow joint letting out a pop of protest.

'One thing's certain – the Jack Cade's mine, at last.'

She swept her hands down with a slap on the draining board, not in triumphant ownership but as a gesture of partnership, rattling a couple of spoons and felling the washing-up liquid. Righting it, she paused, peered at the label and then extravagantly tossed it into the dustbin. She had not intended to buy a lemon-scented variety, since it meant rinsing the plates twice, scented plates being inimical to eggs and bacon. She turned back to the deep-set window where rain spattered the panes, softly at first but more insistently as the sky grew sallow and a thrush sang loudly at the top of the mulberry tree. Soon water cascaded from the broken guttering above, blotting out the view entirely and silencing the thrush.

A collection of photographs and postcards was stuck to the wall between window and dresser. They were so familiar that Rosie barely noticed their subjects any more but now she ran a fresh eye across them, as if to reassess their power to trigger other images.

'I am here and she isn't.' She reached out a small, practical hand and tooled a fingernail round the white border of one, pressing back a turned-up corner.

'I still exist and she does not, except in my head.' The photograph was spotted, smeared a little from being too close to the sink, the faded, misted blues predominating, reds receding. Sally, a tiny spot of tomato-coloured something disfiguring the self-consciously furious brow, an arm about her small sister Rosie, sitting in the mulberry tree perhaps thirty-five years ago, their unripe past faces peering wistfully through large dark leaves. The images answered her summons and flooded over, drowning out the present.


She was blinkered, field of vision firmly framed in navy blue. The triple bands of the enclosed landscape read, from top to bottom: a straight-edged navy cloud dangling an intrusive black spiral into the green and silver centre, where diamond points of light fluttered against a brilliant sky. The bottom band was a blurred sand dune smelling of Lux soap-flakes and above it humped a ridge of curling fibres which moved as she breathed, catching rainbows along their lengths. A red flash, a flare of facets above intruding pudgy fingers, attached to something large and green. She cried out, put her hands to either side and pulled, swimming up to the surface to confront a round pink face with dark brown eyes, inquisitive and friendly. It seemed familiar.

'Mum – MUM! Rosie's sat up by herself!' Sally, her wrist encircled by an elastic bracelet of red glass beads, dropped the mulberry leaf into the pram and ran to the house, pink legs flashing beneath pink gingham skirt, scattering chickens and disappearing out of the sunlight into the dark oblong that was the open back door. This was her first recognition of her sister Sally, from the pram parked beneath a rustling poplar tree in the garden of the Jack Cade Inn, as it was in the late 1950s, as it still was now. Then Rosie had had no titles for the things she saw, no names for the colours, but the pictures were still embedded in her brain.

She'd pushed aside the leaf abandoned on the fluffy cellular blanket and, a godlike baby surveying its own creation, looked out from beneath the hood of the pram at moving trees and clouds and saw that it was good. She waved her hands about as if conducting them, connecting with the loose strip of stuck-on braid dangling from the hood of the pram. She tugged, drawing it to her mouth, felt the hard corded edge against her soft lips and experimentally sucked it.

Rosie made a face at the remembered taste, but how could she have recalled its gummy flavour from such a distance? How could she see him now, Dad – John Craddock – in bright sunshine or in drizzle with a mac over his head, enthusiastically brandishing his little Kodak Instamatic? Every year he wheeled them up into the branches of the mulberry on Midsummer Day to record their birthdays, one before and one just after, till the day Sally, aged fifteen, declined to climb up on account of her long tie-dyed cotton skirt.

'*When* are we allowed to drop this, Dad?' she'd complained. 'We're not fairies! Can't we stand on the front step like normal people? I don't want muck all over my clothes.'

Rosie, ten, who had been wearing shorts and a Red Indian necklace of fake bear claws sent by a Canadian aunt, knees dirty and scabbed with bramble scratches, was hopelessly impressed by her sister's sophistication. She liked to climb trees but she also wished to be photographed in a more adult manner, with feet on the ground, but didn't say so.

Ritual had been important to their father and Rosie often had to plead with a recalcitrant Sally to engage in some sacred ceremonial of his own devising. Understanding how much it meant to him, she had desperately wished him not to be hurt by her sister's refusals. She had been a conciliatory child, had loathed the discord, and couldn't bear it either that it was always her beloved Sal who caused it.

On Christmas Eve, Rosie crashed about in the normally forbidden bar, strumming an imaginary guitar, hoping against hope that on Christmas morning there would be a real one at the foot of her bed, which, every year, there wasn't. She became quite hysterical with excitement as the tree was brought in and set in a bucket; fairy lights, squashy tangerines and gold string were provided each year to hang on the branches.

Sally, suddenly all cool and groovy in a little orange tweed skirt, which gradually receded upwards day by day as she secretly took up the hem night by night, obtusely desired coloured glass balls and flossy silver frost like everyone else.

Dad had made the star himself when he was a child, from silver foil stuck onto cardboard with flour paste, and no other star would do. It had sat in a box at the back of the cutlery drawer in the kitchen dresser, where he rediscovered it when he returned from the war in 1945. A sergeant with a mangled foot, he had survived both the chaos and horror of Dunkirk and the D-Day landings and was now hopeful of the peace. There had been few changes at the Jack Cade Inn since he joined up, and now he fought an interminable battle to retain it as he remembered it before the war when his parents had been the tenants.

Sally became impatient with their father's sentimental insistence on their both halting the decorating and waiting till he limped in, puffing and self-important, to top the tree with the shabby star. Ignoring Rosie's terror at such lese-majesty, Sally once hung up the star herself and nearly suffocated with giggles as she heard the uneven footsteps approaching.

'Well, after all, I can reach it now,' Sally said, blushing to see the smile disappear from Dad's wide red face and the spreading look of martyred disappointment. His expression was frequently martyred when dealing with Sally.

'I didn't know you really *wanted* to do it,' she said guiltily resentful. 'I just thought I'd save you the trouble.'

After the decorating but before the front door was unlocked with its giant's iron key and the customers burst in, it was expected that the girls would sit before the flickering, cavernous fireplace in the bar, each with a sherry glass of ginger wine. Dad sat on their left, smugly smiling, and their mother, Ruby, to the right. As always Ruby seemed a little strained at having to appear to be enjoying herself, and relieved to have evaded the threatening bunch of mistletoe which John always cut from the cooking apple tree and pinned to a beam in the bar. She was shy of the girls seeing her being fumblingly embraced by their father.

Dad would take a long draw on his Capstan Extra Strength cigarette and, after blowing a stupendous smoke ring, would toast first his three 'Christmas fairies' then the Jack-in-the-Green carved above the fireplace. Each and every year the same. Each separate clink of the glass was precious to traditionalist Rosie, abhorrent to the stripy-blonde, long-leggity Sally, who flaunted off to watch the television in their sitting-room, leaving Rosie alone with their parents. Liberated from the frustration of family rituals, Sally danced wildly to the Christmas Special Top of the Pops and brooded on means of escape from the countryside. They heard her skid on a rag rug and crash heavily into a table. They also heard her swear. Rosie was disconcerted by her absence but all the same, waited with bated breath for the miraculous launch of the first smoke ring, since it signalled the actual start of Christmas.

'Don't get in a stew, Johnnie,' said Ruby, hauling down the bottom edge of her burgundy-coloured cardigan as if it might escape and expose something unmentionable. She sat tight and upright. She had been, Rosie had come to realize, a good-looking but bleak woman, who'd remained unreconciled to having married beneath her; her father had been a well-to-do, chapel-going draper and haberdasher from Bellhurst. She never, ever, served in the bar and only laughed on social occasions.

'She's at a difficult age, Johnnie.'

'She's been at a difficult age since birth. She's Miss Sally Madhouse from Middhaze-in-the-Marsh. She's my loopy-lovely-o.' Dad threw back his head as if unconcerned and lips pursed into a perfect fat circle, blew the wobbling blue wreath of smoke up into the candle-lit room. It hung above their heads for only a second before being sucked down by the indraught beneath the carved bressummer beam above the fireplace.

It was hard to dismiss these pictures, each one so achingly well defined. Rosie's skin prickled with gooseflesh at the chilly phantoms. She lit the last of her duty-free cigarettes, blew her own smoke-ring and, sitting at the pitted oak table in the bar, hoping to distract herself, drew up a list of Things To Be Done, the first item of which was 'Ferrets'. It rained, on and on.


The Croswells' black BMW powered through the Romney Marsh monsoon, rolling a muddy, vole-drowning tsunami to either side which engulfed the verges of the narrow road. Vicky Croswell was annoyed by the diversion and her face, as innocently pink and white as an eighteenth-century portrait, glowered ahead through the murk. She had little patience and they were expected at one o'clock for lunch with her own Kadely clan in Winchelsea, intending afterwards to do some house-hunting in the area.

'If I pop in now,' Paddy Croswell explained soothingly, 'it will save one of the brewery staff from having to attend the funeral. It'll only take ten minutes or so – it's just one of those things I *have* to do, out of courtesy. The landlord died two days ago and the pub isn't far, only a mile or two out of our way.'

'I thought you said it was a free-house now? I'm sure they'll be far too busy weeping and wailing to notice if anyone turns up to offer a handkerchief.' It sounded callous but since her father's funeral, over which she still had recurring X-rated nightmares, Vicky self-protectively shied away from anything to do with death, its accoutrements or embarrassing relicts.

Paddy sighed and slowed, creeping along behind a tractor, the road ahead affording no hope of passing. He was the newly appointed Managing Director of Green & Croswell's, still freshly aware of his responsibilities and determined to do everything by the book. It was one of the few surviving regional family-run breweries that had not fallen victim to the massive buy-outs of the Big Five breweries in the 1960s and 70s. Green & Croswell's had an estate of two hundred pubs and a national reputation for good-quality ale, still brewed in the traditional manner. Their survival was due entirely to the stubbornness and integrity, in the face of massive financial temptation, of Paddy's father, George Croswell, now Chairman of the Board.

'Dad would have gone himself if he'd been back from his cruise. I should warn the widow that there are some problems with the freehold title.' He gestured hopefully at the weeping clouds, indicating a little patch of brightening yellow in the distance, and attempted jocularity to relieve his wife's increasing impatience.

'*Voilà!* A ray of sunshine! Don't look so glum, my plum! I

really will be very quick ... that is if I can find the sodding place. I'm sure it's the next turning on the right.' He stretched out his left hand to pat her on the knee, but she twitched it away irritably.

The tractor also turned right into the causewayed lane, forcing them to a crawl for another half-mile, keeping their distance to avoid the blinding khaki-coloured mud spraying up on the windscreen. An oasis of leafless poplars and willows sprouted in the low-lying, empty acres and between them could be seen the terracotta-tiled roofs of a group of old buildings.

'There it is! I've only visited it once or twice before with Dad, years ago, when I first joined the brewery. We went on a tour of all the pubs, to get my eye in. He was particularly fond of it.'

'What a dismal place! Where on earth does it get its customers from? It's miles from the last village.' Vicky leant forward and scowled into the gloom as Paddy, still following the tractor, turned cautiously into a pot-holed, gravelled space in front of the inn and stopped.

'My God!' He switched off the engine and gazed in dismay at the dilapidated range of buildings in front of them. 'It seems to have come down even further in the world than I remembered. Look at the state of it!' He reached behind him and pulled a jacket from the back seat.

'Why don't you stay in the car? I really will be quick and it's only half-past twelve. There's no reason for you to get your hair blown about.' He gave her a placatory grin then, rearranging his pleasant but slightly rabbity features into a suitably grave expression, paddled off after the combat-jacketed tractor driver into the pub. Paddy's rabbityness had been endearing enough to Vicky when he was twenty-five. Now, in his plumper forties, he had come to look more like his mother, Mary, a woman of great charisma and dubious mental stability, but Vicky had to admit the bunny resemblance had also increased. It was not caused so much by the round brown eyes and only very slightly protruding front teeth, more by his manner of moving, with sudden pauses to straighten up and look about him warily, as if suspecting a possible attack from behind.

Vicky yawned and stared petulantly after the men. She had had no intention of accompanying Paddy inside to visit the bereaved in any case. She disliked pubs in general and particularly country ones. If she thought of them at all, they appeared in her mind as those depicted in 1950s B-movies: squalid places stinking of Jeyes fluid, with metal tables and frosted glass, where men in flat caps 'quaffed' and discussed football; worse were the horrendous holes still inhabited, in her imagination only since most of them had long since been swept away, by bogus squadron-leaders and decorated with fly-spotted hunting prints and horse-brasses. Nastier still in her opinion were the faked 'rural' pubs in towns, where bits of brown leaf fell from the nicotine-smoked hopbines garlanding the ceiling, to float poisonously about in one's nice clean Margarita, should one have been fool enough to order such a thing in such a place.

Certainly they would now be unforgivably late for the luncheon party being held in honour of her great-aunt's eightieth birthday and although appearing self-confident to the point of insensitivity, Vicky still retained a justifiable terror of Aunt Jane's acerbic tongue. As she looked despondently at the gap-toothed, tile-hung frontage, the rain ceased and the ground steamed gently in the unexpected warmth of early-spring sunshine. She needed to stretch her legs and got out of the car, curious despite herself. The Jack Cade Inn was a handsome place in spite of its apparent dereliction. The central part of the building consisted of a large but straightforward Kent vernacular farmhouse with a massive central chimney and later extensions to the rear and each end. Knowing that Paddy's 'ten minutes' invariably stretched to half an hour, Vicky also collected a long cream raincoat from the back of the car to cover her pretty almond-green suit and, exchanging shoes for Wellingtons, set off to explore. She was quite shamelessly nosy.

'Garden' indicated a terse sign on a wooden gate, so she pushed it open and went in, and drew a deep breath. She stood on a bare, hen-scratched patch of ground in the centre of which stood an ancient mulberry tree, its wandering, sagging, still leafless branches supported on skewed crutches. It was surrounded by rotting wooden tables and benches and a clutter of rusting farm machinery. To the left, behind a wide encircling ditch and sagging pig-wire fence was an old apple orchard in which a ram browsed despondently. To the right lay a neglected vegetable patch and a huge pond, glittering malodorously in the sudden sunshine.

Something long, low and yellowish shot out from beneath a decaying mound of potato haulms and leek trimmings and raced across the yard with what looked remarkably like a pullet clutched between its jaws. It disappeared behind a range of wooden barrels. There were scattered hutches, duck-houses and chicken arks, brick outbuildings, a range of old stabling set about a Kentish ragstone cobbled courtyard. The land about looked secretive in spite of its openness, half pasture, half arable, and laced with drainage watercourses, channels, narrow dykes or wider 'sewers', criss-crossing the area like silver lines on graph paper, and, unknown to Vicky, all with names of their own: the White Kemp, Sheaty, Tore Petty and many others. Amongst these thrived, unknown to her, the area's other inhabitants: the swans, snipe, frogs, herons, ducks, moorhens, coots, eels . . . She was only interested in the inn itself.

'Good God! It's Cold Comfort Farm,' said Vicky, wandering around the building, sizing it up. Gradually her eyes began to gleam. She had completed various diploma courses in interior and garden design and architectural appreciation, and was unable to prevent herself from imagining the conversion of any place, however unlikely, into an inspirational family domain for themselves and their two children. Although they lived at present in an elegant Regency terraced house, in Tunbridge Wells where the brewery was based, it had no garden and was owned by the brewery and she had long felt the urge to be established in a proper country setting. Her interest had been aroused. She felt the pricking of need in her thumbs; the properties they'd previously visited had already been over-converted and modernised, in her estimation either unimaginatively or in grossly poor taste; Vicky wanted the satisfaction of doing it all herself, making a showpiece for her talents.

As she explored the yard behind the house, ducking beneath the washing line strung across what was quite clearly the private part of the so-called garden, brazenly peering into sheds and under bits of tarpaulin, she had the sensation that she was being watched and, glancing round, caught a glimpse of a face at a window. Too quickly for her to ascertain whether it was male or female, it dodged indignantly behind a drooping curtain.

Still aquiver with curiosity she marched round to the front again. A clump of daffodils had been broken by the recent gales and their brave egg-yolk yellow heads lay draggled in the mud. The inn sign swung crookedly on its iron brackets and the window frames were ill-fitting and peeling.

Momentarily forgetting the reason for their visit to the Jack Cade, she decided to go in and have a quick look around, so as to get a better idea of the size of the interior. In the long room, the solitary tractor driver sat over a pint at a table in the window, gazing dreamily into the distance. Half a tree smouldered on a Vesuvius of ash in the great fireplace, held within bounds by a giant semi-circle of iron, one half of the rim of a cart wheel. Smoke eddied about the room in throat-tickling wreaths. The walls were panelled, painted plain nicotine-cream and devoid of the accumulated brassy bric-à-brac and horse collars usually found in such places.

She could hear a woman's voice coming from behind a closed door to the left but could see no sign marked 'Ladies' and didn't fancy asking the meditating farmworker its whereabouts. Busily taking in the height of the ceilings and the state of the floorboards, Vicky stalked boldly towards the voice and through the door. Paddy's startled face and that of the landlord's widow stared up at her from a round, highly polished table where they sat with cups of coffee steaming before them. Paddy stood up and introduced his wife.

Vicky suddenly recalled with a shiver the doleful nature of the occasion and in a charmingly twig-brittle, off-hand tone assured Mrs Hooke how sorry they all were to hear of her husband's death. Then after a meaningful look at Paddy, she pleaded their lateness and asked if she might use the lavatory, hoping to be directed to some inner sanctum from where she might find the chance to explore a little further.

'It's outside ...' said Rosie Hooke, remaining seated at the table, hand still clutching the handle of her cup. She had an intense, brown-eyed, measuring look, which made Vicky momentarily uncomfortable – she was unused to being summed up and found it offensive.

'... to the right, just behind the woodpile. Take care, the seat's a bit rocky and the chain'll need a good tug.'

Rosie Hooke's voice suggested a larger person. It had depth and colour, was a little husky, and the accent was very softly Kent. Chin-length, stripy dark gold hair hung untidily about her oval face; the expression in the tired and shadowed nut-brown eyes turned to amusement. She wore a black sweater and reminded Vicky of some French actress she had seen in an old arty film on the television. What *was* it called? In black and white, with a woman and two men endlessly tinkling about the countryside on bicycles. What was her name? The same deep-lipped, flat mouth with slightly downturned corners ... Never mind. It would come to her. It was sufficient that Rosie Hooke looked uncommon and was very far removed from the tear-sodden old barmaid whom she had expected. Discomfited at being foiled, Vicky retreated outside – but she had been right, the proportions of the rooms were most promising.

Once bolted inside, contemplating with distaste the flaking whitewash and hammocked cobwebs of the lavatory, she heard a scurry of feet, furious barking outside and a thud of paws as a baying dog hurled itself heavily at the door. It sounded very fierce and Vicky bellowed for help. The dog renewed its barking and scrabbling. The chain came away in her hand as she jerked it and she cast it to the floor in the beginnings of panic, increased by the appearance of a spider the size of a Black Widow speeding past her feet. Her yells redoubled and again the dog gave tongue and scrabbled at the door as if she were a rat to be rooted out. There was no reply. Paddy should have finished his condoling by now. This was very silly. The minutes passed. Imagining a pit-bull at the very least, Vicky stood frozen, avoiding contact with the cobwebs. At last she heard Paddy calling her in the distance and renewed the wails.

'Paddy! *Paddy!* I'm stuck. The dog won't let me out!' It was horribly humiliating.

'All right, darling! I'll fetch Rosie to call it off.' Paddy didn't like dogs much. He added, in an attempt at reassurance, that it wasn't a *very* big dog.

More minutes passed, then she heard Rosie Hooke's calm voice and with relief, imagining the dog to be held securely, she unbolted the door and peered out. A flurry of damp, white, tail-waving collie-cross, its blue-white eyes rolling, threw itself against her and muddy paws were pressed lovingly and firmly against the front of the pale raincoat. Vicky smacked it off viciously.

'I'm sorry, Mrs Croswell,' said Rosie, at last getting hold of the dog's collar. She looked as if she was trying to prevent herself from laughing. 'Trash just loves women and we don't get too many coming out here. My nephew let him out because he thought he saw someone in the back yard. We have to be careful.' Rosie Hooke stood easily, her manner unapologetic, challenging even. Vicky suspected, with a wave of guilty antagonism, that the reasons for her invasion of the back garden had been misconstrued. Paddy hovered behind, irritatingly also unable to stop himself from grinning.

Vicky crisply thanked the woman for releasing her, adding over her shoulder as they walked to the car: 'By the way, I think you've got a ferret loose. It's had one of your chickens.' She felt she had retrieved some composure and her status as MD's wife and folded herself neatly back into the car to wait, slyly demure, whilst Paddy said his good byes. She remembered the name of the actress. Rosie's face, watching them contemplatively as they turned the car around, just slightly resembled that of Jeanne Moreau.

They drove in silence the last few miles to Winchelsea. As they locked the car Vicky fixed her husband with an iron stare.

'You will not, of course, regale everyone with a heavily embroidered version of my getting locked in the lav.' Her voice was acute with annoyance.

'Of course not, darling.'

'It's just that I don't trust you. You told *everyone* about Jenks's jockstrap and I've been teased about it ever since. It's hateful.'

Paddy stifled a smile at the memory of his wife, following sedately behind the headmaster when they'd visited their son's prospective public school. They had for some reason been taken through the empty but still strongly scented changing rooms after a recent rugby match and, on leaving, Vicky had inadvertently spiked a small garment of some sort on her heel and trailed it behind her as she strode after the headmaster. Annoyed by the mirth of the boys as she passed along the wide corridor, trying to scrape off the unknown attachment as she walked, she grew ever more prim. On discovering the nature of the offensively grubby, damp and stained article, she had become crimson with rage.

'For God's sake,' she had said in the hearing of the headmaster, standing on one leg and flapping her foot about in the air, 'get the bloody thing off my shoe!' The headmaster had rushed to her aid, banging his head smartly against Paddy's as he also bent down to help. A name writ large in indelible marker on the greying elastic waistband of the jockstrap pronounced it to be the property of a certain R.A. JENKS. Paddy's sense of humour being on the simple side, he had found the episode disproportionately farcical, more particularly because of her rage, and had recounted the story on every possible unsuitable occasion. He would not be able to restrain himself from using the dog incident either, but he'd try to be careful it wasn't within Vicky's earshot.

Lunch was a buffet affair and contrary to her expectations they managed to slide in unnoticed among the chattering relatives. They were able to pretend they had been there for a considerable while by the time the cumbersome Aunt Jane, a female Torquemada resplendent in tomato-coloured silk and leaning unnecessarily heavily on the arm of one of her great-nephews, reached them on her progress round the room. Paddy steeled himself to give her the required peck on each withered, orange-powdered cheek.

He glanced fondly at Vicky's alert profile offset by the neat little blonde bob, her peaches and cream complexion. Were real peaches ever that delicate a pink? The phrase was better suited to Aunt Jane, instantly bringing to mind the tinned Cling peach segments, bright orange in their gelatinous juice, and the swirl of sickly, off-white condensed milk which had been served on high days at school.

He was returned to the present by Aunt Jane's still youthful voice enquiring first about his gout, which ailment he had hoped to keep to himself, and secondly demanding to know the reason why it was taking them such a fiendishly long time to find a suitable house. Resentfully, he assured her the gout was in abeyance and wondered when he had last heard the word 'fiendishly' used. No one did any more, did they, except perhaps his father?

Vicky and Paddy survived the inquisition with a few tattered shreds of their private life left intact and a grudging respect for

Jane's ability to dominate. She had the knack of converting even the adult members of her family into children the moment they set foot over the threshold.

'Is it necessary for you to keep up with quite so many relations?' moaned Paddy after they had gone the rounds of fourteen favoured cousins. His stomach was rumbling and he was fed up with all the kissing. 'Surely cousinage should be dropped after the thrice-removed bit?'

They were at last summoned to help themselves to the feast laid out in the dark dining-room, where the heavy curtains were only drawn back in the afternoon after the sun had passed round and couldn't fade the dark mahogany of the dining table. Aunt Jane called on her daughters and grand-daughters each to bring a dish of something when she entertained the family and the selection was as eclectic as the monstrous Victorian silver épergne which held court in the centre of the table. Vicky imagined it to have been designed by a whole committee of bewhiskered Prince Alberts: bunches of grapes and disgusting *putti* dangled and lurked uncomfortably in hard gothic arches around the base while corinthian columns held aloft posy holders and little dishes, their cranberry glass liners filled with dusty sugared almonds left over from Christmas.

Vicky had recovered her good humour somewhere between the first glass of champagne and the seventh cousin. The faint odour of stale horse-radish sauce which hung about the dining room held uncomfortable memories of sometimes tearful and always tedious childhood visits, but she shook them off and set about the food, heaping a violently coloured salad on to a gold-rimmed plate and riffling through the crest-encrusted silver for a fork without bent prongs. It was all in need of a good polish.

'Tell me about the Jack Cade. Why has the brewery allowed it to fall into such a state?'

Paddy, who was by now thoroughly famished and serving himself to more poached salmon than was fair to the other lunchers, glanced up in surprise; such interest in anything to do with the brewery was unusual.

'Because it's no longer owned by us – Ben Hooke bought it, some say along with Rosie, in the early 80s.'

'Then what exactly were the problems you wanted to sort out with her?'

'She was the joint licensee. Ben Hooke took out a brewery loan to buy it, two in fact, tied to barrelage. She has to take a certain number of barrels of our beer each month. The repayment date of the loan is in about six months' time. Unless Ben's left enough money for her to pay it off by then, she'll either have to sell the pub, which would be difficult with the tie, or the property will revert to the brewery for the price agreed at the original sale, minus the unpaid proportion of the loan.'

'Is that likely?'

'Very, I would have thought. He was a rogue and a rascal from what I can gather. Apparently Rosie's been working outside the pub for the last few years, just to keep them afloat. Why the interest?'

Vicky looked sideways at him, cunningly, her lips still tightly pressed together. 'Didn't you see the possibilities there? That beautiful old house ... the huge garden ... the orchard? The fact that the sun came out as soon as we arrived? I could do such a wonderful job on it! And, of course, we'd get it quite cheap, wouldn't we, if we offered to buy it before it reverted to the brewery? She surely won't be able to sell it quickly on the open market with this barrelage tie or whatever it is – couldn't we get that bit revoked? And the market is rock-bottom at the moment.'

Paddy looked at her in astonishment, a forkful of salmon wavering hazardously in mid-air.

'Are you quite crazy, Vicky? Think of that beautiful old rectory we looked at last week – now *that* was closer to the mark, surely? And much nearer work for me. The Jack Cade needs thousands spending on it, and in any case the brewery would probably have first refusal if Rosie wanted to put it on the market!' The idea of living on the marsh didn't appeal to Paddy at all. 'It's also quite difficult to get planning permission to turn a public house into a private house, even if it doesn't do much business. Not in the interests of the community and all that.'

'But what community? Or does one miserable farmworker drinking a pint on a Saturday lunchtime constitute a community? It's exactly what I've been looking for. I *want* the Jack Cade. You must find out how many rooms there are and what land. There surely must have been a survey done before it was sold off?'

'Hello, Vicky. Is this a private discussion or can anyone join in?' Rushett Kadely, one of her multitude of younger cousins, stood behind her looking intrigued.

'Oh, hello, Rush,' said Vicky, coolly. In Aunt Jane's estimation, Rush had 'gone native'. His pale blond hair was cropped in convict mode and in defiance of the formality of the occasion he wore an astonishingly nasty pair of shiny, dark brown plastic, mock-croc jeans.

He worked as a record producer and split his spare time between a flat in Islington and a cottage on the coast near Fingle which, it was reported by cousins with whom he was on better terms than Vicky, was extraordinarily sparsely furnished inside: 'Just beds and a woodstove. Almost a hermitage.' He was several years younger than Vicky and she had made it her business to squash him thoroughly when they were children, disliking his candid blue eyes which masked, she was certain, a lack of suitable respect for her. He had mocked her attempts to contain him and she'd responded with vicious pinching whenever possible and had once locked him in a cellar when he was six, together with a dead Labrador that was awaiting burial. They'd suffered each other's company throughout long bellicose summer holidays at her uncle's East Sussex farm, their sniping at each other carrying on regardless of the presence of other distractions and more amenable cousins, making themselves almost sick with dislike.

Angelic of feature and with no apparent animosity, Rushett now flashed a seraphic smile at her.

'Did I hear you mention the Jack Cade?'

'You may have. It depends if you've actually washed out your ears since we last met.'

'Come on, Vicky. Don't be childish. I've just heard from your mother that you're house-hunting.' The Jack Cade was Rush's frequent weekend retreat, an ashram where he found perspective and attempted to darn the parts of his life that had become frayed whilst working in London. His hackles were up protectively, but not showing.

'Yes, we are. I'm fed up with small-town life. As far as towns go it's London or nothing for me, and as that isn't possible it must be the country.'

'What's your interest in the Jack Cade?' Rush looked at her speculatively. 'Hardly the sybaritic environment in which one would expect to find the wife of the MD of Green & Croswell.'

'Mind your own business, Rush.'

'Charming, sweet Vicky. I will indeed. Why is it I'm always surprised when you're rude?'


On the journey back to Tunbridge Wells Vicky proceeded to enumerate the many plus-points of acquiring the Jack Cade.

'It's the right size – it must have at least five bedrooms. It's set right back off the lane and has those beautiful willows and a huge walnut tree behind the stables. Those could be renovated, and there's one paddock at least. How much land does it have? The garden alone must be well over an acre ...'

'Actually I'm not sure that it isn't six acres in all, but I expect the field is rented out.'

'Never mind, I'm sure we could claw it back. There are no close neighbours – it's in splendid isolation. Not too far from the sea. You could even keep a boat at Rye – you know you've always longed for a boat! You didn't see the glorious catslide roof at the back. It looked in extremely good condition, no wavers in it at all.'

'I expect it was re-tiled after the great storm of '87 – most roofs in the area had to be then. That's the other thing – isn't it a bit bleak round there? It must be hellish in the winter.'

'Everywhere in England is hellish in the winter. Did you see the fireplace in the long bar? Its beautiful carved bressummer? That gorgeous breakfast table you were sitting at – I expect she would let some of the furniture go with the pub, wouldn't you? It's far too good to be used as a pub table. I wish I could have seen the kitchen . . .'

'That was her private sitting-room you barged into, and you interrupted us when I'd only just mentioned the reversion clause. It'll all have to be done by letter anyway, which is what I barely had time to warn her about. It's very difficult talking about that sort of thing so soon after her husband's death. And, for God's sake, stop jumping the gun! The place isn't on the market yet, may never be, and don't you think *I* might have a few words to say about where we're going to live?'

'Well? Go on, say them.' She looked at him, not altogether playfully aggressive, noticing the smidgen of watercress stuck to his long front teeth. 'What have you got against it?'

Paddy, negotiating a roundabout, remained silent for a moment. Champagne eventually made Vicky quarrelsome.

'Rosie was born there, in one of the bedrooms upstairs. She was telling me about it when you arrived. Her family have been the tenants since the end of the last century. She loves it.'

'Well, if she can't come up with the money, then she'll have to stop loving it. It's practically falling down. It needs to be properly looked after.'

'I thought you just said it wasn't in such a bad condition?'

Vicky's imagination had sped ahead. She was already super-vising the building of a walled vegetable garden, planting cordon pear trees, tending beehives in the orchard – no, not bees, skip the bees — making game pies and inviting envious London friends to stay. There was certainly room for a swimming pool ...

'It depends whose side you're on,' she said.

# Chapter Two

An icicle of worry jabbed into Rosie's stomach. She felt insecure in the sudden glare of sunshine and returned quickly to the inn with the whitely prancing, insouciant Trash. Vicky Croswell's abrupt appearance had jarred her. She was glad to see the back of them both. With considerable effort she lifted the great two-handed iron poker from beside the fireplace and levered the log a little to one side, letting it slip back with a puff of ash. Back at the bar, she poured half a glassful from a new barrel of Green & Croswell's dark honey-coloured Spring Bitter, holding it up to the light to check that it was settling properly, sniffing and sipping with the discrimination of a sommelier. It smelt hoppy, tasted both deeply malty and fresh, and was ready for the evening trade.

'You look like you need something a bit stronger, Rosie,' commented Sam Dicken from the table by the window, placidly handsome blue-chinned face smug beneath the idiotic red woolly hat. 'Not more bad news, I hope?' Since developing a premature bald patch he rarely removed the hat. The sight of Rosie gave him warm feelings and when in her presence he never took his eyes from her, which she found both touching and irritating. He would, she knew, do anything for her, as long as it didn't entail moving too fast, but she carefully avoided incurring any sort of debt. Did he wear the passion-killer woolly hat in bed with his wife? Poor Chloe. It must be like going to bed with a garden gnome; it was not surprising that they had only the one child. Rosie stifled a yawn.

'What do you mean, *more* bad news, Sam? You know as well as I do that Ben's departure is a blessing.'

She sounded flippant, wishing to avoid further solicitude; it was important to keep conversations with Sam tightly under control, to prevent him from reminiscing about how close he'd been to marrying her himself. To keep a faithful friend, she respected the convention that they would have married if it hadn't been for Ben, and for the sake of Sam's pride's had never actually disabused him of the fantasy.

'Where's the rest of the Eel and Sprocket lot?' she enquired, interested by their non-appearance; the fraternity normally met there on Saturday lunchtimes to discuss angling and anything remotely connected with mechanics. There had been an unfortunate tendency recently for a couple of them to get into a huddle and indulge in Website-witter for which, to Rosie's glee, they had been reprimanded for being boring by the remaining members.

'I expect they thought you'd have shut up shop, out of respect,' said Sam. 'So, it's the King's dead, long live the Queen?'

'We'll have to see. There are problems I didn't envisage. Ben knew how to keep me surprised.' She lifted her Irish-coffee voice light-heartedly but irritably twisted a shred of cellophane from a cigarette packet between her fingers, trying to turn it into a bow but merely achieving a granny knot.

'I suppose I should have cancelled the PPPB meeting this evening but it's too late now. And there's Geoff Pocket's folkies. They asked last Monday if they could come in for a session and I forgot to – didn't want to – put them off, although it seems a bit indecent to carry on as normal.'

Had people expected them to close up till after the funeral? They couldn't afford to shock anyone but nor could they afford to stay shut for more than the Thursday and Friday, either. It was a bit like show business in that respect, she supposed. Sam nodded understandingly.

'Well, if it's business as usual, I'll ring round. There's quite a few who'd be prepared to drink Ben's health, now he's lost it. We all knew how it was, for you.'

Rosie doubted that, and watched patiently as he felt in his pocket, pulling forth a handful of small change, grains of wheat and large galvanised staples embedded in fluff. She didn't care to be reminded of how unfortunately public Ben's behaviour had been. She kept imagining that he was going to walk through the door, cursing. She was still unused to feeling safe.

'I'll have a pickled egg in a packet of salt and vinegar crisps, to celebrate,' said Sam, at last detaching a coin from his hoard.

'Don't bankrupt yourself, will you?'

A sulphurous stink issued from the pickled-egg jar as she prized open the lid and dextrously fished out a brown-stained egg with a long-handled wooden spoon.

'Phooh! Time we got some fresh pickling done! Did I tell you that Aylwin's moved back in?' It was important to let Sam know she was not alone, otherwise he might haunt her with his expectations. 'It's great to have him sleeping in the house again,' she continued, 'and we've just been joined by his girlfriend, Elvira.' Aylwin had barely mentioned her before her arrival, had not at first told Rosie when she had moved into his little flat in Parden, but perhaps that was the way it should be. Extravagant praise of girlfriends by Aylwin had previously seemed to signify an uncertainty, as if he were testing his opinions against himself, aloud. Silence might signify a deeper, more confident pleasure, to be hidden away from others, not spoken of in case it vanished.

It was important to let Sam know she wasn't alone. Rosie brought the egg-and-crisps and her drink over to join him and, keeping the table between them, sank on to a chair, amicable but very still. She looked past Sam, through the rectangular leaded panes of the window to where a green woodpecker hunted beside the driveway, its powerful beak below the scarlet cap alert for woodlice beneath the wet dead leaves and grass.

It was Sam who'd nicknamed her sister Scatty Sal. Scatty Sal had unsorrowfully failed all her O levels and raced through jobs, boyfriends and bottles of vodka at such breakneck speed that their parents could not keep up with her. Dear Sal, too, who'd fought off persecutors bent on throwing Rosie's satchel from the window of the school train, who'd fielded water-bombs as the boys rioted up and down the carriages and had listened, with more patience than she had ever shown their father, to Rosie's confidences.

'It's my belief,' Dad had said, sitting worrying in his shirtsleeves at the kitchen table, 'that she's running two or three at once. We know about that Michael Godley from the Rhee garage. You wouldn't know who else figures, I wonder, Rosie-poso?'

She had denied all knowledge of Sally's doings. That afternoon she'd watched her sister walk calmly down the muddy lane, a hip-swinging vision in best blue jeans and silver platform boots, long stripy hair ironed straight and hanging down her back. She had seen her climb into a waiting car. Rosie was still a schoolgirl then, unexpectedly taking A levels. She had her own secrets, one of them being the much older Sam, and, like Sal, needed to keep certain things hidden from the relentless questioning of their intrusive mother. They both had to resort to extraordinary measures to avoid their doings becoming common knowledge, frequently causing confusion but never falling out with each other.

'Come and see,' Sally had said, giggling at the door of her bedroom that night, eyes alight with mischief. 'Come and see what *I've* got!' She sat on the bed and opened a flat box, rustling carelessly about in the tissue paper, flicking out a mint green silk bra and pants from Janet Reger. 'The bra's too small for me. It was a present. Would you like to have it?' At seventeen to Sally's twenty-three and only used to white cotton everything, Rosie was deeply thrilled and hid the illicit silk in a paper bag inside her wardrobe.

Sam had fast been found too predictable and plodding. He was too narrow a vessel for Rosie to pour herself into and having other potential boyfriends he didn't know about, she had been evasive. In fact she had evaded him entirely with a sudden departure for Dorset to stay with the equally abruptly married Sally.

Conscious of Sam still expecting conversation, Rosie tried to lever herself out of the past again. A death brought memories floating to the surface, dead goldfish turning belly up in the pond, silvery white and bloated. Now she also began to remember, in recurrent toothache twinges, that Ben had once laughed a lot and that she'd once imagined that she loved him.

Sam also was deep in the hitherto, all manner of panting beasts lumbering out of the jungle as he sat admiring Rosie's stillness. It had been that stillness which had initially attracted his attention all those years ago. So relaxed: long legs stretched out before her with ankles crossed, the reticent expression in her eyes, the light catching the sheen on the smooth-as-butter skin of her cheekbone and casting red glints in her hair. He'd taken his son to see *Aladdin* in Folkestone last January and been much struck by the legs of the principal boy. Rosie, although quite small, had such legs and he briefly tried to imagine them fishnetted in tights, the pale flesh trapped beneath the black diamond patterning.

Sam didn't suppose she had had much joy out of Ben the last four years or so, in the sexual sphere, and had often imagined himself . . . she *would* have married him, if it hadn't been for the tragic accident which had killed Sal and the swift defection from all responsibility of Sal's husband, Michael Godley. Rosie had brought Sal's six-month-old son, Aylwin, back to the marsh to bring up as her own. There had been gossip, of course, at the time, that the baby was Rosie's anyway, but he had ignored it, knowing it was malicious since she'd never allowed him more than a kiss on the cheek.

She would *surely* have married him, once she had the impediment of Aylwin, if he'd not been too sure of his ground this time and taken some years to ask. His grandad had warned him not to have anything to do with girls till he was thirty-seven and although he'd just about guessed that had been a joke, Sam hadn't seen any reason to hurry. Rosie's parents had died within six months of each other and between their demises the cursedly exciting Ben Hooke had swooped down out of nowhere like a buzzard on a chicken, plucking the shell-shocked girl from amongst the scattered flock. When Green & Croswell sold off the inn, Ben had acquired both it and Rosie. It had taken Sam a considerable while to convalesce from the suddenness of it. He had the farm, a son now and his devoted Chloe, but Rosie had been his first love. It was sad he had never once been able to tell her how he felt about her.

Rosie, divining by his soppy expression that his silence was to do with regrets she didn't share, stood up abruptly and returned to the bar. Catching up a cloth, she started to polish already sparkling glasses, slowly working her way around outside and inside, holding them to the light and squinting to make sure there were no smears.

'I don't like to poke about and find out what Elvira's background is, but she's very well-spoken.' She turned and reached up to replace the glasses on the shelf behind her and again irritably felt his eyes watching the stretch of her jersey across her back. 'I've got her a part-time job starting next week. Nest has agreed to split my work at the Nursery Garden between us for the time being.'

'Aylwin's got a job, now he's got his degree?'

'Oh, yes. He was sensible enough to grab the first one that came along. I'm sure I told you? He's worked for a printer in Parden since last October. It'll be cheaper for them to live here and I'm very glad to have their company. Aylwin's taken two days off work, and a day for the funeral of course, so he can help me.'

'How's he taking it?'

'Shocked, even if he and Ben had no time for each other.' She did not add that on Thursday night, when he'd arrived home, twenty-two-year-old Aylwin had put his arms around her and asked, in a child's whisper, why was it he felt so frightened now, although he'd wished Ben dead so often? It was alarming actually to hear the words, knowing she'd frequently wished the same and difficult for her when he flitted backwards and forwards from child to adult to child. She'd soothed him as a child, stroked his cheek and addressed him as an adult, admitting that she also was ashamed of having wished Ben dead on occasions.

'Hmph! Beats me why one needs a degree to work at a printer's. It's all computerised, isn't it? You just have to press buttons.' Sam stood up reluctantly, showering crisp crumbs on the floor and shrugging his hefty shoulders. 'Well, I'd best get back to work. I was going to do some spraying this afternoon, but it looks like it's coming on to rain again and the ground's still too waterlogged to put the tractor on it. I'll pass the word round that you're open over the weekend. People like it when you've got musicians in, even if it is only folkies. Keep your chin up, Rosie.'

'I will. It's so high it's practically nudging my nose. 'Bye, Sam.'

Talking to him was agonisingly dull. After he'd gone, she yawned again and, glancing at the clock, thankfully locked the heavy oak door. Apart from three bird-watchers who'd been waiting damply outside at twelve o'clock when she'd opened up and who had left on foot just before the Croswells had arrived, the ever-watchful and gently ridiculous Sam had been her only punter. Two-thirty. It was unlikely there'd be any more customers that afternoon.

Surprisingly to Rosie, Elvira was in the garden, bravely trying to tickle out the glutted ferret from behind the disused cider barrels with a piece of raw pork tied to a stick. Pleased to see the girl doing something useful, Rosie picked her way carefully through the mud to join her and offer advice on its recapture.

'We've got nets somewhere. Can't we drop them over it and roll it up somehow?'

'Not enough room,' said Elvira. 'We'll have to move the barrels.'

'I've put a notice up in the bar, to see if anyone wants to give the little thugs a home. Troublesome things, except with Ben. I think they loved him – he certainly spent enough time with them. I'm glad something loved him.' She'd said too much and became a little shy of Elvira, covering the shyness with abruptness. 'If we can't catch this one – is it a Jill or a Jack? – I'll have to shoot it.'

'Mrs Hooke, you can't!'

Rosie was instantly aware she had made herself sound unnaturally harsh – she certainly could not have brought herself to do such a thing – as Elvira's clear grey-green eyes were horror-struck, the thick dark lashes fluttering in distress.

'You don't need to call me Mrs Hooke. Rosie will do, the same as everyone else. If we can't catch it, I can't take it to the vet to have it put down, can I? We can't have it rampaging about eating everything that moves, though. We'll just have to shift the barrels. Where's Aylwin? Did he get the shopping from the cash and carry? We're nearly out of crisps.' She kicked the wedges from beneath the first barrel and rolled it away.

'After this, I'm going to turn out the desk. I'll need Aylwin's help. I'd like it if you came too, now you're living with us?' There had been no time to fence about. Her acceptance of the girlfriend had been virtually instant. 'There's something important Ben never let on about, you see, and I need to go through all the bills and papers. I expect Aylwin has explained the situation? Ben wouldn't let me touch any paperwork and I need to know what's what. We *all* need to know where we stand.'

Being full of water to keep the wooden staves from drying out and opening up, the barrel was a leaden weight. It gathered momentum on the slight slope and, before Rosie could stop it, rolled straight for the pond, narrowly missing a grey gander snoozing by the edge and crashing into the dark water with a monumental splash.

'Bugger!'

'Look, I'll push and you stop the next one from going the same way.' Elvira flicked dark strands of hair out of her eyes and leaning her slight body against the second barrel, heaved. Her ears, Rosie noticed, were delicately pointed and hung with little silver oak-leaves, and she wondered again about the girl's provenance.

'Quick!' exclaimed Elvira. 'Use that old post as a brake. I can reach him now. Would you believe he's still curled up asleep? I need something to roll him up in. I don't want to get nipped.'

'Take your sweater off. That'll do. He's really rather sweet asleep, isn't he?'

Triumphant, they firmly swaddled the bulging, comatose ferret in the fleecy sweater and after gingerly replacing it in its hutch, went indoors together, Rosie much pleased by the practicality of her new lodger.

She picked up Ben's sacred bunch of keys from the kitchen table and calling up the stairs for Aylwin, set off for the back parlour with Elvira a little timidly in tow.

Above the desk in a gilt frame was an oleograph of Rosie's maternal great-great-great-grandfather, John Poydevin, white-whiskered and podgy, well-upholstered in black and sporting his Waterloo medal on his breast. Ben had bought the desk for ten pounds from the auction of old Colonel Wrigley's effects, in the early days of their marriage: a vast, gloomy Edwardian oak roll-top which had a brooding, sarcophagus-like presence in the room. Rosie imagined that when her back was turned the top would slide up with a rattle and a midget Napoleon would be lying there dead in his uniform. Her father had owned a smaller desk, a little country bureau which Ben had sold without asking her. Dad had kept a jar of sticky bulls-eyes and pieces of butterscotch wrapped in gold foil in the central niche. Sal had been the scruncher of bulls-eyes; Rosie had had a preference for the butterscotch.

Ben used to wait till she'd gone to work before removing things and sneaking them off to auction or else selling them for half their value to an acquaintance or a sharp-eyed customer. Sometimes she didn't notice things had gone for a day or so. It was when she went to fetch a needle and thread that she found her best-beloved sewing table had mysteriously vanished. On returning from a shopping trip, she had discovered the contents of her chest-of-drawers turned out upon the bed and no sign of the chest itself. When she'd stooped in the dark during a power-cut to place a cup of tea beside the bed, she'd found the old night-table with its pot cupboard was missing. Ben had sneeringly watched out of the corner of his eye each heart-wrenching discovery, daring her to complain.

After the loss of the night-table she'd argued the toss and on being for the first time shockingly threatened with a fist, had fetched him a tooth-rattling bang with the flat of a tin tea-tray. Terrified after that first violence, more appalled that the actual blow had come from her, she'd locked him out of their bedroom, an oak-panelled room of corresponding size to the bar-room below and in the distant past used for holding the local leet court in considerable style. She began to control her fear of the rages by imagining them being set to rumbustious incidental music of the type used in early films to accompany dramatic events in stormy weather.

She never again responded to his provocation, understanding by then that he was courting a violent reaction, enjoying watching her hating him. She had learnt to purvey only calm and keep all agitation to herself; unlike her father, she was definitely not made for martyrdom although the effort of strangling her instincts, of never appearing cowed in public or in private, was chronically wearing. Finally, after the last drop of her affection had seeped away, Ben had broken right out of her area of compassion and raged around outside it, quite literally beyond the pale. It had taken monumental determination to hold on to what she still firmly believed to be her birthright. A divorce would lose her the Jack Cade. She would not let it happen.

All through the past year she had been kept going by a deep-seated hunch that she would see Ben out or that he would suddenly have a rational moment and sign up with Alcoholics Anonymous. Now something else was amiss, some blood-sucking thing that was going to spoil all her plans. Paddy Croswell had hinted as much before they'd been interrupted by that strangely underhand little wife of his. Why had she been nosing around the back? Perhaps that was being unfair, though. Perhaps the woman *had* just been looking for the ladies' toilet when she came so boldly through their private garden?

Breathing rather fast, with Elvira's misleadingly ethereal presence in attendance, Rosie turned the key in the lock and pushed up the creaking, segmented lid. Inside was no Napoleon but an orange string bag of sprouting shallots. There was also a half-drunk half-bottle of supermarket own-brand whisky, a collection of broken ball point pens and an Old Holborn tobacco tin, red, yellow and blue in commemoration of the Queen's Silver Jubilee in 1977. It contained merely an assortment of fearsome fishhooks, paperclips and a half-crown piece.

The little inner drawers held further rubbish and a fly-spotted postcard, a softly sun-lit painting of a woman reading a letter – perhaps pregnant, Rosie judged from the wide fall of the loose blue silk jacket. She forgot the waiting Elvira and examined it minutely, wishing to delay uncomfortable discoveries, remembering having once read that the biggest difference one would notice, should one find oneself in previous centuries, was that most of the women of childbearing age would be in varying stages of pregnancy. It was hard to judge the woman's emotions from the faded print. Was she delighted by the contents of the letter, had it confirmed her expectations or was it troubling her? Rosie turned it over: Johannes Vermeer, 1632–1675. It had been sent by her parents when on a rare week's holiday in Amsterdam in 1970. It had once been stuck to the bedroom wall and smudges of Blu-tack still adhered to the back.

A disembodied and tousled fair head appeared high up around the door, with china-blue eyes behind gold-framed spectacles, dimpled chin decorated with faint corn stubble. Aylwin, tall and round-shouldered, rarely came straight into a room, preferring to hover just outside as if expecting to have to take evasive action. Ben had thrown things at him on occasion, most memorably a half-carved leg of lamb followed by a dish of spinach. Like Rosie, Aylwin still nervously expected Ben's death to be apparent rather than actual, perhaps to have been a cruel practical joke and that the monster might still issue abruptly from a cupboard, bellowing insults.

'I've put the kettle on.' He ventured inside, gave Elvira a hug around her narrow little shoulders and sniffed, questioningly. 'You smell different?'

'That'll be ferret,' said Elvira composedly, returning the hug, enjoying the resonance of the young, rumbly voice inside his hard chest. 'The males do niff a bit in the spring.' She giggled. 'Did you ring around, to see if there's anyone who wants to give them a home?'

'I did. The van-driver at the printer's wants them! He's coming tonight. He'll buy all four.'

'*Buy* them?' exclaimed Rosie, her face brightening. 'Good Lord! I thought I'd have to pay someone to take them away. How much?'

'Only a tenner for the lot, I'm afraid. If I were you, I'd offer him a whisky in the bar before taking him out to see them. If they smell his breath they might think it's Ben and won't nip him.'

Rosie chuckled then again drifted away from the matter in hand, staring helplessly at the desk. In rapid succession came images of Aylwin rolling through his early stages: a solid, flaxen-haired baby then a bony, boisterous boy, before entering that dark tunnel of self-absorption that was adolescence, that fearful jumble of hot bedclothes when the world seemed either too tight or far too frighteningly large and empty. Aylwin was now Aylwin again, a little tentatively himself but all heart and brain bones – and gratifyingly, comfortingly normal.

Elvira gave a little nervous cough.

'Come on,' said Rosie, briskly opening a drawer, as if it were the others who were adrift and dreaming. 'Let's get started. We've got to open up again at six, and fit in tea. Let's empty everything out of the drawers and pile it on the table.'

By five o'clock it was all in neat, dreary piles – dog-eared pink bank statements, bills, income tax, National Insurance, and a collection of letters from Green & Croswell. These last dated from the period approximately four years after their marriage, before she had become joint licensee, and concerned the original mortgage and a second loan from the brewery. Ben had never allowed Rosie anywhere near the accounts, right up till the end. She had dealt with the ordering, taking in of deliveries, the cleaning, serving at the bar in the evenings, remembering to renew their licence and apply for extensions, the family cooking, the house itself and the poultry. Ben had dealt with the paperwork, grown large, hard vegetables and drunk whisky. He had also been abusive to any strangers who poked their heads inside the inn and only slightly less offensive to the regular customers.

At first, before the drink problem became too apparent, there had been a little upturn in trade, because, Rosie assumed, there were always people who saw others arguing as theatre. Some people seemed to enjoy meeting a little safe danger when having a night out and found the irrational rudeness a giggle, a floorshow on which they could dine out afterwards – as long as it was not always directed against themselves and they did not have to come face to face with the heartbreak behind it. He'd been intolerable to all Rosie's old friends and she had become isolated, had lost touch with many of them although they accidentally met in town now and then. Her school friends from the grammar were now sensible businesswomen, dentists or solicitors perhaps, or else sensibly married to dentists and solicitors with children of their own who, she thought with a little inward chuckle, would also grow up to be sensible and safe. But that was absurd – there was no reason why their children should not just as likely be crack addicts or astro-physicists. Her finger went up to feel the chipped edge of an eye tooth. If she'd married a dentist she could at least have had it treated free, and perhaps he would have explained why she frequently dreamt that all her teeth had fallen out. He would have banned the butterscotch. She hadn't been able to afford a visit to the dentist for a couple of years. Come on, come on! Back to the distasteful matter in hand.

The income tax, VAT and beer at least were mercifully in order and paid up to date. There was £1,800 in the current account but there was the funeral to pay for, other bills, and apparently no life insurance.

Aylwin leafed through the papers, wondering just how much money Ben had slurped up with his boozing. The bank statements told the sad tale. For the last five years there had been increasingly erratic repayments of interest only on the loan, which corresponded with the start of the period of decline in their takings. This lowering of the profits had been caused not only by Ben's bellicosity and light fingers with the stock, but by the construction of a major new road two miles away. This had converted their area from a quiet backwater to a stagnant pool – or a lovely, unspoilt part of the countryside, it depended on which way one looked at it. The drink-drive legislation, the cross-Channel bootleg trade, duty-frees and yet another deepening recession had all played their part, but most of all it had been Ben's increasingly offensive behaviour that had kept customers away.

They owed approximately £20,000 to Green & Croswell. Rosie looked up and saw distress and incomprehension on the two young faces. Aylwin's eyes, although blue and gently vague, reminded her acutely of Sally's.

'Oh, Mum!' he said, hand jerking out to clutch at her arm. He'd never thought of her as his aunt. 'I thought everything was going to be all right.'

'You're not to tell anyone else about this, either of you,' Rosie said almost fiercely, trying not to panic, 'until I've decided what to do. Not until I've heard properly from the brewery anyway. I don't know how bad it is yet. I can't make out when this loan has to be repaid.' She threw down her pencil and looked up at the woebegone Aylwin. 'It's all my fault!' she wailed. 'I should never have been so soft with Ben. I should have *demanded* to know what was going on. It was easier, to think we were so short of money because of the mortage repayments, not because he was literally chucking it away down his throat.'

'Of course it's not your fault! You couldn't have fought him, the way he was.'

She leant her face on her hands for a minute, pressing the cool palms against the eye-sockets.

'We've got to start planning as soon as possible. See if we can't find ways of getting more custom. Let's make a list while we eat. With the tenner for the ferrets, we've only nineteen thousand nine hundred and ninety pounds still to raise! I don't suppose this friend of yours will want their cages as well?'

Aylwin, noticing that Rosie's hands were trembling, felt a wave of helpless sympathy.

'I'll see what I can do.'

'I'd be grateful. We'll start clearing the rubbish out of the garden, make it look pretty for the summer. No one will want to sit out there the way it is now, like an agricultural mortuary. I've invited everyone back after the funeral. We'll have to sit down afterwards and work out ways of paying this money back.'

Determination, that was the thing. Their finances were going to be as tight as ever, if not worse. Rosie crept into the kitchen and guiltily retrieved the bottle of lemon-scented washing-up liquid.

Upstairs Aylwin, who had undertaken the sorting of Ben's clothes and shoes, sat on the bed and tranquilly watched Elvira take over. A ball of quicksilver, she shot about the room, assessing and dividing garments between hospice shop, bonfire and useful-for-gardening piles.

'Gilbert Bentley would like that tweed jacket. He's in the bar.'

'Then why don't you take it down to him? I can hear the band. I'll finish up here. Would Rosie mind if I cut up this shirt for dusters?'

'I'm sure she'd be delighted.' He leant forward and caught her wrist. 'Come on, stop rushing about and give me a cuddle.'

She wriggled like a puppy then collapsed on to the bed and he swooped on her. The hospice shop pile slipped to the floor.

'This room isn't over the bar, is it?' She struggled from beneath him, and sat up anxiously.

'No, don't worry, it's the back parlour below.' She slid back again.

Downstairs, the Jack Cade was unusually busy and it was nine o'clock before Rosie had a moment to stand aside and make an affectionate but calculating survey of the evening's haul of customers, many of whom had come out that night in order to support her. Before opening up she had been struck by the enormity of the task ahead and it had caused a lump the size of a walnut in her throat, but she'd washed her hair and put on a cheerful red shirt and lapsed unconsciously into the chosen role. The stresses of the day dissipated as she began to speak in the neutral, empty-but-comforting, cliché-and-banter mode expected of her by the older customers, drawing in the lonely, accepting condolences quietly from those who knew and laughing at the jokes of those less frequent customers who didn't. The atmosphere was dense with friendliness, which made her wary; if she wasn't careful it could blind her to problems which needed to be kept in view.

The semi-shaven Brian the Book was crouched with pads of paper and pen in the window-seat, lit by a candle in a gin bottle. Endeavouring to look romantically mysterious, he wore a grubby white shirt and rusty black jacket; his prematurely receding hair was scraped into an exiguous pony tail and he indulged in bouts of ostentatious scribbling interspersed with unfocused middle-distance gazing. His only known published opus was the menu for a restaurant in Purley, which he had once proudly shown to Rosie. His imaginative powers had been given unfortunate licence, medallions of lamb being kissed by garlic before bathing naked in a cristal (sic) pool of vodka and scented by all the spices of Arrabie (sic and yuck, thought Rosie, and guaranteed to send one scuttling for the nearest chippy). He had been reputed to be writing a novel for as long as anyone could remember. People had stopped hopefully asking him if they were in it and now were kind to him, generally considering him a harmless lunatic. Rosie was amazed at how his ego had survived unscathed, triumphant over God knew how many put-downs, a solid stock-character in her imaginary play. Only, she thought, at this rate, Aylwin will write it before I do. If this place closed, where would Brian go to act out his fantasies?

The object of Brian's affectations that evening was the lean girl sitting at the bar, her straight, rust-coloured hair drawn up into a top-knot stuck through with a dangerous fake-tortoiseshell pin. She had a Celtic bracelet tattooed about her left wrist, her name was Amber, she was a garage mechanic and was completely uninterested in Brian. She was even less interested in the conversation of Lenny who perched unsteadily beside her on a stool. Lenny was old, mild and pale, his round face blandly unlined by responsibilities. In his attempts to interest Amber he was rambling through an inventory of the contents of his refrigerator.

'... and I keep a nice little pot of chicken fat at the back, just in case it's needed for frying, and there's a packet thing, one of those home-style, farm-fresh pizzas in the little freezer cabinet ...'

Amber yawned and asked Rosie for another pint and Lenny tried another tack.

'... lost this screw, see, when I was mending the washing machine. I could hear it tinkling while it was spinning my overalls, but *could* I find it? No, I could not ... I had to go all the way over to New Romley to get one just like ...'

Abnormally ordinary, Lenny was one of God's fools, certainly owing his physical survival to divine intervention. Amber raised her eyes heavenwards, grinned fiercely at him and took herself over to join Sam and Chloe Dicken, with whom she brought up the subject of euthanasia.

At another table a couple of lively academic ladies discussed sexuality in cyberspace over large gin and tonics, and Geoff Pocket with his buzzing hurdy-gurdy, a remarkably beautiful tin-whistle player, an Irish drummer and a guitarist were hogging the fire. They had respectfully started their session with a couple of keening instrumental laments, then 'The Leaving of Liverpool' and other shanties where the main theme was one of farewell, but judging the mood of the evening to perfection, had gradually livened up.

Seven vicars had arrived in a minibus for an informal exchange of gossip on their safely distant parishes. Unaware of the gravity of the occasion, they exchanged risqué jokes about matters of moment to the Church of England and laughed immoderately. Two pints ahead of the musicians and delighted by the music, they joined in very harmoniously with 'The

Cuckoo's Nest' and 'Cushie Butterfield', and more forcefully with 'The Wild Rover', bellowing out the chorus: 'And it's No, Nay, Never (stamp, stamp)! No, Nay, Never No More (bang, bang), Will I go a wild roving, No, Nay Neve-e-e-r, No Mo-o-o-r . . .' The vicars, apart from the overweight bearded youngster among them who did not know the words and wore slovenly trainers and sagging, paunch-stretched jogging pants, crashed their stout boots to the floorboards with enthusiasm. Rosie had to beg them to keep the sound level down till the gloomy members of Promoters and Protectors of Proper Beer, the Peepy-Peebies, who were in dour conference in the curtained-off back room, had finished their business. Indistinguishably whey-faced, bearded and heavily built, they spoke ponderously about 'specifics' and 'mashes' and berated failures to meet the required standards for the next issue of their *Proper Beer Book*, the Peeby Bee. They spoke in turn at first, with stiff, Gestapo-like gestures, insisting on demotions in the ratings for the use of fairylights in this pub or total eviction for the introduction of piped music in that one, increasingly interrupting each other until an acrimonious argument began to ferment.

Rosie thought it odd that they were so humourless, but then it was probably their tedious gravitas which had enabled them to hold back the incoming tide of continental lager. They had been uncomplimentary about the 'guest' ale on offer, the only alternative that evening, apart from the various bottled beers, to Green & Croswell's Kentish Stout and the Spring Bitter. This was a sore point with Rosie, who knew she would be able to tempt in more customers if she was only allowed to chose a decent real ale from one of the many little breweries flourishing up and down the country. She had, however, no choice in the matter. Although it was the law that tied-houses should be allowed to serve one beer other than that supplied by the brewery which leased out the pub, Green & Croswell had circumvented this inconvenience. They went to another brewery similar in size to their own and it was, 'You take ours in your pubs and we'll put yours in ours.' Their tenants were then 'encouraged' to take the guest beer they were offered. The one on offer in the Jack Cade wasn't particularly popular and was so variable in quality that she often had to return barrels half full. She would have to find a way of circumventing this, and fast, if she was going to pull in more trade.

Rollo and Sarah Molliner, with whom Rosie had more than a customer-landlady acquaintance, had arrived that evening by bicycle and were introducing darts and short-cut cider to a culture-dazed guest from London.

'Short-cut to oblivion, you see!' shrieked Sarah, missing the board by two feet and embedding a dart in a door. They had enticed Peter Richards away from his cronies as a partner for their friend; Peter had spent most of his life at sea and learnt to play darts on board ship. He could play well when tiddly and if he sensed he wasn't tiddly enough, stood on the balls of his feet and bent his knees, rocking to mimic the pitching and tossing of a boat, thus improving his accuracy.

Sarah had occasionally been privy to Rosie's difficulties, knew of the circumstances of Ben's death and had taken to heart her plea that everything should now proceed as normally as possible. Rollo was less adept at discovering the right note to strike and was distinctly awkward, his slight stammer increasing while ordering the drinks. Rosie tried to set him at ease.

'Ah, hold on a minute, Rollo. I've some eels out the back that Sid Jones left for you. Recent events had put it out of mind.' She disappeared to the freezer in the scullery behind the kitchen and returned shortly holding at arm's length a parcel resembling an exceptionally long and rigid French loaf done up in newspaper.

'Here you are. I've been quite anxious to get shot of them! I swear they're tainting everything else, although they're so well wrapped. I don't like to keep fish next to ice-cream. What are you going to do with them? Jellied or smoked?'

Rollo sniffed the parcel cautiously, as if it might be toxic.

'You're right. Even frozen they're quite pungent. I'm sorry you've had to hang on to them for so long. I'll smoke them; Sarah can't stand being ambushed by bowls of jellied eels in the fridge. Many thanks, Rosie.'

Grateful to her for gently easing him into speech, he deposited the parcel upright beneath the coat hooks and went back to the darts board. It stood to attention for a while, alongside an umbrella, before sagging in the warmth of the room and slithering to the floor.

In the opposite recess, seated in the inn's prized and creaking pair of yew-wood chairs, were a pair of lost Americans. Their hired car had broken down on the main road in the gathering dark and discerning from the sign upside-down in the hedge that there was an inn down the lane, they had bravely walked to it and rung for a cab to take them to the safety of their hotel in Rye. It being their first visit to England, they were still solidly anglophile, but had never before come across beer from the barrel and were wary of its safety. They sat whispering timid consolations to each other, nervously tapping their feet to the music and shooting coy glances of disbelief at the dog-collared carousers.

Rosie pulled over her list and noted down, 'Planning permission for inn-sign on new road. Repaint and re-hang the one in the lane'. Aylwin would do that. He was good at lettering.

The previously barred 'Tiger' Bright had been welcomed back that evening for the first time in six months. It had been Ben who'd thrown out Tiger, a gruesome middle-aged motorcycle enthusiast with lunatic pale, pale eyes and grog-blossom nose, thus depriving them of one of their most regular customers. Rowdy Tiger and his devoted Kittens were a brotherhood, and sisterhood, of once-feared hell-raisers, now more or less grown up and respectably employed although still given to team anarchy in the evenings. That particular evening they were welcoming back one of their number, 'Puss', who had just returned from holiday in Thailand where he had gained the kudos of being the only known person to have actually bitten a live stonefish, of which even the coating slime is poisonous. 'I came to in hospital, see,' he was telling his rapt companions, 'and there were all these geezers sitting on my bed, smoking and playing cards on my stomach.'

Since the Kittens had loyally refused to drink without Tiger, the Jack Cade had lost them as well for a time, till one or two, timidly perfidious, had crept back under cover of darkness. Now they were all happily readmitted and, apart from the incorrigible Tiger, were on their best behaviour.

He gently wound up the Americans, insinuating that the cab would surely charge danger money for crossing the border from Kent into Sussex. Rosie came to their rescue by threatening Tiger with disclosure of his real Christian name, Cuthbert, but was interrupted in her alternate lulling and reproving by the entrance of a chirrupy young stranger. He looked about approvingly and, rubbing his hands together, announced that he was Nick and that he'd come about some ferrets.

'I'll get Aylwin for you,' said Rosie, a sensation of light-headedness coming over her as she looked at the innocent potential ferret purchaser with glee. She felt that the removal of the ferrets would set the family on the path to recovery. 'Would you like a whisky while you're waiting? On the house?'

More words blew lightly through the cosy, hazy room. Geoff Pocket was now singing 'Sally, Free and Easy'.

# Chapter Three

Oliver Ragstaff Potter, dodging impatiently amongst the doddering tourists in Knightsbridge, raced up the steps of the club two at a time, rang the bell and breathlessly stated his name and business to the security guard and was duly ticked off as an expected guest. He was more than a little late for lunch with his mother. He was further delayed on the stairs by an old gentleman with two sticks who was being laboriously heaved aloft to luncheon by a nurse, two steps up and then one backwards.

The wide, red-carpeted staircase was dimly decorated in the manner of an Underground escalator, with framed black and white photographs of founder members stepped up the walls, heroes and heroines of the Resistance, and of General de Gaulle. Oliver expected that as their significance receded with the years, they would soon be decorated with felt-tip pen spectacles and pointed beards, or their noses desecrated with chewing gum. The club owed its existence to the other kind of underground, the former members of which had operated during the the Second World War, but since there were fewer and fewer of these originals each year, it had long since opened its arms to include their modern equivalents.

Ollie need not have worried about being late. He saw as he came into the bar, through a haze of cigarette smoke, that his mother was happily engaged in gin and flirtation with another upright octogenarian.

'Hello, Mum. I'm sorry to be so late. The train was held up by a body on the line near Sevenoaks ...' He bent and kissed her cheek. 'Good afternoon, Colonel. You are lunching with us, I hope?' He shook hands respectfully with the old man.

'No, no. I've no appetite these days. I'm off home now, to have my snoozy. I'm doing well, for ninety, but I do need to sleep. Nice to see you again, Ollie.' His pale blue eyes, although embedded in a nest of thick-grained and deeply creased skin, were clear and looked remarkably alert. 'Goodbye, my dear Felicity.' He kissed her hand, elegantly, and with precise but very short steps, gave the impression of striding away.

'Ollie, darling, you are infuriating. God! I thought for one dreadful moment he was going to accept. He really is the most dreadful old bore. But we're all old bores now. My stomach's been rumbling audibly for the last half-hour.'

Felicity stared at him with not quite focused eyes, due not to gin but to her refusal to wear spectacles in public. With knobbly and nicotine-stained, maize-coloured fingers at odds with their neatly manicured and pink-painted nails, she impatiently stubbed out a half-smoked cigarette in a bowl containing dry-roasted peanuts.

'I know for a fact that he's only eighty-four. Isn't it odd how people pretend they're younger when they're in their forties and fifties and then start piling it on when they get to ... well, my age, I suppose. Now what's this about a body on the line? No one you knew, I hope?'

'Of course not, darling. Now, let's find a table.'

Lunch progressed satisfactorily until Felicity discovered that he had been made redundant from his latest and short-lived middle-management job at an agricultural chemicals firm. It had not been a very satisfying occupation and had made him thoughtful when eating, causing him to wonder which of the company's many products he was currently ingesting.

'Poor sweet. How very dispiriting for you. I thought you were a little subdued. However, it's probably all for the best. I'm sure you only took the job to be near that monstrous little cat Vicky. That's the only possible reason you could have for being in Tunbridge Wells. I was so disappointed when I found out you'd met up yet again. I can't understand why you haven't found some sweet, unmarried girl to lust after. Vicky's just a bad habit, like picking your nose. She's never going to leave her husband, you know that.'

Now that the Colonel had departed and in order to read the menu, Felicity had replaced her bi-focals and scrutinised him with some exasperation, which was unusual since she rarely took him to task or fussed unnecessarily.

The expression on Ollie's fine, good-looking features, only slightly marred by ancient acne scars, was self-protective, a little withdrawn. His eyes were grey, wide-set like her own, and gave the impression of an unsuitably sleepy innocence. The hair, fine and thick though not too long, was a well-cut stack of that peculiarly English shade of silvered hay, not yet mouse and more subtle than blond, in which grey hairs arrive unnoticed. Forty-four, well-travelled, unambitious but with well-founded financial expectations, he had continued to waft, to his mother's usually well-concealed distress, apparently negligently and perpetually indigent, in and out of Vicky Croswell's sphere throughout his adult life. He'd never been a clinger, and had showed early signs of great independence, which made his renewed attachment to the Croswell woman even more unintelligible.

Although tall and broad-shouldered, she thought her son looked a little thin inside his well-cut but tired grey suit, a bit weary even, and there had been no sign of his usual heart-warmingly attractive grin. Ollie now affected a falsely contrite expression, since he knew that she considered the affection he felt for Vicky a perversity. Felicity's irritation softened for a moment.

'Are you very broke, darling? Why don't you let me buy you a new suit for interviews at least? I can easily do that without the trustees jumping on me. I did see old fart-face the other week about trying again to get the trust overturned but I'm afraid it's no use.'

'No, Mum. Thank you very much but you mustn't worry. Humiliating though the situation is, I've got some redundancy money and applied for at least four jobs. Something will turn up. And I haven't really got the time to go shopping.' He had always been scrupulous over never borrowing money from her, however much she wished to lend it, and was not about to start now. 'There are one or two things to be done and I have to catch the four-forty back. I'm out to dinner tonight.' He exuded optimistic busyness far better than he managed contrition. Felicity sighed. She still sighs, he thought, amused, with a French accent.

'The hell cat, I suppose?'

'Would you care for a pudding? I do wish you wouldn't talk so loudly.'

'This is one of the last bastions left where one can speak one's mind.'

'I would have thought it was the last place where one *should* speak one's mind. I thought it was supposed to be all hush-hush, or has that all gone by the board?'

There was a burst of noisy laughter from a group of large young men celebrating at a nearby table, their muscles bulging inelegantly beneath well-tailored suits.

Felicity leant forward and hissed: 'You see the riff-raff that comes here now? They're probably supposed to be rooting out terrorism at this very minute, which is quite ludicrous. Everyone knows that the would-be terrorists are all living just round the corner from Harrods on social security and housing benefit.'

She sat back again and giggled, and Ollie suddenly saw for a second how she must have really looked when she was in her twenties, the early photographs of the person whom he had read about in so many war-time autobiographies at last merging with the face he knew so much later. But then she had been deeply involved, in German-occupied France, in matters of great importance to the war effort. Now here she was, smoothly white-haired and with arthritic hands, a healthy and self-sufficient old lady, widowed, divorced, widowed again, living in a flat near South Kensington tube station. His father had also married twice before. Five times up the aisle between them and only Ollie to show for it. He feared he was a disappointment to her.

'Well, if you won't let me help, I should get back to work.' She was proud to have some work to get back to. 'The coffee here is filthy. See me home and come and have some decent stuff and a cognac with me?'

'Of course I will. I'd love to. You haven't told me what it is you're working on at the moment?'

'Quite exciting. I'm advising on a TV film again, after all these years. What they call period detail. It's odd how they spend so much money yet never seem to get it right. I've told them one or two things about the script as well, corrected them on the sort of expressions people would or wouldn't have used in the 1940s. Isn't it peculiar how the past gets clearer and clearer as one ages, yet one cannot remember the day of the week? I do worry sometimes, though, that I'm reinventing the past.'

'Good heavens! What's the film about?'

She chuckled again, coughed and suddenly looked down self-consciously to examine the palms of her hands, as if expecting to find written instructions on them.

'Me, I think.'


In Fenwick's changing room Vicky Croswell struggled blindly from the suffocating embrace of a lilac velvet dress, snagging hair in a hook and nose on a razor-edged price ticket. Once her breathing was restored, she reinserted herself into less constricting jacket and trousers and tidied her hair.

'I shall have to pay a visit to the gym this week,' she said to herself, flattening her stomach with a hand as she stood sideways, examining herself in the unforgivingly well-lit mirror. 'That's a definite bulge above the waistline. However, if I don't have any lunch and don't pig out tonight, I *might* just get away with it! I deserve a frock after the horror at the dentist's this morning.' She reapplied lipstick but the lower lip at the right-hand side still retained a palsied, pouty appearance after an ineptly administered injection. She noted that the zip on the dress was showing signs of strain but it was too adorable to miss and she bought it all the same and trotted jubilantly through the shopping mall out into the sunshine, stopping to buy a sensationally scented bunch of cream narcissi and ready-made first courses and puddings for eight for the dinner party that night.

The dinner had been intended merely for old friends who also had children shortly returning for the Easter holidays, the last gasp of adult entertaining before Cressie, thirteen, and Harry, twelve, came home. Paddy had spoilt it a little by asking her to invite two virtual outsiders, Peregrine Briggand and his new wife, who had only recently moved to the area. She had, Paddy insisted, met Peregrine once or twice in the distant past but she had no recollection him or of his first wife. But Ollie was coming, and that would jolly things up.

The Jack Cade, which hadn't been far from her thoughts over the last few days, loomed up again disreputably in her mind. It must be revisited, before writing to make an offer for it, before it came on the market. Paddy must be nagged again about finding the survey and the details of the mortgage. She was looking forward to hinting about her find at dinner that night, but must not say too much. Who knew which among their friends might not also be house-hounding and beat her to it? Some people were so opportunistic.

When the children were at home she devoted her time entirely – well, almost entirely – to their entertainment. Although she was less besotted with them now than she had been when they were small, Vicky was almost looking forward to the holidays and had all the usual Easter outings inflexibly lined up: point-to-point on Easter Monday with cousin Minky and her unruly mob. Wednesday was lunch in Clapham with Lally and her rather more polite children, followed by a visit to a West End cinema, if there was a film suitable for such a wide age range of children. Then there were the statutory visits to the dentist and hairdresser. Cressie also had a party to attend, her first proper evening party, so there would inevitably be a miserable trailing around of shops searching hopelessly for whatever unsuitable and esoteric garment it was that she had immutably fixed in her mind's eye.

Then came the bit Vicky fancied even less: staying with the Seagraves in Hampshire for three days' sailing, if the weather was fair. How she hoped it would be foul! She would be tempted to pray to the devil for a hurricane in time to prevent them from setting out. It was odd that the Seagraves loved boats so much, with a name like that. She hated sailing herself, always puked, but felt guilty if she missed one moment of the children's company. If she didn't sail she would have to hang about all day giving free advice to tiresomely competitive Charlotte Seagrave about the redecoration of her awesome mansion . . .

Vicky found she couldn't remember on which level of the multi-storey she had parked the Renault. Five? Six? No sign of the damn' car. It must be level five after all. She trudged back to the lift. Last year Charlotte had written to Vicky with news of the brilliant progress of her own three children: Clara getting eleven As in her GCSEs, Lachlan playing junior hockey for England, Euan tootling his way through grade six on the flute although he was only nine. Vicky had replied, on a terse little postcard, that Cressie had just skied down Everest and that Harry was shortly embarking on his MA in psychology. It was going to be a little awkward, going to stay with Charlotte after she had been so patently rude. Surely the damn' car was on level five? Ah, there it was! She dumped the heavy food bags in the boot, carefully stashed the dress on the seat beside her and reversed out, scraping the white Mercedes on the left as she manoeuvred. Sod it! Served them right for taking up so much room. She drove blithely away without inspecting the damage.

On entering the house it became apparent that Avril, the cleaner, had not put in an appearance as promised. Her money still lay on the hall table. A sock and a pair of black knickers lay on the staircase and upstairs in the first-floor drawing-room, above the uncleaned marble fireplace, a vase of dead daffodils stood, their splitting stems clear of the remaining inch of smelly water and their once waxy trumpets and petals reduced to golden-brown tissue-paper thinness. Newspapers lay in a shuffled heap on the floor where Paddy had thrown them last night. His cigar butt still lay malodorously in the unemptied silver ashtray and there were two dirty coffee cups on the undusted sofa table. It was an un-room, uninhabitable and unwelcoming.

Panicking but tempering her annoyance with caution, she rang Avril and demanded to know what had happened and could she please come in that afternoon instead? Avril claimed to have spent most of the morning in the police station bailing out her son and on the way home had tripped on a kerb, broken a toe and subsequently spent a trying hour or two at the hospital, waiting to have her foot X-rayed. She was unable to walk, let alone clean someone else's house. With the tactful words of sympathy that were due to an irreplaceable paragon clotting in her throat, Vicky replaced the receiver and, cursing, threw open the windows to air the room. The anaesthetic had worn off and her bruised jaw throbbed.

It was after four o'clock by the time the house was straight and there was a moment to glance at the receipt for the Moroccan roast lamb she was intending to prepare for her guests. Vicky let out a wail as she read the first words: 'If not using ready-to-eat apricots, soak apricots *overnight*'. She peered at the packet purchased from the wholefood store that morning to stuff into the boned shoulder of lamb: 'Wild dried apricots from Iran. No preservatives'. Nowhere on the label did it say ready-to-eat ... it would have to be a short overnight, then, from four-thirty to six-thirty. Perhaps if they were soaked in boiling water ... Paddy poked his head round the door of the kitchen.

'Hello, sweet plum. I thought I'd come home early and give you a hand. Everything under control?'

He grinned affectionately and she threw a wild apricot at him.

The spicy apricot and cous-cous stuffing was deliciously moist, having sucked most of the juices from the lamb, but Vicky re-hydrated the meat to her own satisfaction with quantities of red wine gravy. Certainly it was not a disaster. Janie and Gerry Cutt-Norton and Megan Sliverley, whose husband was away on business in Kuwait, compared their offspring's achievements and failures through mouthfuls of smoked trout garnished with slightly muddy winter-flowering pansies hastily snipped from the garden. They touched lightly on animal rights protesters and discussed the inconveniences of the recent flooding with Peregrine Briggand and his very young wife whilst chewing their way through the lamb. They indulged, with Ollie Potter, who had been invited to replace Megan's husband, in salacious gossip about the nervous breakdown of a close friend and the odd sexual tastes of a shadow Cabinet Minister. They were becoming happily boisterous and ribald by the time Vicky dished up the pudding. The candles flickered prettily on the glasses and shiny well-fed faces and a great many opinions flew back and forth across the cosy dining-room table — some pompous and curiously ill-informed (Gerry), some of them designed to cause maximum discussion and argument (Ollie).

Ollie, his usual elegantly untidy self, sat attentively on

Vicky's left, a flattering expression of devotion on his face. Vicky, relaxed and cheerful now her guests appeared to be so compatible, secretly admitted to herself that she was very fond of him; he was incredibly useful. On her right sat Peregrine Briggand, who worked, he told her at length, for an investment trust with environmentally friendly pretensions, checking out the ecological credentials of the companies and their satellites. He was saturnine of countenance, discursive and very hard work, expatiating lengthily on the minutiae of a particular section of his topic and, just when her attention was wavering, planting a little sharp splinter of a question to ensure that she was following his drift. He also sent continual furtive glances slithering down the table to where his wife Fiammetta sat, next to Paddy.

Fiammetta was considerably quieter than the other guests, with pale, straight hair which hung a little limply on either side of a pale and beautiful face, devoid of make-up. She had told Vicky that she had been at school with a Jessica Kadely and enquired if she was a relation? Vicky had sorted through her mental card-index of relations and decided that Jessica must be Rush's youngest sister, and wasn't impressed by the connection. She privately nick-named Fiammetta the 'Mouse-wife' but had not failed to notice when the Briggands arrived that the little cream and green *dévoré* dress she wore was expensively antique, suited her very well indeed and made Vicky's own new lilac sheath look too tight and just a little tacky. Engendering such feelings in one's hostess is not, generally speaking, wise.

While apparently paying the closest attention to Peregrine, Vicky was also surreptitiously keeping an eye on the far end of the table where the Mouse-wife talked earnestly to Paddy in a rapid undertone and illustrated her points with jerky, stabbing movements of her long thin fingers. Vicky was unable to catch their drift but Paddy seemed riveted and had forgotten to refill the glasses, staring enchanted into the little pointy face cocked towards him. Ollie began a colourful anecdote and at the shrieks of laughter at the dénouement, Fiammetta looked up uncomfortably. Ollie, now assured of the attention of the entire table and well used to singing for his supper, commenced an even less likely tale. Megan Sliverley, already slightly pissed, more filthily capped it.

Fiammetta looked disgusted, put down her fork with a clatter and crossed her arms, looking reproachfully at Peregrine, who raised his eyebrows at her then stared down at his plate. Whether he was censuring her or approving of her own censure, Vicky was conscious that it was a little late to call order. Po-faced little madam, she thought, crossly. It was only a joke. Paddy was distressed and wondered why the stories one heard from women at dinner parties were always far closer to the knuckle than anything told by men in bars or clubs.

'Oh, God,' said Megan, smirking and smoothing back the blonde hair which she still wore cut in the fashion of her heroine, the late Princess of Wales, along with a wide pearl choker, ditto. She'd seen Fiammetta's expression and was delighted. 'Oops! I've gone too far again! Was it too much in front of the child-bride?'

'It was unnecessarily gross,' said Fiammetta loudly. 'And I'm hardly a child bride, at twenty-six.'

There was a second's embarrassed silence before Vicky, feeling the evening drifting astray, volubly launched into an account of the discovery of her heart's desire, lyrically describing the delights of the ancient and quite unspoilt house without revealing either its name or whereabouts, whereupon Paddy was unable to resist revealing the fact that she had been held hostage there, in the bog by a dog. Megan sulked but more general conversation resumed and under cover of it, Vicky nudged Ollie with her foot and he turned eagerly back to her. He had noticed her slight discomfiture, seen the little frown lines between her eyebrows deepen for a second.

'Can you be free on Friday week, at lunchtime?'

Ollie, always ready to do her bidding in the hope of getting more than a peck on the cheek, said that he thought he might manage it. The casual tone of his reply was undermined by the alacrity in his rather bloodshot eyes. The idea of taking the yum-yum Vicky out to lunch, for which she would undoubtedly pay, was an unexpected gift. He was greatly enamoured of every one of the little roundnesses of her person which she found so distressing and, having known her since she was twenty, had remained hooked, despite serious attempts to detach himself and even after she had unaccountably married Paddy. Paddy and he had attended Pangbourne Nautical College together but Paddy had been discovered to suffer from colour-blindness and had gone into his father's business, the brewery, while Ollie had gone into the Merchant Navy for some years as a deck officer with P & O.

The problem of a suitably gargantuan income was now solved for Vicky via what Ollie assumed hopefully was a marriage of convenience. Having delightfully met her again after an interlude of three years, and with his passion sadly rekindled, he was unable to understand what was stopping her from at least amusing herself with him now that he had stopped travelling abroad and moved from London. The fact that Vicky remained resistant did not deter; there was always hope.

Although he was obsessed by her, he was conscious of some-times viewing Vicky as a performance where it was necessary, as in the majority of the arts of entertainment, to turn accomplice and suspend disbelief to a certain extent. He was quite happy to put his three-pennyworth of imagination into her act, the cost of a ringside seat, the viewer's share.

Ollie was generally much appreciated by women whose hus-bands often forgot the compliments and other small attentions that help to smooth a lumpy marriage and he managed to deliver these with such discretion that the husbands imagined him to be an amusing and innocuous fellow. The wives, however, secretly thought of him as an escape route in times of stress, each imagining that his would be the broad, attractive shoulder they would turn to should their marriages become unbearable. But so far as love went, he was only interested in Vicky.

'I need to go and have another look at the house I've been talking about,' she whispered, 'to check up on first impressions before we put in an offer they can't refuse. It's an inn at present, you see, and not the sort of place I'd like to go to on my own – a bit echoing and empty.'

'Paddy doesn't sound as if he shares your appreciation of it?' Ollie couldn't help thinking that it sounded a most inappropriate place for Vicky. He thought of her as supremely urban, found it hard to imagine her in the middle of a field, for instance, or feeding chickens. 'Can't he help you get it via the brewery? I do like the way those little pearl danglies jiggle about in your ears when you move your head.'

'No, not yet, to the first question and you know what Paddy's like – everything by the book. He worships rules. It would take forever if we do it that way round and even then it wouldn't be certain. I was all for striking immediately, sending a letter off at once, but he said I must at least wait until he's dug out the survey from the brewery – and till after the old landlord's funeral.'

'You shouldn't have let Megan get away with it,' hissed Paddy as he carried the coffee tray up to the drawing room for his wife. 'Ollie was bad enough but at least he was funny. You should have shut her up before she started. You know how crude she can be. I don't think she ever thinks about anything except sex.'

'Tough!' whispered Vicky, pausing before opening the door for him. 'It's probably because her husband is away so much. Still, if one can't have a bit of fun with one's friends . . .'

'Fiammetta's not used to that sort of thing and we don't know her at all. It was bloody embarrassing. She's the daughter of some obscure Scottish earl and, from what I can gather, she's led a very sheltered life.'

'Then this evening will have opened her eyes a bit, won't it? And there's no such thing as an obscure earl. Mind out! The cream's slopping into the candied fruit. Here, let me take it now!' As she carried it in, she noticed a blue tin of Antiquax and a dirty yellow duster lying on the floorboards where she had left them that afternoon and endeavoured to side-step and nudge them beneath the extravagantly draped cream calico curtains.

Megan had recovered her jollity and was determined to persecute. 'Now it's your turn ...' she was saying hectoringly as Vicky laid the tray on the table. 'Come on, Fiammetta, which book would you least like to be given for your birthday?'

Mouse-wife Fiammetta had not missed the furtive kick and smiled infuriatingly up at Vicky. 'Coffee, how lovely. I was just beginning to feel a little sleepy.' She turned to Megan, taking in the hairstyle and choker, and smiled again, slyly. 'How about *The Wit and Wisdom of the Princess of Wales*?' she suggested and Janie Cutt-Norton choked on a candied cherry and patted her plump chest histrionically, eyes brimming with tears of glee.

It was nearly midnight. As soon as Fiammetta had drunk her coffee, she stood up, dress hanging from her slim figure in graceful folds. Vicky had been mistaken. She was cat-woman, not mouse-wife.

'I'm so sorry, but we both have to get up so early tomorrow morning.' Did she slightly stress the 'both'? Vicky wondered.

'Do you work? What do you do?' she asked, awkwardly, rising from the comfortable depths of the sofa into which she had only just sunk; Lady Fiammetta's departure was a colossal relief but her own dress stayed tightly rucked into little fat creases across her stomach and she heard the smallest rip as the stitching of the zip gave way.

'Yes. I teach philosophy at a sixth-form college, and at the local prison.'

Ben's sister Janice's style of dress had barely changed since the late 60s and, give or take a detail or two, was currently back in fashion. She was long-boned, wore a quantity of smudged black eyeliner and a long and faded yet still dramatic black velvet trench-coat tightly belted around a scrawny waist, but her appearance was nevertheless tentative. The sky was clearing and in the windswept, puddled lane outside the church, Rosie noticed the dragging hem and helped her to catch it up with a safety pin. Janice's knees being wobbly, Aylwin aided Rosie in gently supporting her fragile figure up the wide sweep of steps into the hillside church where, perched precariously on the hard edge of the pew, her long face peered uncertainly out at Rosie through a fairground pony's curtain of coarse, improbably rust-red hair.

'We should have followed the coffin, not gone in ahead. Should we ... shouldn't we stand up when ... when they come in?' Janice enquired tremulously, hopelessly searching Rosie's stony face for an expression of grief equivalent to her own. Poor, poor Janice, thought Rosie, she has no one else to share it with. She's mislaid two husbands and dear little brother Ben was her last relative. That Janice knew of Ben's alcoholic excesses was a fact, but Rosie was aware that her sister-in-law had little understanding of the nature and consequences of them and had been unable to bring herself to believe in the reign of terror to which Rosie had been subjected.

Idiot-brained at the time, she had thankfully let Janice instruct a favoured semi-retired vicar to take the service and had encouraged her to choose the hymns. I *must* make an effort, she thought, some sort of show of sharing in her emotions. She could sense the comforting clump of her customers in the pews behind and softly patted Janice's thin mauve hand. Elvira leant over Aylwin and handed Janice a dry paper hanky, but before Rosie could sympathetically mould her features into any realistic semblance of sorrow she was caught out by the sprighty progress up the aisle of the elderly vicar.

'... *We brought nothing into this world and it is certain we can carry nothing out. The Lord gave and the Lord taketh away ...'* he declaimed in a high, belling voice, whisking past them ahead of Ben's earthly remains. The pallbearers had difficulty in keeping to a suitably solemn pace behind him, passing the well-filled pews at an accelerated shuffle.

'Yes,' said Rosie grimly, slipping a comforting hand beneath Janice's elbow but steadying herself. 'We stand up now.' She suddenly felt very weak.

They sang 'Eternal Father, strong to save' since Ben had been in the Navy, and later, quite unaccountably, 'We plough the fields and scatter'. Janice, who had chosen 'O Thou, from whom all goodness flows', looked startled.

'They've muddled up the numbers,' she quavered, distressed. 'I said number 283, Ancient and Modern. "O Thou, from whom" was Ben's favourite hymn.'

Rosie, who had never known Ben to enter a church since she'd met him, stifled a snort but her own emotions were still more complex than she'd supposed and she was caught out by real tears which welled up, unforced, and a sharp pain in the sinuses which threatened more. It was possible that Janice was investing Ben with her own newly declared Christianity – the 'born-again' variety, she had assured Rosie, as if this was a superior type of addiction. Janice passed her the crumpled damp tissue and looked pleased. A brief shaft of light fell through the bright robe of a stained glass apostle and caught the top of Janice's head, turning the red hair a dusty olive green. There was something endearing about her scrappy, hopeful appearance.

Once back at the Jack Cade, Rosie tactfully escorted Janice into the kitchen since she was obviously quite incapable of facing the crowded bar, her sorrow being at odds with the less sombre mood of the assembled mourners who smelt collectively of wet wool, hairspray and tobacco.

'There now, you sit at the table and I'll make tea. It went off very well, I thought.' Rosie hung her black tweed jacket behind the door, pushed up the sleeves of her sweater and re-filled the giant cream and green enamel kettle. In the kitchen it was impossible to hear the mounting noise from the bar and Janice relaxed a little, sitting back on one of the blue-painted chairs and watching Rosie dolefully as she laid out cups and saucers and the milk jug. They had little in common, had tolerated each other in a friendly enough fashion on their rare meetings but conversation had previously been confined to pleasantries.

'I was wondering if I might have a little something of Ben's?' asked Janice, eyeing Rosie wistfully, as if she knew she were about to be denied any such thing.

'Of course, you must have whatever you like. Were there any particular things you wanted?' Rosie was worried; it had not been only her own furniture that had been sold but most of the possessions Ben had brought with him.

'I thought perhaps that little carved chest which our father brought back from Hong Kong in the fifties?'

'Janice, I would have loved you to have had that chest,' Rosie exclaimed, having disliked its crudely carved and suspicious little fishermen lurking beneath pom-pom trees, 'but unfortunately I'm afraid Ben sold it.' What to do, what to do? 'Why don't you come upstairs with me when you've finished your tea and we'll look around and find something?' She knew she should have foreseen this and was desperately trying to remember what was left. His clothes? Two or three dozen books? A watch and a flashy gold ring with a chip diamond set gypsy-fashion in a star, which he'd never worn? That would have been sold too, if it had not been 'lost'. It lay where she had tucked it away beneath a loose floorboard in the big bedroom several years before in an attempt to save something of value from his onslaught, along with her grandmother's amber and crystal necklace and gold brooch.

Upstairs, Rosie with difficulty prised up the floorboard with a screwdriver and discovered that a mouse had made its nest in the ring's blue tissue paper wrappings. Janice then explained that she felt second-hand rings were unlucky and settled for the watch and a large pink and white lustre Sunderland bowl which had been her mother's and in which Ben had kept bottle-tops, used matches and discontinued currency. Its usefulness had saved it from sale, or perhaps the fact that being constantly under his nose, he had ceased to notice it.

'Oh, Rosie! Are you sure? It means so much to have that bowl. But then, of course, I have my faith, too. You *are* a kind person, and you have all your wonderful memories ...'

'Yes,' agreed Rosie pleasantly, hand clutching the doorknob of Ben's wardrobe, knuckles white. 'I have all my memories.'

Janice slumped down on the bed and burst into tears. Rosie put the amber necklace in her skirt pocket and comforted her as best she could. Then Janice, tears fairly slopping down her cheeks, let it slip that Ben had borrowed three hundred pounds from her some months before and had not returned it. She wailed piteously that she couldn't find a job and was shortly to have to move from her flat in Hythe and what was she to do?

Rosie, stunned into an unguarded moment of mixed sympathy and guilt, and in the fashion of someone picking up an attractive but battered object in a junk shop, convinced that it would come in useful some day, promptly offered Janice a temporary home. She regained control of herself fast enough to stress the 'temporary'. She must be mad, she thought as the invitation slithered from her lips, she'd regret this. I hardly know her and I should have consulted Aylwin. She'll probably try to make us sing hymns before breakfast. To replace one Hooke so immediately with another didn't seem, on the face of it, to be very sensible, but it was either that or pay back the three hundred pounds, which she couldn't immediately do – and she did feel terribly sorry for Janice.

Janice accepted with alacrity and mopping and blotting, followed Rosie downstairs. Rosie was to discover that Janice and paper hankies were inseparable, except when she really needed them, when they were nowhere to be found. When she was both cold-free and joyful, they flopped from her sleeves like wet snowballs. Later, Janice ventured bravely out amongst the crowd in the bar and sipped delicately at a glass of wine whilst receiving commiserations. At about four o'clock she accepted the lift back to Hythe tactfully offered by Geoff Pocket's girlfriend.

'I never knew Ben had so many friends. I'm so pleased that there was such a turnout to wish him goodbye. Thank you so very much for the invitation, Rosie. I'll see you on Thursday week. Any little room will do for me, just so long as it's quiet and out of the way. I don't want to be a burden to anyone.'

Rosie went through to her parlour via the kitchen door and, sitting at the loathsome desk, with trepidation opened the letter received that morning from Green & Croswell, read it carefully and did some furious thinking. It confirmed what she had expected; the sum due by the beginning of September was twenty thousand and thirty-one pounds, failing which the freehold title of the Jack Cade would revert to Green & Croswell at the sum agreed in 1984 when the first mortgage was taken out. She gasped on reading the amount. Seventy thousand pounds! One would be hard put to buy a cottage with that now! The inn was, even in its present state, worth treble, even quadruple. For so long used to concealing her private affairs, it was obvious now that she would have to cast aside pride and ask friends and customers for help. Not direct financial help, of course, begging was out and she'd try the banks for that, but for fund-raising ideas. The one thing that never crossed her mind for an instant was whether it, the Jack Cade, was worth the effort.

She felt a rush of adrenalin. A captive audience was out there in the bar, so she had better make use of it, but what style of approach should she adopt to get across the urgency of the situation? Heart beating double-time, as if she'd swallowed a pint of espresso, she sat staring at the titles of the tatty books and paperbacks on the little shelf beside the desk: Readers' Digests, a service and repair manual for a Ford Escort, *The Elizabethan Age*, which must be one of Aylwin's school text-books. It was unlikely that Ben had ever read it. He'd been a man who lived too entirely in the present second to consider the past, or for that matter the future further ahead than his next drink ... Suddenly inspired, she seized the text-book and hurriedly rootled through it. Tilbury ... Tilbury, Queen's address to Troops at ... page 298.

At five o'clock, hyped-up and stubborn, she rejoined the funeral party in the long room and decisively rang the bell, much to the relief of Aylwin and Elvira who had been rushed off their feet for the last hour and were wondering what had happened to the chief mourner.

Elizabeth I would have been proud of Rosie. Standing with the hearth behind her, she fixed her eyes on a startling hat in the assembly, glanced nervously at Aylwin behind the bar as if seeking reassurance, and then the years of impotence dropped away and she addressed the troops as a warrior queen, startled by her own fluency.

'Dear friends, Aylwin and I would like to thank you all for your kind support today. I know it isn't usual to make a speech at a funeral but there are reasons for doing so, so I hope you will bear with me as a matter of some importance has arisen.

'I need to warn you all most urgently that the Jack Cade is in grave danger of being repossessed by Green & Croswell.' She sounded scornful of such impertinence, and made Green & Croswell sound as if they were the Dukes of Parma and Medina Sidonia. There was a groan at this but she continued. 'To some of you, I am sure, the Jack Cade is an anachronism, but I intend to fight this incursion with every breath in my body, to make sure it stays open as it is now – a cheap country club for a group of much appreciated but eccentric layabouts and also our home, of which, as many of you know, members of my family have been the tenants for four generations.' She'd added an extra generation for good measure.

'In order for the Jack Cade to stay as it is, we need to raise a certain sum of money.' There had been wavering applause at the abuse but there was silence at the mention of money. 'If you feel that the Jack Cade is an asset to the community, then I count on you all to help me fight the brewery and raise the funds to keep it open in the form that you know and love.' She took a breath and waved her arm about airily. Disdain. She had forgotten the disdain.

'Can you imagine what plans Green & Croswell have for this beautiful old inn? No? Well then, how would you like a theme pub, perhaps named The Pig's Knickers, with fake armour, pikes and falchions hanging from the beams, piped music – perhaps Julio Iglesias, flashing lights from fruit machines and squid-rings in batter?' Another groan rose up from the assembled mourners. This was a totally unfair assessment of Green & Croswell's intentions and an unlikely horror but she felt it worth brandishing the appalling possibility before their noses.

Hurrying on a little, since the heat from the fire behind was beginning to scorch the back of her legs, she continued, 'If anyone has any ideas for fund-raising, I would be delighted to hear them and meanwhile I count on your loyal support in encouraging more customers. I've absolutely no doubt that we can win this.'

Her eyes caught Tiger's at this point and he gave a slightly apologetic and shifty smile. Rosie feared she'd gone over the top but there was a round of real applause this time. She looked unusually vulnerable and slim standing there all in black, with Gran's amber-and-crystal necklace about her neck like a gorget. Although she had not actually said that she had 'the mind and body of a weak and feeble woman', nor actually stated that the brewery was an Armada to be defeated, that was the impression that took root in the minds and hearts of Tiger and the Kittens, and of the Eel and Sprocketeers, who recognised the spirit of the speech if not the text. Valiant little Rosie, fighting the big guns. Of course they'd help. Let tyrants fear. Her voice had been kept almost seductively low, but it wasn't a comedy turn – she had spoken with conviction. The idea of being turned out of her beloved home for a pittance was not to be contemplated. This was where she belonged – she would not be displaced. This was her profession.

'All you've got to do, Rosie,' said Tiger, overcome with beery emotion and calmly volunteering everyone without their permission, 'is whistle. Everyone here today would do anything they could to help you out.'

'Thank you,' said Rosie, smiling at him, almost fondly.

Sarah Molliner, grinning and with an anxious-looking Rollo behind her, delivered a hug. 'That goes for us as well.' Then she whispered, 'That was brilliant! I love a bit of insurrection. I want to raise a mob to go and set fire to Green & Croswell's offices at once.'

Rosie left the hearth and went out amongst her buzzing subjects, cheeks glowing, receiving nods and winks and pats on the back. She discovered amongst her relatives two elderly, but still slyly indistinguishable twin uncles with twin ketchup-stains on their black ties, who promised to visit more often. She thanked Nest Kerepol, her employer, for coming and smothered a giggle on overhearing one of her scarce Poydevin cousins greet one of the Bentley girls: 'Hello there! I recognise that face!' and the tart reply, 'Are you sure it's just the face you recognise?'

This cousin and his wife had moved away some years before to Sussex. The wife was the wearer of the hat, the one on which Rosie had fixed an eye when delivering the speech. It was an attention-pleading little black and white pillbox that would not have gone unnoticed at Ascot, with a wide black grosgrain ribbon hanging down behind and its upper deck overloaded with black spotted veil, flapping gauze bow and a grossly shiny black carnation. For the remainder of the afternoon the hat was constantly in view, sailing valiantly about the crowded room beneath its trembling garnish.

The Hat's husband was most interested in Rosie's predicament and suggested she could do with a few new ales.

'I know you've got Green & Croswell to contend with, but

there are ways and means, you know.' He tapped his nose in a fashion that could best be described as avuncular, dug out his wallet and found a card. 'Try this chap. You won't believe it, but he's the ex-head-brewer from Green & Croswell themselves. Had a little disagreement with them about six or seven months ago and walked out. He's just set up his own small brewery and is looking for custom, but of course Green & Croswell have barred all their pubs from using his as a guest beer so he's a bit short of outlets locally. I've tried it and it's very good stuff. He might do you a special deal. He's guaranteed to be discreet. My company did the wiring for his new set up.'

Rosie thanked him and slipped the card in her pocket.

Rush Kadely had attended the funeral out of curiosity. He was tactfully dressed, almost unrecognisable in suit and dark tie. The majority of men attending were likewise disguised; their suits were less well-fitting than Rush's, due to their having been bought, in most cases, to last all foreseeable weddings, funerals and visits to bank managers, regardless of alterations in fashion or in girth.

Rush stood quietly out of the way, observing and occasionally exchanging a few words or nodding to an acquaintance: Sarah Molliner, a local farmer, a JP, Sam Dicken the faithful hound, weird Amber, the elegant local butcher and the shrewd Seth and kind Phylly, who owned the Eeldyke Inn some miles away.

In Rush's eyes the Jack Cade was a strangely enchanting parallel world, remote from the click and sparkle of modern technology; a sanctuary for those irritated by the squib-like pops of shallow sound-bites or the mindless strobe flashes of the media. Each time Rush walked through the door he knew it for an organic entity operating in an entirely different time-scale from the world outside. What Rosie had in the Jack Cade was something many operators of multiple pubs did not understand: she had the brand loyalty of her customers, not entirely to the beer they drank, but to the environment in which they drank it.

Now rapidly integrating her address with the scrap of conversation overheard at Great Aunt Jane's birthday lunch, he wondered what bitchy cousin Vicky was up to? Could she want to buy this place, perhaps, and turn it into a des.res. for herself and the Croswell puppies? He could imagine how it would look after she had got her acquisitive little paws on it: smothered and swagged with straw-coloured dried flowers and inhabited by delicately battered painted furniture, the garden thoroughly box-and-bay-tree-ed, cluttered with pretty eighteenth-century seats, Edwardian glass cloches and, for all he knew, Stuart wheelbarrows and watering cans. Vicky always overdid her effects. It would be typical of her to want for herself alone that which was at present enjoyed by the many. It would be pleasurable to stick a pin in her plans and pop them. He wondered who was the delicate little girl helping Aylwin out behind the bar? He'd not seen her before. It was time to mingle and find out more. He put down his coffee – he never drank alcohol in daylight hours – and waded in.

'Hello,' he said in Elvira's ear as she exhaustedly melted into an empty chair and sank her teeth into a substantial cheese and plum chutney sandwich. 'My hobbies are manipulation and teasing. What are yours?'

She stared up at him, took in his appearance, noted the plain grey suit and his air of easy, unthreatening sexual energy, decided he was pretty but a poser, and finished her mouthful before smartly replying: '"Tending thrashing machines and wimbling haybonds."'

Rosie was so tired she could barely get out of her clothes. Leaving them lying like a black stain on the floorboards, she fell into bed to find that someone, probably Elvira, had kindly provided her with a hot-water bottle. The faceted crystal beads of the necklace were digging into her neck but she couldn't summon the energy to unclasp it before falling into a coma.

In their room across the landing, Elvira lay beside Aylwin and gently smoothed a hand over his lusciously curly head, over and over again, exploring the little folds and furrows of his ears with her finger tips. Unimaginably soothed, he turned and found her luminous face examining him in the thick dark.

'Isn't it quiet?' he said. 'I'm sure I can hear Rosie breathing. I'm sorry to have brought you into the middle of all this.'

'It can't be helped. Was it never quiet like this when Ben was alive?'

'Not often. Even if he'd stopped shouting and whining for a while or was asleep, there was an echo of it in your head for hours afterwards. Rosie used to get terrible headaches. You've missed a bit, just on the right – it's aching to be stroked too.'

'Are you a little sad about your uncle? I mean, he *was* sort of your father?'

'No! He never was!' Aylwin said vehemently, sitting up. 'I was at least seven when Ben married Rosie and I can remember Gran and Grandpa and how different it was, before *he* came.'

He lay down again with his head pressing a little uncomfortably on Elvira's bony shoulder. 'But he was all right, I suppose, until a few years ago – never bothered me much. He was sort of joky, laughed without thinking first at things I said. Irritating, but not unkind.' Aylwin paused and then sat up again, his upper body a large white oblong in the dark.

'The thing I *hate* is how he's left us both feeling guilty. It's so unfair. I didn't understand how dreadful it must have been for Rosie because I was at university most of the time Ben was at his worst. I think she protected me from him so much that she stopped me learning what he was really like. I feel now that I deserted her when she needed me most. But I'll make it up to her. As long as you're quite happy living here? It won't be forever but she needs us at the moment. She can't possibly run the inn all on her own.'

'I'm quite happy here. I wouldn't mind staying forever. It's a very special place.'

He yawned and reached for her hand. 'I've got a photograph of my mother and Rosie together when they were young, sitting in the mulberry tree. Sally was wearing short white boots – very innocent. There's another of her alone, in a rowing boat on the Military Canal. She was pretty, like Rosie, but looked a bit discontented. She didn't want to stay here forever.'

'Do you mind, not knowing about your father?'

'No, I don't think I do. If I did know, it would hardly change my life, would it? I think that not knowing makes some people quite desperate, but I'm just curious, occasionally, that's all. Stop fidgeting and go to sleep. I've got to work in the morning and it's after midnight.' He slipped his arm across her gently, as if to restrain her.

'You're the one who's fidgeting! Anyway I can't stop it. I'm too tired to sleep. My legs keep bicycling and if I close my eyes I see piles of coffee cups to collect up. How do you think Rosie feels? She must be a little sad, surely, and so worried about the future?'

Aylwin grunted. 'I don't quite know how she feels. She has the most equivocal expression on her face sometimes. I don't know how I feel, either. It's all so fresh. What did Rush have to say? You were talking for quite a while.'

'He wants to help Rosie . . . Aylwin?'

He could not resist her and immediately there was a change of mood and a certain amount of rustling, creaking and giggling, cut short as he put a finger very gently over her lips in an effort to stop her waking the unrouseable Rosie.

# Chapter Four

Having been forced to operate in an overtly passive fashion for so long, Rosie now ran an intimidating schedule, graph-plotting daily rises in the takings, planning small festive events to further improve them and cleaning the place so thoroughly no one could find anything. Her outpouring at the funeral had drained her and she became unable to mouth more than crisp, single-minded practicalities. Aylwin was anxious about her state of mind but Elvira deduced that in spite of the financial worries, Rosie was riding high on determination and imagined that she needed to keep busy after the too sudden descent of peace.

Breakfast and supper at the Jack Cade, when the three of them ate together, became increasingly fraught as methods of raising extra income were serially proposed and blackballed. The majority of the customers patronised the Jack Cade because games machines, pool tables and taped music were absent. Rosie had long ago fought that battle with Ben and won. The place must stay unchanged because, however hard she tried to dismantle and rearrange the edifice of its tradition, she simply could not envisage it any other way – and in any case, there was no money available with which to effect a change. Serving food had been rejected since according to the hygiene regulations they would have to fit out a ruinously expensive kitchen and install indoor toilets.

'Bloody stupid,' remarked Rosie, indignantly tossing the

booklet from the local council's department of environmental health into the molten maw of the Rayburn. 'Surely anyone can see it's more hygienic to have them outside the building, not inside? And anyway, look at Seth and Phylly over at Eeldyke, how well they do and they don't serve food either. No, this is a drinking and talking place. People can't talk with their mouths full.'

After a few more suggestions and rejections they agreed, two to one, to offer bed and breakfast, since it was allowed that the breakfasting guests might take their food with the family in the kitchen without too many regulations. Aylwin was the dissenter. Making conversation to complete strangers at a quarter to seven in the morning sounded utterly repellent to him, but it was pointed out that not many guests would leap from their beds at that hour and if Rosie were to hand over her outside job entirely to Elvira, she would be free to cook a second sitting at a more convenient time.

Once made, the decision gave Rosie the sensation of being in control for the first time in a long while, but she was conscious of this being an illusion and swatted the pleasure factor smartly on the head before it got the better of her. She added it to the list of Things To Be Done each evening (it now extended to three sheets of her large, clear handwriting) and each morning on waking chanted it like a litany, worrying that the items were not being crossed off fast enough.

Aylwin had loosed a subterranean groan when he heard that Janice was coming to stay. He pointed out that Ben had unkindly told them that his sister had once been introduced, like a computer virus, into a perfectly workable 1960s commune and that after two years she had caused so much well-meaning destruction, she was its sole remaining member. He also commented that he supposed she would ease the burden for Rosie until things settled down. Rosie had thus far regarded the imminent arrival of Janice as the burden but, put that way, she now appreciated there might be advantages for herself as well as for Janice. She could do with an extra pair of hands in the bar.

They cleared away the supper and Rosie dragged them

upstairs to inspect the bedrooms, there being six in all. She hadn't visited the two in the attic for some months but knew what she would find. Neither the electricity nor the incontinent 1950s central heating system, installed by her father after a modest win on the football pools, extended so far up the house. By the light of Aylwin's torch they could see that in one room the lathe and plaster ceiling had collapsed onto a jumble of dispirited chairs-in-waiting and in the other the beige flowered wallpaper hung in sad, mildewed shreds, probably since the departure of the last live-in helper in 1940. They stared, unable to think of anything to say, uneasily breathing in the depressing odour of old, damp plaster and ancient dust. The rooms had been in retirement for too long and were, for the moment, quite out of the question for B and B usage. They shut the doors and returned to the first floor, where the second largest room, at the top of the stairs and next to the cavernous bathroom, was earmarked for the guinea-pig guests.

Aylwin, despatched to look out some paint, unearthed a large tin of pale blue emulsion from beneath the clutter in the stables. It had an aged layer of glutinous brown substance on its surface when opened, but once whipped up with the egg beater, it served well enough for the repainting of Ben's old room, now re-designated as Janice's.

Elvira had firmly opted to be part of the enterprise. Unlike Aylwin's previous girlfriends, not only could she catch a ferret and cook and was impervious to the sea of mud which still surrounded the inn, but she could sew as well. While Aylwin slapped on paint in Janice's room and Rosie served in the bar, Elvira ran up neat curtains for the guest room made from an old summer dress of Rosie's (denim-blue cotton chambray), lined with the thicker parts of worn-through sheets. She disembowelled Rosie's inherited rag-bag containing three or four generations of shirts, dresses and dress-making scraps, and with permission cut out the useful lengths, tossing the lot into the washing machine. Rosie's immaculate parlour temporarily became the sewing room, mounded with multicoloured off-cuts, coffee mugs and bird's nests of thread. By the time the paint-slopper had worked his way

round the bedroom, piles of neat ironed six-inch squares lay on
the parlour floor, waiting to be machine-stitched into strips and
thence into two patchwork counterpanes of cream and blue prints.
The strips were steadily joined, a pattern of squares and crosses
magically emerging as an engrossed Elvira whirred and snipped
into the early hours of the morning, delicately manipulating the
antiquated electric Singer sewing machine, so early a version that
its designers had enamelled it black with gold curlicues like an old
hand machine. Aylwin was vastly proud of her.

Rosie woke muzzily the next day and found herself anxiously
listening for sounds of Ben stirring along the landing. Chadwick's
*The Decipherment of Linear B*, a coffee-stained paperback left behind
many years before by a customer which she had been reading
before she slept, having spent the night with her in bed now lay
shamefully scuffed and dog-eared beneath her shoulder. Having
spent a dark night hovering between sleep and wakefulness,
she was unsure which was which and a trifle morose. She
had also been disturbed by cloudy visions of Sally and had
dreamed infertile, arcane dreams in which she sought to unravel
important cuneiform instructions and endlessly added columns of
silver figures embroidered on a black velvet background, always
arriving at a different sum. Sally appeared behind her, shook her
head sorrowfully and told her to do them again.

With her face poked into the pillow, she lay in the centre of the
wide bed, knees drawn up beneath the bedclothes, shutting her eyes
tight against the bright scarlet of the counterpane and the golden
pattern of the creeping sunrise on the pale plaster of the wall
opposite. She was still tired and wished to be transported by magic
straight down to the kitchen where crisp bacon and toast on a hot
plate would be waiting, without the intervening dreary necessities of
leaving a warm bed, dressing, feeding Trash and seeing to the poultry.
It was one of those dawns when she was unable to see further than the
breakfast breadcrumbs and did not wish to cope with the exigencies

of her new household. But it was daylight now when she rose; it would soon be Easter and although still very wet, she convinced herself the weather *was* getting gently warmer.

Optimism rose further as she opened the kitchen door into the watery world. As the pale yellow sun rose over the low mist into the clearer sky, ricochets of light were reflected from hazed puddles and dykes and flashed from ponds and raindrops, flooding the thick moist air.

'Ponds used to be called flashes, I believe,' she said to herself as she unloosed Trash, who danced outside his kennel, rattling his chain. 'It smells, if not of spring at last, at least a promise of it. Sheep, wet earth, and a top note, as they say when selling perfume, of narcissi. Why do we imagine spring bursting in with a tarara, when it nearly always sneaks up, apologising?'

After completing the outside chores, Rosie checked the bar, retrieving from the backs of chairs the assortment of clothing left behind by the customers and hanging them up in a prominent place so that hopefully their owners would recall what they had lost and take the damn' things away. A flat tweed cap, a dusty black fedora, a pink cardigan and a lumberjack shirt full of holes joined the lonely dinner jacket and creased Hermès scarf on the coat pegs.

The scent of bacon filtered through from the kitchen and by the time she'd restocked the soft drinks shelves, it was crisping on the stove and Elvira was moving swiftly about making coffee and laying the table. Someone was looking after Rosie, and that hadn't happened for a long while, so she later ignored the mess in the parlour and was most impressed when shown the near-completed patchworks. She had begun to feel warmly intrigued by Elvira.

'They're masterpieces! They'll look perfect in the spare room. The only things we'll have to buy new are the duvets and linen.'

'I've been through the linen cupboard as well. Aylwin said you wouldn't mind? No suitable sheets but there are loads of other treasures. There's an Edwardian striped cotton skirt that's asking to be worn, and look at this cloth, for the chest-of-drawers in the guest room. It's *real* lace. All the stains have been got out and it's been starched.' She looked up at Rosie, a grin on her face.

'Aylwin's got the scratches off the chest by rubbing them with a piece of walnut and the drawers have been lined with clean paper, although I'm sure bed-and-breakfasters don't actually unpack their things, do they? But I suppose we ought to give them the opportunity.'

Frowning at finding a long hanging thread, she snipped it off with her little white teeth and looked down at her handiwork with satisfaction.

Rosie examined the neatly stitched together fragments of other people's pasts, happily identifying some and shuddering at others, like relatives in a photograph album. She paused in the middle of this self-indulgent nostalgia, wondering if it was preferable to allow people to initiate the telling of their own stories rather than asking too many direct questions? She'd caught a glimpse through the open door of Aylwin and Elvira's bedroom the other day and was surprised that someone so neat in person could be so chaotically untidy with their things. Well, that was Aylwin's problem, and anyway he probably didn't notice, and Rosie had been brought up not to pry. Her father had once said that people told him more than he wished to know in any case, without any further digging on his part, and running a pub had made him the unwilling repository of many awkward secrets.

'You're a very good sempstress,' Rosie ventured, stroking the patchwork. 'Where did you learn to sew like this?'

'Well, *not* at agricultural college,' said the surprising child. 'I only went there to please Dad – no sons, you see, and he hoped I'd take an interest in the farm. It was horribly hearty and chemically unsound so I dropped out.' Elvira looked up again, showing signs of pleasure at having been asked. 'I'd rather make a living sewing, if possible. I'm afraid I'm an anachronism. I'd really prefer to work at home, you know, have babies and a garden? It's a pity we haven't got the time to quilt these properly, on a frame, like Provençal *boutis*.'

Rosie stiffened at the mention of babies, and what on earth

was a *boutis?* She felt herself constricted by panic, like a waisted hour-glass with the sand rushing through, pushed by the weight of grains behind, and had to force a smile.

'Oh, God! Look at the time! I'd better bustle. Where's Aylwin? We must get off to work. His car won't start so I'll drop him off at the station. It's all getting a bit complicated but I'll be back with the van at lunchtime so you can take over at the nursery. Perhaps you could open up the bar at twelve? The new brewery man is visiting early this afternoon, so if by any chance he turns up before I get back, cling on to him like a leech.'

Janice arrived, hesitantly, in a taxi on the afternoon of Thursday, 4 April. Her belongings were packed haphazardly, chinking in cardboard boxes, seeping untidily from carrier bags and escaping from red plastic sacks. She was understandably weepy as Rosie helped her upstairs with her possessions and provided coat-hangers and encouragement. Rosie noticed that there was something slightly obsessional about the manner in which Janice laid out her belongings on the dressing table, arranging and rearranging bottles and jars according to height, and hair brush, comb, tubes of make-up and several eye-pencils according to length. She draped a silver chain with a large crystal pendant on one knob of the looking-glass and a little blue enamel crucifix dangling from a ribbon on the other, and placed in the middle a small glass ashtray with Monet's water lilies printed on it. She gradually stopped sniffing and began to chat.

'I feel this room — I really *feel* it welcoming me. Is it very old, this back bit of the house? Mediaeval perhaps?' She paused, portentously. 'I sense great age echoing about me. I was the Lady of Shalott in my previous life.'

Oh, help, thought Rosie. We'll have to tread carefully here, not to stamp on her dreams.

'Yes, it is old,' she said, non-committally. 'It was supposed to have been built around an old chapel. You can see the remains of it in the kitchen, an arched stone doorway into the scullery. I've been told it's Early English.'

Janice's religion, Rosie rapidly discovered, consisted of a hoddle of beliefs tacked and battened on to a wobbling base of Christianity, decorated with gilded finials of neo-Celtic mysticism and censed with superstition and aromatherapy. She listened patiently while she hung up Janice's catholic collection of silk blouses and then suggested they might go downstairs and eat. Janice followed her down, pausing on the stairs to look about her with dramatic awe and run her hands caressingly up and down on the smooth banister. She was welcomed rapturously by Trash and more cautiously by Aylwin.

'No, no, that's far too much for me! I have so little appetite.' She looked archly up at Aylwin who obediently halved the doorstep of bread he had been cutting for her. 'No, I really couldn't eat a whole plateful, just a little spoonful will do me. One potato, thank you. I hardly ever eat meat. It's a real treat. And it's still so early . . . I don't usually have supper till eight o'clock.' She knocked the water jug with her bangle, making the glass chime, but immediately stopped the ringing with a finger, saying anxiously, 'Oh, I'm sorry! Every time one does that, a sailor drowns, you know.' Seeing blank looks on the faces about her, she explained that that was one of her mother's sayings, though of course she didn't believe it.

Perplexed, Rosie watched Janice as she sat at the kitchen table, poking delicately about in the stew at first and breaking the bread into ever smaller pieces before nibbling them like a red squirrel, then accepting the offer of a large second helping, eating more bread, and finally demolishing, with not too much urging and little lapping sounds, two industrial-sized portions of apple cobbler and custard. Rosie was convinced that she had managed to eat more than the rest of them put together and wondered unhappily if Janice had been eating enough before? She felt the tapping of temperate affection for this scatty, questing, middle-aged child.

'And is the house haunted?' asked Janice, addressing Aylwin.

Rosie tried to signal 'No!' by kicking him but missed and stubbed her toe on a very solid chair-leg.

'I've not noticed anything *in* the house. There's a child that walks outside past the parlour window sometimes.'

Janice gasped at this curtly described phenomenon and immediately questioned him. What sort of child? How old? A boy or girl? Was it in period costume and if so which period? Doublet and hose . . . stiff petticoats?

'It's hard to tell,' said Aylwin, unconcerned, taking off and wiping his spectacles. 'It doesn't hang around to be described, it just goes past, sort of looking in.'

'I never knew you'd seen it,' said Rosie jealously. 'You never said.'

Janice was the last person to tell about such a thing; she looked the type who would know just where to contact bell-ringing, incense-burning exorcists.

Rosie most definitely didn't want the apparition exorcised since, shamingly, she was the only member of the family who'd never had the privilege of witnessing it, a fact that aggrieved her, as if she'd been excluded from a club. Even bloody Ben had seen it, or had sworn he had. Members of the family, her parents, had said perhaps once a year, 'I saw the child again today,' as if reporting a sighting of the irregular emergence of a well-known recluse. It caused no further comment than a raised eyebrow and a knowing, 'Oh, did you?' It was not wondered at, or spoken of to outsiders. It was a fact that some people thought they saw it and a fact that they all thought they saw the same phenomenon. It was also a fact that there was no pattern to its appearances. It didn't appear to herald anything in particular, wasn't a harbinger of death nor, quite definitely, a bringer of prosperity.

Janice was frustrated in her attempts to ferret out more details of the phantom and whilst continuing to stuff her thin face, evinced a keen interest in Aylwin and Elvira and asked them so many personal questions that Rosie felt it would shortly be necessary to intervene. Aylwin showed the unmistakable signs of withdrawal. He muttered evasive replies to the unwitting intrusions and his blue eyes closed childishly in distress. Eventually, merely grunting a response to the latest in the barrage of enquiries, he mumbled that he had some work to catch up on and making urgent, raised-eyebrow faces at Elvira to suggest she might care to escape too, pushed back his hair and decamped to the peace of their bedroom.

He gently removed a heap of her underclothes from his desk and a pile of books from the top of his aged computer and slouched over it for a while. When Elvira failed to materialise, he turned it on, waiting patiently whilst it whispered mouse-in-a-wastepaper-basket warming up noises. He then commenced a short story. 'Intruder', he tapped out and underlined, then beneath that, 'by Aylwin Godley'.

Not exactly an awe-inspiring name, he considered, staring glumly at the cluttered bookshelves, the reams of dog-eared notes from both school and university, works of reference, novels, Rough Guides to Norway and Greece, his *Widsith* essay in a blue folder, notes on the *Dream of the Rood* in red.

Green Anglo-Saxon dreams were part of another life. He had moved to a different level, up or down he wasn't sure, and although they would have enjoyed the independence of the small flat he'd rented in Parden, it had been drably uncomfortable. Elvira hadn't said much about it in the few weeks they'd been together there, but he was certain she keened for lawns and bowers, fruits and flowers, and would prefer the lark as a morning alarmer to the gravel trucks rumbling past the bedroom window, shaking them awake at half-past six in the morning. The view from their window had been despairing; ever more acres of land engulfed by industrial estates, feeder roads and shopping 'villages'. Aylwin's love for Elvira was epic and he hadn't considered for a moment that Rosie might not find her as enchanting as he did himself. Now her arrival was a fait-accompli, he felt he had been quite right not to worry about it.

While he was upstairs, thinking up the first line and wondering if 'prurient' was too forceful a word to describe someone like Janice, downstairs Elvira was imperturbably coping with the nervous cross-examination: she came from Herefordshire and had met Aylwin at a party in Leeds. That was months ago, just before he'd graduated. She was twenty, which Rosie was relieved to hear, and had been born on a Sunday. 'You know the rhyme,' she said, '"The child that is born on the Sabbath day, is bonny and blithe and good and gay?" That's why I'm called Elvira. From the play, *Blithe Spirit*?' She then switched from acquiescence to a bewildering non sequitur of a counter-attack.

'Did you know, Janice, that Thursday was named after the God Thor, and Tuesday was named after the God Tiw? And that Tiw, who was Thor's younger brother, had his hand bitten off by a wolf?' Aylwin must have fed her that little morsel of information. There was a lull while Janice struggled to digest both this and the crunchy brown scrapings from the rim of the pudding dish, then began again.

'I think it's time we cleared the table,' said Rosie firmly, standing up, cheeks aching with suppressed laughter. 'I've got to tart my face up a bit and change into a skirt before opening. By the way, Elvira, I've had an idea. I was always told that the inn's only been named after Jack Cade since the early nineteenth century, when it was taken over by a man with revolutionary aspirations called Jack Sparr. Before that it was the Seven Stars, I think, but we might do a bit of research and see if we can't come up with something to interest the local paper? Free advertising – it might attract a few more people.'

She turned hopefully to Janice. 'As it's your first evening and you must be tired, I thought we'd leave the workings of the bar till tomorrow? You could watch the telly, if you liked? It's in the back parlour and there's a fire lit in there and some books. Or you can come through and keep me company?'

Since no more food was forthcoming, Janice was now nibbling on a fingernail. Her eyes took on an anxious look and she fluttered her fingers faintly over the red fringe.

'What do you mean, show me the workings of the bar? Do you want me to *serve* in there? I mean, I couldn't possibly! I'd be far too shy.' There was a clucking sound in her throat as she protested, putting thin hand to heart as if suffering palpitations at the very idea, and adding bravely but with a lack of enthusiasm: 'Couldn't you give me a few little jobs to do behind the scenes . . . something menial perhaps? Cooking, or even washing floors?'

Rosie told her not to worry. She hoped that when it was suggested a second time, as with the pudding, Janice might agree if given enough time to consider it. They couldn't afford a passenger, even if they were under an obligation to her because of Ben's debt. Tomorrow she'd get Janice to help sort through the cupboards to find things for Aylwin and Elvira's pitch at Fingle car boot fair on Easter Monday. With fine weather, they should raise enough cash for some new china and an electric kettle for the guest room. Spring cleaning time, on top of everything else. The whole place needed stripping down and scrubbing. She wondered if neolithic woman, as the days grew longer, had suddenly been overcome by the urge to clear out all the old deer and rabbit bones from the back of her foetid cave?

This is our cave, she told herself, and Janice hasn't got one of her own. I think I'll get used to her. I *will* like having her here.

Rosie had an appointment with the bank in Parden at midday on Friday. This entailed taking time off her morning shift at the nursery and a re-jigging of their carefully orchestrated sailor's hornpipe of arrangements for travelling to and from work – the sickness of Aylwin's antique Mini Traveller had been diagnosed as terminal and the only other means of transport were Rosie's ex-post office van or the erratic train.

The horrors of borrowing money had been impressed upon her as a girl and ever after the act had loomed as large a sin as theft in her mind. She had, with reason as it had turned out, been horribly uneasy when Ben had taken out the second loan. By the time Elvira had delivered her to the station she had temporarily overcome her scruples and become seriously optimistic. She was tidily dressed in the business-like black jacket and skirt she had worn for the funeral and hoped she bore some resemblance to the neatly suited, briefcase-toting women she saw stepping out of trains in the evening, their hair still as neatly styled as it had been when they left home in the morning. She had abominably plastered her own hair with unaccustomed hairspray. When she caught sight of herself reflected in the carriage window and nervously patted it, it felt just like grade one steel wool.

The church clock across the road clattered its teeth and struck twelve as she entered the room and a very young man, whom she at first took to be an underling, hastily hid a copy of *Loaded* beneath a file on the bleak teak desk. He proceeded to disenchant her as she nervously outlined the potential of the bed and breakfast trade and less confidently produced the hastily assembled accounts for the past six months. The young man, pink-faced, bland and perhaps twenty-five or thirty – she could not quite gauge his age – fiddled with his pen as if bored and kept pushing glittery gold-rimmed spectacles back up the bridge of his nose with an index finger. By the time the clock's hands had cranked themselves round to ten past Rosie had finished, and he, waxing more powerful in the face of her hesitation, became short on sympathy and long on technical jargon, from which she managed to decipher 'no chance'.

In view of the lack of an acceptable business plan, a loan of that magnitude was not to be considered. He then stood up and peered out of the window, pulling down the slatted blind with one finger and jingling keys in his pocket with the other, acting the detective inspector. The figures she had produced, he continued, apparently addressing the street outside, were unpromising and the collateral of the inn itself was not hers to offer since she had previous mortgages on it and onerous ties, and money was not lent to pay off other loans. He turned back but spent a little time feeling inside his inner jacket pocket as if searching for his warrant card, still not meeting her eyes. He was amazed, really amazed, that the brewery had been so lenient with them for such a length of time and had not already repossessed the property.

'I suppose your bosses have already lent everything to the

second cousin twice-removed of some third-world minister of housing?' Rosie snapped. 'So he can buy a flat in Belgravia.' The clock struck the quarter hour and she stood up abruptly, half-blinded with indignation, wrathfully grabbed back the file of unimpressive figures and walked from his obstructive presence.

The bank's electronic doors hissed apart too slowly as she strode out and she cracked her forehead on them, stumbling against a pushchair being jerked backwards up the steps by an equally frustrated young woman. 'I hope you're not going in there to borrow money,' Rosie said, 'because they haven't got any.'

Well acquainted with disaster, firmly believing that fate placed trip-wires across the road if one was foolhardy enough to imagine something a certainty, she'd carefully primed herself, to no avail, not to expect success that morning. She hadn't believed herself, it turned out, but she recovered a little on the walk back to the station wilfully aborting the foetal depression and stopping at Woolworth's to buy half a pound of butterscotch as a comforter; it would be only too simple to give in.

'There's another version of things somewhere and I shall find it in a moment,' she muttered, blowing her nose. 'I didn't really think he'd lend us the money so easily or if I did, it was very naive.'

The station was new and neutrally modern. There was no shortage of matt stainless steel surfaces and cold blue paint. There was however a complete absence of staff to consult should the information on the monitors prove incomprehensible and several benighted Japanese travellers hurried back and forth, anxiously accosting everyone with requests to be put on the Wye train, which had already left. It was some time before it was discovered that it was the Rye train they were after, for which, like Rosie, they were far too early.

The steel walls were posterless, which was boring since she liked to pass the waiting time by making anagrams and the possibilities of TOILETS and SUBWAY were limited. The cafe was spotless, the saffron yellow Danish pastries were expensive, all the chairs were taken and she was not allowed to smoke. Outside on the platform, a low, bum-aching, tubular stainless steel rail was the only form of seating and Rosie squatted miserably on it, trying to keep her knees together and watching sympathetically as at least four people walked slap into the cafe's clear glass electronic doors. By the time the welcomingly mud-spattered marsh train chugged in half an hour later, she had converted HASTINGS to NAGSHITS, GINSTASH and NITSHAGS and was pretty desperate to be at home.

She walked the two miles back to the Jack Cade from the station in her best green suede shoes, spirits and feet further dampened by a sudden shower. Elvira, hearing the irritable banging of the kitchen door, popped her head around from the bar, eyebrows raised.

'Any luck?'

'No. Not a sausage,' said Rosie, kicking off her shoes so hard that one of them went flying across the room and hit an ageing swede in the vegetable basket. She tugged at the damp, stained toes of her tights and mumbled, 'Not a single penny, pfennig, franc, farthing. Not a Euro's chance in a corner shop. Bugger them!'

'Oh, I am sorry. At least you've tried ...' Elvira registered the real disillusion on Rosie's face, caught her moment of angry despair and flew across the room to hug her.

'Guess what? Janice has overcome her coyness and has been helping me in the bar. She's quite happy to be left in charge for a while, it's nearly empty anyway, so you can stay put and recover. We've eaten, but I've put out a slice of the chicken pie and there's a baked potato just about ready in the oven. I'll go and change then get to the nursery. You mustn't giggle when you see Janice, though. Promise?'

Rosie noticed with surprise that Elvira was wearing the Edwardian skirt and that it fitted snugly round her little weasel waist. She managed a watery smile. Aylwin had better watch out, she thought. Others would soon be after Elvira. It was pleasant, having her about, like a daughter of her own, in spite of the engulfing waves of needlework, the little piles of material, off-cuts and pins left to trap the unwary in the arms of chairs. She removed from the table a half-finished cushion cover of overlapping fish-scale patches, ran her hand over the surface to check for needles and sat down to eat.

After eating she pulled an ink-stained copy of Keats's poems from among the cookery books and sat moodily with her feet against the hot cream enamel of the stove for half an hour, reading, accompanied by the punctuating pings of the cold tap dripping into the saucepan in the sink. She was still too irate with the bank to remove the pan and found it difficult to concentrate.

Her father had owned an almost complete set of Kipling, in faded soft red cloth with an elephant's head impressed in gold on the front cover, a tiny lotus flower held in its trunk and an Indian swastika in the background. They were good for making rubbings, onionskin paper laid over the elephant and gently scribbled on with coloured pencil. The pig-eyed elephant always came out quite clearly, like a rubbing of a penny. Dad had never read anything else, not even the five or six paperback Agatha Christies and the copy of the *The Robe* which had belonged to her mother; Ruby also read *Woman's Own*, passed on to her by the postmistress at Rhee, and took books out of the travelling library occasionally, but latterly read only those which confirmed her own experiences and prejudices. There had also been a *Pears Encyclopedia* kept in the kitchen, which always fell open, scattering loose pages, at the much-thumbed medical section.

The only other reading material in the Jack Cade, before she started her own collection, was a tiny, spineless Volume Two of *The History of Tom Jones – a Foundling* by Henry Fielding Esquire, printed for C. Cooke, No. 17 Paternoster Row. Its leather front was oak-smoked with age, and beginning at Book VI with '*In our laft book we have been obliged to deal pretty much with the paffion of love . . .*' ended with Book IX '*If therefore his bafeneff can juftly reflect on any befides himfelf, it muft be only on thofe who gave him his comiffion*'. Rosie knew it by heart. The original owner had done some calculations in pencil on the fly leaf and noted mysteriously on the end paper: '*How much will she be given?'* The book had been discovered beneath a floorboard in her parents' bedroom, the secret place which had at a later date been used for Ben's ring and the necklace. She had been twenty-five before she found out the rest of Tom Jones's story.

As a child she had, very slowly and frequently uncomprehendingly, read the Kiplings, even the boring ones, beneath the bedcovers with a torch. She had pored over Agatha Christie in the lavatory, ignoring her mother's embarrassed knockings on the door as she devoured *Murder in Mesopotamia* for the third time. Later still, she began rapaciously to explore the worlds of others in an attempt to exclude for a few hours the more mundane happenings in her own. She'd been encouraged to stay on at the Grammar to do A level English and Biology, and there had even been talk of university but it hadn't happened. Aylwin had happened, and the world had closed in around her again. Now Rollo Molliner kept her supplied with books and had recently lent her *The Buddha of Suburbia*, which was so far removed from her own adolescence as to be hilariously exotic.

Even if she'd been stationary for most of her life, had been hefted to the Jack Cade like a mountain sheep, bound by habit to its own slopes, she had at least imaginatively voyaged. As for actual travel, over the last few years Sarah Molliner had shown her London on furtive day trips where Rosie had screeched with laughter at the price tags on dresses in Harvey Nichols, clothes only previously seen in the pages of the rare *Vogue* and *Harper's* which turned up at the doctor's waiting room, and had wandered speechless with dread between the root-rent, subfuscous mausoleums in Highgate Cemetery. They'd attended a raucous red and yellow gathering of Punch and Judy puppeteers in Covent Garden, sung 'Jerusalem' to William Blake in Bunhill Fields, been to the Whitechapel Gallery and St Paul's Cathedral. Once Rollo had met them and taken them to an oyster bar in the City, and together they'd plumbed the dank depths of Gordon's wine bar, drinking vast glasses of Sauvignon whilst watching the sad burgeonings and deaths of extra-marital office romances as they waited for the train at Charing Cross. From the top of London buses she'd once seen in through a window in Camden and caught a glimpse of a naked man throwing a cup across the room, and had looked down on derelict slate roofs and seen a triumphant scarlet snapdragon blooming in the choked-up guttering.

It was disconcerting, seeing those thousands of closed, intent London faces and knowing that she would never get to know any of them and that they would never know her, or care.

... and we went on holiday to St Ives when I was seven, she thought, putting the book face down on her lap and trying to comfort herself, unconsciously rocking back and forth on the creaking rush-seated chair, and, I went to Poole with Sally, and Malaga the year after Ben and I married, so I've at least flown once, and been on ferry trips to Boulogne. It's not as if I'd never actually been away.

It was cheaper to get to France and closer than London and she'd won a double Eurostar ticket to Paris from the local paper. That last trip had been kept a nerve-wracking secret from Ben; instead she'd taken her cultural guru, French-speaking Sarah. It had been quite intoxicating, prancing about Paris together, and Rosie had returned explosive with things to tell but having invented another reason for her absence had had to keep silent till Ben was asleep and then, unable to restrain herself, telephoned Aylwin late at night to pour forth all the exciting details of the Musée d'Orsay, of buying a cheap but beautifully well-fitting dark purple skirt, and of eating something called *Gâteau Berrichonne*.

She was interrupted at two-thirty by Janice. There was a young man who particularly wanted to have a word with her. Rosie sighed, closed up the virtual and trotted through to the bar to find out what was passing for reality in Middhaze.

Whilst impatiently waiting for Ollie to arrive on Friday morning, Vicky had her nose stuck into the old building survey of the Jack Cade which she had at last wrested from Paddy. She breathlessly turned the pages of the red folder as if it were a thriller and muttered to herself, like Mr McGregor gloating over his bag of baby rabbits, 'Seven and a half acres! Six bedrooms, and four of them double! Kitchen, fourteen feet by twenty, scullery and wash-house!' She skipped over words such as 'dry-rot' and 're-pointing' but was enraptured by the lilt of 'double-hung sash windows', thrilled by the poetry of lathe and plaster with timber studding, unappalled by the absence of guttering at the rear and the deterioration in the ceiling of bedroom five – 'total replacement recommended'. She exulted at the mention of 'stone archway in kitchen area, possibly thirteenth-century, requiring some attention from skilled stonemason'. She must get in first, she must!

The doorbell rang and she reluctantly set the papers aside to coo over later. Her other homework had been attended to. On ringing the local planning department and, without admitting an interest in any particular place, sounding them out on the procedures involved in decommissioning a licensed property, she was advised it might be difficult although certainly not impossible but that there would be many factors to take into consideration. That was enough for Vicky. Her name had had some bearing on the formation of her character. If not quite impossible, then she would do it.

Ollie, early for once in his life and operating in full romantic mode in tune with the soft spring day, brought her a bunch of lightly crushed mauve and yellow freesias as a thank you for the dinner. She had ordered him to dress suitably recessively for the occasion and he had complied with chameleon ease. Most of his clothes were on the rough side of shabby.

The journey was more or less tiresome to her since he would keep suggesting deviations: a detour through this village or a drink at some other place he happened to know, perhaps a walk on the beach afterwards?

'After what, Ollie?'

'After whatever. After noon, after visiting this Jack Cade chap, after sex . . . ?' He was, as usual, enraptured by her inaccessibility.

'You never give up, do you?'

'You'd be livid if I did. Think back, how annoyed you were

when I arrived at one of your parties with Lizzie Portley! I have to have some amusement, you know, whilst waiting for you to see what a glittering future I'm offering.'

Vicky ignored him and stared primly out of the car window at a suddenly fascinating flock of sheep.

She was disturbed to see that a newly painted sign swung from its post above the hawthorn hedge on the road, but was reassured by the continued dilapidation of the inn itself. There were two cars and a motorbike outside, and once inside, they encountered Elvira introducing Janice to a beer barrel. Janice had changed into what she considered suitable attire for a barmaid: a white blouse with tucks and rampant frills and a long, drooping dark green skirt, cinched tightly around the waist with a wide red plastic belt. She had piled the scarlet hair on top of her head and looked grim and determined, as if unwillingly preparing to serve double *absinthes* to the customers of the Moulin Rouge.

Elvira had come out in sympathy with her, secretly hoping Janice might look less outlandish if she herself dressed up for the occasion, and wore a long white apron over the striped skirt discovered in the linen cupboard, gracefully kicking aside its thick hem and pinked ruffles as she stooped to the beer barrel taps. It had been Elvira's suggestion to the dithering Janice, after Rosie had gone on her mission to the bank, that it would be a treat for Rosie not to have to wolf down her lunch and come straight into the bar on her return. She had been 'training' Janice since half-past ten and, overcoming the older woman's initial nervousness, soon discovered that beneath Janice's tremulous exterior there was a fast brain for figures and that the absence of a till was no trial to her.

'Now, that's the Green & Croswell's Spring Bitter, one pound seventy, and the honey-roasted peanuts, fifty pence.' Elvira took Tiger's money, showing Janice the drawer where the change was kept. 'See, bowls for the change and a box for the notes. If it's a note, don't put it away in the drawer till you've passed over the change, so there are no arguments about giving them change for a five when it was a ten they gave you.' She turned and smiled with complicity at

Ollie who leant tall and nonchalant against the bar, looking pleasant and slightly raffish in a long, grey raincoat which reached nearly to his ankles. He, in turn, was intrigued by their corporate uniform.

'Good morning. What can I get you?'

Vicky stared avidly about her. She was perturbed by the extraordinary nature and high level of staffing and to see there were more customers than she had anticipated. A rosy-cheeked group of walkers in serious socks, their knapsacks and mud-encrusted boots piled behind the door, sipped half-pints by the fire and ate their own sandwiches. A stout fellow with mighty shoulders and a shock of curly greying hair chatted to the lunatic-looking woman behind the bar while an ancient monument, flat-capped and bow-legged in blue dungarees worn beneath a tweed jacket, warned him to have nothing to do with women till he was thirty-seven. A glum and greying couple sat speechlessly opposite each other, occasionally coughing. They made alternate self-important little rigmaroles of finding handkerchiefs and spectacles and of folding and unfolding maps. Retired civil servants, thought Vicky, with nothing left to say to each other. How grim that would be, to run out of conversation at that age, with still another possible twenty years to go ... But I must stop gawping and assimilate. I was expecting it to be almost empty. It isn't exactly busy, but there are more people here than one would hope for. Where can they all have come from?

Two middle-aged men came in just then and stood in the middle of the room, patently amazed by their surroundings. They were dressed in adult baby clothes, the pastel stretch towelling showing every bulge to its disadvantage, and Vicky shuddered at the sight and quietly drew Ollie's attention to the carved beam.

'It's a Green Man in the centre, do you see, in all that carved boskage?' she whispered. 'Isn't it wonderful? Do you understand why I've fallen in love with the place?'

'Yes. The joint's jumping – I expect the death-watch beetles are line-dancing along the rafters,' said Ollie ironically, shaking back his hair and looking about not particularly enthusiastically, but seeing she was most definitely serious, he tried again. 'It's stunningly atmospheric. Is that the right thing to say?' He coughed exaggeratedly as smoke from the fire blew across his face and then stared briefly at the beam in question. A dark and pointy face, its nose battered and grainy, stared slyly back at him from slanted eyes through a carved mask of stiff leaves, flanked at each side by two further foliated bosses depicting a pair of foxes. Ollie looked away, uncomfortable.

'We obviously can't eat here,' he hissed, 'and I'm ravenous! When you've sopped up enough cider and measured up for curtains, we'll go to Rye, shall we, and find a restaurant? I think that's the nearest to civilization round here. I'd even settle for fish and chips.'

'Please keep your voice down and do stop going on about food, Ollie. We've only just arrived! Forget you're in a pub for a moment. Don't you think this would make the most unbelievably beautiful drawing-room? Now, according to the plan I've got at home, that door over there leads into the part they use as a cellar, and on the other side ...' She dropped her voice again and giggled, side-tracked.

'That woman looks exactly like *La Goulue*, doesn't she? Do you think if we la-la'ed and clapped she'd do a can-can and show us her frillies?'

'I don't think I want to see her frillies – is that the one who rescued you from the lavatory? She looks like a horse on the way to the knacker's. The younger girl's pretty, though ... hasn't she got a tiny waist? What a bizarre place – effortlessly ancient. Not like those places which look as if they've had difficulty in retreating far enough into the past to satisfy their owners? In a way, it's sort of a disease, this passion for making everything look old, isn't it? But then, it began in the eighteenth century with all those hired hermits in fake grottos and Marie Antoinette's make-believe farm. The Victorians had it badly too: romantic mediaevalism. We're aware of what's being lost and are disturbed by the future, just as they were. Did you know, when you insisted on buying that useless, worm-eaten wooden dough-trough for your kitchen, that your action was a symptom of an illness? The sign of a civilisation in decline? Or is it perhaps just an attempt to retain one's sanity when faced with too rapid a change? I wish I'd known it was fancy dress . . . Your cider seems to have gone down very fast. Would you like another one?'

'Yes, I would like another. And, no, that isn't Rosie Hooke.' She hadn't been listening to Ollie's ramblings. She didn't want to leave so soon. Rosie's absence was a bonus. Vicky had been anxious that her imagination had rampaged, that the Jack Cade might turn out to have been a figment, but it *was* real, dignified and as solid as remembered and it would be hers by the end of the year, by means fair or foul, regardless of Paddy's timid protestations.

Ollie eventually dragged her away after a surreptitious inspection of the dereliction at the rear of the building, and once back in the car was surprised by her sudden and cider-inspired little burst of passion. Vicky still retained an edge of unpredictability which aroused him and for the briefest span of time he forgot the intervening sixteen or seventeen years since he'd last managed to induce in her any physical manifestations of affection – he had been her brief final sexual fling just before her marriage to Paddy. He smiled a little ruefully at the thought that it was not really mankind Vicky found a turn-on but houses: pediments and cornices, mathematical tiles, bricks, mortar, king posts and curtains, were her erotica.

Vicky was on an imaginary zenith of her own, thinking incautiously, just for a moment as he pushed his hand between her thighs, of an alternative life and how exciting it would be to move into the Jack Cade with Ollie rather than with Paddy. Risk . . . everything was a risk. Ollie had been the most nearly dangerous of all her early acquaintances and his continuing keenness was very touching but she must not allow herself to become impractical.

At that moment Rushett Kadely drew up beside Tiger's motorbike, yawned and rubbed his hands over his eyes. He had been working late into the night at the recording studios for the past two days and had left London early for the weekend, eager to introduce a little mutually beneficial fund-raising scheme to Rosie. He'd given the matter a great deal of attention since her plea for assistance after Ben's funeral.

It was the cut of the fair hair, the shape of the shoulder, that drew his attention as he was about to turn in at the door to the inn. As Vicky came up for air, he saw he was not mistaken but restrained himself from going over and rapping smartly on the steamy window to give her a much-needed shock. Rush recognised neither the elderly blue Saab nor her mop-headed groping partner and slipped inside unseen with a little chortle. He was still grinning when Rosie appeared in the bar, summoned by Janice.

'Hello, Rosie. I was hoping to find you. I see you've just been visited by the grand Mrs Croswell.' Rosie looked a bit washed out, he thought, which was hardly surprising. She stiffened slightly at the mention of the name Croswell.

'Back again, was she? I wonder why? I was having lunch and missed the pleasure of her company.' She looked sharply up at him. 'She isn't a friend of yours? Janice, thank you so much. You seem to have managed very well! Why don't you go and have a coffee? I'll take over now.'

'I've met her here and there,' said Rush, lightly evasive, staring curiously after the departing Janice, 'but she's not quite what I've come to see you about . . . or rather, maybe she is, since I've an idea to kick off your fund-raising. Something to help save you from Green & Croswell's clutches.'

Over a cup of thinly flavoured instant coffee made by Janice, sitting in a patch of sunlight in the window seat, he outlined the plan which Rosie, cautiously excited, promised to put to her family for their immediate consideration. He made further notes, then drove away to his hermitage.

It was clouding over when he arrived and a curlew rose from a field and flew across the horizon. Rush sniffed the air for the scent of salt and walked round the house, examining things; the overflowing water-butt, the orange lichen on a fence-post, the snub noses of miniature tulip bulbs growing through the stony soil. He was home, and banging shut the door behind him on the greying skies and impending rain, set about lighting the wood-stove.

The interior of the small house was very plain indeed and cleanly white: walls, floors and woodwork. The only hints of colour came from the curtains and divan covers of pale, blue-grey linen, a large, faded nut-brown and black Afghan rug upon the floor and a bright pink plastic rose, which he'd found on the path in Fingle graveyard, tucked on top of the circular white-framed looking-glass.

The absence of possessions was calming, and deceptive. All around the room alternating with the divans were low cupboards, locked, which hid his past history and which, from time to time, when suffering from crises, he would open and lovingly sort through and tidy, like a squirrel counting its cobnuts or, perhaps, a traveller consulting a guide-book.

He took a handful of CDs from his small leather briefcase, selected one and drummed his hands on the kitchen windowsill while the kettle boiled, listening to the extraordinary male voice weaving like raw silk through the pounding accompaniment. Very odd, very odd indeed, not unlike a cross between a Mongolian throat-singer and a counter-tenor. Koumar Ramsbottom from Middlesborough, alias Mel Plunket, could be big. Very, very big. A millennial sound with deep roots?

Chuckling at his own pomposity, Rush searched out a packet of Monsooned Malabar coffee and a cardamon pod which he carefully cut in half to release its aromatic seeds into the brew.


'Rush Kadeley wants to use the back field in early May, to hold a private party with marquees and bands.' There was a suppressed excitement about Rosie as she leant forward in her chair and surveyed the three faces turned expectantly towards her, their knives and forks poised in the air as they sat over plates of roast chicken and spring greens.

After Rush's visit, Rosie had unexpectedly recovered both strength and humour and taken advantage of a break in the weather, spending what was left of the afternoon cleaning out the chickens and turning over the drying earth in the vegetable patch. Her creamy skin was pinkened from the glow of the sun now setting behind the orchard. Elvira, although she had the cruel eyesight of the young who take note of every tiny wrinkle, each little sag and softening, thought Rosie looked remarkably beautiful for someone of her age, even if she hadn't removed her wellingtons and had a streak of dried mud on her neck.

Aylwin, politely holding out a greasy wishbone to Janice for her to pull with him, was curious.

'Is he paying rent for the field? Oh, you've got the bigger piece. Quick, quick! Make a wish.'

'Better than that. He *says* he'll guarantee us half the profits! He promises a minimum of £500, thinks at least four hundred people will be coming. If it's a success he'll organize another one in July. By the way, the silencer's gone on the Rotorvator. It sounds like a Chieftain tank.'

'I'll get it fixed at the weekend. And I'll do the Rotorvating anyway – you'll put your back out, struggling with the thing.'

'Thank you, Aylwin. I have to admit it's a bit heavy for me. I didn't realize when I started on the job. Once it gets a will of its own and heads off down to the Land of Oz, it's incredibly hard to get its nose up again. The old patch has never been so deeply dug. But come on, tell me, what do you think of Rush's idea?'

Aylwin looked as if he might have reservations. 'It sounds a bit too good to be true. It's got to be a very exorbitant rave, if that's what it is? Why is he being so generous to us? What's our part in it? Do we do the drinks and things, set up a beer tent?'

'No, we don't do anything. He told me he was organizing the party anyway but that this would be a better place than the one he'd first booked. He'll be arranging absolutely everything. All we have to do is be discreet – he doesn't want gate-crashers. And from what he said it sounds considerably more sophisticated than a rave. We could provide bouncers, perhaps?' She giggled, knowing it all sounded a bit unlikely, but leant forward eagerly. 'Anyway, I'm asking you all first for your opinions. I think we should go for it. We'd have to get old Ted's sheep out of there a few days before, and clean it up – Rush says he wouldn't want his guests dancing about shin-deep in sheep shit. The thing that attracted him is the privacy, no neighbours to complain and no one being able to see what was going on from the lane because of the trees. They'll be in leaf by then. It'll be attended by a lot of people from the pop music world, you see.'

'Ooh!' said Janice, translucent, blood-red currant jelly dripping from her fork into the voluminous frills on her thin chest. 'Who do you think?' Transported back to the late 6os at the mention of pop, she shimmied to the Hollies, even ultra-coolly shared a joint with Donovan, barefoot on a beach in a little purple Biba dress, catching the wind in her blowing mane of coppery hair.

'Those sort of people usually want to be *seen* partying, don't they?' asked Aylwin. 'What makes him think they'll come trooping down to this neck of the woods to party in such seclusion?'

'He seemed certain they would. He's bussing them all down here. He'd got it all planned out and we walked round the area together with him taking notes – bus parks and toilets and all that. It's a five-acre field; there's plenty of room. He wanted to put up a tent right round the May tree in the middle, but I told him that if it was actually flowering at the time, people would suffocate with the smell. It's not the best of things to have in an enclosed space. Anyway, he'll phone on Sunday night for our answer.' Rosie stood up and stacked the plates.

'It's very unlucky to bring May inside houses.' The alarmist Janice had come out of her reverie. Proverbs clattered from her lips like plates in the kitchen. 'It brings death.'

'As I said, it has a very foetid stench in a confined space, I expect that's why it's considered unlucky. There's usually some practical reason for these superstitions. I've not had time to make a pudding. We could finish those crumpets ... I really fancy a crumpet and marmalade. Aylwin, would you mind taking your socks off the breadboard and nipping into the bar to stoke up the fire? And I need another dozen Newcastle Browns from the cellar before you go and do your stint at the typewriter. How's it going anyway?'

'I'm having a break from writing this evening. I've got to the stage where all the interesting bits of the story are complete and I'm a bit frightened of actually joining them up.'

It was very warm in the kitchen and Rosie yawned. It had been a long day and there was the evening session to be got through. The wind was rising, humming through the tiny hole in the thick window pane where Aylwin had once carelessly let fly with an air-gun.

'I hope it's busy tonight so I don't have to listen to any more of Loopy Lenny's fund-raising ideas. I know he can't do joined-up thinking but he suggested a beer-mat auction! Apparently *he* collects them, but surely no one else does? And last night Brian the Book thought we should hold our own Olympic Games . . .' She stopped and put her head to one side and looked consideringly at Elvira's little sharp-sweet face. 'But, perhaps that's not such a foolish idea as it sounds . . . I'd automatically binned it because it came from Brian. Where's my list? I think I'll write that one down. In fact, I think it's positively brilliant!

'Elvira, I'm afraid one of the geese has had a go at Aylwin's best shirt. It pulled it off the line and ate half the mother-of-pearl buttons before I could rescue it. Could you be a sweetheart and look out some replacements from the button box while I change my clothes? I'll sew them on before it gets busy in the bar.'

It must have been a goose folk memory, she thought, the bird distinguishing mother-of-pearl from plastic. They needed extra calcium whilst laying and had helped themselves, being also partial to lime plaster off the stable walls and rotting wood, as well as grass and corn. She must remember to take a basket of goose eggs through into the bar that evening to sell. She sighed. She was accustomed to this state of constant financial insecurity but was beginning to find it enervating. It was pleasant though, having company; there were surprisingly few tensions. Aylwin and Elvira just got on with their lives, helping out when they could and Janice, in spite of their misgivings, her inconvenient beliefs and endless paper hankies, was proving to be a very sweet-tempered woman.

# Chapter Five

Aylwin and Elvira set out at seven o'clock in the chilly grey of Easter Monday morning for the first car boot fair of the season. Rosie's van sagged unhappily beneath the weight of their wares and they were obliged to unload two boxes of books and a pair of defunct paraffin stoves before leaving.

As they unloaded they were besieged by dealers whose hands flickered over their offerings, delved into boxes and rudely turned up chairs to inspect their bottoms for woodworm. Elvira, bumble-fingered with the early-morning cold, became frantic since she couldn't keep track of them and shouted that if they weren't allowed to unpack in peace, they'd put the whole lot back in the van or double the prices. No notice was taken and during the mêlée she lost and had to assume stolen a little china box with a silver thimble in it, and was most upset.

However, by nine o'clock the sun came out, they'd more than recovered their pitch money and had made enough for Elvira to sprint round the other stalls to see if there was anything suitable for the B and B room. She staggered back to Aylwin with a large gilt picture frame which to his amazement she immediately sold again for three times its purchase price. The profit was invested in six pairs of unused Egyptian cotton sheets and eight pillowcases, all still tied up with neat green ribbon bows.

Aylwin, still half-asleep, found the whole affair a bit beneath his dignity at first, particularly when people insisted on dickering over such tiny amounts. A man kept asking would he take ten pence for a saucer marked twenty and Aylwin became bored and said it must have been wrongly priced, it should have been a pound. The man grumbled but paid the pound. The psychology of it eluded Aylwin and he escaped from the stall and hunted down large quantities of off-white emulsion paint at a knockdown price, and for fifty pence purchased a children's picture book, *The Gremlins* by Flight Lieutenant Roald Dahl. He thought it was interesting since it was about the Battle of Britain and the pictures were by Walt Disney, from a war-time cartoon production of which he'd never heard. Elvira was unimpressed when he produced a Royal West Kent Regimental metal cap badge, a prancing horse with the word 'Invicta' in a scroll above it.

'I thought we were only supposed to be buying things for the inn?'

'Aha! But Grandpa was in the Royal West Kents. Rosie might like it. They've disappeared now – amalgamated by the Government years and years ago. It's very pretty, don't you think? And it was only thirty pence for the beret it was attached to. I only bought it because my head was cold.' He looked pleadingly at her. 'They'd overlooked the badge because the beret was in a box of old boots and was inside out.'

The level of poverty exhibited by some of the stalls was depressing: battered and grubby plastic toys and lidless sauce-pans, ubiquitous brown stoneware mugs decorated with ochre-yellow daisies, a ripped leather jacket or worn work boots and an assortment of country and western LPs laid out on a dirty blanket. Aylwin miserably imagined everything gone wrong, the Jack Cade repossessed and Elvira and himself once again attending a boot fair, not with the unused contents of the china cupboard and sheds but this time in dire need, with all their personal, precious and private belongings laid out on old bits

of carpet. How easy it was to slide down the scale – at least
the marketing man's social scale on which you were classified
according to profession or lack of it. He wondered where a
writer stood in relation to a printer.

There was a change in the clientele as the morning progressed; the hungry dealers drifted away to be replaced by eager,
well-breakfasted, grey-haired ladies, pouncing on decanters and
peering at maker's names on the backs of plates, hustling their
husbands away from useful carpenter's tools in order to take
charge of yet another bulging carrier bag of doubtful goodies.
Later, the families arrived and wandered pointlessly up and down
in the sunshine with dogs and pushchairs, barely looking at the
stalls and intent on refusing their wailing children anything.
Aylwin watched, shocked, as a woman slapped and swore at
tiny children whose only fault appeared a natural desire for
that particular broken blue plastic lorry or this tawdry dolly.
He bought the doll and rushed after a weeping little girl to
give it to her, only to be told: 'F ... off! You a pervert?' by
her Sycorax of a mother.

Embarrassed and angered by her belligerence, he wandered
off to sulk on the beach behind the cars. It was all good copy,
he supposed, and he brought out a notebook and biro. Hunting
gulls floated above, their heads turning back and forth as they
mechanically scanned for scraps beneath them. The sea was
churned and choppy and a fishing boat pitched and rolled
in the middle distance. Feeling sympathetically seasick, he
loitered and ambled back through the stalls and bought a
cup and saucer, which Elvira later despairingly assured him she
had sold to a dealer only twenty minutes earlier for half the price
he'd paid. She was keen to prove to Rosie that their trip had
been worthwhile and felt he wasn't taking it seriously enough.

'Ah. I knew it looked familiar,' he said guiltily, and was eager
to make amends. 'I thought it would be easier to sell a pair, you
see. It's a different world here, isn't it? Quite cut-throat, in its
way. Why do people bother to have children if they're going to

be so poisonous to them? Is there any coffee left in the Thermos? There's a van selling hamburgers somewhere about – I can smell it. I'll find it and get us some, shall I?'

'Why have you got a doll sticking out of your pocket?' She tugged at its matted and fibrous orange hair.

'It's a present for you, daft girl. I thought you could call it Green & Croswell and stick pins in it.'

In spite of these purchases and the odd mistake, their take was an outrageously successful ninety-eight pounds. They returned home harmoniously at twelve o'clock, in a near-empty van, extremely pleased with themselves and hopeful of congratulations.

At lunchtime on Tuesday, Rosie returned from the nursery garden with a gift from its owner, the ever-generous Nest, three boxes of ruby-red and only-slightly-bruised double daisies to sell to the customers. A personal letter sat on the top of a stack of junk mail on the kitchen table. The envelope was of importantly thick cream paper and, suspecting further condolences, she left it sitting there till after the gratifyingly busy lunchtime session. Trade was definitely picking up and without Ben's alcoholic depredations their takings over the past week were encouraging.

She organized Janice with emulsion paint, brushes and rags, and ignoring her protestations that she wasn't any good at decorating, encouraged her to start work on the guest room. She herself intended to spend the remainder of the sunny afternoon planting out onion sets and garlic. Already gum-booted, in old jeans and the thick blue sweater which she wore when gardening, Rosie took the letter into the parlour and shut the door. The light in there was soft on the creamy walls. The desk had been de-Benned, her own current correspondence was now filed in the pigeon holes and she had dusted, polished and smothered its ugliness with three bunches of primroses; it was all gratifyingly business-like. She could hear Janice upstairs, trotting about on the floorboards and trilling 'I am an ocean wave, my lo-o-ove . . .' off-key. Relieved that she was settling in so well, Rosie ripped open the letter.

The child walked past the window and glanced in, its head just above the sill; a colourless regard, palely interested, as whitely querying as Keats's wan primroses gathered at midnight. It was at the transient instant so very normal that although her brain began, slowly, to register surprise, the vision was gone before the goosebumps had risen prickling to the skin's surface. She had wanted to call out, 'Wait! What do you want?' but it had gone before the words were arranged. She understood now why there had been so little fuss made about it. A child, perhaps ten years old and blonde, its body appeared solid with no hint of Victorian ectoplasmic butter muslin. It was not threatening yet it was out of place, disturbing, perhaps like catching sight of someone one thought one knew on *Crimewatch*.

Rosie closed her eyes for a second and opened them again to read the letter in her hand. That at least was real.

13th April

Dear Mrs Hooke,

In spite of my connections with Green & Croswell, I am writing to you on a purely personal level. I understand that it is likely that you will be putting the Jack Cade on the market shortly and, bearing in mind the difficulties of selling such a property with its urgent need for modernisation and its barrelage tie, we would like to make you a prior, private offer to purchase the freehold.

We are confident that we can come up with a price which, since we will be seeking planning permission to turn it into a private house, will be more than could be obtained on the open market as a public house and certainly far more advantageous than the price agreed by the brewery should it revert to them in November.

Perhaps you would care to consider this and then discuss it with me? I am free at any time this Friday, if that would suit. I look forward to hearing from you.

Yours sincerely,

Victoria Croswell

Rosie read it twice more. It was as clear as gin, the handwriting round and confident, and it came from what she assumed was the Croswells' private address.

She marched up and down in an unusual fury, the floor-boards squeaking in protest.

She wants to get hold of it cheaply before it reverts to the brewery. She *assumes* it will revert. She assumes, quite rightly, that we're in deep financial dogshit. She knows the brewery might then decide to retain it as a pub. They might also re-let it or remove the barrelage tie and sell it as a private house on the open market, although they'd also need permission from the Council to do that. But she won't wait till then, perhaps because she knows that to satisfy the brewery she'd have to pay almost full market value? But he's the MD, so you'd think he'd be able to sort it to their advantage. People like them know people on planning committees, but even then it would be dodgy ...

Rosie stopped pacing and fuming. She stood by the window, inspecting the rough palms of her hands thoughtfully, turning them round and looking forlornly at the uneven fingernails.

Ben allowed us to be trussed up like chickens by that damn' brewery. Even if we sold it to her, the mortgages would still have to be paid back and then what would be left? And what would I do? I belong here and running the inn is the only thing I know. It isn't a question of money. I'm not leaving except by force! Damn her, and damn her sneaky little offer. I don't even want to know how much she's prepared to pay. We've already decided. Nothing's changed.

She knew by heart every crack in the plaster, the texture of each beam, every damp patch, door-latch, worn brass handle and egg-cup of the Jack Cade Inn. She knew the window pane in the scullery where long ago someone had scratched their name, *Iohn Amys*, with a diamond. She remembered where her mother had lost her wedding ring while cleaning out the rabbits and the place behind the red-currant bushes where Sally had fallen and cut her knee on a piece of glass one Whitsun. She now knew the child too.

How continuously her thoughts turned to Sally. Why did it seem easier to recall long-gone Sally than Ben, whose death was so much more immediate? Sally had never been far from her thoughts in all the years that had passed since her death, but lately she seemed to be ubiquitous, popping up night and day, any place, any time.

Rosie was aware of being foolhardy and knew that the decision was an uncharacteristically emotional one, but without waiting to talk it over with Aylwin and with rage breeding an unusual clarity of thought, she sat and wrote a prematurely defiant reply to Vicky Croswell, announcing an inability to understand from where she had got the impression that they needed to sell the Jack Cade. It was not for sale and never would be. They would save themselves.

The nearest letter box was at Middhaze proper, the small settlement a mile up the lane, consisting of five or six cottages, and further on Sarah's house, set about lumpy fields and the ruined east wall of a defunct church – a perpendicular cardboard cut-out standing on a mound and reflected in the dark water of a dyke below. The last post was at three-fifteen and before she could lose her nerve, Rosie ran upstairs to the paint-bespattered Janice to tell her that she was going out and instructed her on what to do when the Green & Croswell beer delivery arrived.

She slipped on an old donkey jacket and set off in the sunshine at a great rate on her bicycle with Trash cantering along behind. It was a relief to get away from the house into the positive sunshine and she swerved joyfully round fallen willow branches and bounced over treacherous rain-filled holes in the crumbling tarmac. She would post the letter and visit Sarah Molliner and sound her out on the possibilities of Brian the Book's Olympics. A fresh perspective on the events of the past two weeks was needed.

Rosie zig-zagged back and forth over the strip of grass which grew along the centre of the lane, trying not to think about the letter in her pocket. The moth-eaten hawthorn hedges were showing life-green patches; lambs with sunlight shining pinkly through their baby ears stared nosily at her through the gaps as she rattled past.

The brick-built letterbox stood opposite a pair of cottages where lived Lenny in a state of tenuous truce with one of the Kittens. The same wide dyke that flowed behind the field at the inn joined the lane at that point and ran alongside it for a further mile.

Sarah Molliner was crawling up its bank, red with exertion, long curly blonde-grey hair slipping out of an untidy granny-knot at the back of her head and clinging wetly to her cheeks. She appeared a trifle scatty, standing there in rose-pink trousers and a necklace apparently made from tiny Christmas decorations, a dripping length of washing line in one hand and a mud-spotted manila envelope in the other. Sarah stuck a booted foot firmly on the rope while posting the letter and waited as Rosie drew up breathlessly and dismounted, the panting Trash dancing about her as she dispatched her own letter with a little moan of agony.

'Was that something important you've just posted? I haven't seen you since the funeral – are you keeping a step ahead of the bailiffs?' Sarah's question was not insensitive; she had a friendly, intelligent face and it was now concerned. 'Has anyone come up with some shatteringly brilliant idea to save the Jack Cade? I've been wracking my brains without success so far.'

'Not yet, but there are one or two things on the simmer.

That letter was to turn down an offer that would have saved us financially, but lost us the inn. I feel a bit light-headed, foolish even, about refusing to even discuss it.'

Rosie pointed in disbelief at the shallow black bowl of a boat, floating unreliably in the water below them at the end of the rope. Trash growled at it.

'Don't tell me you came out in that thing?'

'Yes. Isn't it funny? It's a coracle. If one isn't in a hurry, it's a great way of getting about. The only trouble is that it's so low in the water it's impossible to see over the banks and guess one's whereabouts. If it wasn't for the height of the church ruin I wouldn't have known when to stop paddling. I'm also terrified of meeting swans – they're so aggressive at this time of the year.'

'But where did you get it from?'

'An acquaintance of mine in Somerset makes them. I bought it from him. I haven't quite got the hang of it yet and could probably have walked the quarter-mile in less time, but then the wind was against me. Why don't you follow me on your bike back to the house?' Rosie watched, intrigued, as Sarah stepped gingerly into the coracle, rocking about dangerously before arranging herself plumb in the centre of the seat.

'That's the worst bit, climbing out and in. I'll race you!' she called up, weaving and splashing the paddle about in the water in front of the boat but going about in a tight and unintentional circle. 'Damn! Two minutes on land and I've lost the knack. I could get seriously seasick in this. Ah, here we go!'

Rosie arrived first and waited for Sarah on the bank at the end of the garden, offering to help haul the boat out. But Sarah refused, crying out that it was light as a feather, it was only tarred canvas, and she could easily carry it. She flipped it bottom up and, hoisting it on her back like a water-beetle's carapace, wavered across the grass on thin legs, staggering under its wet weight, to heave it finally onto a peg in a lean-to shed to drip dry.

'I'm shattered! I think it probably has its limitations as a form of transport, but it's very good for the muscles.'

They lolled contentedly on a green garden swing seat in the large sunny studio, a converted brick farm-building separate from the house, drinking unfamiliar green gunpowder tea and staring at Sarah's latest creation. She was a sculptress. Her medium was glass and although larger commissions were sometimes carried out at glassworks in the East End of London, the majority, being intricately constructed from many small sections, was completed there in the studio. Dazed, Rosie had once watched Sarah and her assistant working when the furnace was roaring and been enthralled by the apparent danger of the molten glass and hellish, eyeball-searing heat.

Sarah's extraordinary constructions sparkled in the atriums of office blocks in the City. Magical seats of apparently solid crystal shone out at the end of yew-lined vistas in the gardens of private mansions, and a giant chandelier was gently swung, by the aid of a tiny electric motor, from the ceiling of the new People's Museum of the Twentieth Century in Llanelli. Its drops had been handblown into moulds in the forms of people with outstretched arms. It was an apotheosis of carefully tuned, softly tinkling figures representing, she had hurriedly told its startled commissioners, the very men and women involved in the manufacture of the museum's exhibits during the past hundred years. She admitted later to Rosie that she had thought that up on the spur of the moment and was quite smug about its political correctness, but the sculpture had in fact been inspired by one of William Blake's illustrations to Dante's *Divine Comedy*.

'Now, tell,' she said, plumping up a cushion and kicking off her boots. 'What's been going on?'

Rosie explained the projected party and the Games, which brought a rapturous response.

'The Romney Marsh Olympics – Rosie's Games! But that's brilliant! You could run it over a bank holiday weekend – there's one at the end of May, isn't there? And sell tickets for watching the events – you'd need three or four taking place each afternoon.' She waved her arm expansively. 'You can sell concessions for side-shows and charge the entrants a little as well.'

'Could you organize coracle-racing, do you think?'

'Of course! There must be others in the South East.' Sarah's eyes glittered. 'I'll track them down, get a list of customers from the man who made mine.'

'I thought we could get a charity tie-in, make a donation out of the profits, then it'll be easier to get publicity ... We could have silly things like marshman steeplechasing or pole-vaulting dykes, and a proper tug-of-war. Men and maids of Kent versus Kentish men and women!'

Although buoyed up by Sarah's enthusiasm, Rosie was still intimidated by the amount of organisation the event would require. Sarah waved that aside impatiently.

'You must delegate. You've been functioning on your own for far too long: trust people. They're all dying to help. Put one person, with a second-in-command, in charge of each separate event. I'll have a word with Rollo about public liability and weather insurance, see if he can get you a good deal. That's very important. And we'll have to find someone to bankroll you for expenses. That man we brought round to the Jack Cade a couple of weeks ago, the night the musicians were in ... he's rolling in money and adored everything about the place.'

She looked fondly at Rosie. 'You've had so much to put up with for so long. I get very airy-fairy working here alone all week. Do you know, after Rollo, of course, at present the Jack Cade is my sanity, my contact with the everyday world? I'd miss it desperately if it went under and became a snooty private house, with white post-and-chain railings across the front and brick pillars with concrete pineapples on top. If you do your utmost to prevent that happening, I'll do the best I can too.'

\*      \*      \*

The air was still early-April warm when Rosie returned home and it was not too late to get some gardening done. She hurriedly dashed together the ingredients for a lamb stew and set it in the oven. She made Janice a cup of tea and praised her painting, adjusted the soft spile in the top of a new beer barrel in the bar to allow the foam from the still working contents to ease out safely and then, collecting a radio from the parlour, she at last escaped into the garden.

She placed the radio on a tree stump and started planting, preferring that day the sound of human voices, wanting words rather than music. The oily word 'connubial' slipped from the tongue of the broadcaster, its syllables slyly, falsely promising comfort but suggesting hard labour. She'd missed the first part of the sentence, and now they were off on another topic.

'Received pronunciation' was what they called the accents of these confident voices. But how else could they have been expected to acquire it? By theft, perhaps? Rosie saw no reason not to speak as her parents had spoken and unconsciously expected everyone else to do the same.

The grey-and-white-barred Marran chickens in the orchard scraped and bowed, uttering soft purring croaks of affected surprise as they routed out a wire-worm or woodlouse. There were a few oddities amongst the flock, interbred bantam hens and a cockerel named Baldur the Beautiful, whose cape was such a vivid shade of iridescent green that he could be seen from a considerable distance. 'Vivid', that was a good word. Bright and alive, the repeated 'vi-vi' giving it lightness but ending on 'd' for strength. A vivid imagination, a vivid face. The violets by the orchard fence were vividly purple and smelt of musty, long-gone great-aunts. She would pick enough to fill an egg-cup and put them in the kitchen, to see if the smell conjured up the same thing for Janice. Aylwin and Elvira were too young to remember the existence of violet-scented aunts.

She stooped and pressed each onion bulblet firmly into the light, rich, alluvial soil, using the length of her own foot as a measure, and like a priest bidding farewell to the individual members of his congregation, gave each one a little pat and whispered benediction. Now there was a different discussion in progress on the radio between an earnest young man and a hornet-like interviewer.

'Ahem ... So why do you think this particular study of popular culture is so important?'

'Because it defines major factors in the collective interests of a large percentage of the population, the young in particular, who are alienated by the elitist intellectualism of the so-called "high" culture.'

Rosie dropped an onion inside her boot.

'I see. So, you do agree at least that there *is* a high culture, even if you don't like it? Isn't popular culture merely the "if you can't wear it, smoke it or dance to it, it's of no interest to us" culture? Totally commercially generated? Big business? And isn't it just as exclusive and élitist in its own way as "high" culture?'

The interviewee was silent for a considerable time, so while waiting for his answer Rosie sat on the grass and shook the onion out of her boot.

'Participating in it is a rite of passage.'

There was a snort of disgust. Rosie planted the recovered onion with extra care.

'That's a load of nonsense, and you know it!' The inter-viewer's voice was hectoring. 'A passage to where? By saying participation in popular culture is a particular passing point in one's life,' here the interviewer spat out the alliterative 'P's with venom, 'even you are assuming you must pass on to another point as you get older. Or do you expect to stay young and sexy forever? And what is that further point if it isn't *higher* quality thought, music, art, etcetera? Why not start with the best in the beginning? Why are you so terrified of making quality judgements?' The voice became fainter; the battery was running out.

It was a rhythmic job, planting onions. Rosie occasionally threw aside a runt bulb, a pebble, a rusted nail or ancient piece of flaking oyster shell. The diatribe on the radio was now reduced to faint tweetings. A robin appeared. She unearthed what looked like the mud-encrusted handle of an ornate Victorian poker. 'Are you ancient high or pop?' she addressed it, rubbing it with her thumb before slipping it in her pocket along with the greenish farthing found earlier.

She and Sally used to go on treasure hunts, armed with trowels, along the edge of the field where there was a line of depressions indicating old rubbish pits; they unearthed quantities of blue and white china, rusted enamel pans and iridescent glass. Sometimes the glass had been distorted in the heat of a bonfire, the patent medicine bottles transformed unrecognisably to writhen forms of ice green or cobalt blue. They found, and fought over, a broken silver teaspoon with a deep split in the metal of the handle, just above the bowl, and in snatching it from each other, snapped it. Rosie kept the handle, since it had a delicate feathery R engraved on it and Sally kept the bowl. Finding things, however useless, helps one to believe in Providence.

How would Sarah's glass be classified? It was simple to look at and understand, so it should be popular, but then it was the product of years of training, thought and experience, wasn't it, and a particular visual genius, which probably meant that it was high? Was it the depth of thought and the amount of effort allied to genius that went into producing 'great' art that scared people off? And what was genius anyway?

Rosie finished planting the onions and sowed three rows of spinach beet and parsnips. Sarah had said that the inn was her sanity. Well, it was hers too, only more than that ... in some sense she *was* the inn. She could no more sell it than sell herself. But then came the disturbing thought that that was what she had actually done in marrying Ben. She had sold herself then, complaisantly enough, in order to keep it.

She was the Jack Cade's keeper and would remain so. *The innkeeper.* She kept the inn, it kept her in, she kept in it. She would tell them all at supper that she'd seen the child.

On Tuesday evening, Vicky was in an acrid mood as she dressed to go alone to a private view of an arts and crafts show. Megan Sliverley, who had been her intended companion, had sinusitis. Paddy had pleaded working late, and when she'd tried to summon Ollie for escort duty, he was unaccountably more interested in going out for a drink with Jos Sliverley. The wimpy children had loosed a whinging jeremiad, producing at least ten reasons each why they should not be forced to attend, which was a pity, since she felt it was time their sporting activities were balanced with a little culture.

Rosie's letter declining to discuss the sale of the inn had arrived that morning. Unnerved by its confident and dismissive tone, Vicky burnt the toast and shouted at Cressie but resolved to leave it for a week to gather her energies before trying again. Perhaps a personal visit this time would be more useful – a little more pressure perhaps, an insinuation that the brewery was already unfavourably reviewing their case?

She had ascertained from a reluctant Paddy that the Jack Cade's manner of repaying their mortgage left a lot to be desired. It was quite evident that they were in trouble. Even he had been surprised to discover that it was apparently his father, George, who had insisted there was nothing to worry about and had instructed that they should be left alone, so long as the interest came in. There must be some way in which she could smoke out the source of Rosie Hooke's confidence?

Anyway, now it was which shoes to wear with which skirt and bugger everything else! Vicky felt she must attend, having recently been inveigled into becoming a Friend of the Arts Trust organising the show. A Friend of a great many organisations and charities, with a catholic register of commitments of this sort, her annual subscriptions to these institutions amounted to a hefty sum. Although she had long since lost interest in raising money for a certain historic building, or for stewardship in perpetuity of a colony of dormice and had fallen out with the Charity Ball committee, they all still benefited since she never remembered to cancel the various direct debits.

'One might as well be living in Ireland,' she moaned as she left the house in the drifting mizzle and ran to the car, a seed pearl and peridot necklace bouncing against her generous grey cashmere-clad chest.

A woman in a large van was patiently waiting for a parking space in a side street near the gallery and Vicky, feeling aggressive and on the right side of the road to take advantage of the departing car, manoeuvred smartly into it. Adolescent words were exchanged.

'I hope you rot in hell!'

'You look as if you're rotting already!'

The other woman, eccentrically dressed and now speechless, stamped back to the van and drove off. Once inside the echoing creaminess of the gallery's minimalist foyer, Vicky shook off the little unpleasantness with the rain drops, signed the visitors' book and grabbed a glass of acid white wine. She began a predatory prowl about the exhibits which were arranged in screened-off sections, each already crowded with its artist, chattering acolytes and past patrons who were, as is usual at private views, obscuring the works on show from everyone else.

Vicky was searching for a painting to fill a gap in the drawing-room or perhaps some large ceramic object to place on the Regency console table between the windows, but conversation with the producers of the artefacts was daunting since they appeared to speak another language. She'd once been guilty of an ire-inspiring visit to an artist, during which she'd held a swatch of curtain material up to each painting in turn, trying to find one that matched, and then announced condescendingly that she'd buy two of the pictures if he painted the frames a russet pink, to match her sofa. She had not been able to understand why the man had thrown a paddy and it wasn't until later, in the comforting surroundings of a favourite wine bar, that Janie Cutt-Norton had gently explained that it was perhaps the other way about? One was supposed to buy a painting because one liked it for itself, or at least give the poor artist the impression that there was more to one's choice than a fortuitous colour match, and *then* arrange the furnishings to complement it. Since then Vicky had tried to deal more carefully with the fragile egos of artists; they were so tetchy.

She was standing entranced before a jeweller's stand when she overheard a breathless conversation on the other side of the partition. She picked up a bracelet and casually admired it whilst listening.

'I'm sorry I'm so late. Some cow nicked my parking space and I had to park miles away and make two trips in the rain with the boxes. Anyway, I'm here now. Thank you so much for giving me a hand – let's get the show on the road!' It was definitely Ms Rot-in-hell and that explained to some extent why she had been so rude. Vicky replaced the bracelet and picked up a necklace, gold fish hanging on a fine wavy hoop of gold, and looked up and smiled encouragingly at the blonde girl who sat quietly beside the stall. The girl's nails were painted iridescent drake's head green and were busy with a polishing cloth and a silver ring.

'Might I try this on?'

'Of course you may. Here's a looking glass.'

There were tinkling sounds from next door and disembodied little cries of: 'That's it!' 'No, an inch more this way!' 'How's Rollo?' 'There, that looks immaculate.'

'Guess what?' the disappointed parker continued. 'You know that lovely inn near us on the marsh, the one you took Rollo and me to when we first went to live there? No, not the Eeldyke, I mean Rosie Hooke's place. Rollo and I spend an inordinate amount of time there at weekends because it's within walking distance. Well, perhaps you've heard already but Rosie's in financial trouble and the inn is under threat of being sold, as a private house, would you believe?'

Vicky froze, her face reflected in the glass, incredulous. The girl caught the look and was puzzled as it passed from incredulity to venom. Vicky recovered and pointed at another necklace, dragging out the jewellery session to hear more. She lowered her voice.

'No, perhaps not. What about that one? I think silver looks so much classier with grey, don't you?' The girl bent and lifted a silver version from its brown velvet case and handed it to her, resecuring the gold one. They were joined by another potential customer, searching for a ring.

'Yes,' the voice continued. 'We're all going to help with events to raise money and stop it. The first one is going to be a big private party, renting the field behind in May. And she's planning something else, a sort of rural pastiche Olympic Games for later, at the end of the month. It's all quite inspiring. You must tell friends to visit, boost her trade a bit.'

'Hello, Victoria. Buying some crown jewels?'

She spun round and there stood Janie, grinning.

'I'm thinking about it. Isn't this attractive?' She smiled again at the little jeweller, ingratiatingly this time. 'What are these pale green stones?'

'Hang on a sec. I'll ask my mother. I'm looking after things for her.' To Vicky's horror she slipped round to the next-door stand. 'Mum, I'm really busy here, can you come for a minute?'

Thankfully the woman who emerged was not the one with whom she'd had the parking contretemps, being tiny, older, and an expert saleswoman. Janie watched, astonished and gloating, as Vicky was fluently lauded, gently cajoled and teased into producing a credit card. It was most unusual since Vicky always knew exactly what she did and didn't want and normally made short work of those who offered the latter.

Vicky was so distracted by what she had heard that the delicate hand-made silver chain dangling an assortment of flowers, birds and aventurine and turquoise eggs, was rustled into tissue paper and presented to her in a little silk bag with a drawstring almost before she became conscious of the fact that she'd bought it. While this was happening, Rot-in-hell called out that she was just going back to the van since she'd left behind a vital piece of something. As she passed, Vicky kept her face turned to the beamingly successful little woman in front of her, saw how pretty she appeared in a similar necklace and was unable to prevent herself from beaming back, although she did not feel at all like beaming. She wandered casually with Janie to the next stand, still in a fog as to how she'd come to spend so much and dazed by the worrying nature of what she'd heard.

The next stand was twice the size and in a central position. Its occupant was plainly someone of considerable rank in the artistic hierarchy for only three objects were displayed in the space, the sides of the stand being occupied by large black and white photographs. Centrally, on a sky-blue cloth, beautifully lit and apparently floating, three spheres of glass rotated and deep in their thunder-and-white clouded interiors drifted, by wizardry, a gathering of miniature glass people. As Vicky and Janie stared, momentarily awed, a small crowd began to gather around the stand, likewise struck.

There was a pile of cards and leaflets on the empty chair, and Vicky took one of each. Sarah Molliner was the guest artist for that year's show, she read, and then her eye ran down an impressive CV and price list. She whistled.

'I have to get on, Janie. I was supposed to be buying a picture.' She must move on before Rot-woman returned and recognised her.

'Wait a minute. They're heavens, aren't they?'

'Extremely over-priced heavens, if you ask me.' Vicky whispered back, not quite quietly enough. 'Come on, if you are coming.'

'And how do you over-price heaven?' said a man behind her, coldly. 'One is, above all, paying for the imagination.'

Vicky, pink in the face, removed herself as fast as possible, indignant. She had not meant the flip comment to be overheard and being rudely scolded by strangers twice in one evening was a bit much. She had another glass of wine with Janie in the less crowded centre of the room, and a chat with an aquaintance from her evening classes in upholstery.

'That's better,' Vicky said, finishing up the wine in one gulp. 'It's such a relief not to have to listen to any more crap about art.' Out of the corner of her eye, through a parting in the crowd, she saw Fiammetta and Peregrine Briggand just arriving, followed almost immediately, most surprisingly, by Rush. She let out a moan and bidding a hurried farewell to a startled Janie, headed for the opposite exit.

Was it a law of nature, Vicky asked herself irritably as she bumped her way back and forth out of the parking space, that the person one most wishes to avoid will appear by unsympathetic magic in the unlikeliest places: in the queue at the delicatessen counter of a supermarket in the next county or at a private view which one had expected to be more exclusive? Tunbridge Wells was not a haunt of Rush's, but he was quite possibly acquainted with Rot-in-hell, since she appeared to inhabit the same area. That was also a little worrying.

Some eighteen months before, Fiammetta had been made temporarily vulnerable by fluctuating finances and was fast sinking into one of her cyclical sloughs of despondency. She had been swiftly pounced on and entrapped by Peregrine. At the private view that evening, her meeting with Rush was irrationally electrical. They had sensed each other standing side by side in front of Sarah Molliner's bewitching balls of glass, turned and stared – stared so avidly that Sarah, who knew them both individually, offered to act as a lightning conductor and introduced them.

Neither of them dared to touch, fearing a short-circuit. Fiammetta thought furiously and looked around nervously in

Peregrine's direction. They had been at the show barely half an hour and he had already shown signs of being eager to leave. Now he had fallen behind her and loured threateningly over the previous stand, interrogating the jeweller about the mechanics of her craft. How very dark he was, how black-haired, beetle-browed and grim in his charcoal suit. In a second or two he would look up to check that she had not strayed too far ahead. 'Wait,' she mouthed at the golden seraph beside her, 'just a second.' She returned to Lucifer and without any apparent sense of urgency, miraculously persuaded him she wished to buy a birthday present for him in secret and suggested he might wait for her in the bar of the Cafe Rose across the road?

The ensuing conversation with Rush was panicky, both aware that they had too much to say and absorb in too short a time, but a further meeting was furtively arranged.


In bed that night Vicky dreamed that she was in the Jack Cade with a circle of antagonistic women standing close round her in black legal dress. They wore monstrous grey wigs like clouds and threatened to make her eat bowls of loathsome porridge but she escaped by distracting their attention with the necklace she had bought, rattling it temptingly before their noses and then throwing it down and running away in the opposite direction whilst they scrambled after it, gobbling like turkeys. She thrashed about so much that Paddy nudged her and she woke up, breathless and triumphant.

'I've won!' she cried. 'I'll get it.'

'What's the matter, plum? You're talking gibberish. If you are going to shout in your sleep, you might at least say something I could tease you with in the morning.'

'I was dreaming about turkeys.'

'That's all right then. I thought I heard you mention Ollie.'

# Chapter Six

On the Thursday after Easter, Ollie, finding himself one morning reinvented as a gumshoe, received his eavesdropping orders in Vicky's drawing-room: he was delegated to attend the Jack Cade regularly until he discovered the date and timing of the private party.

'But, Vicks, there's nothing you can do to stop it, surely? If that is what you intend? Anyway they're hardly going to raise enough money to pay off their debts by giving a party.'

'I thought you were unemployed at the moment, Ollie?' she reminded him, inclining her body slightly further away as they sat together on the sofa, partly to insist on a proper distance between them in order to avoid being pounced on and partly to hold back the incipient bulge above her snakeskin belt. She'd been a bit heavy with the Easter eggs over the weekend.

'I've offered you a wage. It's not, I admit, as much as I'd have to pay a proper private detective, but then you're hardly experienced in that field, are you?'

'It's not the money, it's the principal of the thing.' Ollie was hopelessly swayed by her proximity and noticed with pain the physical retreat. 'I feel a little mean deceiving them.'

'Bollocks. You've never shown any sign of having principles before. I *will* get the place eventually, even if that Hooke woman doesn't sell to me directly. All you are doing is facilitating – helping us to get it at a lower price.'

'Oh, all right.' He supposed she was right. He knew intimately to what degree denial merely increased desire.

'"Amorality"' Potter at your service. But what are you planning to do, when you find out?'

'I'm going to wreck it.' She sounded calm, looked calm, but gave a violent little jerk of her foot. 'I've got to have that house. My whole happiness, Ollie, depends upon it.' She stared for a moment into his face, wide-set aquamarine eyes a little heavy-lidded for the merest instant, and he felt a lurch in his stomach. It was a look that slayed him and he dragged his own eyes away to fall, gloomily, on a little group of family photographs in silver frames. Paddy and Harry, Paddy and Cressie, Paddy with the Prince of Wales on a visit to the brewery, Paddy and Vicky skiing . . .

He knew he was being monumentally mucked about but were it not for Vicky, his days would be very dull now he was unemployed. He had keenly attended job interviews the week before but hadn't managed to get across his keenness and had not made the short list for any of them. He wasn't despondent but desperately desired Vicky to be grateful, to wish to please *him*, for a change. If he could help her obtain this wretched inn, he might get a foot on the ladder, or even a leg over. Over the years he'd tried everything else to keep her attention; long absences, other women, devotion, the cold shoulder, hot breath – but it hadn't occurred to him to cure himself of the obsession, which was as unaccountable to everyone else as it was to him. Now Vicky was becoming as possessed by the Jack Cade as he was by her.

'How? I mean, how will you wreck it?' He was half-shocked, half-interested and leant closer.

Vicky glanced at her watch, sprang up from the grey-and-cream-striped silk sofa and dug about in a little needlepoint bag for an envelope, which she handed to him.

She was enjoying herself and smiled most engagingly; doing something positive to attain the dream pumped an airy freshness into her. She was of the generation and persuasion that thought automatically, and without any modesty whatsoever, when presented with any potential acquisition or service: 'I'm worth it.'

'I don't know how, yet. Something will come to me. Let's find out when and what it is first. If you should see Paddy, not a word of this. He'd be appalled. Now here's your lolly and you'd better get off. It's ten-thirty and it's a no-no for you to be seen here when the children get back from tennis coaching.'


Thus dismissed, Ollie clattered down the Croswells' stone steps and stood leaning against the white-painted iron railings for a minute, considering how he should proceed. He came to the conclusion that if he were to engage in undercover work he would at least need an alias and a suitable topic to use as a wedge to open up conversation; well, perhaps the former was not strictly necessary, but it would make the whole thing more amusing. He could pose as a writer researching a particular subject, which would give him a reason for being in the area and some credibility as a regular visitor over the next week or so. He headed for the library, spending the next hour and a half diligently cramming into his head all known facts about Jack Cade's Rebellion of 1450.

He'd heard of the revolt, of course, but was hazy about its causes. His whole concept of British history had been distorted at an early age, as had previous generations', by the childhood reading of his grandfather's copy of *1066 and All That*. This, the Second Peasants' Revolt seemed to have been supported equally by the Kentish upper-middle classes and was aimed, as ever, at heavy-handed taxation and the corruption of greedy, bribe-taking officials who'd surrounded the weedy Henry VI and blocked all access to him. Henry VI was manifestly a Bad Thing. Jack Cade's origins were, Ollie learnt, indeterminate. He came from Ireland, said one source, from Kent or even Essex, said others, but styled himself Captain of Kent. Ollie kept finding himself side-tracked by delightful details, such as the fact that the venal Duke of Suffolk had been beheaded in a boat and his body dumped unceremoniously on the sand at Dover.

The final spur to the uprising appeared to have been a rumour spreading throughout the county that Henry's Queen, Margaret, intended to revenge herself for Suffolk's murder by depopulating Kent. I wouldn't have liked that if I'd been a popule, thought Ollie, industriously taking notes. I'm not surprised they revolted at the thought of their farms being converted into royal hunting forest.

Jack Cade had gathered his forces a mere ten miles from where the inn stood, had marched on Maidstone with a growing army, joined by men from Sussex and Essex, and thence on to Blackheath where the Sheriff of Kent, Sir William Crowmer, and his father-in-law, Lord Saye and Sele, were summarily tried and executed.

Jack Cade appeared to have had insufficient control over his vast mob and lost the sympathy of the citizens of London who rose up against the rebels, by now drunk with power, stolen gold and probably beer, and expelled them. The rebels had been for the most part pardoned, since they had never ceased to be loyal to the King, but Jack Cade forfeited his pardon by attacking the castle at Rochester on the way home for tea. He had fled, been caught by one Sir Alexander Iden and died of his wounds, possibly at Heathfield in Sussex, or possibly at Hothfield in Kent; there seemed to be some disagreement on that last point.

Those were the fragile bones of the matter. A powerful force intent merely on obtaining justice, reduced to a shambles by poor leadership. The entire episode had taken place between the beginning of May and mid-July. It might well be possible that Jack Cade had been in the area of the inn or even stayed in it, since quite a number of insurgents had been raised from

Romney Marsh and its surrounding villages, but then it was unlikely that the place had actually been an inn at the time. Ollie was however well pleased with what he'd found. He slipped the notes into his coat pocket and left for the marsh.

It was fortunate, he considered, that he hadn't been seen by the landlady in the company of Vicky and that the exotic barmaids, on duty that day when they had made their earlier visit, were unaware of her identity. That could have made things difficult, now that she'd blown her cover by writing to the redoubtable Mrs Hooke.

It was a typical early-spring day on the marsh, gusty, with fitful showers and infrequent but transfiguring flushes of sunshine. The road approaching the Middhaze turn-off was obscured by dense smoke and as Ollie turned up the lane, he was enveloped in a billowing, stinking cloud from a mountain of straw litter that was alight and smouldering in a field. He braked, but not soon enough, realizing too late that it was also typical that a flock of sheep had escaped their field and were milling invisibly about in the smoke, baa-ing and coughing. Before he was fully aware of what was happening, he had shunted one of them.

Blinded by smoke, heart thumping with anxiety, he leaped from the car and examined the casualty. It was a large ewe and it lay unmoving on its side beside the car. He hoped it was merely stunned. What did one do under such circumstances? He couldn't exactly give it the kiss of life. Should he do a runner or, more responsibly, find the owner and tell him, and then perhaps be forced to pay extortionate compensation? He bent over it, wringing his hands. He had never been so close to a sheep before and was surprised it was so large and heavy. He had vaguely expected sheep's wool, when actually on the sheep, to resemble a barrister's wig: stiff, pale grey and tightly curled. This was soft and tacky in his hands and he couldn't move it, nor could he breathe or see more than a yard ahead. In the distance he heard a fire engine, so he got back in the car and crawled on a little further, barely aware of the whereabouts of the verges and constantly nudging frightened bundles of fleece. Suddenly he was out of it but was faced with a baa-ing and reproachful Greek chorus of ewes and lambs, their bizarrely slit-pupilled eyes accusing.

The fire engine's siren sounded close behind him but it stopped the other side of the smoke and, poking his head out of the window, he could hear shouting.

'You've hit one of them!' said a voice.

'Couldn't be helped!' said another.

Ollie wound up his window again and, stifling a sudden urge to run back and come clean, drove on, arriving at the Jack Cade three or four minutes later, still shaken but relieved to have had the guilt shifted to broader shoulders. A lorry stood outside the inn and there was some activity taking place in the garden to the right – male voices, a lot of grunting and the scraping sound of shovels. There was also a newly painted sign, executed with eye-catching panache, announcing Bed and Breakfast. A broad man in a red woolly hat burst through the door as Ollie was about to enter and lumbered off across the drive at a lurching run.

Ollie was annoyed by the growl from the white dog lying in front of the fire. Undistracted this time by Vicky's presence, he was startled by the pleasant familiarity of the long room. Hesitating on the threshold for a second or two, he became conscious of the factors which enchanted: an essential, otherworldly calmness and a sense of permanence.

There was also the intriguing presence of Rosie Hooke, if it was indeed her. A woman in red jeans was standing on the bar, a tea-towel in her hand, attempting to catch a blue tit which was perched on a lampshade, its tiny beak gaping with exhaustion and fright. She had lovely legs. In no way did she fit the description issued by Vicky, who had insisted on a resemblance to some old French film star – he couldn't remember which one since he hadn't really been listening, but it had caused him to imagine a highly painted old dame with blood-red nails and chicken-skin neck wrapped in chiffon scarves.

'There, got the little darling! I'm always scared they'll dash their brains out on the window panes.' She smiled down at Ollie.

'Would you mind helping me down and opening the door again, so I can throw him out?'

Ollie found the voice bewitching. It had a quality that compelled one's attention, regardless of the commonplace words, and although his hands stank of salty sheep, he eagerly put one out to steady Rosie as she stepped from bar to chair and chair to floor, and obliged with the door. Once on the ground he found she was much smaller than he'd thought in spite of the intriguingly lengthy legs, about five foot five perhaps, but very nicely proportioned, very neat indeed, and he put Vicky's description down to jealousy. Aware that he also reeked of smoke, he felt bound to explain why but left out the bit about hitting the ewe.

'I thought I heard fire engines. I knew the Wycliffs' sheep were out – Sam Dicken just went out to help round them up. Now, what can I get you?'

It was simple after that. He explained how he came to be in the area, staying in Parden to research Jack Cade for his first historical novel, and although he blushed slightly when explaining, almost came to believe it himself. Rosie was immediately enthusiastic, mentioning that a journalist was visiting that lunchtime to do a piece on the inn and as he probably knew more about Jack Cade than she did, perhaps Ollie would like to meet her?

'It's free publicity, you see. She might mention you as well, and get something in about your book. It's only a local paper, though.'

The man in the woolly hat returned. He breathed heavily as if he'd been running and glanced suspiciously at Ollie. He plonked his great hands down on the bar in a proprietorial fashion, cleared his throat and seemed to be about to interrupt when the red-haired woman whom Ollie had seen on his last visit appeared and hung irresolutely at the door behind the bar. On this occasion she was more sensibly dressed in a thick orange sweater embroidered with pink butterflies – a sickly E-number orange, a pink reminiscent of prawn cocktail.

'The men have finished laying the turf, Rosie. What shall I do? Shall I send them round for a pint or can they come through the kitchen?'

'Yes, of course they shall have their beer, but send them round by the front, Janice. I don't want mud all over the kitchen flags.

'Got them all back in again, have you, Sam?' she said to the woolly-hatted one, and not waiting for an answer, returned to Ollie to explain they'd been having the garden returfed, ready for the summer.

'It had got into a real mess over the years, with the poultry being free-range. They've got cosy new arks now and a proper goose-house a neighbour built. It's a good deal – free turf. I only had to pay for the labour.'

'How did you manage that?' Ollie was still entranced by the voice and being made privy to any information at all gave him hope that he might insinuate himself without difficulty.

'Well, it's like this ...' she leant forward conspiratorially, dark eyes sparkling '... they had to lay turf on a new industrial estate in Surrey – purely cosmetic, to make it look nice for some big-wig who was going to open it yesterday morning. The thing was, the building wasn't nearly finished and as soon as the very important person had left, all the turf was to be stripped off again and carted off to a landfill site, to rot. Such a terrible waste – and all paid for by the construction company. I'm not the only one who's benefited.'

She looked up as the muddy turf-layers appeared, wiping their feet and rubbing their hands on overalls, grinning in anticipation of pints and cash payment. They were followed by a young couple in cycling waterproofs, and a girl who swished across the room breathlessly in a long black coat, notebook in hand and a silver stud in her eyebrow.

She hurriedly apologized for her lateness and immediately produced a small camera from within the folds of the coat and fussed about efficiently, eventually posing Rosie in front of the fireplace where she snapped confidently a couple of times and then proceeded more uncertainly with the interview for the local paper. Ollie leant against the bar, sipping and listening, as the woman, needing constant repetitions of facts and assistance with her spelling, jotted down the essentials.

'An old chapel, right? A bricked-up stone archway in the kitchen, the old west doorway of the chapel, right.' She kept repeating that she needed an angle to hang the piece on, and halfway through, in desperation at discovering the right coat-hook, Rosie brought Ollie in on the conversation.

'This is ... I'm sorry, I don't know your name?'

'Oliver Potter.'

'This is Oliver Potter who's writing a novel about Jack Cade. He'll be able to tell you more about the historical details.'

Ollie was by now thoroughly enjoying his visit and launched into an embellished description, full of blood and mire, of the life and times of the ill-fated Captain of Kent, unaware that the girl was struggling to keep up.

'... and, of course, it's perfectly possible that he stayed here in this very house, or in the house then on this spot. One can almost feel his presence, don't you think? I'm sure his ghost might at any minute walk through that door, brandishing a halberd and encouraging the customers to leave their ale and follow him to London to seek justice from the King. That was Henry VI. No, sixth – VI. You've put Henry the Fourth in your notebook ...'

The girl, awed by the dramatic presentation and pleased at last to have dug out something sensational from this intractable interview, looked gratefully at him. She drained her glass of white wine and said that that was just the interesting angle for which she had been looking. Now she must get back to file her copy. She shook hands with both Oliver and Rosie, who was stifling a giggle, in fact several giggles since she burst into full-blown laughter as soon as the door had swung shut.

'That was a masterstroke, Oliver! I'd never have thought of dropping a ghost into the muddle. She's the daughter of one of my regular customers, you see, who owes me a favour. I think it's her first assignment.' She paused for a second, looking a little anxious. 'Journalists love ghosts, don't they? It'll be interesting to see what she writes. The paper comes out on Friday.'

Ollie, whilst trying to appear modest, noticed she had the most illuminatingly attractive eyes and happily accepted a free drink. Although he had started out the visit in a light-hearted enough manner, he now became slightly uneasy at the falseness of his position.

The young couple had crackled off their waterproofs and were sitting in the corner, arguing.

'Of course the Beilbys won't speak to us. They know all about those quinces you stole from the Jehovah's Witnesses.'

'But that was ages ago,' objected the woman. 'And anyway, they were just going to waste, rotting in the grass in the back garden. I could see them from the bedroom window.'

'That's no excuse. It's still a bit much, stealing their quinces and then offering them quince jelly as a Christmas present. You should have asked! People are funny about that sort of thing round here.'

'Weekenders!' Rosie whispered. 'They've managed to upset just about everybody.' She smiled again or appeared to since her mouth did not widen much, but her eyes looked amused. Ollie reciprocated but decided it would be best not to make any further overtures at that point. He needed her full confidence and mustn't be precipitate. Although he appeared to have been accepted at face value, it would take a visit or two or hopefully more before he could indulge in any serious probing. There was no great hurry to finish the job, as he explained to Vicky on the phone later that afternoon.

'It's vital I don't make her suspicious or she'll clam up. I'll go back tomorrow evening. She's a canny little thing. As I was leaving, a coachload of chemists turned up. The driver was lost, had been looking for a pub called the Eeldyke where they were expected. She persuaded him that it would be shut by the time he got there and he might as well bring his passengers in to her inn for a drink instead.'

'How interesting,' said Vicky, 'and did you glean anything of importance during your time there – for which I was paying?'

'So far, only that the garden was being returfed. She's expecting to be busy this summer. She's just been interviewed for the local paper but didn't say anything about being broke to the journalist. She got me to tell them all about my book. Oh, yes, and I hit a sheep in the lane.'

'That was careless. I hope you don't expect me to pay for it? What was that about a book?'

'Don't worry. I pretended the fire brigade had hit the sheep, and I invented the book as a cover.'

Vicky sighed and put the phone down. Ollie might be willing, but it was not apparent that he was taking things seriously enough.


The Jack Cade put on a different act altogether for Ollie's next visit, on the evening of the following day. The interior was transformed into a low-lit and mysterious cave, with only the softest murmur of conversation audible which faltered a little as he entered. Two or three small groups of drinkers sat widely spaced in the shadowy periphery and two solitary old men, who although they nodded to him as he came in, sat silently staring into space, undecorative obelisks one at either end of the long bar, each with a little pouch of tobacco before him and a minute roll-up smouldering between clenched lips.

Having taken up a place at the bar but feeling uncomfortably alien in spite of his even further dressed-down appearance of black jeans and old leather jacket, Ollie bravely turned his gaze back into the room. Eyes, which had pierced the back of his skull while he was ordering a pint, were suddenly averted and the gentle muttering recommenced. He had been found harmless, he hoped, possibly even a welcome addition.

Rosie handed over his small change with an encouraging smile, thankfully seeming disposed to chat.

'Everyone is very quiet, aren't they?' he almost whispered.

'I suppose so. But then, so few of this lot will speak to each other anyway.'

'Surely in a place like this everyone knows everyone else?'

'They do, but they can choose not to, if you see what I mean?' She leant forward and whispered confidingly, 'The fishermen over there − proper fishermen, not anglers − don't speak to farmers, and the farmers, on the other side, don't have much to say to fishermen, although they're quite chatty with merchant bankers. No one much speaks to the pikies by the fire, mainly because they don't speak to anyone but themselves, and Albert and Gilbert,' she indicated with a swift nod to left and right, 'they're old lookers, used to be the best of mates since childhood but haven't spoken to each other for eighteen months, not since Albert won first prize for his medlar jam at the Rhee Flower Show. They're cousins. They'll go on coming in here but will probably never speak again.

'It'll jolly up in half an hour or so, you'll see. How's your research going? Are you comfortable in your digs in Parden?'

Ollie assured her he was more or less comfortable in his imaginary room and Rosie looked a little disappointed, perhaps having been fishing for a customer. He was unhappy with the idea of getting to know the family any more than was necessary − he supposed there was a family − he'd had the impression of a supporting act in the wings. The red-haired woman, the pretty girl. He discarded the notion that it might be more fruitful to his real researches actually to stay in the Jack Cade since there was the ever-present fear of being sussed out and it would be difficult, if he got to know them too well ... Difficult to do what? he asked himself crossly. Difficult to then do the dirty on them?

The room began to fill and soon was gently heaving with people who were not so reluctant to make themselves heard. He found himself engaged in a conversation, subtly engineered by Rosie acting as if she were a literary hostess and the Jack Cade her *salon*, with an American couple. They had presented her with a card announcing their identity: Paul Palmer, Professor of Classical Studies at the University of Hanabogle Bay, and partner-in-perpetuity, Mary Coussmaker Palmer. Ollie rapidly became out of his depth, historically speaking. They were a bit too politely intrigued by his non-existent novel. He fudged and side-stepped for what seemed an interminable five minutes before managing to extricate himself, turning the conversation to eco-scares and the remote possibility of rising sea-levels obliterating the marsh entirely. Being in the process of buying a cottage on the coast near Fingle, the Palmers were a little rattled.

Ollie was rattled too and had another beer, although he knew that he must be careful, having to drive back to Tunbridge Wells that night. The natives appeared more approachable now and, regaining confidence, he was drawn apparently by osmosis into a noisy group of scruffians who appeared delighted to find a talented raconteur in their midst. He obliged with a couple of the exceptionally dreadful naval stories for which he was famous and managed casually to drop in that he had heard Rosie was giving a private party. Misunderstood in the midst of the racket, whether wilfully or not he didn't know, he found himself instantly invited to one that night.

'You want to come to the party? Shall we make him an honorary Kitten?' There was general table-thumping approval. 'We're off to the Eeldyke first, to tank up till closing time and to get some take-away beer. Amber's coming. You can follow her.'

Thus it was that at half-past three in the morning Ollie found himself in what seeemed to be a ploughed field beneath icily brilliant stars, a bottle of Newcastle Brown in his hand, amid a milling tribe of tattooed and pierced unknowns of both sexes to whom it seemed, although he had no recollection of it, he had sworn affection. Appearing to him alternately satanic and benevolent as they drank and lurched to the accompaniment of a thumping rock band, they scuffled, bonded and passed out around the centrepiece of a gradually spreading bonfire fed by tree-trunks and various items of furniture donated for the occasion.

Earlier he had been slumped on a rain-soaked plush sofa beneath an elder bush with Amber, who had been ferociously eating his ear, but the sofa was doomed to feed the fire and they were turfed off. Clouds of smoke and steam from the smouldering upholstery drifted up into the dark, mingling with the smell of a pig, or perhaps a missionary, being roasted over a pit of coals somewhere behind a shed. By now too out of it to feel the sodden state of the seat of his trousers, but vaguely hungry, Ollie lost track of Amber and stumbled off in the general direction of the pig.

Staggering shadows rippled across the walls of outhouses and carnivorous individuals attacked the half-cooked pig with penknives, but the heat was too fierce for them to grab more than a sliver at a time. He was passed a sheath knife encrusted with pork fat and mud and told to help himself. He was still swaying indecisively, wondering whether to risk second-degree burns when Amber, in demonic mode, loomed up. Her long face glistening in the torrid heat, she wrenched a whole french loaf from the jaws of a passing lurcher, tore it in half, and seeing him still havering, took pity, gently removed the knife from his waving fist and swiftly slashed a collop of meat from a haunch, handing the resultant sandwich to him with a grin. He was by this time suffering from Hieronymus Bosch-like visions and felt impelled to make certain there were no small people entrapped between the slices.

'... the grossness of it all was very interesting. I woke up in the dark in the back of this van, outside another pub. It was quite alarming. The owner of the van, Ossie – that's short for Ocelot, most of them are named after cats and he looks like Albrecht Dürer's self-portrait, all flowing gold ringlets – had gone to work the next morning without knowing I was asleep inside and he'd been to Hastings and back before he discovered he'd got a passenger. Ossie was having a lunchtime drink with Phylly, you see, she's the landlady of this other pub, and they heard me banging on the back of the door. He was very kind and drove me back to where the party had been to find the car.' Ollie did not mention his alarm at finding that Amber was asleep in the van with him.

'I'm not in the least impressed,' said Vicky, tight-lipped. She was trying to be serious and stare reproachfully into his grey, seedy face, but only just managed to smother a smile as he sprawled across the spotless kitchen table and buried his pounding head in his arms – he was too stinkingly filthy to be allowed any further into the house but she had at least poured several cups of coffee down him while still under the impression he had been involved in a car accident. The feeling of having him at her mercy was invigorating.

'I am not in the least interested in the social mores of this group of New Age fellow travellers. When is this private party being held? You hadn't forgotten, had you, that that is what you were supposed to be finding out?'

'I'm afraid I still haven't a clue.' He looked placatingly up at her and ran his hands through dirt-darkened hair, knowing it held a porcine stench. 'I can't rush this. At least I'm beginning to get known. They'll forget I'm a foreigner in a few days' time and really open up. I promise to find out before Sunday.'

'You smell quite disgusting.' Vicky shuddered. 'You'd better get off home, for a bath.'


'Rosie said I was to give you this, if you came in. She's had to go out,' Janice said, passing over the folded Friday local newspaper and pointing at an article and photograph alongside the shortlist of winning entries in the Middhaze Spring Flower Show. 'It's not quite what she was expecting, but she thinks it won't do any harm. Did you enjoy Tiger's party? I heard you ended up at the Eeldyke Inn. You came in once before, didn't you?'

'Oh? Yes, with a business colleague a while ago. Let's have a look at this.' He was a little embarrassed, still had a slight headache and was vaguely disappointed that Rosie wasn't around. He'd begun to look forward to his visits and was even finding a little amusement in Vicky's irritation at his inability to come up with the goods.

The photograph of Rosie showed her full face just in front of the bressummer. The carved leaves standing proud round the Jack in the Green had been caught in the camera flash, so although the Jack's face was hidden, Rosie was startlingly haloed, beguilingly glorified like Daphne caught in the act of turning into a bay tree. The leafy coronation had given her a most seductive appearance.

'"*Local Inn Haunt of Revolting Peasants*"', he read aloud. '"*Is it true that the Jack Cade Inn, near Middhaze in the secret depths of rural Romney Marsh, is haunted by the ghost of the leader of the peasants' revolt back in 1381? Landlady Rosamund Hooke, who has lived here since 1450, firmly believes so.*"' Ollie's voice began to tremble with mirth. '"*On windy night's the doors slam and a white figure strides through, calling for ale and brandishing a hulpert to stir the revolutioneries. This apparently peaceful, thirteenth-century Inn*"* — I know Rosie said fifteenth-century — "*has many tales to tell and is well worth a visit for a quiet drink in the newly* *landscaped beer garden which will be opened in the summer with a celebration match of Dwyle Flunking between regulars of the Jack Cade and the Eeldyke Inns. Most noticeable in the bar with its wealth of beams is the portrait of Jack Cade carved into the fireplace. The times were bloody and on his return from London where he was pardoned by Henry V, Jack was murdered on Hothfield Common."'*

Ollie smiled broadly. 'Well, you never know what might happen on Hothfield Common, so I've heard, but it might have been Heathfield.' Janice stared blankly at him so he read on. '"*Mrs Hooke offers Bed and Breakfast. Staying with her at the moment is Mr Oliver Potter, a local historian who is researching a novel about Mr Jack Cade.*"' He gave a weak giggle.

'She won't get too many customers wanting to stay here if they think they're going to be woken up in the night by a phantom with a hulpert.'

He laid down the paper and stole a hopeful glance at Janice. 'Rosie isn't cross about it, is she? I'm certain neither of us said there were actually ghosts, although, as they've made her out to be about 550 years old, I wouldn't be surprised. Whatever do sub-editors do, if they don't sub-edit?'

'No, she laughed about it. And while she's been out, we've had three telephone bookings for the B and B, one person for tonight and a couple for Saturday and Sunday. She'll be pleased about that. They'll be her first customers.'

She may be pleased but Vicky won't, thought Ollie, taking his drink and the paper over to a window seat. She's going to get severely annoyed if I don't come up with something soon. But they're such decent people ... a trifle eccentric but very decent. He found himself staring out of the window, watching a solitary figure passing along the lane, an old man, his dark coat tied with orange string, a sack on his back. Where could he be going to on foot? Where had he come from? Then a steel blue Mazda turned in and drew up outside the window with a spurt of gravel, annoyingly blocking his view, and two young men leapt out, conferred and collected a briefcase from the back. They had that casually confident sense of purpose that Ollie found unnerving in people so much younger than himself. The white dog didn't growl at them when they came in, he noticed.

'Hi there, Janice. Rosie about?'

Janice, flustered by their sudden appearance, ran her fingers spider-quick through her red fringe, fluffing it.

'It's just that Kieran here wants to have a butcher's at the field site, work out a few things for the big night? OK if we go round and walk about? We need to measure up the access and sort out one or two things.'

Janice assented, and preened a little, finding it necessary to sneak a hand inside the neck of her cardigan and haul up a bra strap.

'You will shut the gate behind you?' she called out anxiously as they disappeared again.

'Is there going to be a party?' asked Ollie, breathing out a breeze of relief at finally releasing the words of which he'd been struggling to rid himself for so long.

'Well, yes, but it's private. He's giving it, the fair-haired one – if you can call that hair. It's not really anything to do with us. He's just hiring the field.'

'Sounds like fun. Perhaps it's his birthday. They looked very busy. When is it to be?' Ollie turned over the newspaper and began to read as if he were just making conversation and was not particularly interested in the answer.

'Early in May.' Janice was inspecting her face in the tiny mirror stuck to the wall behind the bar. 'I've just got to slip out to the back for a minute. Will you ring the bell for me if anyone comes in?'

'Of course.' Damn the woman! As soon as she'd gone he wandered up to the bar, glass in hand, and scanned the area above the barrels where various notes were pinned and there was a shelf with notebooks and a glass cockle pot of pencil stubs and biros – perhaps a calendar, or an appointments diary?

He realized he should have thought of this right at the beginning. A large calendar with a picture of romping lambs was staring him straight in the face but the page was of course still turned to April. Listening carefully for sounds of footsteps, he nipped behind the bar and lifted the page, feeling like a dirty old man lifting a skirt. There in red felt-tip pen were the words '*R. Kadely – Party Set-up 6 a.m. – Start 9. 00 p.m.*' on Friday, 3 May, and the whole of the day was slashed through with a red squiggle. Kadely ... what a coincidence. It must be one of Vicky's spider's nest of cousins.

He could have found it all out five days ago, if he'd been thinking straight and not enjoying himself so much. Perhaps if he hadn't been so entranced by Rosie ... There was a low growl behind him and the white dog stood there, blockading him behind the bar, its wet, black-blotched pink gums and glistening white upper canines revealed beneath the sneering lip.

Ollie saw himself for a second as a desperate but resourceful cartoon cat, entrapped by a fang-gnashing bulldog. An animated deception was required and he made a lightning grab at a bag of pork scratchings from the box on the table beside him and hurled them over the dog's head. Oh, relief! The dog leapt after them. Heart pumping, Ollie slipped back to the right side of the bar, snatched up his glass and quickly sat down again in the window seat where he assumed an attitude of relaxation and stretching out his legs, began writing on the new notepad he had acquired in order to give credence to the researching author tale. Caught between triumph and annoyance with Vicky for putting him in this absurdly demeaning situation, he was scrawling '*I fooled you, you effing hopeless hound*' over and over again down the page, like a child writing lines as a punishment. The dog was still excitedly nosing the packet across the floorboards when Janice came back into the room.

'Wicked Trash! How did you get hold of those?' Janice, her face newly made up, bent over to pick them up. Ollie glanced up, surprised.

'I wondered what all the rustling was. Does he like them? Here, I'll buy him the packet.' He was looking forward to adding to his expenses: 'Pork scratchings for ferocious dog – forty-five pence'.

Trash stood nearby, wall-eyes watching suspiciously as the packet was ripped open and a large piece of what resembled hard, yellowish polystyrene was dropped at his feet. Ollie noticed that his hands were very slightly shaking. Espionage, he decided, was not a skill he had inherited from his mother. He forced his voice into friendliness.

'There you are, you humbuggery old humgruffin!' Trash polished off the packet and lay down beside him grinning, tail thumping the floorboards. Ollie drained his pint and returned the paper to a coyly smiling Janice, asking her to give his regards to Rosie.

Janice was sad to see him leave. She thought him a lovely man, in spite of his clothes. Tall, with easy good manners, a beautiful face, even if it was a little thin – the slight scarring added humanity to the good looks – and such lovely thick hair. Growing up in the hairy 60s, she'd never come to grips with the hideousness of the semi-shaven skull; when she was a child it had only been poor little boys with nits who'd had their hair cut so short.

Now a month into her sojourn at the Jack Cade she was more content than she had been for years. It was gratifying to be needed and accepted by the family. She had unusual erotic dreams about Rush Kadely that night, in spite of the hair shortage, and woke up blushing.

'So, we've got less than two weeks.' Vicky stood tautly by the tall windows of the drawing-room, biting a hangnail and watching a woman below in the wet street, a pooper-scooper in her hand, trailing self-consciously along the railings behind an incontinent Great Dane.

'People shouldn't keep such enormous dogs in towns. How embarrassing and disgusting it must be, cleaning up behind them.'

She turned back to Ollie, who lay back indolently on the sofa with his feet on the coffee table, smoking one of Paddy's cigars and coughing a little whilst admiring the rear view of her. How neatly rounded she was, how softly curved her hips.

'I suppose,' Vicky continued, moving a vase and picking up a pinch of fallen white petals, pouting a puff of breath at the dust – Avril was still unfit for duty, 'I suppose one might have to get a dog in the country. I expect I shall be forced into it by the children once I've got Cade House. I fancy a Jack Russell.'

She rolled the petals into a little ball and flicked it at him with a complacent pussycat grin and leant forward to remove his feet gently from the table, breasts brimming from the deeply cut neck of a silky pearl-grey cardigan. She was pleased, so far, but had already passed to the next obstacle.

Ollie blinked. 'You've already renamed it? Aren't you moving a bit fast?'

'I have to move fast. You're absolutely certain, are you, that it's Rush who's giving the party?'

'That's what it said. And the men who visited the inn yesterday ... one of them had one of those beardlets that looks as if it were glued on, like a little stripe of pubic hair down his chin, and the other, very alert and bright-faced, had round blue eyes like a cherub and very short fair hair.'

'That's him. Any resemblance to a cherub ends there. If Rush is giving it, it's probably one of those all-night rave things where they take drugs and spend the night looking as if they're all swimming up for air, but are glued to the same spot. Cressie says the music's called house, broom-cupboard, sink ... that sort of thing. Now, I want you to hire some roughs to cause an upset at the party. I've got to stop them from making any money.'

Ollie, caught by surprise, jerked upright, coughing a little more emphatically.

'Who? How rough? Where from? And do raves still exist?' He was alarmed, having hoped his part in the action was over and that a reward, or at least a whiff of one, might shortly be coming his way. The children at least would not be used as an excuse to throw him out of the house. He had ascertained earlier that they had been safely delivered back to their respective boarding schools, well fed, well entertained and horribly fit after all the tennis and sailing.

'Do use your imagination, Ollie! You obviously have the knack of mingling with just the right sort of people. I thought you might try Hastings? I believe there are several biker hang-outs there. You must go and make contact, offer whatever it takes. I'd go myself, only it's not something *I* could be seen to be doing.'

'Why do you want me to hike all the way to Hastings? Aren't there any local ne'er-do-wells here you could employ?'

'The further away from home, the better.'

'OK. But I think we're beginning to tread dangerous ground.' He looked doubtfully at her determined little face. 'Have you ever thought, Vicks, that once you've got the house, all those people will have nowhere to go and relax and meet their friends?'

'Don't be stupid, Ollie. There are hundreds of other pubs. Anyway, I could open it once a year and have a fête in the garden. They could all come and see it then.'

He hooted with laughter. 'And pay their respects to you as lady of the manor? I don't think that would be adequate compensation somehow. This is positively the last errand, Vicky.'

Once back in his flat, away from Vicky, against whose unexpected arrival he kept the bedroom in a state of optimistic tidiness, Ollie belatedly began to wonder how he had managed to get himself involved with this, this . . . shabby was the word which regretfully popped into his mind, this shabby enterprise.

Until his redundancy, he had occupied the larger flat on the same floor but forced to trim expenses, he had moved into this apartment, two small rooms and bathroom at the top of a large, much-divided plain stone house with an uncompromisingly plain slate roof, much like many others in that part of the town. There were other peripatetic tenants, he'd noticed, who over the past year had exchanged their badger setts according to their means.

He wrenched the sash window up and leant out of the sitting-room window, above the rear garden, from where he could see the flat top of a high and unneighbourly holly hedge which spinily divided the garden. A yellow tricycle lay abandoned on the grass beneath. A lone grey sock, his, had lain across the top of the hedge for a month, spitted firmly on its prickles out of sight of everyone but himself, blown away when he attempted to dry a pair on the windowsill in an emergency. A speckled, iridescent starling now approached the sock, peered at it, pecked, decided it was not good nesting material and flew off. The sky was absorbent, sock grey, and spat contemptuously in Ollie's eye when he looked up. He shut the window and sat down on the green velvet sofa. Intended for a far larger room, it took up most of the space and if he stretched out his legs, his feet came immediately into contact with the black iron grate.

He perceived himself as a sad suitor, doomed to perform ever more eccentric and illegal tasks in the hope of a transmogrifying kiss from the proud princess. What was it that kept him so tied to her apron strings? Merely unsatisfied lust? Vicky was a woman who frequently rose to outright arrogance and occasionally appeared to scrape the bottom of the barrel of pettiness; it was the bits in between when she was such fun, so charmingly sharp and sexily bossy-booted that he wished to spend every moment with her.

I am allowing myself to become ridiculous, he thought bitterly, letting myself be used like this. I wouldn't take this from any other woman. I am becoming a miserable droog.

He wanted Vicky, but for what? Just another affair, another
chance for her to slither from his clutches, making last-minute
excuses as she slithered back to the financial security of a doting
husband? Oh, God, now he was thinking of her in terms
of a snake. He felt both sympathy and resentment towards
Paddy. And why was he enamoured of such a serpent? Perhaps
because she had been a part of his imagination for a very long
time and he was too nervous, at the moment, of the empty
middle-aged future to disengage himself entirely and become
his own man again.

Is this all that's left of me? he wondered peering into the
fridge. How thin I've become on the inside.

He dragged out a packet of plastic-looking ham and made
a sandwich from a stale sliced loaf, adding lashings of masculine
mustard from a tube. Once fortified, he would watch the
lunchtime news and answer the advertisement for a Senior
Manager for *Ange et Caramel*, the food firm who had recently
set up a distribution point and offices in Parden. His French
was good, and he would quite easily regain his interest in food
once he had employment. Afterwards he might, just might, drive
off to Hastings to find an amateur terrorist or two.

# Chapter Seven

The town was unfamiliar to Ollie and came upon him from all angles. Large Edwardian houses shambled up and tumbled down steep-sided valleys, trapped between serial post-recessional attempts to hoist themselves, both financially and culturally, above the run down and tacky excitements of a seaside resort and the sad remnants of the British fishing industry. It appeared also as a microcosm of an up-but-never-quite-coming London Borough, with high Victorian terraces, either gentrified and smartly painted or with their rendering cracked like dirty icing and crumbling down the hillsides beneath the whirling seagulls. A mêlée of the arty and the mundane, flats and bedsits, fish and chips, tiny and hopeful vegetarian restaurants hung with art students' angst, piss-artists, unemployment, chain stores, chain smokers, DHSS, foreign English language students ... all helplessly, hopelessly entangled, yet alive, kicking and edgy.

The neat and articulate mingled with the unspeakable and incomprehensible. Crusties begged in the underpass and affluent young women with shiny hair trotted from Debenham's with glossy carrier bags. Obese, trailer-park drearies in tracksuits grazed their way along the streets on tidal waves of burgers and bubble gum. The expensively casual and literate loitered in antiquarian bookshops whilst disfigured substance abusers lurched from tattoo parlours. Warehouses bulged with overpriced domestic detritus, most of it decorated with orange crocuses and labelled 'Clarice Cliff'. Old-fashioned rock and candyfloss shops fought for space with the ubiquitous tinkling New Age crystal emporiums from which issued CD sounds of mating whales.

Beautiful and ancient houses staggered, stunned, away up the Old Town's narrow High Street, resigned to being part of a Heritage trail. '*You are now in 1066 Country*' warned a Tourist Information leaflet as if alerting the reader to Norman bandits. Posters raised issues, advocated rights, advised on the whereabouts of Irish bands or paint-your-own-plate classes. Camden-by-the-Sea, thought Ollie, reconnoitring the hilly streets in the persistent drizzle, repelled, enchanted and constantly deflected from his purpose, the town's salty smell drowned out by patchouli-and-vanilla-scented candles and exhaust fumes.

For some considerable time his search appeared fruitless and his earlier confidence was waning when he was at last directed to a suitably gruesome thug-venue. In near desperation he blantantly approached a group of likely-looking gentlemen muttering together in a dark corner.

'If I wanted to hire some people to cause a bit of disruption,' he asked, his accent carefully tuned to Radio Essex, 'nothing violent, you understand, just a bit of aggro, who would you suggest I ask?'

The man he had addressed looked faintly puzzled.

'I'm sorry, old chap. What did you say?'

Ollie repeated the question in a shout to be heard above the music. In black leather, unshaven, with handkerchiefs tied round their foreheads apache-style, they had looked the part but it turned out he had approached a group of accountants out on a jolly. He was sniggeringly redirected to a vast, brightly lit cafe in yet another part of town where, after being passed from person to person, and quoting the name of the last man he spoke to on each occasion like a password (Brengun sent me ... Big Les says you might ... Sharkie says you are ...), he at last discovered, succeeded in convincing and buying the services of, a suspicious group of six potential disrupters.

Once they were convinced of his seriousness it was all far too easy. Contact numbers were given. One-third cash up-front agreed on, to be paid before the party in the vicinity of the Jack Cade on the evening, and the place and time of the final pay-off agreed. They were not to be seen at the inn beforehand. Think SAS, he urged, rather than Rambo. They were to arrive at ten-thirty, disrupt the electricity supply if possible and do a bit of minor terrorising without actually laying hands on anyone. One bruised head, one scratched nose or torn dress and the rest of the cash would be forfeit.

After he had telephoned Vicky to report his success, Ollie wandered along the seafront in the twilight amongst aimless gangs of blank-faced, identikit teenagers, wondering if even their mothers could tell them apart. The grey sea slapped up rattling pebbles and hissed as it sucked them back again. It was a soothing sound, but he didn't feel soothed.

Back in the Old Town where he had left the Saab, he queued for fish and chips and crossed the road to eat them in a small children's amusement area, sitting on a low wall along with parents and grandparents who shrieked encouragement at tiny offspring racing round a brightly lit miniature go-kart track. There was a small boy of three or four who was laughing so madly with pleasure as he raced round and round that his eyes were shut. His little spectacles and glowing face reflected the flashing sequence of the coloured lights, red-green, blue-yellow, red-green, blue-yellow, each time he passed the point where Ollie sat with his fish cooling in the scrumpled paper, wishing it was himself circling so ecstatically. The midget cars slowed and rolled to a halt and the child stumbled out, undismayed by the ending of the adventure and still laughing, limbs quite limp with excitement.

Ollie became pensive. We're good at breeding, he thought, which is what animals are supposed to do – breed and die. But we all seem laggardly about the dying. Where will all these children live, with their multi-re-hipped and elbowed, re-hearted, re-kidneyed and corneaed great-grandparents refusing to go under and taking up all the space? I don't think I want any children. We've short-changed the next generation and we've only ourselves to blame if they refuse to look after us when we're old.

He became very glum and felt an urge to visit the Jack Cade again, just to make certain that it, and Rosie, were still there. It was only eight-thirty. He could be there by nine-fifteen, although in atmosphere it was light years away from this indifferent twinkling seafront. But better not.

Rosie noticed that Rush's mind was elsewhere as they sat together in the Jack Cade, settling the final arrangements for the forthcoming party; he repeated himself often and kept glancing distractedly out of the window into the dusk.

'As I said, Rosie, none of the guests will be visiting the pub, they'll be taken straight into the marquees in the field, through the screened entrance at the side ... What's the time, do you know ...? The only stipulation is that none of your customers gate-crashes. Tell them it's a convention of hotel-keepers or something equally boring.'

He peered anxiously through the twilight, burning up the damp air with blowtorch blasts of impatience. The headlights of distant cars flared and disappeared as they wound across the flatness. Having bullied himself into confidence for so many years and found the assumed self-assurance so rewarding, he had nearly forgotten the agonising tension of wanting and waiting in uncertainty.

Fiammetta was driving like a bat out of hell, away from Tunbridge Wells and towards the marsh. She was astonished when she thought about her marriage now, how few rational thoughts she had had about it before the event. She was making up for lost time as she drove, thinking clearly and furiously.

Peregrine, with his interestingly analytical approach to life and persistent, dark solidity, had seemed, at the time, someone with whom she had more than sufficient in common to make a go of it. She'd imagined herself as rather cynical, as having few illusions about life and thought Peregrine and herself, if not deliriously 'in' love, at least well suited in both mental and physical aspects.

She had woken up one morning with an alien trader who was quite out of stock of whatever it was which had attracted her in the first place and with many new varieties of qualities and defects of which she had no need or which actually repelled her. A stranger, moreover, twenty years older, who checked up on her every move, who questioned and fought her inclinations in almost everything. He treated her merely, she was convinced, as a form of mental exercise, someone to be constantly reasoned with as if weight training in a gym. He manipulated her to the point of exhaustion and winning was enormously important to him. She was no Katherina, did not care for Petruchios and could not allow her entire life to be restructured into a game of chess to keep him amused.

Not having been keen on her prison teaching job, Peregrine had acquiesced only because it was unlikely she would have any social intercourse with her male students after classes. Naively, she had hoped to show the inmate students the relevance of philosophy to their lives, to help them to question everything, to reason, and to travel beyond the immediate advantage to themselves of any action, looking ahead to the repercussions and consequences. Some of them already had degrees, several of them more than one, in other subjects. It was dispiriting to arrive home from the prison after an afternoon spent wrestling moral conflict and rational choice with a group of A-level lifers of varying ages and degrees of criminality, the highly intelligent majority of whom ran circles round her if she lost concentration for a second, to find Peregrine waiting for her with a mind unstretched by his present occupation, so alert and relentlessly inquisitive that he resembled an electric cattle prod.

Fiammetta, although she willingly shouldered half the responsibility for the serious error of marrying him and was sorry, did not intend to suffer the consequences.

She arrived at the Jack Cade just a little after sunset. A skinny crescent moon had risen in the still greenish evening sky; she had already chosen to be unfaithful to Peregrine, if not this particular evening then soon, very soon.

The door of the inn was impatiently flung open and Rush stood beside her, almost scrabbling at the car door handle and speaking fast as she emerged from the frowsty car into the fresh evening air.

'You found it! I'd almost given up hope, thought you'd never get away! How did you manage it?'

'Peregrine's having supper with friends in London. He's staying the night. I'm "attending a meeting, to do with work". I was careful enough to put it in my diary, which is just as well because I caught him checking.'

It was there in the understandingly subtle light of the Jack Cade that they began to disentangle each other's old lives and find their places in the new arrangement.

Rosie, glancing across covertly now and then, felt quite wistful. How delicate they were with each other, how close their heads were across the table and yet how determined not to touch. The sense of tense potential between them was far more erotic than other cruder cuddlings and gigglings she had witnessed from behind the bar. Their enjoyment of that tension was almost tangible, as taut as the strings of a musical instrument, yet next time she turned her eyes to them, between serving a bottle of John Hop and a bitter shandy, Rosie found she had missed the moment of defusion. The nervous pizzicato had abruptly halted and the girl had become almost languid while Rush was leaning against the wooden back of the settle, laughing.

A draught of jealousy swept down the back of Rosie's neck

and she felt like crying. Ben, more a slap-and-tickle sort of man, originally jovial, loud and apparently uncomplicated, finally crude, had never been someone to set the heart fluttering, although for all the wrong reasons that sensation had come about later as he Jekyll-and-Hyded, a jinking jinx who bucked terrifyingly about the tiny arena of the inn. Was that what had irked Sally all those years ago, the smallness of the stage? Which of them were audience and which actors?

They were here of their own free will, the customers choosing which thoughts and actions to make public, she choosing to watch or perform herself. It was not a job in which one could be recessive or she at least could not be.

I'm the director, perhaps. I can set the mood of any particular session. How much of that stems from position and how much personality? Have I really got the willpower left to save the theatre from the bulldozers? And why? If I start doubting now, I've lost. That's how it's always seen: an attack, 'assailed by arrows of doubt', siege engines, arbalests and mangonels fairly chucking it down on one's head as if it was always something to be resisted. Doubt is sensible. Time to review the options, etcetera. Perhaps this is just the interval in the battle scene? The bit where everyone stops for a gulp of lemonade in the wings? I'm tired, or I wouldn't be thinking about it, I'd be doing it. And what about sex? I'm free again. I'm not old, even if Rush and his new girl over there made me feel ninety just now. Come to think of it, I've never seen him with anyone before. He usually comes alone.

She imagined her hair greying and rheumatic twangs emanating from her knees as she bent to turn the tap on the barrel, and caught an unflattering glimpse of herself in the little mirror on the wall as she passed it on the way to the cellar to fetch more tonic waters. She was frowning and her eyes were disappointed. She looked like Sally.

Returning with an armful of bottles Rosie gave another surreptitious glance in the couple's direction and read their intentions although she could not hear them above the general chatter.

'We *must* go now.'

'I think we must.'

Their drinks unfinished, they were cautiously hurrying, gathering up a jacket, the girl's bag, a packet of cigarettes and a lighter, patting pockets for car keys although barely taking their eyes from each other for a second. Rush turned and waved a hand in Rosie's direction as he left. His face was dazed, she saw, and weighted with lust.

Ah, well, she thought, a little acidly, acknowledging that she was suffering from jealousy. Another one bites the dust.

Their abandoned table was swiftly re-occupied by another pair, both young and very tall. The man, Francie, was flamingly red-headed; the woman, Bea, with a calm beauty belied by the fact that she appeared to be having a quiet but fierce argument with her partner. She had her elbows on the table and long fingers held up, tips together before her lips, as if to mask the words which she rapped out in a terse undertone. Suddenly she relaxed, grinned and put a hand on his arm, pointing to the door. The redhead stood up to welcome a much older, white-haired, Scandinavian-looking man, with suntanned face and ski-slope nose.

Rosie knew them well, although the Norwegian, Canute, had only recently become a customer. She began to think she had seen everyone in the world before and felt bitterly lonely, eager for closing time. Depression began to prowl about like a wolf. She was tired and wished that just one of the people present had come in to see her personally, for herself. Snuff your candle, sir? Go on, out, out! Recorded time says it's only nine o'clock but this evening I do wish you'd all shove off and leave me to my own last syllabubbles as I drown in beer. Time, please. Time for self-indulgence in your own time, not mine, although I know you're paying for it, dear customers – and some of you *are* very dear and I need your lolly. Pull yourself together, Rosie. Look at the script. Assemble the scraps and keep going.

'Hello, Sam, pint of the usual? Campari and lemonade for Chloe?'

\*     \*     \*

Ollie supposed that there were about fifty people absorbed into the long room of the inn, but it did not seem overcrowded. The windows were open on to the warm darkness and the great fireplace had been cleaned out and lay empty, waiting for the first evening chills of distant October. The curtain across the rear room was drawn back and revealed the unlikely sight of a group of fishermen sitting about a table, playing bezique by candlelight.

Rosie stood behind the bar, her face up-lit and motionless as if meditating while Janice hustled to and fro behind her. She resembled a seventeenth-century painting, a card-playing Madonna, golden in a scoop-necked long-sleeved red top, absorbed in sorting out her hand. She looked up at Ollie, slitty-eyed as if coming out of a trance, and beamed like a child with a present. He had to shake off the feeling that he had just come home from the sea.

He felt welcomed, wanted, and miserable. Perfidious Ollie, he thought, con-man, spoiler. Rosie was as desperate to stay in the Jack Cade as Vicky was to evict her. He could feel their two separate needs pulling him apart, and suddenly it was Rosie's that were paramount. How, for God's sake, had Vicky managed to keep him anchored for eighteen months, in Tunbridge Wells of all places? He'd been secured like the fleet of the pirate queen who allegedly kept her ships moored to her big toe – or was it tied to the bedpost? Either way even when asleep, she would feel the tug if someone tried to steal them.

'Hello, Oliver. It shows, doesn't it, that there's no such thing as bad publicity? That hilarious article has done the trick. I'll have to hire some ghosts or everyone will be disappointed. Look at the crowd tonight!' Rosie leant forward and lowered her voice and he caught the smell of butterscotch on her breath as he bent towards her.

'What can I get you? There's something special under the counter, if you'd like to try it? Here, have a taste and see what you think.'

She bent below the bar and brought up a half-pint glass with a taster in it and handed it to him. He had no idea why she was being so furtive but happily sipped and agreed to a full pint.

'That's Ned Rother's bitter. I'm only supposed to sell the one the brewery sends but this one's been on for twenty-four hours and I've sold two-thirds already. I'm so glad you came in – there's something I wanted to show you and I need to ask your advice.'

'Go ahead, Rosie. I'll help if I can.' He would, he decided, do almost anything to undo the mischief in which he'd so willingly become entangled. The object which she pulled from a drawer behind her and discreetly placed in his hand was wrapped in a piece of striped cotton rag. It was heavy and metallic. A figurine, gold-coloured, about five inches high, with a little spike at its base which prevented it from standing upright but clearly meant it had been at one time fastened to something. He looked questioningly at her.

'Where did it come from?'

'The onion patch! I found it the other day and forgot about it till this morning. When I washed it, you see, I thought at first it was brass, a poker handle or something, but it isn't, is it? I mean, it does look mediaeval, doesn't it? I know the Victorians did pseudo-mediaeval stuff – gothic revival, I mean, all those churches – but this, it looks . . . it looks so lively.'

'No, I wouldn't think it was a handle of any sort. It might be bronze?' He scanned its smooth, uncorroded surface carefully in the dim light, admiring the crowned and waving curls around the symmetry of the face. There were faint traces of darker metal showing through the gilding clinging to the cheeks, the intricately modelled folds of the robe and the tiny hands placed one on the breast, one across the stomach.

'Could you take it and find out for me? I'm so busy at the moment. I just wondered if it *might* be valuable.' Rosie looked bizarrely beautiful with her unconventional face a little flushed, excited even. 'It's odd. That patch has been dug and planted over and over for so many years, you'd think Ben might have found it before. It was lucky I didn't do it any damage with the Rotorvator.'

'I could take it to a local museum first, perhaps. Then, if it can be identified and has any value, I could put it in an auction for you? In fact, it might be best if I took it straight to an auction house.'

'That would be kind. I'm hopelessly busy at the moment, organising these Games. Any little amount extra would help enormously. Although,' she looked a bit sad and hesitant at parting with it, 'perhaps it shouldn't be sold? It might be the Jack Cade's patron saint or my own guardian angel, mightn't it?'

'Don't worry about that now. Find out what it is and if it's worth anything, then make up your mind. Have you got a piece of paper? I'll write you a receipt.'

'That's not necessary. I'm sure I can trust you.'

Ollie's hand shook as he rewrapped the statue and slipped it into his jacket pocket. 'You shouldn't trust anybody, particularly with something like this. I'd like the piece of paper, please.'

She tore off a sheet of paper from a pad behind her and he fished out a pen and wrote his name and address on it. 'Received by Oliver Potter from Mrs R. Hooke of the Jack Cade Inn, Middhaze, Romney Marsh, Kent – a gilded metal (bronze?) statuette found in the vegetable garden of the above property, for investigation into its value.' He added the date and his telephone number and Rosie beamed again and tucked the piece of paper behind the fateful calendar.

'And how goes the book?'

Book? Oh, shit. *His* book. He mercifully remembered in time his alter ego, Oliver Potter the historical novelist, and managed a casual, 'Oh, pretty well.' She smiled again but there being a press of people needing serving, had to turn away, not hearing his throat-clearing and hesitant beginning, 'Rosie . . . ?' He knew with a shiver that he had been about to ask her if she ever got away from the inn, and . . . then what? He seemed less and less to be operating under his own volition.

She was busy for some time and when next she looked up,

hoping to continue their conversation now that there was a lull, felt an unexpected jolt of disappointment for Ollie had disappeared, leaving his beer half-drunk.

'When I came to stay with your sister Jessica, you were too grown-up and grand, being an undergraduate, to take any notice of us! We were fourteen and wanted you to play poker with us.'

Fiammetta sat cross-legged on the floor of Rush's happily desecrated hermitage, dressed in a navy-blue silk slip, with a wide-blown scarlet tulip tucked behind her ear. She was lining up the tokens from a battered Monopoly set, the silver battleship leading the flat iron, the top hat and the boot. Other games and toys lay scattered around them. Rush had been drugged by her finely tuned love-making, but gradually coming to, had now unlocked his private hoard for her amusement and lay beside her on the rug.

'I'm trying to make amends. I *do* remember you, though, excruciatingly well.' He gently pulled her foot out from beneath her and examined her toes, one by one. 'You and Jess were nightmarish, and never left me alone. Terrible, skinny girls with secret eyes, befuddlers of the truth. Secret gigglers, secret readers of other people's private letters, secret thieves of my T-shirts. I remember having breakfast in my room to avoid you. Now I think I might starve if I don't breakfast with you every day forever. How on earth did you manage to turn into a philosopher?'

'I'm not a philosopher. I try to explain other people's philosophy to students. I'm very far from promulgating any thoughts of my own, since they aren't on the syllabus. By the way, I've still got your T-shirt, the one with "A spliff a day keeps the doctor away" printed on it, and I never expected you'd become a musician.'

Rush put her foot down and picked up the other, stroking it softly as if it were a cat. 'I'm not a real musician. I just organize other people's music, make the best of them, process it so they can sell it to other, other people. I like all the technical side. Do you promise you aren't going to go home?'

'I'll have to, tonight.' This had to be done properly. She couldn't cope with leaving Peregrine till it had all been carefully planned. She'd married him on the spur of the moment, a disastrous decision. It needed to be unravelled more thoughtfully this time or divorcing him might be just as intractable. 'You mustn't worry, I'm definitely leaving. It would have happened anyway, even if I hadn't met you.' She leant back on her hands and considered Rush gravely. 'I'm frightened of our uncovering each other too fast. It's better to unwrap people like one does in Pass-the-Parcel, little bit by little bit, don't you think? Tell me about the party. Can I come?'

'Of course, but I don't think they'll be playing Pass-the-Parcel. So what happens when you get to the toffee in the middle of the wrappings?'

'I can't imagine. Do you know something – something quite different? I met a cousin of yours, Vicky Croswell, a month or so ago. We went to dinner at her house.'

Rush had been leaning on his elbow, and suddenly sat up straight. 'And what did you think of her?' His voice was so chilly that Fiammetta looked up in surprise.

'*La grande bourgeoise*? Her husband is too nice for her. She went on, just a bit, about an exceptionally beautiful old house she was going to buy. She was trying to cover up an awkward moment. The odd thing is, you'd noticed there's a carving on the fireplace at that pub where we met this evening? Well, she raved about this place in the middle of nowhere, with just such a carving. A Jack-in-the-Green, or Green Man. It must be the same place. Is it up for sale? She made it sound as if it were a stately home and she'd already signed the contract.'

'Over my cold corpse! Or rather, quite a lot of cold corpses. I had an idea she was after it and now I'm certain. She'd put in five bathrooms and smother the garden with topiary and tennis courts. But there are moves afoot to save it from her. My party is one of them. Vicky married for money and she's been a dissatisfied cow ever since. Before that she was just a cow. Now, I want you to listen to this, and tell me what you think.'

At first Fiammetta simply hooted with laughter as the unbelievable sounds of Mel Plunket's version of 'Silver-eyed Sally' pulsated through the room.

'My God! Quick, quick, play it again!' she demanded, doubled up with delight. 'It's an atom-shifting voice, isn't it? Can he produce that live?'

'You'll hear him on Friday night. He's part of the entertainment. Almost better than Freddie Mercury, don't you think? His first album is due for release next month. I think he's going to be a major transitional factor between pop culture and Schubert.'

More shrieks of laughter, further entanglement of limbs, more exquisitely extended loving.


Paddy was relieved to find Vicky in a sunny mood on the morning of 3 May. She had been somewhat preoccupied recently.

'Since you've got your AGM this evening, Janie and I are having a girls' night out. Megan's coming too, since Jos is in Karachi.'

'Where are you going?'

'Oh, just out to supper and then for a drink. Is there a buffet thing at the AGM as usual? Good. Then I don't need to leave you anything. I don't know what time we'll be back. Megan's found some new place in the country she wants to try.'

'All right, my plum. I expect I'll be lateish, anyway.' He'd enjoyed the peace which followed his parents' departure on a lengthy classical cruise, but George Croswell had now returned and in between lyrical descriptions of Delphi, Paphos and *souvlaki*, was poking his nose into things that no longer concerned him at the brewery and aggravatingly questioning this and that, prefacing each sentence with, 'I know it's your pigeon now, old boy, but if I were you ...'

Nothing on earth would keep Vicky away from the Jack Cade

this evening. She had borrowed a short reddish-brown wig, having first ascertained from Janie, who had long ago been troubled by *alopecia areata*, that it had been dry-cleaned although Janie rattily assured her that it wasn't catching. She would wear jeans and a black T-shirt belonging to Cressie and so remain unidentified. She had not told Megan and Janie the reason behind the visit.

The front door clicked as Paddy left the house and she rushed up to their sunny bedroom and, scraping and pinning back her own hair, essayed the wig. She stared at herself-yet-not-herself in the Regency-style mahogany mirror and was amazed.

Good God, how ordinary I look! Now what could I be? An assistant at a supermarket check-out, perhaps. I think I'll need a darker lipstick, something jammy.

She rustled about in a drawer for the large striped sponge bag in which she kept several years' worth of unfortunate cosmetic purchases. Glitterati eye shadow, Pussycat Promise eyeliner, gold lipstick, lipsticks called Coffee Pudding and Natural Nougat ... why did I buy those? Scrabble, scrabble, Lancôme, Chanel, Max Factor, Estee Lauder, Rimmel ... and here we are – Damson Darling ... there, that's wonderful. I am quite literally unrecognisable. All I've got to do is keep my voice down ... 'Oh, my God! I do wish you *wouldn't* creep up on me like that, Paddy! I thought you'd gone to work. I was just trying on ... well, I was just ...'

She began to laugh for his expression, mirrored above the dressing table as he stood behind her, was one of hypnotised fear ... as if she were a fox.

'How do you think I look? I thought it would be amusing for a change tonight, to see if brunettes have any fun at all.'

'You look like Avril.'

'Nothing wrong with that, I suppose. She's really quite good-looking.'

'I came back to change my shoes. There's something sharp in the left one, sticking into my foot. Could you perhaps pop them into the mender's for me if you're out shopping this morning?'

'Is it worth it? Why don't you just throw them away?' Vicky

was now experimenting with the Glitterati eyeshadow, bending forward with her jaw slightly dropped and her eyes narrowed and dabbing with a tiny brush. She had no time for the offending black brogues that Paddy was tendering.

They were his favourite shoes, gently worn in, the leather conforming with exactitude to each toe, lovingly polished and cared for. He helplessly raised his eyebrows at her lack of sentiment and thrift and went meekly downstairs, re-shod in a newer pair which squeaked.

Just after sunrise, at 6 a.m. on 3 May, lorries rumbled through the gate beside the Jack Cade. It was fine and warm and the ground was firm and dry, although the newly mown grass sparkled with dew and fine drifts of mist floated over the surface of the dyke.

Plans were consulted and posts were hammered in, the confines of the site being demarcated by fluorescent orange tape. All possible access to the Jack Cade was cordoned off and alternate signs warning 'Deep Water' and 'Do Not Proceed Past This Point' were mounted alongside the dyke, which acted as a semi-circular boundary on the far side of the field. Floors were laid, spotless white marquees erected, the vast main one after all enclosing the May tree which showed quantities of tiny pearl buds but was not sufficiently advanced in its flowering to smell at all strongly. A wide covered way soon extended from the lane, around behind the garden of the Jack Cade, to the marquees.

Rush had not arrived but by mid-morning the electricians had moved in, followed by stage builders. At mid-day the decorator's van appeared, with rolls of green, black and purple gauzy material and box after box of flowers; the accents of Benenden and Cheltenham Ladies' College floated out lackadaisically from the top of step-ladders, mingling with and good-naturedly mocked by those of Inner London comprehensives as their owners crawled about at ground level with toolboxes. Chairs and tables were delivered. Generators throbbed.

The colour scheme disappointed Janice, who had been wandering ecstatically about the site in the bright sunshine, tripping over ropes and getting in everyone's way. By the afternoon she'd donned a pair of olive-green-and-orange-striped hipster pants with wide flares in honour of the occasion and had, more successfully, astonished some of the electricians by suddenly sicking up a past vocabulary.

'It's all happening, man,' she said, nodding wisely and leaning so close over a boy that her red hair carelessly brushed his shirtless shoulder. 'This is where it's at.'

The young man, who was intent on unravelling a mass of writhing electrical cables, gaped up at her, bewildered.

'If you say so.' Then he gave a gap-toothed grin and added as an afterthought, 'Cool trousers! Do you know what? I just heard a cuckoo. I never heard one before.'

After having insinuated herself into the main marquee and embarrassingly overturned a bucket of proteas and dark purple tulips, Janice busily reported back to Rosie.

'It all looks a bit funereal to me. They've got black ostrich feathers on the tables, and black candles in those things with glass shades. I expected it would all be fluorescent pinks and limes, like sets on the telly.'

At one o'clock a party of workers descended on the inn and swiftly drained a barrel of beer before leaving to continue with their hammering, straining, shouting, heaving and stapling. So many mobile phones were in operation now on site, that it was hard for their owners to find a quiet place from which to issue or receive their orders. Rosie, who had with difficulty fought down her own curiosity and kept out of the way, spent a considerable amount of time fending off and reassuring locals who stopped to question, for they were unable to see through the trees from the lane exactly what was occurring behind the inn, and certainly something of moment *was* happening and they quite naturally wished to know exactly who, what, why and when. She explained several times, trying to play it down, that it was not a rave to which anyone could go, but a private party. More like a wedding reception, she added, and nothing to do with her. She was stunned by the apparent chaos and began to fear for the sanity of the man in charge, Kieran, the one with the Mohican beard. And where *was* Rush? Also her mind kept drifting back to Oliver Potter, round Ollie, up and down Ollie.

Rush arrived, completely calm, at six o'clock, followed by Fiammetta in a bit of a state, at seven. She had four boxes and two suitcases forced into the back of her car, for she had left Peregrine and tonight, after the party, would move into Rush's house. He introduced her to Rosie and the rest of the family and took them on a conducted tour of the set-up, an eerie world of long interconnecting white canvas corridors and huge spaces, far larger than anything Rosie had envisaged. Sound testing was agonizingly in progress, and the ear-splitting whistlings and wailings even penetrated the walls of the inn. Things were gradually winding down, and soon only those dealing with sound systems, security and catering were in evidence.

Rush and Kieran sat in the pub and toasted the success of the evening, and on the arrival of three gentlemen in bulging dark suits disappeared into the back room to make further arrangements for the place was teeming with voyeurs, Sam amongst them. Aylwin and Elvira were back from work and after a hasty meal were helping to serve the nosy-parkers.

At nine o'clock, Janice was to be found in the lane, eagerly scanning the coaches and limousines with smoked glass windows and their allegedly illustrious passengers, who disappointingly disappeared straight into the covered tunnel. She retired indoors again, whereupon there was a roaring above and a helicopter landed in the dusk, lights blazing like a Venusian invader. With a little squeak of frustration, Janice slopped a glass of wine vaguely into the hopefully extended hand of its purchaser and fought her way out again through the buzzing crowd to see if she could at last spot a serious contender for stardom.

Those inside the inn could hear the thumpity-thumpity bass of the music in the marquee but they might as well have been in a different country. Vicky was enjoying her incognito but was having difficulty not letting slip to Megan and Janie that she had been there before. Now was not the time, as they stood at the bar, elbow to elbow with and jostled by all sorts of unspeakable people, to divulge that this was the building she intended to transform into her new home. Not all the drinkers were so uncouth and hairy, however, in fact quite a few of them would pass unnoticed in Vicky's favourite wine bar in Tunbridge Wells, and there in the window sat that arty woman, the glass sculptress, and the man she was with looked irritatingly presentable.

'Rosie! An urgent message from Rush. The caterers need more water – can they come through the garden and stick their hose on the kitchen tap again?'

The voice caused Vicky to swing about sharply and there stood Fiammetta a couple of feet away from her. Unmistakably Fiammetta for she was wearing the same green dress she had worn to Vicky's dinner seven weeks before. Rush – Fiammetta, Fiammetta – Rush? Where was the jealous and tediously financial Peregrine? He was not the sort of person one would associate with a rave, surely? And were there caterers at raves? Fiammetta looked in her direction, seemed as if she was about to smile, as if she knew her, and then halted, puzzled, and turned away. Vicky smugly patted her wig but suddenly felt a qualm. Had she quite misjudged the affair after all?

The partyers were also well-insulated, unaware of the inn's existence or even their own whereabouts and caring even less. The buffet had been raped, replenished and pillaged again and Mel Plunket was leaping up and down in his separate little tent, loosening up. He felt slightly nauseous, as he always did before performing, but his band lay on the floor, smoking and professionally unconcerned, and the two backing singers were fussing over each other's hair extensions. It was not the time to throw a wobbly. This was the most important venue he'd ever played. The real beginning of his career.

The three men to whom Rush and Kieran had earlier been

speaking in the inn discreetly worked the floor. During Rush's necessary absences, Fiammetta had been allocated a minder in the form of Rush's assistant, Violet, a short and boisterous girl with such huge breasts that Fiammetta feared she would overbalance when she bent down to rescue a stray tulip. Violet's sole aim appeared to be to ensure that Fiammetta did not talk to anyone for more than thirty seconds and after a while it dawned on her that thirty seconds was more than enough.

The live entertainment was due to start and there was a lot of networking, table-hopping, showing off, of bare flesh and tinted glasses. The tent wall was open down one side on to a large, specially constructed terrace beyond, with more tables and further dancing space beneath the rising moon. Many of the male guests appeared to be accompanied by identical tousle-headed blondes with strident, urban-squalor voices and not enough underwear.

Mel wandered on to the stage after the band with his shirt hanging out, looking as if he couldn't care less whether anyone listened to him or not. He was pretty, in the catamite style, an almond-eyed young man with dark cropped hair and a slim, oh-so-smooth, muscular body. The restless crowd amongst the flickering black candles in the semi-dark cave before him were vampire bats to be placated. They wanted blood. Well, he'd give them as much gore as they wanted. He took the mike and a deep breath and summoning up a long, vibrating roar, was off with 'Silver-eyed Sally'.

It was certain that the Jack Cade had never heard such a volume of sound before, at least not since the Battle of Britain. Its timbers vibrated, the glass in the panes hummed and outside in the dark, squirming across a board laid across the dyke, Ollie's hired band of spoilers halted uncertainly.

'Let him finish. He's bloody brilliant!'

'No, come on. Timber and Steve should be at the electrics by now. Let's do the biz and be off.'

Just as the roar of appreciation at the end of his first song died down and Mel, now glistening with sweat, prancing and preening, commenced the second number, the sound failed, then the lights went out and after counting to ten, the black-balaclava-ed thugs erupted on to the stage. A mike stand was snapped across a knee; Mel was carried shrieking off-stage by an eighteen-stone heavy who, mindful of his brief, very gently set him unharmed on his feet in the dark and patted him on the head. The other members of the group strode amongst the candle-lit tables like gorillas, beating their broad breasts and roaring, stuffing handfuls of delicate pastry barquettes of caviar into their mouths, yanking off a tablecloth here, up-ending a wine bottle there, dragging cigarettes from lips and dropping them into drinks. There was also a little mooning . . . it was surprising how much they managed to do before the security guards woke up to what was happening.

Half the guests at least imagined it was a stunt and burst into further cheers and applause, screeching with laughter and clapping; the other half had been enraptured by Mel and would have been extremely annoyed by the interruption if they hadn't been as high as jumbo jets on the new designer drug which had been hawked about that evening and were feeling incredibly . . . incredibly . . . well, fantastically whatever. There was squealing as a table went over and in the distance a siren was heard. The sound was heard first above the bedlam by the three keen-eared, besuited gentlemen who promptly disappeared. Rush would have been tearing his hair if it had been long enough for him to get a grip on.

Steve, Timber, Keg, Blue, Blue and Barney McGrew melted away beneath the tent flaps, dragging yards of green gauze and a bunch of tulips behind them as they burst through the taped barriers. They stumbled into the previously self-effacing but now hysterical pushers who were urgently divesting themselves of their remaining little tablets by throwing them into the dyke.

Blue flashing lights twinkled through the trees to the right, drawing level as the last pocket was emptied and the last little plastic envelope ditched, and carried on, straight past the inn, to a reported car in a dyke two miles beyond Middhaze-in-the-Marsh. Brightly bobbing in the moonlit and sluggish water of the Jack Cade's dyke was a fleet of little purple and green pills.

Tiger and the Kittens, along with three unknown women, had gathered outside in Rosie's vegetable patch to listen more closely to Mel the Magnificent. They had seen the lights go out and heard the rumpus, heard also the furious cackling of the geese, the startled, belching baa of the old ram and the crashing sounds of the interlopers leaving via the orchard and had lumbered into pursuit. It was Tiger who felled Timber, cracking his head against the knobbly trunk of an ancient Ribston Pippin, and with one arm round his throat, painfully ripped off the balaclava and whispered hoarsely in his captive's ear: ''Allo, mate. Your gran knit this, did she? What you up to then?'

'Nothing much. Just a bit of fun. Get off, you bastard! I've got 'alf a salmon tucked inside my shirt.'

'Well, effing do nothing much somewhere else. This isn't your patch.' Thump. 'Effing get back to effing Sussex!' Tiger let it go at that, since he was a bit out of condition and breathing heavily. He also urgently wanted to see if he could make it with one of the posh bits they'd left beside the spinach in the veg patch. That little one in black was quite a cracker, as far as he could see in the dark. Sadly they'd all of them disappeared by the time he returned.

The electricity supply was restored surprisingly swiftly and the festive atmosphere in the main marquee soon picked up again. Rush made an announcement, the caterers replenished the buffet, order and alcohol were restored to the tables and although Mel complained that his nerves were shredded, he good-humouredly agreed to go on stage again and finish the session. Rush and Fiammetta went over to the Jack Cade to reassure Rosie, but it was past closing time and they found her wiping down the tables, unaware of the ruction. Elvira was collecting glasses and Janice and Aylwin were counting the stupendous takings in the kitchen.

'Here we are, Rosie. It looks like you've had a good night! The party'll be going on into the small hours, I'm afraid.' He slipped a hand inside his jacket and brought out a wad of notes. 'This'll make you sleep better. I thought you'd prefer cash in hand.'

# Chapter Eight

It was in the cool dawn, when all the guests had departed and after much yelling and searching about the misty, near-deserted party site, that his weeping drummer and the two remaining and recalcitrant security men found Mel. He was in the dyke, face down in a mere three feet of water. A couple of bruised black tulips floated beside him like exotic waterlilies and a piece of green gauze trailed from the heel of his snakeskin boot. Clustering, clinging against the outline of his body in the water, gently swayed a few unsinkable green and purple pills, along with a half-eaten onion bhaji.

'I keep telling you, he hadn't a care in the world. He played first at ten o'clock, then did a bit of mingling with the guests — schmoozing they call it, you know, meeting useful people and all that — and he had some supper . . . I saw him eating an anchovy salad. I saw him dancing. We had a chat together.'

Rush rubbed his eyes and passed dry fingers over drier lips. There was a powerful sickly scent of May-blossom in the marquee and outside the tent people were waiting for the all clear from the police to start taking it down. Poor, poor Mel. He'd hoped so much for him. This, also, was hardly the start to their alliance for which he and Fiammetta had hoped.

'No, I had no reason to think he was on drugs although he may have been. He played a second set at midnight. He was very pleased with everything, himself included. No, I mean he was excited. No, he's nice enough; I liked him and he had every reason to be pleased. He went down very well.' Christ, what an unfortunate phrase! 'I mean the audience raved about him. He isn't a drinker and hadn't been in the business long enough to make any enemies. No, I don't know of any relatives, but the drummer was his best mate – he'll know.'

The detective inspector also looked tired and not a little bored. Bodies in dykes were not so very uncommon and there were no signs of violence. A serious traffic accident further up the road had prevented an officer from immediately attending to an anonymous call reporting a fight. The officer had driven past on the way back; the pub had been shut and dark and the security man at the entrance to the private party had denied that there had been any trouble and suggested that the call was most probably a wind-up from some local annoyed by the loudness of the music. Rush Kadely seemed an entirely reasonable and responsible fellow, and backed up other accounts that Mel Plunket had been alive and well long after the alleged incursion. They'd have to wait for the pathologist's full report after the autopsy.

'Mel and the others were going to stay the night in the tents and leave in the morning. I last saw him round about two-thirty in the morning – this morning, I mean.'

Rush's skin was grey-tinged with tiredness. Fiammetta, who had also been interviewed, was now asleep in Rosie's guest room.

'Well, that's all for the moment, Mr Kadely. Except, perhaps you can help me with this?' The detective inspector pulled out a clear polythene packet, beaded on the inside with moisture and containing a small crumbling green and purple pill. 'Have you seen one of these before?'

'No,' said Rush, dully. 'Where did you find it?'

The policeman didn't answer. It had been found inside Mel's

shirt. He hadn't noticed the coincidental correlation between the colours of the pill and the decor of the party.

'Isn't that a shame!' said Janie, carefully checking over the wig, puffing it up into shape and putting it back in its box. She might need it again one day and, not trusting Vicky to return it, had dropped by that morning to collect it.

'Isn't what a shame?'

Vicky was brunching on toast and Gentlemen's Relish, and wincing slightly as the crunching echoed in her head. Paddy had gone off to play a round of golf. The night before, after depositing a merry Megan and Janie at their respective residences, she had sat fuming in the drawing-room, drinking brandy till Paddy returned. She had been driving and it was at her insistence they'd left the Jack Cade before closing time, much to her companions' annoyance since they were having a prodigiously good time and couldn't understand why Vicky, who had set out that evening in high spirits, had so suddenly nose-dived.

She had discovered from the uniformed giant guarding the entrance that the tickets were all pre-paid and had cost £100 each and, after a little probing, that the members of a rather well-known, even to her, rock band were in attendance. After the party's resumption, there was no point in staying on in the inn. She'd spent a lot of money to no effect and was unfairly furious with Ollie. Her phone call reporting a fight to the police, made during a visit to the irritatingly spotless and repainted Ladies, had produced no results.

'Isn't what a shame?' she repeated, finishing her third cup of coffee.

'Didn't you hear? On the radio. Listen.'

'. . . after a party at the Jack Cade Inn at Middhaze. Police are treating the circumstances as suspicious.'

'I missed the beginning. What's suspicious?'

'Someone called Mel Plunket – isn't that who everyone was

talking about last night? – he's drowned. They said he fell in a river at a party.'

Vicky's face, already a little pale, turned chalky. She hustled off Janie and the wig and ran upstairs, furious with fright, to telephone Ollie.

Ollie waited with mounting apprehension for the local news on television that evening but Mel's death was treated as a minor item and few details were given that he did not know already from Vicky. Please God, it wasn't anything to do with his mercenaries. Damn Vicky! Damn her! That he might be implicated was scary enough, but the thought that he might actually be responsible for someone's pointlessly early death was deeply disturbing, intolerable, unbelievable. Having flagellated himself for weakness for days, now standing by the open window of his flat, listening to a wood-pigeon cooing in the early-evening sunshine, he trundled out a rack and tentatively laid himself upon it.

He had become an aimless, shiftless bastard. Self-opprobrium, however, would not help Mel Plunket, whoever he was. Ollie visualized the tracing and apprehending of the mercenaries, imagined the police getting closer and closer, sniffing at his door. His own arrest for conspiracy to murder. All the interrogation scenes from all the police serials he had ever seen on television began to re-run, twice as brutally, in his brain. He wouldn't last five minutes. I did it! I admit it! Termination of recorded interview. No, it surely could not get that far? There was no motive. His life – he, at least, still had one – must be redefined. And Rosie, the lovely welcoming Rosie, deserved better from him. He recalled her face as he'd last seen it, that cryptic, preoccupied madonna look. He imagined her banging on the window of the police van and yelling 'Traitor!' as he was brought to trial. He imagined her also visiting him in prison, the bright brown eyes sad but forgiving. Unlikely, but she might have hidden depths. At least he felt she *had* depths. Vicky's soul, he had always been aware, was to be discovered about two inches down in a pile of rubble. And he, Ollie, was just as shallow.

'. . . how awkward for you, but perhaps the Hooke woman might lose her licence if they find out it was to do with drugs.' Vicky had actually said that on the phone after castigating him for the pathetic nature of the disruption he'd organized.

'. . . and you might at least have made sure they mucked up the electrics for the rest of the night. They were only out for about fifteen minutes . . .' He'd crashed the receiver down and overcome by a despairing inertia, turned on the tiny TV to sit there watching a war-time drama set on board ship, keeping a score of nautical anomalies in an attempt to regain his composure.

Ollie sat up suddenly, remembering Rosie's statuette about which he had so far done nothing. He was due in London to lunch with Felicity on Monday and would take it with him then, if he was still a free man, get it checked out at Sotheby's or somewhere like that. Too small, too plain to be of any great value. He didn't hold out much hope.

He barely slept that night and when he did was troubled with dreams of his mother making cakes and blowing up balloons, probably the only two things which he was quite sure she had never done in her life.


That Saturday morning, a long-faced Janice reminded them all several times in a voice of doom that she'd told them May-blossom was unlucky. If she says that deaths go in threes, thought Rosie, grimly, I'll have to send her to bed for the rest of the day. They were all glum, their delight in Rush's lunatic generosity having been flattened by the disaster. The death of Mel Plunket, so far unknown to the public, was not yet to make the front pages. The local press was busy with the Parden May carnival and the fact that the May Queen had gone down with chickenpox. They remained unaware that several celebrities of cult status had been anywhere near Romney Marsh.

At three o'clock Rosie closed the inn's door on a lunchtime session that had been blossoming with gossip and ripe with speculation. Perhaps for the first time in her life desperate to be somewhere else entirely, Rosie immediately bundled into the van with Aylwin, Elvira, Trash and a yawning and reluctant Janice. She drove four miles off to one of those special spots which she thought of as peculiarly hers but which, today, she wished to share. The terrible sadness of the drowning of the young man, the intermittent sleep between the comings, goings and doings of the past twenty-four hours, had unnerved all four of them and they now clung together, united in the need for comfort.

'The thing is . . .' Rosie said as they set off in hot sunshine on the stone track that ran alongside a wide, froggy, reed-edged channel '. . . the thing is I feel that all that wonderful money Rush has given us seems, well, slightly tainted somehow – the sun's quite fierce; I wish I'd brought a hat – I feel we've gained it at the cost of a death.'

'I think you're being a little over-scrupulous,' said Aylwin, deftly disengaging a bee from his hair and throwing a stick for Trash. Trash ignored it and rushed down the bank, disappearing barking into the water after a moorhen. 'It simply could *not* be your fault. It doesn't appear to be anyone's fault at the moment and until we hear from the police, we mustn't worry about it.'

'But I *am* worrying. If trying to save the Jack Cade has caused someone to die unnecessarily, then I am responsible, originally. It happened on my land. And I still don't understand where the roughs came from or why they should want to break up the party. Tiger told me at lunchtime. I thought it was just a power cut, but apparently there were four or five of them out there in the dark, waiting to cause trouble.'

'Yes, I see what you mean, about being originally responsible. But it was a contingency, wasn't it? Like you suggesting we all come out for a walk, and while we're plodding along, a goat might fall on Janice's head from a plane and then you'd say *that* was your fault? You must see it's ridiculous, Mum.'

'Yes, I suppose it must be.'

'A sky-diving goat isn't a very good example of a contingency, is it?' said Elvira, using a piece of cow parsley as a fly swat. Janice glanced up automatically and nervously.

'Why does this goat have to fall on *my* head? Oh, listen. There's a cuckoo!'

'Well, *my* head then. There it goes ... See, over there? I'm sure I read once about a goat falling out of a cargo plane and sinking a fishing boat, but it might have been a cow and it might have been in India.'

They had turned away from the waterside and now followed the edge of a field. The pollen from acres of mustard-yellow rape, too intrusively brilliant to gaze on in the sunlight, caused Janice to sneeze chaotically and Elvira proffered a lacy handkerchief. Larks sang, a tractor droned in the distance but apart from these there was only the sound of their footsteps and heavy breathing. Rosie, in red T-shirt and trousers, moving fast, as if driven, led the way and then Elvira floating gracefully along in a long sea-green cotton dress, followed by Janice, complaining about the pace, in emerald and violet. Like Kurdish gypsies, Aylwin thought as they strung out ahead of him in their bright, unsensible clothes. Comical, tragical, pastoral.

Ahead the track turned again and led through a green wheat field up to the base of a huge irrational hummock, a great bank rising smoothly thirty metres or so out of the near sea-level land on the inner edge of the marsh. It was crested with stunted trees and hawthorn bushes and a footpath ran up the gentle slope, through the crop, to the flattened summit and down the other side. A hare leapt away in front of them as they started to climb, then a pheasant clattered up and Trash wavered, gave chase to the hare but was outpaced in ten seconds as his prey's dark ear tips vanished into the wheat.

Aylwin bent and retrieved a piece of black pottery, then a

stone with a hole right through it. He turned to look back and below, where fresh water had once run past the island and the salt tide had flooded up to meet it. Near here Norwegian and Danish Vikings had brought their longships inland in the late ninth century, murdering and maiming as they came. At one time it must have been almost impossible to reach except by boat. He liked to think that beneath the calm fields a long boat's carved prow, perhaps even the legendary dragon's head, lay waiting, preserved deep down beneath the silt.

Rosie gathered speed and gained the top and a perspiring Janice, determined to keep up, gasped.

'It's a graveyard! How creepy! But why, right up here?'

'There was a church here once,' Aylwin explained. 'They still hold a service once a year. And it's the least creepy place I know, in the daylight.'

'But where's the village – where did these people come from? What happened to the church?'

'Down there, look, over to the right a bit.' He pointed. 'That's all there is of the village, and there's the "new" church. They rebuilt it with the stone of the old one, up here.'

'And every night the stone which they'd brought down the hill the previous day, mysteriously flew up again . . .' said Elvira, giggling.

'How did you know?' asked Rosie. 'It sounds like the usual builder's excuse for running over time.'

'Aylwin told me! Listen, a curlew.'

'Look, look at the view!' they cried out to each other, elated, shading their eyes and all pointing in different directions for they were encircled, in the centre of a fish-eye lens; the semi-circle of the rising Weald lay behind them, then to one side a church tower in the middle distance and beyond, open marsh all the way to the sea.

Some ideal places have the power to belittle worries, and it felt immeasurably good to Rosie to be higher up, as even so little height as this gave unexpected perspectives and a false and heady sense of immortality to those who are used to living at sea-level. Well-distanced from the happenings last night, she wandered among the thistles and the leaning grey eighteenth century gravestones which, although fallen, were quick with elegant script and cherubs, skulls and flowers spattered with orange and black lichens, warm to the touch. She ducked round sycamores and saplings to the sad remains of the great weeping ash tree. Dad, limping and puce in the face with effort, had brought them panting up here long ago for picnics, had unwrapped greaseproof packets of sweating cheese sandwiches and brought out a warm bottle of lemonade from an army knapsack. He had sat on a fallen gravestone, smoking, whilst they played in the tree.

The tree was wrecked by gales and decay and its trunk was split and bulging with black fungal growths. A strong new stem with smooth grey bark had sprung up from the crumbling base, so it was at least regenerating. One huge branch lay rotting on the ground, that one which she and even the diffident Sally had sat astride, wildly bouncing up and down and pretending they were riding a prancing horse. It was easier to recall the tree, exactly as it had been then, than either Sally or her father. She too now sat on the gravestone and smoked, watching Janice flittering about. Janice's chronic, childlike clumsiness caused her to trip in rabbit holes and stumble over graves half-hidden in the slippery grass. She squawked as she was stung by nettles and kept up a burbling flow of questions and comments which no one answered, but she did not seem to mind; she was happy, captivated by the 'romantic aura' of the place, she said. Nearby, Elvira lay with her head on the dozing Aylwin's lap and sang, admirably un-self-conscious.

'I want to be buried up here,' said Janice, flopping down beside Rosie. 'It's such a secret place. Can anyone be buried here, or do you have to be a local?' She envisioned a trail of black-draped mourners winding up the hill behind a rose-strewn coffin made of ebony and a threnody, if a threnody was the right thing, hanging in the air.

Rosie had once imagined herself buried here too, and now

imagined an eternity spent listening to a thickly muffled Janice asking questions beneath the soil.

Aylwin said he had once spent a night there with a friend, in a tent, for a dare. 'It's quite different then. It feels unsettled, rustling, and the trees squeak in the wind.'

'Did you last the night out?' asked Elvira.

'No way! We ran off screeching at midnight, filled with gothic dread! I lost my torch and galloped after Jerome, petrified of being left behind in the dark. We practically rolled down the hill in our haste to get to our bicycles at the bottom!'

'I remember you coming home that night with Jerome', said Rosie. 'There was mud and chocolate all over the kitchen floor. What happened to Jerome? I liked him.'

'I still see him, two or three times a year. We used to have terrible arguments. Mostly about girls, I think.' Aylwin turned to Elvira. 'I went to the local comprehensive, you see, and Jerome went to a public school where there weren't any girls – they only came into the sixth form just as he was leaving. He thought it very unfair. He also used to say that one of the differences between his school and mine was that public schools didn't on the whole find it necessary to squash the geniuses in order to build up the pillocks.'

'Did he think he was a genius?' asked Elvira.

'No, he didn't, and he wasn't. Perhaps it was something he'd heard his father say. He read archaeology and after a stint as a motorcycle courier in London, and a working trip to Mexico, he got taken on last year by one of those archaeological programmes on TV. You can see him occasionally emerging from a wet trench clutching a muddy tibia, trying to get his face on camera. He gets to speak every now and then.'

Aylwin laughed, but Rosie had not missed the wistful note. He wasn't as happy with his job as he pretended, she knew, but he didn't have to stay at the printer's forever. She was asking so much from all of them but once she'd made secure the Jack Cade ... It was gloriously warm for early May, soporific ...

Stupefied by the fresh air, she lay back on the grass, felt her eyelids grow weighty, shut them and saw blue patterns dancing on a rose-pink background; she focused intently on the expanding and contracting shapes, and nodded off.

'Rosie ... *Rosie!'*

Oliver Potter, who had been holding her around the waist, squashing her so tightly against him that she could feel each one of his ribs, breathed in her ear and slowly faded, along with the scent of warm, clean but musky man in warm, clean shirt. Not like those youths who sometimes came to the inn, stinking of the cheap, soapy, cat's pee aftershave that flattened the taste of the beer ... Oh, God! Where am I? Aylwin was shaking her arm.

'It's nearly five o'clock.' He hung over her, dark and faceless against the bright sky. It had been Aylwin who'd smelt so delicious. 'We ought to go. There's Mr and Mrs Lamb from London booked in for tonight, if you remember. Hey! Don't go back to sleep.'

'No, I won't. I hadn't forgotten the poor Lambkins. Their room's all ready and they're not due till nine o'clock.' Rosie spat a piece of leaf out of her mouth, brushed down her red cotton trousers and looked up reproachfully. But she didn't get to her feet immediately and sat a moment longer, a little dazed and very thirsty. The sun was dipping and was in her eyes. A supine Janice lay still fruitily asleep, her long brittle hair, recently re-dyed the colour of plum jam, thrown out fan-wise in the grass. Her morello-cherry mouth was open, letting out occasional little whiffling snores.

Elvira rose up from behind a tombstone some distance away, arms up, gracefully rolling dark hair into a knot, the back of her crumpled dress unbuttoned. Rosie, suddenly wide awake, guessed with an inward giggle that Elvira and Aylwin had taken advantage of her and Janice's exhausted sleep to make love, instinctively risking both that the exhausted aunts wouldn't wake and that no one else would climb the hill that afternoon.

'Magical,' said Elvira, hand in hand with Aylwin as they

ambled slowly down again. They were still communicating sensually; a little possessive touch on Elvira's collarbone to flick off a ladybird, the removal of a blade of grass from Aylwin's neck, feeling between each other's fingers. 'But odd how we all forgot, up there, about last night. I stopped thinking about it as soon as we arrived, without trying. No one else mentioned it.' The sun had caught her shoulders and across her cheeks and nose.

'It'll still be there when we get home, the gloom. Probably more police, more questions. But, yes, it's a good place to be when things are grim at ground level. Worries seem so insignificant up there.' Aylwin squeezed her hand. 'I'm hungry.'

Rosie scrubbed potatoes, Elvira and Aylwin tidied, swept and restocked the bar, and Janice, after laying the table for supper, wandered out to the empty field. She was interested in death, and half-expected she would in some way sense its recent presence. Deserted, the grass flattened and scuffed, there remained only a short length of blue and white police tape, a few cigarette butts on the ground behind where the caterer's tent had stood and a piece of purple gauze ribbon tied in a bow on a branch of the May tree. The contractors had cleared up well and had perhaps taken with them whatever emotion it was she'd expected to feel.

In the field across the dyke, a swan was walking. They had a lumbering gait on land, so contrary to their elegant passage on the water, but there was something eerie in the way this one travelled round and round in sweeping circles, pausing now and then to stretch its neck upwards as if it were about to shake its feathers before continuing to turn about. It was not the swan-behaviour Janice had come to expect since becoming used to their constant local presence. Her long shadow leapt ahead of her as she crossed the grass to the bank to take a closer look but it seemed unaware of her across the water and continued stretching and touring. On the ground lay a bunch of flowers, florist's flowers, pink tulips and white daisies in a frilly cone of cellophane printed

with a white lace pattern. There was a card pinned to it; she
stooped to read.

*'To the incomprabel Mel, with love from Flash'.*

She turned to go back to the Jack Cade, but someone else
was clambering over the iron gates from the lane clutching
another bunch of flowers. A skinny girl with fluffy blonde hair
approached and Janice waited.

'Is this where he was drownded?'

'I suppose it must be.'

'Sad, innit?' said the girl, reverentially placing her bunch,
more pink tulips, alongside the other. 'Flash – that's the drummer. I saw them at a gig in Maidstone.' She sniffed. 'My dad's
waiting for me in the lane. He thinks flowers are a waste of
money. He wanted a drink, but the pub's shut. We heard about
it on the local rajo.'

'Ah,' said Janice, unable to think of anything else to say.


'How did the girl know where to come?' asked Rosie, passing Janice a plate of fresh whiting fried in butter, with an
extra-large helping of steaming buttery potatoes, smothered in
lemon, chives and parsley. 'Did she say she'd been a friend of
his?'

They were sitting quietly at the kitchen table with the low
afternoon sunshine pouring in through the open door, lighting
up the parts one never thinks of looking at, glowing on a
spoon dropped beneath a chair, catching the irregularities of
the flagstoned floor, showing up the dog hairs on the rag rug
in front of the stove.

'No. She just thought it was sad. She'd heard about it on
the news.'

'Then more of them will be coming,' said Aylwin, at which
point there was a cough at the door and another young woman
and an embarrassed-looking boy stood outside on the stone step,
clutching yet more flowers in crisp cellophane.

'Sorry to butt in on your tea, but could you tell us where to put our floral tribute? Where it happened?'

'This is grotesque,' said Aylwin after the third interruption.

'Ted wants to put his sheep back in. I'll collect the other flowers from the dyke and bring them back to the entrance. We can't have people in and out and over the gate. Sooner or later one of them's going to leave it open, and anyway the sheep might eat them. They all seem to be pink tulips. Are tulips poisonous?'

No-one knew.

After supper Aylwin wrote a sign to tie on the gate and when it was in place, Rosie collected the five bunches of flowers and stood them up beneath it.

*Flowers in Memory of Mel Plunket*

*Leave here, please*

By Sunday lunchtime the car park was full and the long bar and sunny garden were again populated with the curious and the prurient, including a pair of unnecessarily truculent tabloid reporters elbowing out the regulars and trying to melt down Rosie and Elvira's leaden discretion. The Jack Cade was being impinged upon by the outside world for the first time in years and its inhabitants were not enjoying the ill-gotten fame.

'Janice, be a love and do some clearing up? Sam says the flowers are edging out into the lane and are being driven over, and there's a dog loose somewhere.' Rosie lowered her voice. 'And call Aylwin to come and help us serve these ghouls.'

'But he's upstairs, writing.'

'Tell him I'm sorry to interrupt but I really, really need him. And I'm nearly out of glasses.' She raised her voice again and called out over the chatter.

'Who owns the Airedale running loose in the field outside? If it starts worrying sheep, Ted has a right to shoot it. You have been warned. Oh, Rush! How nice to see a familiar face. It's chaos here, as you can see. Before anything, could you dash round the garden and try to find the owner of that damn dog?'

'I'll give you a hand, shall I?' Fiammetta coolly stepped behind the bar and started serving. Rosie was startled.

'You've done this before?'

'I used to serve in a pub when I was at university. Yes? Two pints of snakebite coming up. Rosie, Rush has heard from the police . . .'

Rosie glanced up sharply and put her finger to her lips, warning of the presence of interested interlopers.

'It's OK,' Fiammetta whispered back. 'It *wasn't* foul play. Natural causes, not even drowning. An undiagnosed heart condition. It could have happened at any time. I know it's still very upsetting, but at least we can stop thinking it might have been murder. Rush was terribly worried, as you must have been.'

'Two pounds ninety, please. Thanks. Hello, Brian. No, I'm afraid I can't read your short story just at the moment, but if you leave it with Elvira when you go . . . Yes, we are just a bit busy.' Rosie returned to Fiammetta, relief evident on her face. But she thought a minute before answering.

'It's not pleasant, is it, how relieved we all feel to be let off the hook? The poor boy's still dead, however it happened. Oh, help! *Rush!* Don't bring the dog in here . . . Trash'll go for it!'

Too late. There was a turmoil of snarling and yelping, a whirlwind of brown and white fur and a chair went over. The dog fight had the welcome effect of thinning out the customers and Rosie leant thankfully against the bar, face pink with exertion and her hair all over the place but she was at once confronted by another gentleman of the press.

'Perhaps you could spare me a moment now, Mrs Hooke? What kind of people were they, the ones who tried to break up the party on Friday night?'

'That's the first I've heard of anyone trying to break it up.' Rosie became uncharacteristically flustered.

'Could you tell us how you feel about Mel Plunket's death?'

'No, I couldn't.'

'But you must have some feelings, surely?' The reporter was bossily censorious and insistent. 'A young man, sensational singer, bright future before him, drowning suspiciously on your property?'

'I didn't say I didn't have any feelings,' she snapped. 'I said I couldn't tell you about them. And there were no suspicious circumstances. We've just been told that it was natural causes. You seem to know more about it than we do.'

A camera flashed, dazzling Aylwin just as he looked cautiously around the door from the kitchen.

'Psst! Rosie? Janice is holding a reporter to ransom in the kitchen. She found him poking his nose into the pantry and she's got hold of the flogger. I think you ought to come at once and do some damage limitation.' The flogger, a large wooden mallet used for knocking the spiles and taps into beer barrels, was gently wrested from Janice's irate hand.

Monday started quietly. Elvira and Aylwin went out to work, Janice cleaned the kitchen and Rosie, blank-minded for once, planted out leek seedlings and sowed Little Gem lettuces and the french beans.

By twelve o'clock she was up a ladder in the sunshine, re-puttying a first-floor window frame at the front of the house, wishing that Oliver might come in for a drink that day. Beneath, Sam Dicken was unnecessarily holding the ladder, admiringly close to her legs, irritatingly over-protective.

'Why don't you let me do that, Rosie?'

'Because it's your lunchtime. You go and have your pint and leave me to it. I promise you I'm quite capable. There are only three more panes to do.'

Exasperated, she turned and looked down on him, standing so patiently beneath her in his overalls. A large gloup of linseed-scented putty fell off the end of the knife and landed on his hat; the summer having arrived, Sam had cautiously discarded the red woolly one and now wore an infinitely more fetching wide-brimmed khaki thing.

'Sam, how do you feel about organising a hay-bale pitching competition for the Games?'

He smiled up at her and said it would be no trouble but clung fast to the ladder, reluctant to be dismissed. Then Elvira drew up in Rosie's van and leapt from it, brandishing a newspaper.

'I just had to come back and bring you this. Fourth page, look!' Rosie sighed and carefully descended the ladder, avoiding Sam's helping hand.

It wasn't Mel who'd hit the headlines. '*Lady Fiammetta slums it!*' There was a photograph of her and Rosie behind the bar. Fiammetta's head was helpfully arrowed. '*Lady Fiammetta Briggand rolls up her sleeves to help landlady Rosie Hooke in a crisis. Following the mysterious death of pop star Mel Plunket in the early hours of Saturday morning, the quaint Jack Cade Inn was besieged by grieving fans bearing floral tributes . . . a riot erupted as tractors tore down the rural lane, flattening bouquets and scattering mourners.*'

'Triple tripe! How did they find out who she was? And why are they interested in Fiammetta? It can't, surely, be just the title? Perhaps she's notorious in some way and we don't know it. I'd better ring Rush, though, and warn him. All right, Sam, you win. Here's the putty knife.'

Rosie was aware, indeed had been apprised by Rush himself of the nature of his relationship with Fiammetta and of, if not the title, her status as a fleeing wife. There was a muffled explosion as she told him the news and just as she put the receiver down, a darkly furious man burst in through the door. This was becoming farcical. 'I knew it,' she muttered, 'I've lost control. I'm in the middle of someone else's dreadful play.'

In spite of Peregrine Briggand's forceful but immaculate politeness, Rosie could feel the blast of icy wrath like frostbite on her face. *Never get embroiled in your customers' private business.* That's what her father would have said. Free-range Sally would have loved all the excitement. Rosie braced herself and gave the man a pleasant smile.

'I'd like to have a word with your new barmaid, if you don't mind?'

'I haven't got a new barmaid.'

'Come, come. You look like an intelligent woman. This is very important. I was shown her photograph in a newspaper this morning. She was working here yesterday. I will not be palmed off with lies.'

Rosie had never actually heard anyone say *Come, come* like that before. It was charmingly old-fashioned, and she inadvertently smiled again at this wronged husband who'd popped up from the pages of a Regency romance.

'I've seen the picture too. The woman who helped me, very kindly and unasked, was a customer. Doesn't she look pretty?'

'She didn't come unaccompanied.' It was a flat statement. 'Who was she with?' Peregrine leant forward aggressively, the forbidding hedges of heavy dark eyebrows forced together as if to prevent his nose from escaping upwards. Trash circled, snarling unpleasantly.

'I've no idea.' Rosie looked at him blankly. 'It was extremely crowded. Packed out, in fact. First she was here doling out pints like a professional. Then, as things became quieter, here she wasn't.'

'Does she visit regularly then?'

'Can't say as I've noticed.' The grander he became, the more rounded and rural did she. He glared at her, certain that she was pretending innocence but failing to prise anything further from her, he stormed out, leaving behind, she swore afterwards to Aylwin, the smell of brimstone and scorch marks on the floorboards. She grabbed the phone and pressed redial.

# Chapter Nine

'You should have heard him, Ollie. He's a terrifying man. Viciously polite. He'd been through their joint address book, phoning all her friends and then relations and acquaintances, which is when he tried us. I felt I ought to tell him that Rush might be involved. I was quite drained afterwards. I wouldn't like to be Rush when Peregrine catches up with him; I distinctly got the impression that it was his pride that was badly damaged, rather than his heart.' Vicky gave a little snigger at her own perceptiveness, which Ollie found infuriating.

She had come, for the first time ever, to his flat, late on Tuesday afternoon. His voice on the entryphone, coming after a long pause, had sounded odd, but that was to be expected after the terse words which had passed between them on the phone on Saturday. She walked up the wide pink-carpeted staircase, up and up, past the blank white-panelled doors of other apartments, past a large and hideous brown and gold Japanese vase on the second landing. She stopped and examined this, wondering at its neurotic ugliness, the cluttered squirling patterns of raised white dots and the demonic faces lowering from behind brown and terracotta-coloured paeonies.

She now sat for the first time in Ollie's small, plain third-floor sitting-room. A biography of Coleridge lay face down across the arm of the green sofa, showing a facet of him of which she had been unaware and which surprised her. A yellow and blue Ikat cushion had been flattened where he'd been lying. A few CDs were stacked neatly on the small table along with a pile of papers and unopened letters. Tidy. She'd never thought of him as tidy either, then realized uncomfortably that throughout their long relationship they had met on her terms, in her own surroundings, and she really knew very little about how he lived, or his interests.

She had come prepared for a little muted, casual seduction, as little as she could get away with in order to effect a reconciliation and a continuation of their fragile, indeterminate arrangement. She was a little worried after the sharpness on the telephone, perhaps, but blithely confident that she would eventually smooth things over satisfactorily and recover the situation, even if it meant going to bed with him.

She was quite excited by the idea of it, now that it might be necessary. She wore a white sleeveless linen blouse, with just the right number of buttons undone, long green linen wrap-around skirt and bare feet in little lilac snakeskin sandals. There being nothing else to admire, she had effusively admired the view but now it was blocked by the long, dark silhouette of Ollie looming against the window, arms folded, staring down at her. His fair hair was ruffled and spiky, his feet were bare, he wore black jeans and T-shirt and looked . . . how did he look? She was unable to make out, with the bright light behind him, that his expression was curiously forbidding.

'Aren't you going to offer me something to drink? It's a long way up all those stairs and it's awfully warm for May.' What was the matter with the man? He hardly seemed enraptured by her presence. How to get him back on track and purring again?

'It's a dear little room, isn't it? Is that the bedroom through there?'

'I've only got some bottled lager, French stuff, I think.'

'That'll do, then. I need . . .' She needed Ollie to be on her side. She raised her arms and casually raked through her hair. Her armpits were whitely smooth and velvety but she had not yet managed to soften the stiff dishevelment too carefully constructed by the hairdresser earlier in the day. She looked predictably delectable to Ollie and since there was nowhere else to sit, he reluctantly came and sat beside her, thighbone to thighbone, opened the beers and handed her one. This, he thought, might be interesting.

'*We* need to think about the next ploy, Ollie. It's the Games, isn't it? The opportunities are better there. Of course, all this publicity the Jack Cade is getting is terribly counter-productive to our plans. We need something to put the customers off. How about a food-poisoning scare? Rats? Something like that? Or drug-dealing?' she rattled on. 'It is a relief, isn't it, finding out that the poor boy hadn't been murdered?' She sounded brightly, tightly compassionate. 'You didn't know? I wouldn't have done if Janie hadn't phoned me and mentioned it . . . this morning. She listens to local radio a lot.' In fact she had known since Sunday night but it hadn't occurred to her that he might not have found out too.

'You've known since *this morning*? A relief? Oh, yes, it's a relief all right.' Ollie put down his beer and slipped an arm behind her warm back, forcing her to edge towards him, but she came without resistance. Saturday, Sunday, Monday, Tuesday . . . Long hours spent thinking that he had played a part in killing someone. A very long time, but he had deserved the misery. There was a square of sunshine on the shining skin of her shoulder, a parallelogram of brightness running across the dusty back of the green velvet sofa. Vicky smelt expensively fresh and citrony in the hot afternoon air; she felt loose, soft. The sun caught the tiny gold hairs on her forearms as she moved closer again. Soon, he expected, there would be the well-known tremor of opposition following which she would leap up and change the subject, rat-tatting out some smart dismissive remark. But it did not come. Instead buttons slipped from buttonholes with an unlikely smoothness, garments were flung aside and she lay there, surprisingly and beautifully white-blonde naked, moaning a little to encourage him, looking up at him with a complex expression in which complacent triumph surfaced through a layer of greed. It was the complacency, more than anything else, which suddenly repulsed him, actually made him want to throw up.

Ollie, his mind as usual several paces ahead of his body, wrenched himself away with difficulty, reached for his jeans without looking at Vicky again, struggled into them and walked, uncomfortably, across the room to the window, thrusting up the sash and leaning out, as if to take a gulp of unpolluted air.

'Ollie! What's the matter?' He leant so far away that Vicky imagined he was about to throw himself out. 'Ollie! Ollie?' Indignant then panicky.

He half-turned towards her and it was clear that there was nothing wrong from an anatomical point of view but she had never before seen contempt on his face and it was a second or two before she understood that that was what it was.

'You'd *let* me, wouldn't you? Just in order to get your own way? It's the patronising "let", the allowing, I don't care for. You don't give. You certainly don't give a toss about me. You don't care about Paddy. You probably don't give a damn about your own children either, as long as they don't show you up. You've known since this morning and you let me wait? As long as you manage to get Rosie Hooke slung out of the Jack Cade, you'd do anything.'

In order to see him, Vicky's head was twisted round at an awkward angle. She gasped and grabbed at her skirt, and sat up, protesting.

'Ollie!'

'Go on. Go back to poor moneybags Paddy. I just needed to find out if you'd go the whole hog in order to keep me in line and get what you want.'

'Bastard!' She was kneeling up, struggling with the buttons of her blouse, which were more reluctant to be done up than they had previously been to be undone. She snatched up bag and sandals and ran for the door, turning, as if to give him a second chance or perhaps to loose a final shot, but he had turned his back again, a wide-shouldered back, tense with fury.

With a mewing wail, Vicky ran out of the door and thundered downstairs. She paused by the Japanese vase, an Antiques Roadshow horror probably worth a thousand pounds, and malevolently thwacked it so hard with the high heel of one sandal that it cracked from rim to base. She waited a second to see if it would fall apart but it didn't and she continued down, stopping in the sunny white hall and hopping a little on the black and white tiled floor as she fumbled hot feet back into the sandals; one of the four large white doors that opened into the hall moved half an inch, then wider, and a gaunt old lady stood there, walking stick in hand, flat, navy-clad chest festooned with gold chains, flat lap covered in cat-hairs, narrow pink split of a mouth querulous and sunken eyes disapproving. Vicky stuck out her tongue and crashed the front door behind her.

In the street, breathing in the rush-hour traffic haze of Tunbridge Wells, she castigated herself for cowardice. God, how humiliating! You idiot! You've mucked it up, and badly. You should have stayed to fight your corner. But it's impossible, fighting when one's starkers. You'd have talked him round if you hadn't been so confused. I mean, there you were, prepared to sacrifice all, to give him what he's always wanted, the best time he's probably ever had in his life, and he ... Idiot! Idiot! It'll take you days to wheedle him round now, to get back to where you were. She was still certain that she would be able to do so, never having seen Ollie in a real temper before.

But where were we? I misjudged his feelings about the Mel Plunket thingy, didn't realize quite how nervous he was about being implicated. That's all it is, of course. I suppose I should have told him on Sunday afternoon, when I knew it was all a fuss over nothing, not waited till today. But there wasn't time on Sunday, was there? We had the Carringtons for lunch and they didn't leave till nearly six and it's so damn' hard to get any time to oneself, let alone to make a phone call, particularly a private one, with Paddy being so *there* . . . And Ollie wasn't in all day yesterday, so he can't have been worrying that much, surely? I'll bloody well have to manage it without him, if the stupid bugger's going to be so prissy. But if he doesn't come round at all, if I've really lost him this time . . . Oh, hell's teeth and arsenic!

She viciously flicked a black flying insect from the front of the creased white blouse and, firmly suturing her emotions, set off unsteadily round the corner to her car. She would indeed do anything so long as she got Rosie Hooke out of the Jack Cade.

After she'd left, Ollie continued to lean out of the window. He contemplated the grey sock, still lying bereft on top of the glistening holly of the hedge. He thought hard about the sock and the ache subsided, desire wilted. The sock had been joined by an orange Frisbee; there had been a sharp shower of rain in the night and it was now being used as a bath by a sparrow, the bird's fluttering and dipping sending out rainbows of tiny sparkling drops. He studied the yellow plastic tricycle on its side in the flowerbed beneath. The act of studying, taking in each detail, assuaged the self-imposed physical frustration.

It was weird that although the tricycle appeared to be moved about the garden, left in a different place each day, he had never actually seen or heard a child riding on it, and unlike the other occupants with whom he was on friendly terms, he'd never even met the people in the ground-floor flat.

Vicky had gone, but there was neither sorrow nor pleasure. He was cured. Cut loose. How did it feel to be free? It surely ought to feel better than this dull sense of decreasing alarm, as of hearing the fire brigade in the distance, safe in the knowledge that it wasn't one's own house on fire. The most continuous human factor in his adult life, apart from his loving yet impartial parent, had ceased to exist and he felt nothing. It was so obvious now that he had been marooned alone on an island by his unfortunate obsession. Were all obsessions unfortunate? He supposed they tended to obscure and exclude other people, other opportunities that might be worthier or more satisfying.

A middle-aged woman came through the open french windows beneath and padded over to the yellow tricycle. She picked it up and moved it from the flowerbed to beneath a laurel bush, taking some care in its placing. She arranged it as if it were a tub of lilies, standing back and considering the effect of its new position. Her hair was neatly cut and dyed blonde, the dark parting showing. She wore black trousers and a white sleeveless blouse, just like the one Vicky had worn for such a short time that afternoon, but her arms were shorter and plumper and he could see even from so far above that they had been sunburnt deep pink, little flashes of white flesh showing around the armholes as she moved the bike again, trying another place. If he'd been until recently quite barking mad, he had not been alone and that was a most comforting thought. He wanted to wave and call out to her, but stopped himself. It would not be nice for her to find that she'd been spied on. He withdrew from the window and very quietly eased the sash down, only to throw it up noisily and lean out again.

'Hello!' he called. 'Isn't it a beautiful afternoon?'

The woman jumped regardless of his precautions and stared up at the shock-headed, bare-chested man waving from the window three floors above. She waved back.

'Yes, I suppose it is. Or it would be if it wasn't for the pigeons.' She grinned up at him and then turned back to the rearrangement of the tricycle.

Ollie could see no signs of pigeons, but was heartened by having made contact with a stranger, however insane.

Breathing calmly, he took a long shower, cut his primaeval-looking toenails, ironed a shirt, picked up and replaced the cushions and rescued the Coleridge from the floor. He lay down again, shutting his nostrils to the faint lemony scent of

Vicky that hung about the upholstery. It reminded him, now mixed in so thoroughly with the familiar, condoling scent of the sofa, of washing-up liquid. He returned to the book.

He was unable to concentrate. He put it down again, and stretched elastically. It was astounding to find that his own '... *Volcano beneath a sea always burning, tho' in silence*', unlike poor Coleridge's passion, had extinguished itself at last. Had Coleridge known that there were actually volcanoes beneath the sea, or had it been an inspired guess? He began to construe his own past state of mind regarding Vicky as a means whereby he had held at bay any serious emotional demands from other people, a useful tool in preventing himself from reliance on or love of anyone else. It was possible now to consider giving up this midget's flat and finding somewhere else to live, as far as possible from Tunbridge Wells. There were possibilities of movement, physical and mental, in any direction. He was clean, de-infested and freshly released from a tight but trivial bondage. An *imagined* bondage. Time to toss away the black leather straps and spiked buckles corseting the brain.

What time was it? Jos Sliverley was back from Abu Dhabi and would perhaps like to meet up for a drink later. Jos was a good man, interesting, possibly influential, but Megan rarely let him out of the bedroom when he was in England. There should be a letter any day now from *Ange et Caramel*. Yea or nay? The job had sounded attractive, within his capabilities, with plenty of to-ing and fro-ing across the Channel, but there had been a great many applicants. He must, *must*, get back to work of some sort; his temporary idleness had been a contributory factor to becoming embroiled in Vicky's schemes.

He remembered at last that in the pocket of his jacket was the receipt given him on Monday by Sotheby's for Rosie's small bronze foundling. So concerned had he been to keep up appearances while lunching with his mother that he'd almost forgotten his mission and then, returning on the train, still so caught up with his own guilt, its outcome had evaporated from

his memory. It was six-thirty. Sod trying to extricate Jos; it was
time to go and break the good news to the delightfully friendly
Rosie. At least it would be some sort of recompense for whatever
damage had been caused by his slimy deception. The main harm
had mercifully been only to himself.

Ollie drove down the lane to the Jack Cade with the low red
sun flashing blindingly at him through the gaps in the leafy
hedges, accompanied by a favourite tape of the heart-breaking,
bronchially grating whine of Tom Waits's *Rain Dogs*. He adjusted
his own voice: '... blind love, bl-i-nd love ...' he croaked
happily, slowing down to look curiously at the untidy hillock
of flowers by the gate, only guessing their import as he drew
up outside the inn and switched off the engine. Brought sharply
back to earth, he wondered how he might warn Rosie of Vicky's
intentions without mentioning his own involvement?

Both upstairs and downstairs windows all stood wide open
to let in the summer and people were drinking in the garden.
There was a delirious scent of freshly mown grass. He grabbed
a faded blue linen jacket from the seat, tried to smooth back
his rampant hair and almost broke into a run to get inside, so
eager was he to see Rosie and tell her the news.

An immense blue and white Staffordshire jug was placed in
the empty fireplace, stuffed with a maenad's arrangement of wild
pear and cherry blossom, buttercups, cow parsley and overblown
pink tulips, a confetti of fallen petals littering the hearthstone.
Some sort of committee meeting, or perhaps a post-mortem, was
taking place in the right-hand side of the bar. Rosie sat at a table
with her back to the door and hadn't see him come in. Also at
the table was the girl who had served him so sweetly on his first
visit with Vicky, a tall, fair young man in spectacles, and three
more people whom he hadn't seen before, all either engrossed
with lists or talking at cross purposes.

Ollie was greeted as an old mate by Tiger Bright who,

hoisting his tattered combat trousers over his porky loins, followed him in and slapped him on the shoulder, standing beside him at the bar. Janice gave him a winsomely toothy smile and whilst waiting for Rosie to finish her confabulations, he stood listening inattentively to Tiger and Ossie's mundane chat. He tried to eavesdrop on the proceedings at the nearby table whilst avoiding being trapped in conversation by a conspiracy theorist from London recently arrived on a quest for the grave of a Russian Grand Duchess.

'*They* don't want us to know, you see, *they* want us to believe they all died at Ekaterinberg. Now this book I've just read says that it's certain she's buried in a cemetery somewhere near here ...' His irrational eyes burned with paranoia.

'... the throttle cable snapped, and there I was, stuck, because Tabby's Suzuki was back at the farm ...'

'... And who is going to take on finding a sponsor for the water-sports? Chloe? Richard? Oh, thanks, Richard. That's one more thing sorted. Now let's see. Tea tent – Mrs Rigsby, Hermione and Minerva. Jenny Taggle dropped out when it dawned on her it was a rather bigger event than she'd imagined. I think she had some idea that a few carrot cakes and a Victoria sponge would do the trick, but she's going to supervise and sponsor the bowling for the half-pig, which is very generous of her. She says her pigs aren't fetching much at the moment. We're agreed, are we, that all tea-tent profits go to the children's charity? Beer tent – that's your pigeon, Aylwin, plus helpers. Food tent, apart from the concessionary stands – the Indian restaurant at Fingle has agreed to do something there. Now, Rollo, your list.'

'Right. Lavatories, stalls and music. Portaloos ordered, tick. Stalls: Nest will be doing a plant stall, manned by Lucinda, tick. There's room along the central avenue for two more ... Geoff Pocket's band will be playing in the beer tent for an hour on both days at lunchtime, tick, and I've collared a student string quartet for the tea tent on Monday ...'

'So we had to wheel out Puss's old Honda . . . Yeah, crotch-deep in manky mud. The old stress levels were beginning to edge up a bit. I was just getting going when the pigs turned up . . .'

At last Rosie was standing, neat figure bent over the table, shuffling papers together. She must have become aware of his presence then since she swung around, grinned and stuffing the papers into a yellow file, came towards him, clutching the file to her chest. He was struck by the fact that her small face was never quite familiar, there were slight variations each time he saw it, different accents on the evenly pale-gold surface of her skin according to the light, or her mood. Not an easy face to learn or to remember accurately.

'We need to talk privately. The little statue?'

'Oh, yes!' The pupils of her eyes widened a fraction. 'Just let me stick these papers away behind the bar and get a ginger beer. I'm quite dry with talking.'

'I'll buy you the ginger beer then, if I may?'

'Of course you can! Thanks. We'll go to the back room, since nobody's taken it over yet. Is it good news?'

There was anticipation, hope in her face; it was most agreeable, being the bearer of good news. He tried to remain poker-faced and followed as she crossed the room. Gently pushing aside the threadbare curtain to the dark, panelled back room and leaving it open, either for the sake of light or possibly to forestall curiosity, she sat down, so excited that the ancient chair picked up the tension of her body and squeaked in protest.

'Now, first of all here is the Sotheby's receipt in your name.' Ollie produced it with a magician's flourish.

She held out her hand for the paper and gazed at it, then looked up, nervously. 'I'm not sure what this means. There's no price here or anything? "Gilt-bronze figure of a saint. Fourteenth-century cross-finial"? *Fourteenth* century? So very old? Is it really worth something?'

'Well, what they told me was that they'd have to do some

further research on it themselves. They'll get in touch with you very soon, to discuss the reserve price, if you still want to go ahead and sell it? Luckily there's a sale of mediaeval items, particularly metalwork and enamels, coming up at the beginning of next month and they want to put it into that. The person I spoke to was very intrigued when he learnt it had been found in a vegetable patch on Romney Marsh, particularly in association with an ancient chapel. It's not precious metal, so there's no problem with treasure trove or anything.' He couldn't tease her any longer since he could see she was becoming stiff with anxiety.

'And?' She had guessed he was drawing it out, leaving the best bit till last.

'Well, the chap was a little cagy, but estimated £3,000. It's not the sort of thing that turns up every day. He thinks it's the figure of a saint; he showed me something similar in an old catalogue.'

'Ooooh!' Her hands flew up to her mouth. She sat so still that Ollie noticed a paleness and a narrowing of the third finger on the left hand, where a wedding ring had once sat. Did widows remove their rings and if so, why? In order to forget an unhappy marriage? To signal availability? Too tight, too loose? Lost, even? 'Lost' was an odd way to express a bereavement when one thought about it ... 'I lost my wife.' It sounded as if the person was temporarily missing, absent for a day rather than dead, as in 'lost my wallet' and they might turn up at any time beneath a cushion. It might, he supposed, have originated from expectations of resurrection, of being reunited in heaven?

Rosie hadn't been a widow for very long, but she'd not appeared particularly distressed on the few occasions they'd met. She had always worn red, as she did now. Was that out of bravado, or a favourite colour? It suited her colouring, gave her authority, made her the focal point of the Jack Cade, like a circus ringmaster. But she wasn't flashy; in fact she wore no jewellery at all. That was a good red she had on now, not guardsman's warning scarlet, more . . . he searched for a suitable description and romantically settled on weathered rose-hip. She was compelling certainly, without being anything other than she was, artlessly, uniquely Rosie, which was itself the core of the attraction. He was not sure how his next move came about but it came slowly, fighting its way through an ambush of caution.

'Rosie, do you ever get away from here? Out, I mean, for a drink or dinner, somewhere else?' She paused so long before answering that he thought perhaps she hadn't heard him above the hum of talk and clinking glasses in the main room, and was grateful.

'No, you're right, I rarely get away from here.' A veil had slipped over the jubilant brightness.

'Would you care to come out with me? On one of your less busy nights, perhaps?' He had not consciously intended this at all.

They were both distracted by the crystalline tinkle of a breaking wine glass. As Rosie turned aside to watch Janice rush out with pan and brush to sweep up the pieces, Ollie could see her using the interruption as a thinking space.

'Yes,' she said, tentatively and very softly, turning back to him. 'Why not? Wednesdays are quiet.'

'Tomorrow? If I called for you at seven? We could have supper in Rye.'

'Oh, yes! I'd really love that.' Then she looked slightly alarmed by her acceptance. 'I must get back to work, Oliver. There's a programme on digging up Anglo-Saxon cemeteries which Janice wants to watch, and she needs a break. Thank you so very much. You've no idea what a help it would be if the statue brought in so much money! But we can talk more about it tomorrow, can't we?'

But they barely touched on the subject of the statue on Wednesday evening. Post-acceptance, the night before, Rosie was uneasy at the sheer unlikelihood of going out with Oliver Potter.

'Perhaps I only know how to do pub-speak!' she wailed to Aylwin, who shook his head in disbelief. 'What happens if he wants to talk politics or discuss some book I've never read, or the state of the nation? Well, I can tell him a thing or two about the rural poor, that's for certain, but that doesn't sound the sort of thing one talks about at dinner. I haven't been taken out anywhere for years. My hair! Perhaps Elvira could help me with my hair?'

On Wednesday morning Ollie received the offer of the job in Parden and immediately accepted. He arrived at the Jack Cade that evening with every intention, should the right moment present itself, of confessing his misdeeds.

Having assumed high spirits as a means of covering an attack of dry-mouthed fear, Rosie, wearing green, her haywire hair smoothly blow-dried by Elvira, flew out of the wide front door like a child from school.

'I never thought to hear myself say it, but I'm very glad to be getting away,' she said, leaping into the old Saab, settling in with such flattering appreciation that he had not the courage to risk changing her mood. She was different yet again, vibrating with a metallic energy which he recognized, surprised, as nervous.

'This evening in particular, or just generally?'

'This evening in particular. You've no idea how rare it's been lately to be with *just* one person. I always feel my attention is being stretched in twenty different directions. Which way are we going? Drive me off quickly before I remember there's something I haven't done and run back inside.'

With a chuckle, Ollie drove off with a little spurt of gravel.

'The table's booked for eight-thirty. We could go and have a drink at the Wipers first?'

'So you do know Rye?'

'Yes. A friend of mine had a boat there some years

ago. I used to do a bit of sailing with him from time to time.'

'There's a Norwegian – Canute, of course, only I think it's spelt K-n-u-t – a tall old boy who comes in to the Jack Cade quite often. You might have seen him? He has a boat there, moored right up in the town. He's staying for the summer. He's promised me a trip later in the year, because I've never been sailing.'

What was her relationship with this Canute? Ollie, caught himself feeling proprietorial; he would have liked to be able to offer Rosie a day's sailing.

They sat on a bench in the pub's garden just beneath the Ypres Tower, watching the masts of chugging fishing boats, and the occasional white sail, dodging behind the buildings and trees as they passed up the narrow river channel on the high tide. Rosie began to relax and Ollie's irritated conscience settled down enough for there to be few real tensions or constraints on conversation. There was no raking through of unhappy childhoods, remarkably few what-will-they-think-of-mes or I-shouldn't-have-said-thats. Their respective pasts were merely sketched in for the time being since they were set in the present moment of each other's inclinations.

The air was damp with dew as they sauntered through the narrow streets to the restaurant. Rosie was pleased by the neutrality of its white surroundings and thankful for the lack of copper kettles and heritage beams. Her inhibitions were on the run and she openly studied Ollie as he ordered the wine: casual, urbane and yet slightly untidy, his hair never quite sitting in the appointed places. There was a very small patch to the right of the long chin he'd missed when shaving which, for whatever reason, she found touching, and although she felt it was lowering to notice missing buttons, one was missing from his open-collared white shirt.

Ollie was convinced afterwards that it was Rosie who had witched away any guilty hesitancy he might have had. Rosie feared having her head turned and didn't at first imagine that his attentiveness was more than habitual good manners, but enjoyed it nonetheless. Surrounded by the muffled clickings of cutlery and plates and soft murmurings and rustlings of the provincial British tentatively enjoying sophisticated food, they did not notice the curious and even envious glances darted at them in the half-full restaurant.

Gently exploratory with the first course, they became liberally hilarious with the second, confidential over the pudding and positively conspiratorial with the coffee. Ollie rather hurriedly explained, to avoid enquiries, that he had been forced to abandon the history of Jack Cade because he was about to embark on a new job and the research was taking up too much time. It was at that minute that he also decided that he would, in actuality, write about Jack Cade. Never mind if it had been done before. He would do it better. He imagined a round ceramic plaque like those they'd noticed on houses on the way to the restaurant, commemorating famous artists and writers: *Oliver Ragstaff Potter, Novelist, lived here,* and the dates. He saw it in his mind's eye, disturbingly set above the front door of the Jack Cade.

It was a shame, Rosie said, that he'd had to postpone the book. It had sounded an interesting project.

'... tragic, though, since Jack was murdered? Aylwin, who's always lived with me, apart from his time at college, is set on becoming a writer, but he has a full-time job and a woman in his life and although he's been writing short stories, he doesn't get the time he needs. He helps me out a lot and Elvira can't cope with him coming home from work and shutting himself away for hours. He's too besotted with her to leave her alone for long anyway. They're very sweet together. I hardly ever detect the bubbling sounds of boiling emotions.'

'I don't suppose,' Ollie said, 'that you get much time to yourself, either. What do you do, when you have time off?'

'I used to get on a train and go to a town I hadn't seen before, explore it and see if it had a nice museum. I love looking at the bizarre things people found useful in the past. Sometimes I used to just shut the door behind me and walk – walk anywhere.' Having any time to herself at all was a recent innovation, and looked like being a short-lived one.

'I found a lovely little museum the other day, in Whitstable. The best thing in it was ...'

'... the brass diving helmet?' Rosie interrupted him, having once visited the place and guessing, intuitively knowing, what would have taken his fancy. He was astonished and a little alarmed.

'However did you guess? Yes, the massive, shining brassy helmet. In spite of its practical purpose, it had the air of a reliquary, with its dim glass window. I felt it might not be empty, that there might be a giant's head inside staring out at me staring in. What thing did you find there that you liked?'

'The Roman dishes, the ones that were recovered in the nineteenth century. Red samian pottery, washed or trawled up in such quantities that every fisherman's wife in Whitstable had one. It was the fact that they called them pudding pans and actually used them for making rice puddings in that seemed so delightful.' Her first course had arrived and it was so pretty that she took her time examining it before tasting. 'I'd love to be able to cook crab soufflé in a Roman dish.'

'What else do you like to do? I don't suppose you get time to do much reading, for instance?' He was probing a little clumsily and blushed very slightly, not wishing her to think he was assuming she was uneducated.

'You'd be surprised! A friend once said that coming to the Jack Cade was her escape, her sanity. Well, reading's mine.' She didn't want him to be embarrassed by his assumption that she was uneducated. 'I'd have been the first person in my family to go to university, to read English if ... if certain things hadn't happened.

'Anyway, it must be difficult,' she continued hurriedly, forking up the soufflé with enjoyment, and rapidly finishing it, 'deciding what area to write about. I love a good old-fashioned moral dilemma, but now that there don't seem to be so many ... I mean, I know that's only one possible area to cover, but it used to be quite a big one, didn't it? I think the Victorians actually enjoyed being thwarted by codes of behaviour – would it be rude of me to ask if I can taste your squid? I've never tried squid – I mean, there are excuses for everything now; someone or something else is always accountable for one's behaviour. It must be hard to decide what line to take. Ah! Mmm. That's not at all what I thought it would taste like! I thought it would be fishy.'

'Do you think people who've been repressed by rigid moral standards develop more interesting psyches than the children of the let-it-all-hang-outs? That repression breeds the ingenuity needed to find ways round the forbidden?' He was watching her with the greatest pleasure.

'If a person can't see there's anything wrong with a particular action, then there's not much more to be said about it, is there? One can only sweep up the pieces and hope that eventually one of the other characters in the book will be strong enough to prove them wrong. Baddies are always going to be more interesting to read about than the pure, aren't they? And there's no reason why the repressed shouldn't be just as wicked, if not more so, than those who don't appear to heed any rules.'

Ollie wondered if that was what had attracted him to Vicky? The up-front, no-humbug ruthlessness? He wanted to get off the subject of morality. It might present an opportunity to broach the subject of his own lack of it and he wasn't quite ready for that yet.

'I suppose that practically the last dramatic things people have left to pit themselves against are the elements, but it's deeply uninteresting to read about people struggling against a force that isn't even trying to outwit them, just going about its normal business and totally unaware? I mean, one can say "Good God! How awesome!" but there it ends.'

'I know what you mean. Suffering because you've actually put yourself in a dangerous position on purpose doesn't exactly tug at the heart strings. It's an unnecessary bravery.' Like me and the Jack Cade, Rosie thought sadly. But she was there to forget about the inn and mustn't start talking about it. They were still excavating their own viewpoints and preparing them for each other's examination.

'But *moral* dilemmas again,' she continued, waving her fork for emphasis, 'if there aren't any restrictions to rub up against and no one is shocked by anything, it must be impossible to be truly sensational, even if you wanted to. Like on the cover of a new book: "So-and-so's Sensational New Novel! A Real Lid-lifter on the World of Waste Disposal Operatives!" It's always just more extreme violence, more corruption, more boringly explicit sex. I've never really wanted to be shocked in the first place, and where do we go from here? Soon, nobody will watch the news unless the newscasters are in the nuddy and we'll all start getting nostalgic about classic snuff movies.'

Ollie laughed and Rosie smiled indulgently at the waiter who had given her a curious glance as he delicately delivered a plate of lamb sweetbreads and appeared to be hovering.

'Perhaps it's cyclical,' Ollie suggested, 'and the voyeurs will push so far they swallow their own tails and strict puritanism will seem as exciting to the decadent as bondage or cannibalism. Were you brought up to repress things? Were you repressed?'

'I have to say I was repressed now, in order to keep you interested. Oh, Ollie! I love these! And look at the little tiddly carrots! Do you think we really are more immoral, compared to our parents, or were they just more secretive about what they did?'

'I think they were just more secretive.'

That point, of course, was the perfect opportunity for Ollie to come clean, to explain about Vicky, but he was still unable to force himself to take it; schoolboy's criminal instincts were warring with adult honourable intentions and, since he was driving, he was short on alcoholic courage.

Rosie wondered if she had been repressed, remembering her mother's strictured lectures on what nice girls did or did not do, without ever explaining 'what'. What Sally had seen as repression, Rosie had barely noticed, being deaf to all warnings and forbiddings, incommunicado in a diver's helmet.

'My mother used to be embarrassed by actors kissing on Coronation Street,' she divulged. 'She wouldn't have known where to put herself if confronted with all the groping and bouncing on screen now.'

'We seem to be busy inventing new repressions of our own, had you noticed?' asked Ollie. 'Media repression. Food police repressing junk food scoffers, whether fat or not – I really fear being forced to eat muesli every day and having fashion police measuring the width of my trousers. Consumerist police forcing down bedtime doses of statistics. Repression by Political Correctness – I know that's laudable in intent, but isn't there something patronising about it, almost insulting to the very people it's supposed to protect?'

'*"You can't possibly take care of yourselves, so we will make laws to protect you."* Is that what you mean? Yes, that is a bit patronising when all that's being asked for is respect, because if you've got that, then the rest should follow, a balancing of rights and responsibilities. I'm worried, too, about the idea of its being enforced by law, of making things worse, but then I'm lucky. I can't imagine what it must feel like to be shouted at or beaten up because I look different.'

'I can't see that it's possible actually to enforce respect, though, however much it's needed, since it's an abstract thing. Sadly, some of us are always going to abuse whatever power we've got ... and anyway, for those who've been denied it for so long, it's understandable they should want to take their turn at axe-wielding, but it would be easier to manage if people wouldn't claim racial or sexual discrimination when all that's at issue is a case of personal antipathy. I suppose it's hard to tell the difference if you're out looking for offence. I'm trying not to be a smug white male brushing something unpleasant under the carpet, but it's getting close to having the thought police. What are you thinking about at this moment? Can I refill your glass?'

She was thinking what a neat, inquisitive, nose he had. 'I don't suppose that the legal sulking which some women go in for does much good. Of course it's necessary to make real toads sit up and think twice, but on the whole it just seems to make quite nice men more resentful.'

Ollie's grey eyes were sparkling at her most unresentfully. It was as simple as talking to Aylwin. There was also the minute but definite tug of a physical rapport as well, she sensed; a hopefully mutual, gradual awareness of the fact that sex might be a future ingredient. This intrigued her considerably, since it was a sensation she had not felt for a long while, but she hoped the fact that she had no immediate plan to add it to the recipe at this stage was also mutual.

'It's the desperate lack of humour,' she went on. 'I had a good howl the other day, reading about a woman who'd accused a colleague of harassment because he'd had the nerve to ask her out to the cinema *twice*. She admitted he hadn't leered at her or anything and that previously they'd been quite friendly. He'd just asked her out, she'd said no, she was busy, so he'd tried again a couple of weeks later, hoping she was less busy. She'd complained because she thought it was harassment and he'd been sacked. It's called the victim culture, I heard it on the radio. Time to stop laughing.'

'You're no one's victim, certainly. And I'm very relieved I only had to ask you to dinner once. I shall try not to leer, though women can leer too, you know. Would you tell me if you saw me leering? I'd like to know in case I find myself doing it unconsciously.'

'I don't think you can leer *except* unconsciously. It's not the kind of expression you can put on, on purpose, is it, like sympathy or surprise?' She choked, laughing, since all three expressions immediately flitted across his face. 'I'm so glad you did ask me out. I allowed myself to be a victim once, but it was depressing. Like drinking old cold tea all day.'

'I can't imagine you've ever come across much discrimination, of the racial sort, on Romney Marsh?'

'No, I haven't. Oh, I'm wrong. There's the gypsies, of course. There's definitely a "them and us" situation when we meet.' Rosie then recounted, without rancour, how she'd bandaged a child's grazed knee and found later that whilst she was busy with Elastoplast and Savlon in the kitchen, the child's parents had liberated a bottle of Gordon's gin from the bar and broken into Ben's van, making off with the new lavatory for the bathroom.

There was no indignation in her voice, just an acceptance of the way things were. She sat still, with her hands in her lap, looking back at him with brown velvet eyes, which he at last realized held the key to the chameleon quality of her face. It lay not in those still features but almost entirely in the alertness of the eyes. They, by themselves, hinted, offered, smiled, pondered, appreciated, mocked, suggested or slammed an inner door in distress.

'They're different,' Rosie admitted, 'in that they don't *want* to belong to our society at all, and there are times when I don't blame them. No one would mind, though, if they were self-sufficient.'

'Perhaps just taking what you need is self-sufficiency so far as they're concerned?' suggested Ollie. 'I was really thinking more of racial tension on grounds of colour.'

'I hardly ever saw a black face until I first went up to London, when I was about eleven and we went to Madame Tussaud's, so I can't speak about its absence or presence with any authority. I expect we feel less threatened by cultural engulfment than people in cities; perhaps some racial harassment may be caused more by fear of that than by lack of respect? Here, you have to get on with the people around for practical reasons, even Tiger Bright and his rantipoles . . .'

'Ranti-whats? What does it mean?'

'It means wild and reckless persons. I found it in the dictionary accidentally, when I was looking up something entirely different. Anyway, as I was saying, here you have at least to be intolerant quietly, like that evening when you came in and it was so quiet? Do you remember? You can't just be rude and disappear off into the crowd. You are the crowd and have to make do with what you've got in the way of company. It must be like that, on board a ship? I'm sure rows break out, but they must be contained for everyone else's sake. What about you? Have you ever been a victim?'

'Yes. In fact I've only just stopped being one. It was quite easy, after all. But I've been a bully too.' He was intentionally lowering his guard, preparing for the announcement of his guilt. He prayed for a second, but all that he blurted out was, 'What would you like for pudding?'

Another chance missed out of the several he had now been offered – but things were going so well. She might storm out. He couldn't bear that.

'I'd like the ginger sorbet, please.'


Rosie paused outside in the dark and looked in at the kitchen window, like the ghost child, before coming in. She saw Aylwin's gold head bent over the table, reading in a circle of soft yellow light amongst a scatter of mugs, papers and half a packet of biscuits, and felt a surge of affection and gratitude for him. He checked his watch and turned a page. He looked up, startled, as a glowing Rosie waltzed in through the back door, tripping on the doormat and hugging herself with pleasure.

'Were you waiting up for me? Where are Elvira and Janice?'

'Elvi's just gone up to have a bath and Janice is watching the telly in the parlour. She spends a lot of time in there, hoping to see the child. No, I wasn't waiting up. I thought you might be later than this. I wasn't actually sure you'd be back at all. Isn't your posh Mr Potter coming in?'

In spite of his protestations, Aylwin's voice was growly with relief. It had been odd for them that evening, lacklustre and rudderless without Rosie.

'Cheeky devil! Not *my* Oliver Potter at all, but it might be nice if he was. He had a long drive home ahead of him and I didn't want to flummox him with all you lot! I've had a wonderful time. I ate crab soufflé and sweetbreads. I drank lots of wine, and completely forgot, for once, about you poor things all sweating away here! I forgot about cleaning lavatories. I even forgot about money.'

She twirled about the table, aware that she was unfairly embarrassing the disgruntled Aylwin and teasingly enjoying the fact; then she calmed down a bit and put her hands on his shoulders and leant her head on his curly chamomile-scented locks.

'You've been at my shampoo again! It's all right for you, my darling. You and Elvi get out together quite often, off for a drink now and then, don't you? Don't worry. My head hasn't been turned – well, only two-thirds to the left, I promise. If you hear of anyone wanting to rent out a place, a cottage or something between here and Parden, let me know. He's got a job there and wants to get out of Tunbridge Wells.'

'Poor posh Mr Potter. Out of the frying pan. Does he know what Parden's like?'

'He's only working there, like you, and he's just plain Oliver Potter. You can't be posh with a name like Potter. It's a stupid definition anyway. He's ex-Merchant Navy, ex-publishing, ex-whatever ... You'd like him – he's interested in books and writing. He's been round the world thrice, been made redundant twice ... He's called Ollie.'

'Whatever for?'

'Don't be chippy. Do you want more tea, my love? I'm going to make some. And do you know anyone with a metal detector?'

'Yes, as a matter of fact, I do. What for?'

'Oh, the questions you ask! What for? To go over the vegetable patch to see if there's anything else there, of course! Another statue, a bishop's gold and amethyst ring, more Battle of Britain bullets.'

'Mum! You've just poured the milk into the teapot! Can't you wait till the onions are harvested? You've planted it all. You'd have to dig up your seedlings too.

'Oh, damn! So I would. But we could try the area that I've left for the leeks. Do you realize that with the party money and what we might get for the statue, and the fact that this month and next we'll be able to pay off an extra five hundred pounds out of profits, we'll be down to owing fourteen thousand? If we can get it below ten and still keep up all the payments, I could try again to borrow the rest and the austerity regime will ease up. By the way, how did it go this evening? Any problems?'

'Nothing to speak of. Brian overdid the beer a bit and left on his bike just before ten-thirty, but he fell off it somewhere between here and Middhaze Church and when he got on again he couldn't remember which way he should be going and turned up here again at closing time. He was riding very slowly with a torch held between his teeth. I drove him home in your van.' He looked up at her regretfully. 'I'm sorry I was surly, Mum. I really am glad you've met someone intelligent. I've set up the new barrel of Ned Rother's bitter and the front of house is all locked up.'

There had been some difficulties that evening with a group of baying and hooraying Henrys on a stag night pub-crawl, with which saga Aylwin didn't wish to worry her, not tonight anyway. The problem had been dealt with by a suddenly fierce Janice who had refused to serve them any more and eventually thrown them out. Elvira had recounted the scene with awe. Janice, in a voice raucous with suppressed fright, had told them to bugger off because they were upsetting the other customers, several of whom had indeed already left. They'd departed, squaring their shoulders, shouting and staggering into the night. They had been scary, unlike the usual stag-nighters with their drunkenly misplaced bonhomie that most people could laugh off; more insolent, aggressive, intentionally disruptive.

'Bless you. I'll go on up then.' Rosie turned the key in the door and shot the bolts, then locked the door into the bar. 'Goodnight, and thank you for looking after things. It was brilliant to have an evening off.'

'We should have made sure you had one before. We didn't think. And Janice too.'

'Oh, Lord! Do you think I'm exploiting her?'

'No, of course not, Mum. She gets paid for her sessions, doesn't she, and Elvira too?'

'Yes, of course. I meant that they might feel obliged to do them.'

What was it Ollie had said about people in a position of power? Rosie had never previously thought of herself as having any, but now, of course, things were different . . . had she allowed herself to become a tyrant?

'Janice knows she can come or go whenever she wants, Aylwin, but I can't persuade her to take time off. She can't drive and won't ride the bike, and although I've promised to take her to the station whenever she wants, and collect her too, she won't go. Perhaps you might persuade her? What's that you're reading?'

'*The Lost Gods of England.*'

'How many have gone missing? Good night, my love.'

# Chapter Ten

'My hair's all tangly. Can't you brush it out for me?' No, she could not. Sally's head was repellently untouchable, swathed in bright green bandages, and her voice was deep and froggy, full of dredging effort. It was another woman impersonating Sally, lying in the shadowy, white-sheeted bed.

'Mike's not the father. He knows ... knew that when we married. There's ...' Sally stopped, opened brown stray-dog eyes and gave a smile, wicked, her normal self. 'And what were you up to this evening? I saw you, sneaking into the car and driving off. Having fun, Rosie-posie? I wonder ...' There was a terrible, painful cough and Rosie felt with certainty that there was no more to come, felt helpless, unsupported, stricken.

The dream was fading and Rosie, already rapidly rising in a smoky spiral from the recurring nightmare, with lungs bursting, began to section off this dwindling scene from reality, sat up in an icy sweat in the dark and turned on the bedside light. At the back of the house, Trash was barking, but stopped as soon as she was conscious of it, so it was probably just a fox. The conversation in that particular dream always ran along the same road and Sally rarely completed a sentence, never said anything Rosie didn't already know. But why expect the dead to prophesy? She'd not been there when Sally died, but in Mike and Sally's cottage, looking after the baby. She'd dreamed this dream so often that it was too familiar to cause malaise for long. Sleepless, she got up, slipped on a sweater and creaked across the roller-coaster of uneven oak floorboards to hang out of a window into the early morning chilliness, shaking off the remnants of horror.

It looked as if there might have been a wayward snap of frost, a bitter chill, as in *The Eve of Saint Agnes*. A barn owl drifted across the field on the other side of the lane and completed the illusion of winter − for all she knew a hare '. . . *limped trembling through the frozen grass and silent was the flock in woolly fold* . . .' What else could she remember from that highly coloured poem of Keats's? '*Her eyes were open, but she still beheld, Now wide awake, the vision of her sleep.*' But Rosie's dream had not been of a lover, of Porphyro, it had been of the dreadful Sally, and she was forty-one-year-old Rosie, not the virginal Madeline. It wasn't the Eve of Saint Agnes either; it was May, not January.

The owl flitted back across the hedge and abruptly predatory instincts of her own emerged; yesterday evening unrolled like a strip of negatives which she could hold to the light, seeing each separate little picture and inspecting Ollie from every angle. She was suddenly shaken to pieces by desire for him. The clear sky paled, stars fading as she watched. It must be nearly five o'clock. It was very still, but the dawn chorus was getting up steam. She slipped back to the warmth of bed, to attempt to relive the night before and try some divination of the future.

It had been simple, really, to get used to the lack of sex after she'd shut Ben out of her room. There'd been no one who'd stirred her up and she wasn't the kind of person who made do with whoever was around just for the sake of it, needing the mental and emotional component in order for the physical to function. She would prefer none at all than half-cock humping. She giggled. The Jack Cade had been her lover.

The sun rose, she was awake and restless so dressed and came downstairs at six o'clock and before feeding the poultry, tidied the long room, wiping the tables, polishing the Jack-in-the-Green over the fireplace till the dark wood blossomed. The Jack's worn nose already shone since people felt compelled to run their fingers down it in passing, but now Rosie rubbed up the entire grain-ribbed brown face, gently forcing the duster between the deep carving of the rigid leaves and honing the fat brushy tails and sharp snouts of the attendant little foxes.

She swung open the front door to draw out the stale smokiness of last night. The sun poured through and a million motes danced in the morning air. A dead cockerel, Baldur the Beautiful, lay on the doorstep.

Appalled, with tears welling up in her eyes, she stood there for a minute with the soft weight of him in her hands, helplessly smoothing the dry, dead feathers and looking desperately round for an answer. His head dangled, the red comb and wattles already dulled, and a tiny gout of dusty, thick blood hung from its beak.

Trash was still chained and in his kennel, but it was Trash who had woken her earlier. Rosie walked slowly round the back, with the bird still in her arms, dreading what she would see and expecting carnage. She imagined Aylwin had forgotten to lock up the the birds the night before, but no, arks and goose-shed beneath the late pink bubble-bath of apple blossom in the orchard were firmly shut, there was no sign of any disturbance. Shaking, she crossed the yard to fetch the feed from the corn bin, and found a half-empty beer glass sitting on top of it. Although it was now fenced off, one of their customers had last night invaded the private part of their garden.

'But why? And who?' demanded Rosie at breakfast, tears barely dried on her cheeks. 'Foxes don't break chicken's necks and leave them untouched as presents on the doorstep.'

Elvira glanced at Aylwin uneasily, who looked at his plate and then sideways at Janice.

'Is there, by any chance, something you're not telling me?'

After hearing their account of the unpleasant louts who'd

visited the night before, it seemed likely that the two events were probably related. But the chicken hadn't been there when the last customers left, nor had it been there when she'd arrived back in the evening at eleven-thirty. Or had it? The front light had been out, and she'd whispered goodnight to Ollie and run straight round to the kitchen door.

Later on in the morning she reported the incident to the police, just to register the event, not out of any expectation of redress. She also rang Sarah. There was a lingering, burnt-toast taste in her mouth.

At the hermitage, things were not unfolding smoothly for Rush and Fiammetta either that Thursday.

'There's a car coming up the track, but it's not the Molliners'.' Rush had been sitting by the window, watching a curlew through binoculars. Fiammetta, delicate and summery in a white shift dress, was painstakingly adding the finishing touches to a salad, placing little bitter lance-shaped leaves of sorrel around the edge like a laurel wreath and scattering the top with daisies. She was enjoying the absence of Peregrine-type questions, as to why she had chosen those particular herbs, and whether their arrangement had any significance to her state of mind or body. She laid blood-red tomato quarters in a line across the green and stood back to admire it.

'It's a dark green Rover.'

Fiammetta screeched out 'Peregrine!' and nearly knocking over the precious bottle of balsamic vinegar, joined Rush at the window. 'Yes, it is! Oh, misery! I can't face him now, not with Sarah and Rollo arriving for supper at any minute. What shall I do?'

'We'll have to face him together. There's nothing he can do except shout a bit.' Rush put his arm round her and hugged, pleasingly protective. 'Come on. But you're shaking! We knew he'd find out soon where you were, didn't we?'

'But not *so* soon. I've not even been with you a week! Come away from the window. Who can have told him? Don't let him in! He'll spoil it all by being too reasonable.' Rush saw that she was really frightened, although perhaps enjoying being so, and he became a little more cautious himself.

The car scrunched to a halt on the shingle drive, the front wheels extinguishing the flame-coloured tulips.

'Run upstairs, Fi. I'll deal with him.'

There was a thunderous banging on the door and Fiammetta retreated halfway up the stairs, white pointy face peeping cravenly through the banisters. 'He's not always reasonable,' she called out in a shaky voice. 'He sometimes gets excited when he can't get his own way.'

Rush tiptoed to the door. '"Hickamore, Hackamore, On the King's kitchen door!"' he said, opening it suddenly, and the burly Peregrine, fist raised in the action of banging, stumbled heavily through into Rush's waiting arms. Rule one, he thought. Grab and maintain the surprise initiative.

'Where's my wife?' barked Peregrine, embarrassed, curtly shaking off Rush's embrace.

Rule two. Instil guilt.

'She's hiding upstairs,' said Rush accusingly. 'She's quite terrified of you.'

Peregrine hunched his shoulders, fingered his tie and jerked his chin forward, disconcerted by this lightweight, angelic-looking individual standing so suspiciously un-belligerently in front of him.

'That's ludicrous. There's no need for her to be terrified, of course. But I must insist on seeing her. We obviously need to talk. Alone.' He did indeed seem very reasonable.

'You can't insist on anything. It's up to her whether she speaks to you or not.' He went and stood at the bottom of the stairs. 'Fiammetta! Your husband wants to speak to you. Do you want to speak to him?'

'No! I don't.'

Rush turned back to the heavily breathing Peregrine.

'There, that's quite simple.'

Peregrine's eyes were busy taking in the ascetic style of the room, and had become fixed on Fiammetta's pile of essays on one of the low cupboards along the wall. They were surmounted by her familiar bag, the large and sagging green basketwork bag that she took with her when she was teaching. He had the feeling, seeing it there, out of context, that it was his and began to edge towards it to reclaim it, but Rush danced back and cut him off. Rule three. Force the opponent to make the running? He was inventing these interesting Rules for Dealing with Irate Husbands as he went along. He waited for Peregrine to speak again.

'I am determined she will speak to me. I'll go upstairs.'

'No.'

'You stinking little pimp! I'll have you for enticement.' Peregrine took a step towards him but Rush stood his ground.

'Good Lord! "Enticement"! How neolithic. Don't tell me that's still a legal possibility? It does imply that women have no volition of their own, doesn't it? And Fiammetta seems to have plenty, *now*.' The emphasis on the 'now' was intended to enrage, a carefully planted *banderilla* in Peregrine's muscular neck. Was he being aggressive too early?

'By all means consult your solicitor,' Rush continued. 'Fiammetta has consulted hers. As she told you in her letter, she wants to divorce. Amicably, if that's possible.'

'I'm damned if I'm going on talking to you about our private affairs. How can we divorce when she won't even discuss things with me? When she hasn't even hinted at her reasons for leaving? She must come home with me now, at once, and discuss this silly little escapade sensibly.'

'It's the discussing that she finds so exhausting. She'd rather let someone else do it.' Rush was feeling a little sorry for Peregrine, who'd only lost his temper once and was trying very hard indeed to regain it and behave.

'I really do think it would be best if you contacted her by letter, for the time being.' Rush was getting a little impatient. He glanced round, saw beyond the wide doorway into the kitchen the floral salad on the table and glanced at his watch. Rule Four. Don't let your attention wander for a second.

'We're expecting friends for supper, so if you wouldn't mind . . .'

This was the last straw for Peregrine. That Fiammetta had friends he didn't know about, that she was calmly preparing to entertain them with this poisonous cherub only a few days after leaving him, while he was miserably shamed by her behaviour and humiliated by the asinine photograph in that tossers' newspaper . . . He became the Minotaur in search of an Athenian maiden for supper and lunged at Rush, knocking him to the ground and aiming a kick at his ribs. Fiammetta, who had crawled out onto the landing on her hands and knees unseen, screamed. Rollo and Sarah came in through the open door, bearing gifts.

After Peregrine's departure, the evening proceeded jerkily at first, since Rush was winded although otherwise unharmed and Rollo and Sarah had been a trifle startled. Fiammetta was not unnaturally distracted by events but she rescued the smoked fish pie from the oven and proceeded with the entertainment, a mite subdued.

Rosie, Sarah informed Rush, had also been having trouble.

'She was out for the evening, you see. They killed one of her chickens.'

'Rosie out? There's an oddity. I always imagine her as actually being part of the physical substance of the place, like the one brick you pull out to tumble the whole edifice, its keystone. I wonder who she was out with? Did she divulge that?'

'No, and I was so upset for her, about the cockerel, that I forgot to ask. She adores her chicks. To hear her talk about them you'd think she almost laid them herself. But it is a bit of a coincidence, after the thugs at the party and the bothersome stag party last night.'

'Isn't it? I wonder . . . No, it can't be. We'll have to keep an eye out for her, won't we? We can't have her being scared into selling the Jack Cade; she's got enough worries without being bullied, and whatever would we do without it? Of course, it might have been the dreaded Fingle bunch.'

'No, Rush, they'd have taken the whole lot, not left one dead. And I don't think they're into voodoo.'

'What have you been roped in to arrange for Rosie's Games, Rollo?'

'I'm in charge of an obstacle course. It's being erected properly, by the army. I've got ten people already who've put down their names. What's yours, Rush?'

'I'm in charge of all the frogs.'

'Frogs? Are you racing frogs? I thought it was strictly human events?'

'Actually, it's four events, two on each day. Frog March-ing, Relay Leapfrogging and Frog-Hopping which is actually pole-vaulting the dyke. All to be carried out wearing flippers. There's also Frog-pulling. But Fiammetta is doing that, aren't you, Fi? She's organising two French Tug-of-War teams to come over from Calais. We thought we'd run a book, place bets on whether her friend from work, Maria, who's a lusty lass, can seduce any of them before the end of the day. That's if there are any worth seducing. The Jack Cade team starts practising in three weeks, but Maria has been practising for years.'


Vicky put down her gin and smiled sweetly at Peregrine who loomed, darkly incongruous, on her pretty sofa, powerful legs encased in pristine summer-weight grey wool suiting drawn up a little protectively, his large hands cradling his drink perhaps a little nervously. He sweats a lot, she thought, in spite of it being so cool in here, and his cuff-links are far too large. I wonder if cuff-links follow the adage about dogs – the bigger and fiercer they are, the more emotionally insecure their owners? Anyway,

I'm sure he can be managed. She had easily discerned the will in him to cause damage to anything or anyone concerned with the alleged abduction of his wife.

'It's awfully valiant of you, Peregrine. It's horrendous to think of young people – it could be my own Cressie or Harry one day – being corrupted by drug-dealers. I'm certain it's been going on for ages in the Jack Cade. Probably smuggling as well. You know the area? Well, old habits die hard, don't they?'

She arched her neck towards the door, as if expecting someone. 'I'm sorry Paddy isn't back yet.' He was, she knew, paying a visit to his mother after leaving the brewery and wouldn't be back till at least six-thirty.

'You've actually reported to the police what I told you? How lucky you knew someone senior in the Force to whom you could pass on the information. Discretion in something like this is so important. Paddy or I might have done something ourselves, I suppose, but the situation is a bit tricky, with him being the MD. It might have looked as if we were harassing the landlady. Still, we won't mention it again.'

Involving other people in one's ruses meant one had to deal with their hang-ups and power complexes. Mercifully it was these very things which had placed Peregrine in her hands.

He nodded vigorously, but didn't say anything. He was a bit alarmed at finding himself alone with such an attractive woman and looked uneasily at the unspeakable, glittering Vicky. The curtains at the french windows stirred a little as a breeze got up and the ice clinked coolly in their drinks. It was only four-thirty, and he had been expecting no more than a cup of tea.

'Now,' continued Vicky, carefully, 'I was quite astounded when you told me that Fiammetta actually *was* with Rushett. A lucky guess on my part, wasn't it? It won't last, of course. Just an infatuation, I expect, on Fiammetta's part. But you mustn't underestimate Rush's staying power.' (Or pulling power, she thought crossly.) 'The more you bother them, the better.'

'It's very sweet of you to take an interest in helping me with my little problem.' His voice was slightly strangled. 'If there's anything I can do for you, you only have to say.'

'Oh, Peregrine, I will, I will.'

Failing Paddy's return, Peregrine left shortly afterwards and Vicky went down to her husband's study, made a phone call, and swiftly wrote a letter on his PC, slipping out in the car to catch the late post collection. The day might have started badly but this was a satisfying end. Ollie had been fearfully rude to her that morning when she had rung in an attempt to mend fences. Well, not so much rude, more indifferent. That had hurt more than a little, that and his refusal to see her. She was unused to being bereft of his consoling company. Indifference was something up with which she would not put!

On Saturday, 11 May, Rosie was up at dawn, taking advantage of the sleeping household to work on the proliferating paperwork involved with the Games. It was a task roughly equivalent to the arranging of three large village fêtes and a point-to-point in seven weeks but she had found her métier, and although the back parlour was filled with parcels of posters, the round table and the desk disguised by a multicoloured mosaic of letters and files over an underlay of Elvira's bits of cotton and the inevitable pins, she was unfazed by it. She didn't like to enquire too closely of Aylwin how he had managed to get the posters printed free.

She opened the window and stood there drinking hot sweet coffee, still fretting over the murdered cockerel, but these sinister worries were larded with quite salacious thoughts about Ollie Potter. She had to force herself to settle down and concentrate on the matters in hand: several letters confirming grateful acceptance of offers of assistance. A new marquee hire company had offered a wonderfully cut-price deal so long as they were allowed to use the occasion to advertise themselves. It was amazing what was offered if there was free advertising involved.

There were the advance bookings of concessions to be sorted, spaces allotted and sponsors to be thanked. Two large plans of the site were pinned on the wall, one for each day of the event, showing their back field and the adjoining one which had been loaned by Sam Dicken. The plans were smothered with stick-on labels in emerald green, fluorescent orange, pink and red. All permissions were sought and the police had been alerted to potential traffic problems.

She had wondered if it was wise to hold the Games so early in the summer and at such short notice, but had conceded when Sarah had pointed out that those involved might go off the boil if the arrangements were too long drawn out and that the very ones ones needed to help might be away on holiday in August.

Finished, apart from a list of telephone calls to be made on Monday morning, she laid the breakfast table and went out into the garden.

It was another perfect May morning, until the postwoman rattled up on her bicycle and delivered the weekly copy of *The Publican*, and another letter from Vicky Croswell. This time it was an execrably impersonal computer-written letter, raising the previous offer by a paltry two thousand pounds, not enough to make Rosie hesitate before returning to the house to write to decline and again throw Vicky's letter in the waste-paper basket; then she changed her mind, retrieved and re-read it. There was something subtly different about its tone, which was not so impersonal after all, less politely patronising, more hectoring. *'Perhaps you would* now *reconsider, in the light of recent adverse publicity and future difficulties, my increased offer of . . .'*

The publicity surrounding Mel's death had not in the least been bad for business, and although there was the coming inquest to consider, they had already been told that it was a heart attack. What particular future difficulties did the woman refer to? The difficulty of paying back the money? The 'now' leapt out at Rosie; it did not infer 'now', at this time, it implied 'now that' something had happened. Did the letter and murdered Baldur the Beautiful go hand in wing? The thought arced suggestively across her brain, but she was forced to put her reading of it down to paranoia, smoothed out the letter and carefully filed it.

Aylwin and Elvira slept late on Saturday mornings, and the B&B guests who'd been staying since Thursday night were late risers. It was a blear-eyed Janice in a dressing gown who came out to Rosie at about nine o'clock in the garden, interrupting her hoeing the leeks. Rosie had been droning under her breath in rhythm with the scraping of the hoe, first *'Green peas, mutton pies, tell me where my Sally lies, I'll be there before she dies, green peas, mutton pies'*, and on encountering a particularly firmly rooted patch of creeping buttercup, sliced through their roots viciously and changed the refrain to *Frère Jacques*: *'Vick-y Cros-well, Vick-y Cros-well, Dormez-vous? Dormez-vous?'*

'Your lovely Mr Potter is on the phone.'

Rosie whooped with delight, clanged the hoe to the ground, ran indoors and, as Ollie seemed intent on visiting her, suggested a walk on the beach since she wanted some stones for the garden.

They went to Littlestone, Rosie having persuaded Ollie that in order to assuage her conscience over having a couple of hours off, she would have to stop on the way at various newsagents and deliver bundles of fliers and entry forms to be inserted in the local newspapers and displayed in the windows.

'If we return by a different way, we can knock three or four more off the list. Would you mind?'

Ollie assured her that he would drive her to Scotland if necessary. She wore a straw hat, in the speckled shade of which she looked to him more interesting than ever. There were few people about and they walked first along the tide-wrack line, not speaking much and poking at the brown weeds and tangled blue nylon shreds of rope, then rolling up sleeves and trousers, headed further down the beach and paddled along on the edge of the retreating, still icy sea, selecting shells and glistening wet pebbles, absurdly aware of each other's bare feet. Hers were neat-toed, lightly gold-skinned like the rest of her, and Ollie's were vulnerable and white with shock at being released from boots and socks, the latter leaving a faint pattern of impressed stocking stitch across his insteps.

'I need only white stones,' she said, bending over to snatch a beauty before the sea dashed over it and it was lost again, 'for putting round plants in pots.' Her strange striped hair was bright tawny-gold in the sun.

'How big? Like this?'

He indicated a pebble with a toe.

'Yes, that's about right. I wish I'd brought a bigger bag with me. I always seem to go home with half the beach. There's something irresistible about them but I must admit, however carefully they were originally chosen, they usually all end up on the gravel outside the Jack Cade.'

It was the vulnerability of his feet, and perhaps the openness of the beach, which made Rosie decide to unload her suspicions as they wandered about until, unable to bear it any longer, he stopped still and interrupted her mid-way through the explanations, just after the chicken incident.

'I think I ought to tell you that I know Vicky Croswell.' Heart, or foot, in mouth.

'You do?' She stopped still, staring at him, letting fall the little handful of stones, pattering them back into the sparkling swirl of water round her ankles. 'Does her husband know about this? But then there's no absolute proof it's her. Is she the sort of woman who would stoop to killing chickens?'

'Yes, she is. Not personally, I would imagine, but she's capable of arranging it. I'm sure Paddy knows nothing about it, if it is her causing the trouble.'

Ollie's heart was beating rather fast. He knew he was spineless, was the lowest form of mollusc. Clamming up – how apt that was. But at least the *omerta* was cracked; the rest would come at another time – would not, could not, come out now.

'Thank you for telling me that.' Rosie didn't seem to want

to know any more. 'Look! There's a whole dead seagull. It's huge! Look at its great sweep of wing, all draggled. How big's an albatross? Could it be one?'

Did she realize the discomfiting effect of the mention of albatrosses on the guilty? Did she know the poem? Had she guessed he was holding something back? Christ, was she going to suggest hanging it round his Ancient Mariner's neck? She was looking up at him sideways, the wide mouth smiling curiously. Again her face had changed. He felt that was what she'd thought of doing and, irrationally, that she was aware he knew she'd thought it.

'Do you know *The Rime of the Ancient Mariner*?'

'I know it, what it's about, not *know* it by heart. I know it's by Samuel Taylor Coleridge. Now here's a pretty stone.'

Was she teasing? No, for God's sake, of course she couldn't have guessed what he was thinking. He must laugh the idea away. He squared his shoulders and declaimed, striking the necessary absurd pose and flinging his arms up to the sky, wild-haired and eyed, startling a circling herring gull which sharply veered away with an indignant squawk:

> '"*Ah well a-day! what evil look*
> *Had I from old and young!*
> *Instead of cross, the Albatross*
> *About my neck was hung.*"'

'Do you know it all?' She was hugging herself, and laughing.

'No, sadly, just odd bits. My grandfather knew great chunks by heart and recited them when he'd had too much brandy. It's surely meant to be declaimed aloud, rather than to oneself. It was electrifying. I loved the frightening bits best – when spirits take hold of the bodies of the dead crew, "*the ghastly crew*", and help him sail the ship home. There's a ghost boat too, suns and moons rising and setting all over the place, snow-fogs and Saint Elmo's fire flickering about the masts. The visual imagination, the essence of nightmares, was quite intoxicating for a ten year old. An astounding man, Coleridge. So was my grandpa. I'm reading a biography of him at the moment ... of Coleridge, not grandpa. Here! Is this one interesting enough? It looks like marble.'

'Perfect! I've seen Saint Elmo's fire, the night before the 'eighty-seven hurricane. It danced about all over the poplar trees. It's coming back to me now, the *Ancient Mariner*; we read it at school. There's the wedding guest, trying to get into the feast, but the Ancient Mariner won't let the unfortunate man pass till he's been told the entire story? That's who I felt sorry for, the wedding guest. That's also nightmarish – the dream where you're late for a party and everything conspires to stop you getting there – only one shoe, an unwanted phone call that goes on for ages, a missing skirt, the wrong bus, and gradually it dawns on you that you're never going to get there, that you've missed it, it's all over, at which point you wake up.'

'That's been my life, till now. I've just remembered the last verse ...

> *"He went like one that hath been stunned,*
> *And is of sense forlorn:*
> *A sadder and a wiser man,*
> *He rose the morrow morn."*

'*He*'s the wedding guest, of course.'

'So *that's* where "*a sadder and a wiser man*" comes from! Do you know, I never thought I'd wander up and down a beach talking about poetry?'

'Neither did I. I can recite Keats too, you know. I'll save it for later. I think you are a very rare inn-keeper.'

'I love Keats. How odd you should mention him today. There might be swarms of us inn-keepers, all reduced to buzzing nursery rhymes and clichés, imprisoned in our hives beneath giant knitted hive-cosies, forced to breathe in the steamy idea of the warm and friendly barmaid. Fluffiness, not cleverness, is what's needed, and I can't be cosy. Not many men drop into the pub and want to discuss *Endymion* after a hard day's work on a tractor. And if they did, they'd want to tell me what they thought about it, not listen to my opinions. My ears get so full of listening sometimes that I feel the drums will burst. Oh, God! What's the time? Ollie, I've got to get back soon. Aylwin and Elvira want to go in to Folkestone, for the food shopping and the cinema and I like Janice to have back-up.'

Aylwin had put in a little doorbell by the bar, so anyone serving could summon assistance or ice from the kitchen should there be a sudden shower of customers, but it wouldn't do Janice any good if she did not get home soon.

'So soon? We seem to have quite a haul of white stones. Enough for four or five pots? Here, let me carry them.'

They touched briefly, withdrew, dropped the bag, then touched again. Rough, smooth, warm, cool, sea-cleaned and salty-sticky, the fingers lingered. They were examining each other's hands, the inadvertent becoming the designed. I like his wrists, the gold hairs. I like her palms, pink and cupped. I like the freckles, I like the blue scar on the thumb, I like, I like. Eat Me, Drink Me.

Rosie's hat blew off, cartwheeling away across the beach, and she pounced after it. It was not until after brown Ben had died that she knew she fancied fair men better. Ollie picked up the bag again, and when Rosie returned, laid his arm around her shoulder, not clutching, just resting it there, and they climbed back up the slope of warm, slithering shingle to the car, speechless, still barefoot, carrying their stony booty, shoes and something else.

Rosie came out of a long unfocused stare. Her eyes had been fixed on the two men, strangers, their backs to the fading light at the window table, but they had blurred as she thought of the morning at the beach. Standing hot and bothered behind the bar with sandalled feet on the cool beer-slopped tiles, swatting away mosquitoes, she had been trying to steal a moment in which to reinvent the frissons of discovery, accurately recall Ollie's face, neck, width of shoulders, hands, legs ... It was hard to keep her mind on the job since the remembering of every detail of him seemed so devastatingly important.

Now that these two had firmed up in her field of vision again, she recalled why her attention had been drawn to them. Their quiet behaviour had become even more sharply defined and disturbing. They nursed their bottles of Carlsberg, barely spoke to each other and appeared to be awaiting an arrival or a happening. They seemed bored yet lazily registered each coming and going from the inn, glancing up as people drifted in and out from the garden. Rosie kept them under surveillance.

'Same again, Gilbert?' She took another bottle of low-alcohol beer from the shelf behind her and poured it for him, carefully tilting the glass, thinking that there was something not quite right about the two men – in their late twenties perhaps, in the wrong dark leather jackets, their jeans the wrong pale shade. They were well matched, urbanly uniformed. There was a similar person, more heavily built, leaning back against the bar nearby, apparently at ease but from whom emanated a fly-repellent after-shave. His fair head was unusually cleanly barbered and his back pockets bulged. He chatted intently to a young woman who wore a T-shirt printed with pink roses, which did nothing to alleviate the heavy muscularity of her weight-trainer's arms. His sharp face was sideways on to her, but he was watching outward.

'Same again, Johnnie?' The air was close although door and windows were wide open and there were sounds of clinking glasses and laughter from outside. It was getting dark now and she caught the flash of distant lightning.

'Flowers for Mel Plunket? Outside, please, the gate on the right. Oh, hell! I've run out of ice. Janice, I'm going to the kitchen to get ice, and more sliced lemon.'

'Hello, Rosie, we'll have to come inside. The mosquitoes are fearsome. Two halves of cider and an orange juice, please.' The three young women, Mary, Mary and Marsha, floated away in their long summer skirts, their three quite distinctive and powerful scents competing in toxicity with the fly-repellent, the interaction resembling formaldehyde.

On the right-hand side of the open door sat Gilbert's cousin, eighty-six-year-old Hilda Bentley who had once been Rosie's father's weekend barmaid. She sat sipping her weekly rum and blackcurrant and fanning herself with the pink parish magazine, partly to alleviate the heat, partly to waft away the noxious smoke from the pipe of her even more ancient and portly husband Louis, seated solidly beside her in his smelly ginger tweed waistcoat and shirt sleeves. It was only the rising fumes which pronounced him alive, not dead and stuffed. Hilda sat firmly, as if it would take God Himself to shift her, knees wide apart, exposing knee-length pink drawers beneath her thick wool tartan skirt. As a gesture to the warmth of the evening she had removed a couple of her habitual seven cardigans, exposing one of sage green, dashingly darned with turquoise at the elbows and neck.

'Rum and Coke? Two pints of Ned Rother's special beneath the counter? How's your mother, Liam? Is she getting about again? Oh, I am glad to hear it. It must have been awful for her, stuck up that monkey puzzle tree . . . Rush and Fiammetta! Brilliant! I need to speak to you both, when you've got a moment. Games-talk . . . Oh, Major Penny, I'm afraid the Spring Bitter isn't ready yet. Would you like to try some of the special . . . only a tonic water?'

She was surprised to see him there in the evening. The Major was their local borough councillor and dropped in infrequently, always at Saturday lunchtimes. A tall man, narrow as a needle, with an energetic Adam's apple, he seemed on edge this evening, a little self-important, Rosie noticed. He rather brusquely brushed off Liam Carter's enquiries about his chances of obtaining planning permission for a workshop for the manufacture of marionettes and went to sit on his own in a corner.

'Good evening, Canute. Hello, Bea and Francie.'

Two bikes roared up and there was a burst of laughter outside where a posse of Kittens were assembled in the twilight. Rosie peeped again in the direction of the strangers. They were showing signs of becoming more animated, which was peculiar since they'd barely touched their drinks although they'd been sitting over them for an hour.

When Tiger arrived, Rosie signalled that she wanted a quiet word. He managed to squint at the aliens without moving his head too far in either direction or stopping speaking and whispered back, 'It's the Filth, Rosie. The Plod. There's another of them outside admiring the pots of pansies. Undercover. They stick out like pricks ... I beg your pardon, like sore thumbs, I mean. What you been up to?'

'It's more what have *you* been up to? I thought they looked as if they were used to wearing uniform. Is it someone in particular, or is it drugs they're after?'

'I wouldn't know, but I'll just go and get a few of the boys in, shall I, and see if we can give them a run for their money?'

'No! Don't be a loon. *Don't* antagonise them. I've got a licence to look after, Tiger. Remember that, please. Just warn your friends to behave and make sure it gets out to those who aren't your friends as well. I'll speak with the police in a minute. It's not fair. They're putting people off.'

Tiger sidled out, and in again about ten minutes later, followed by a few of the Kittens. They slunk suspiciously quietly into the stuffy back room. There was nothing unusual about this, except their drawing of the curtain behind them, but three or four minutes later there occurred what Janice would have called a 'kerfuffle'. Two uniformed policemen strode in and closed the door. The strangers made a con-certed rush towards the back room, rudely pushing through the crowd and over-dramatically rattling aside the curtain, ripping it.

The following silence was broken by titters from those at that end of the room who could see. Rosie could not from behind the bar but then came a wild shriek of laughter from Fiammetta who, craning her neck, was near enough to glimpse the tableau set up for the police.

It was a macabre, even shocking sight. Laid across the sagging table, sardine-wise and presenting to the viewer three rough heads alternating with two pairs of boots, were Tiger and four Kittens. All were quite still and had their eyes shut. Hairy tattooed arms and blackened fingers clasped bouquets of wilting flowers to their leathery chests. A candle guttered and smoked at each corner, on the floor. There was silence until Tiger could no longer hold his breath. He quivered and sat up with a roar, ruining the scene.

'All right. The joke's over, Mr Bright. Would you gentlemen resurrect yourselves, get off that table and follow us outside immediately? Everyone else remains inside. Come along.'

Rosie shot Tiger a venomous look as he passed her with his escort; he was smirking and modestly clutching the flowers before him like a naughty bridesmaid. An excited buzz ensued, reports being passed back from those craning through the windows.

'Ooh, look! *Two* police cars and a van! They're searching them. It's going to take forever, Tiger's got about twenty-six pockets in those combat trousers. They've found half a Marmite sandwich and a bag of six-inch nails so far. And a packet of condoms. Well, *I'm* not coming here again. I didn't know it was such a rough house. It looked very tasteless to me. They've got dogs with them. They're arresting Tiger – no, they aren't, they're letting him go. They're letting all of them go! Rah! Rah! Ra-ra-rah! Oh, what a shame. Is it all over? Someone ought to tell Tiger to shut up, or they'll re-arrest him. They're coming in with the dogs.'

'Well.' Major Penny coughed a little nervously. 'It seems as if the poor police have been given false information.' He sounded sheepish. Rosie swung round on him.

'What do you mean? *Given* information? By whom, and about what? Are they looking for explosives? Hey, get out of here, will you!' An oversprung springer spaniel was tugging at its handler and had stuck its horrid wet nose up her skirt. Rosie, unusually pink with both indignation and the foetid heat, stared furiously up at the wilting major.

'If they're looking for drugs, they're unlikely to find any. If I found anyone dealing in here, they'd be out on their ear. What I want to know is *who* told you there was something going on? This is the latest in a series of attempts to ruin my business and it had better be the last! Come on, Major Penny. You knew this was going to happen. That's why you're here. You know it's *never* been that sort of pub.'

Major Penny, magenta with embarrassment, wavered between self-righteousness and apology and proceeded to dig himself a very deep grave.

'I was telephoned by someone yesterday, and had no reason to believe that the information was incorrect so, as was my duty, I immediately passed it on to the police. They were very interested, since I gather they had already been alerted to the matter. They're having a crack down in the area at the moment. I am very sorry you've been inconvenienced. I just came in to see for myself what was going on and never imagined for a moment that you knew about it, you must believe me. Instead I find the place its usual charming self, if slightly more popular than in the past . . .' Rosie was unimpressed by the inept flannelling '. . . quite like a party, in fact.' He looked about helplessly, as if expecting succour. 'By the way, where did they get those flowers from and how did *they* know about the raid?'

'The undercover officers were obvious to everybody, I would have thought. Not many men come here to drink bottled lager. Tiger's not a dealer and he wasn't expecting a raid till the police were spotted. If anyone *was* dealing, this is the very last place they'd choose to do it!' Rosie was beside herself with rage and fright. 'Whoever telephoned must have been winding you up. I expect the flowers came from the pile left for the poor boy who died last week. They must have posted them through the little window in the back room and then sauntered in empty-handed, innocent as kittens. Now, if you'll excuse me, I want to have a word with the officer in charge. There's the little matter of the damaged curtain.'

Rosie lay spreadeagled across the bed, listening to the fading grumble as the thunderstorm moved slowly inland. The power was off and a lighted candle stood on the table, flickering in the draught of the freshened air from the window. Outside, everything dripped. What a week! Months of silence then — boom! War had broken out and shrapnel rained down on their heads.

After closing time the door was locked and they'd sat with Rush and Fiammetta at the long oak table in the candle-lit bar, drinking whisky and mulling over the probable identity of their ill-wisher. Various things had come to light, the most important being that Fiammetta had recognised Vicky and Janie Cutt-Norton in the Jack Cade on the night of the party. Rush had rocked his chair back and forth, staring at the ceiling, considering the options. He had been of the opinion that it was quite definitely Vicky in the woodpile and now there had been a further letter, perhaps a word to Paddy might be in order.

'He's a rather nice, straight sort of man. This wouldn't be the first time Vicky's embarrassed him. He'll make sure there's no further trouble. I'll do the deed myself, if you like? I'll ring him at his office on Monday morning.'

Rosie, unable to guarantee that she would not lose her temper, had agreed that it might be best if he did, and gone off to bed.

Not all of the week had been so dire; there were the interludes with Ollie which were hours embossed and gilded, raised above these pathetic skirmishes with Vicky Croswell. There had been so little time to sit and think about what she was engaged in. She was propelled forward by that momentous initial decision to refuse to budge from the inn and could not now apply the brakes.

Other women have time to have their hair cut, their toenails painted, lay themselves down in darkened rooms wrapped in white towelling dressing gowns, with slices of cucumber over their eyes, she thought. Or do they? Perhaps it's a fantasy purveyed by magazines? Look at me and marvel. A tie-in with the growers of cucumber and manufacturers of white towelling dressing gowns? I doubt Ollie would notice if I'd cucumbered my eyes or not. I'm on a mission. It'll only take another month to find out if it's possible to complete it. I *must* stick by it and not indulge in ifs and buts. There *aren't* any ifs and buts. It's what I want, what we all need, and there are so many other people involved, I can't let them down now.

It was unsettling, an almost guilty sensation, knowing that she was in possession of a place that made another person quite deranged with desire. Rosie rolled off the bed and, taking up the candle, looked at the bedside clock. Half-past midnight. It was necessary to read for half an hour or so, to unwind before falling asleep, but more candle power was needed. Feeling her way along the landing, she liberated one from the guest bedroom and lay down again with a paperback that had won the Booker prize some years before. 'Sparkling', it announced on the back cover. 'An original and entertaining novel, full of deep insights'. She re-read a few pages to remind herself of the sequence of events but her eyelids drooped in the trying light and tired of the entrapping fronds of kelpy metaphors and too sleepy to disentangle the thin, gelatinous themes which wriggled through it like elvers, she crossly threw it aside.

Has my life ever had a theme at all, even a skinny one? she

wondered. So far it's seemed to consist of lying beneath a stone and heaving upwards, without ever being able to get free. Just as it begins to shift, Vicky Croswell comes and sits on top of it.

She snuffed the candle and almost immediately fell asleep, the acrid trace of the hot waxy smoke tickling her nostrils.

# Chapter Eleven

Paddy put the phone down in his office at the brewery and swivelled around in his chair once or twice, brushing against the straggling spider plant on the window sill. His hands were tightly clasped across his stomach to contain the sinking sensation and assuage the swift curdling of his last cup of coffee. He was slow to anger and the understanding of the information which had just been passed to him came trickling through like some unpleasant seepage from a drain. It was a very bad start to the week. He could try to discount it, of course, since he was aware of the cousinly antipathy between his wife and Rush and this just might be some nasty little vendetta on Rush's part, but Paddy knew deep down that it was unlikely.

Rush had been clinical on the telephone, detailing the incidents with dates, times, and their various deleterious effects on Rosie's nervous system. The antagonism had always seemed to come from Vicky's side first. He would have to get the truth of it from her. If it were true, it could put a very large question mark over the integrity of the brewery. Paddy shuddered as he envisaged the local, or even national, press coverage should this become public knowledge. How could she have actually crossed the border into criminality? How could she have been so obtuse as to implicate them all in this? Had Vicky gone completely insane?

He told his assistant that he would take an early lunch and left the office on foot, needing the half-hour's walk in which to fortify himself for the ensuing scene. Vicky was up in the drawing-room, engaged in constructing an ambitious flower arrangement in an eighteenth-century, brass-bound wine cooler. *His* grandfather's brass-bound wine cooler. Bits of ornamental cabbage and *Eucalyptus gunnii* were strewn across the polished floor which was also liberally spattered with water, short lengths of florist's wire and chunks of some damp green spongy stuff.

'Good heavens, Paddy. What are you doing back here at this time of day? What do you think – isn't this a refreshing change? I've gone back to lovely 1950s Constance Spry arrangements! Those glass tubs of jammed in flowers, all cut across the bottom at the same height, are so boring and commonplace ...'

She had not even turned round to look at him.

'Stop fiddling with the damn' flowers,' he bellowed. 'I want to talk to you.'

She turned, a stem of some grey-leaved ferny thing in hand, staggered by the unmannerly tone of his voice.

'How cross you sound! Have you got another attack of gout?'

'NO! I haven't got bloody gout! Vicky, have you or have you not been recently engaged in various acts of intimidation?'

She felt herself go cold then rather hot. He noticed the change in her complexion, the rosy ears above the little gold bows which he'd bought her last Christmas. She said lightly that she didn't know what he was talking about and turned her back again, continuing clumsily to push the flowers into place, stabbing in the fern behind the cabbage where it waved about uncertainly, like an aigrette on a turban.

'STOP farting about with the flowers! Have you? There has been a complaint.' He would not tell her from whom just yet and could see she was caught off guard.

'I don't know what you're talking about, Paddy. How could you think that ... I'm sure Rosie Hooke has lots of enemies –

doesn't that sort of thing go on all the time? Inter-pub rivalry, you know?'

'No, of course it doesn't. Why should it? Publicans tend to be on good terms with each other, particularly in the country.' Then he pounced. 'And if this is nothing to do with you, how did you know I was talking about the Jack Cade?'

'Oh, Paddy! We want the Jack Cade, don't we? It was all just a little bit of fun to unsettle her — you know, push her into thinking it might be worth her while to accept our offer.'

'Don't be ridiculous! She turned it down flat, didn't she? Or have you made another one I don't know about? It's hardly "fun", is it, to massacre her chickens? Is it "fun" to worry some-one half to death? Is it "fun" to try to wreck someone else's party, even if it is your cousin Rush's? Don't you see what you've done? Not to mention the dire effect it would have on the brewery if it got out that you were trying to ruin a tenant's business in order to acquire the place yourself. Can you imagine how I feel, discovering that my wife is engaged in a little light ethnic cleansing? Because that's what it amounts to, you know.'

'Don't exaggerate! It's nothing to do with the brewery!' she snapped back, at last abandoning the flowers and moving as far away from him as possible, arms folded defensively, behind a little Sheraton chair.

'So far as Rosie Hooke is concerned, you *are* the brewery, since you were making use of information you acquired from me to get what you wanted. Don't you understand, you little bitch, that this could make us look very bad indeed?'

Paddy slumped down on the sofa and put his head in his hands for a second; it was beginning to ache with tension. 'What I can't understand is where you managed to hire these troublemakers? Or were they unsavoury friends of yours I don't know about, out for a little light amusement? And giving false information to the police is not a laughing matter. I suppose we might expect a visit from them at any minute, to see you about wasting police time.'

Vicky paused for a moment, watching Paddy work himself up into a very uncommon state of rage. A fierce bad rabbit. She wasn't worried about the police, since she had not approached them directly and therefore could not be held responsible if various people had acted on her well-planted gossip. It was pleasantly surprising to her that it had been acted upon so swiftly. Peregrine and that boring old friend of Megan's mother, Major Penny, could carry the can. She *could* tell Paddy that Ollie had been the mainstay of the plot and that he had in fact instigated it, but then if he was prepared to go so far for her, that *might* just hint that there had been something more to their relationship than the old friendship inferred by Paddy, mightn't it? She decided that however much she'd like to dump him in the shit, it might be wiser to leave Ollie out of it, for the moment.

'Paddy, I'm really sorry. I just thought ... I thought ...' Her bottom lip trembled expertly.

'You quite obviously didn't think at all! It's quite an extraordinary approach to have taken. I'm shocked and furious with you, I really am! I know how much you want the damn' place, but you certainly won't get it by behaving like this. In any case, it all seems to have been counter-productive. Now is there anything else to be dragged up or is it just this last week that you've been indulging in Serbian practices?'

'Just this last week, I promise you. There isn't anything else.'

'Then we'd better not admit to anything, but absolutely *nothing* else must occur, do you understand?'

'Yes, of course. I see now how stupid and dangerous it's all been. I just got carried away.'

She'd intended to look a little crestfallen, but thankful that she hadn't had to resort to tears, accidentally beamed at him instead. The storm was abating.

'Shall I finish this and make you some lunch? How about a nice slice of game pie and some salad?'

'I don't want any bloody lunch!' He had noticed with dismay how short-lived had been her repentance. 'I've already got indigestion. I hope to God that Dad doesn't get to hear about this. He'd explode!'


Ollie visited Rosie after his first day's work with *Ange et Caramel*. It was his familiarisation period, this first week; he was expected to be in at ten a.m. and could leave again at four p.m. which he did happily, with a briefcase bulging with computer print-outs and a pile of files to study.

Charles Caramel, all steel-rimmed spectacles and neuroses, the junior partner who commuted to England twice a week, was inseparable from his mobile phone and appeared to be in a Gallic tizzy over reports of an incipient blockade of Channel ports on the French side. He was setting out immediately on a doubtful mission to liberate half a ton of ewes' milk cheese. Ollie had consequently been left in the hands of his secretary Angélique.

Contrary to her all-in wrestler's build and ferociously crop-haired appearance, she had, after an initial tetchiness, been most affable and had prepared a luncheon for him consisting of large slices of some of their exclusive goodies and a bottle of white Burgundy. They'd got on famously and Ollie had found himself just about capable of restraining his thoughts from galloping ahead to the Jack Cade.

For once in his life, he had absolutely no idea how to progress with a woman. Rosie and he were, it seemed, on hugging terms, but he felt his instincts had wavered off course. She led him through the previously unknown, untidy and homely private side of the inn, where all rough corners had been comfortably smoothed by generations of previous inhabitants and all defects ignored for so long that they had attained cult status. Trash did not so much as sneer at Ollie as he stood on the flagstones of the high-raftered kitchen. He was absorbed in each movement of

Rosie's body as she laid a tea-tray, fascinated by the hair which was now scraped up on top of her head, a delectably dishevelled little haystack with small soft strands escaping round the nape of her neck.

She took him to the room she called the 'back-parlour' while the kettle boiled. Order was evident amongst the Ben Nevises of paperwork and he listened admiringly while she made a couple of phone calls, her acumen disguised by the sultry voice which appeared to unravel Gordian knots. She then put all aside and he carried the tea-tray out, to sit side by side with her beneath the mulberry. Rosie enquired, politely, about the new job and then proceeded to describe the funny bits of the abortive police raid, and Rush's phone call to Paddy.

Ollie immediately became uneasy. She had laughed it off but how sinister it must all have appeared to her. He hastened to assure her that Paddy would undoubtedly put an immediate stop to it but could not help being smugly intrigued by the thought that more might be brewing at Green & Croswell's than small beer. He swiftly changed the subject.

'That's a splendid little cockerel over there. Is he any particular breed?'

'A Jack Cade Special. He's the slightly less charming sibling of the one that was murdered. He has fighting cock in his ancestry. Those stilty legs are Old English Game, and the vicious spurs. He's a descendant of the bantams we've kept here for years and years. My sister Sally had his many-times-great-grandparents; they were her especial pets.'

'You mention Sally a lot. Were you very close? Would you tell me about her?' He was tensely aware of Rosie sitting so close. Although she wore no earrings he could see that her ears had been pierced, and the tiny mutilations were touching, made him want to stroke them, to soothe away the worries he had been instrumental in causing.

'She was a bit of a wild woman; at times she didn't seem to be very rational.' Rosie laughed at his rather broody expression, mistaking the cause. 'We're not alike, not at all. Everything she did was exciting to me, although one couldn't help wishing she wouldn't do some of the frightening things she did. Her whole aim was to get away from the inn. She was lovely to look at – beautiful, I thought – but she didn't seem to realize the effect she had on people. I still miss her.'

'What happened, or would you rather not talk about it?' He hoped she would and in endeavouring to disengage his gaze from her ears, became fixated instead on her dark eyelashes. Like her sister, she obviously had little idea of the effect she had on others.

Rosie did prefer to talk about it. Talking distanced her from the events and kept them in proportion. Intent on her explanations, her eyes followed the questing cockerel as he searched for tasty nibbles in the grass, announcing his discoveries to the hens and, a benevolent despot, standing back to give them first peck. With her attention distracted, Ollie felt more able to stare at her profile, becoming more finely attuned to the ins and outs of forehead, nose, the strangely sexy, slightly downturned mouth, rounded chin ...

'Sally ran off to Dorset with a garage mechanic, Michael Godley. She was already pregnant and they married away from home, without telling anyone, which upset Dad dreadfully. He was a great traditionalist and had hoped, I think, to marry her off to a rich farmer's son; he'd imagined walking her up the aisle of Old Romney church, all peachy blushes and white tulle. Do you really want to know all this?'

Ollie nodded. He wished to know everything pertaining to her family and to her, in the minutest detail. There was a small brown mole on her collarbone, he noticed.

'I was eighteen, it was summer and I'd just finished my A levels. Sally had just given birth to Aylwin and asked me to stay with them, to help out and to have a holiday. A month after Aylwin was born, she and Michael went out for a drink and left me babysitting. They had a row, Michael never said what about, and they left separately. Only Michael came home. Sally had stayed on and taken a lift back with a girlfriend. They had a car smash. Sally went through the windscreen.'

'Oh, God! I'm sorry. Don't go on if it upsets you.'

'No, it's all right. It *was* twenty-two years ago. In fact, if I sound a bit detached it's because I've been through it a million times in my head since then. She died the next day. I managed to see her that morning. She'd said, before the accident, that Michael wasn't Aylwin's father and that Michael had always known it. Now she said that the real father had given her a lot of money, a sort of pay-off, which was why they'd been able to rent the cottage and not some poky flat. I was a bit stunned, but Sally always had something else up her sleeve to confound one with, a little store of naughtinesses to enliven things. She was unkind sometimes, careless of people's affections – I hope because she didn't believe how much she was loved.'

Rosie spoke slowly as if spelling it out for herself, her index finger, the only restless part of her, tapping out an obscure code on the arm of the bench.

'She was going to tell me something else, the name of the father or perhaps something else entirely, but Michael came in and wanted to sit with her, and she never finished what she was going to say. We knew it was touch and go and he was desperately in love with her, in spite of everything. He was with her when she died. What happened after is blurred, but we arranged for her to be buried at home, here in Middhaze.'

Dry-throated, she gulped at her tea before turning again to meet Ollie's attentive grey eyes.

'The church is long-gone but the graveyard is still conse-crated. There are six generations of Craddocks buried there now, possibly more. Michael and I and the baby travelled back here for the funeral by train. My parents were inconsolable; I wanted to help them, to tell them that I loved them too, but they never got over it. I *had* to. After the funeral Michael Godley literally walked off into the blue, without saying goodbye. He never even came back to the house. We never heard from him again. Letters and phone-calls to the address in Poole went unanswered, so we gave up trying. My mother had fallen to pieces and I wanted to look after the baby.'

'Wanted to or had to? Is that why you didn't get to university?'

'Both, I suppose. The offer of the place at Manchester was let slide. It was a shame, but only because I would have been the first person in my family ever to go to university. The exams had been taken at least partly to please my father and now he didn't seem too interested, it wasn't a great sacrifice on my part not to go although I did become stuck here, in a way. At the time it saved me from having to think about what to do with my life. Just take over the Jack Cade, keep it going and keep quiet. Most people thought the story was moonshine – they imagined, probably still do, that Aylwin was mine and I'd gone off after Sally to hide the pregnancy from Mum and Dad. We've still no idea who his father is.'

'That's very sad for him. Do you mourn the lost opportunities as much as you mourn Sally?' Ollie draped his arm again about Rosie's shoulders. 'The father gave her money? Did Michael keep it himself?'

'I try not to think about what might have happened.' She sighed and leant back and there it was again, that deeply delicious smell of warm, clean Ollie. 'I suppose it does seem tragic and it was, at the time, very. But there was this gorgeous baby and perhaps Sally *wouldn't* have made a very good mother ...? I don't know how much money there was. I hope it was better for Aylwin to grow up here, and at least *he's* got his degree. I got an awful lot out of that – I became a parasitic learner, used to feverishly read his books and essays in the vacations to see what I'd missed and drive him nutty with questions.'

'And your husband?'

She considered him seriously for a moment over the rim

of her cup, her nose wrinkling as if at the sudden recall of a sour smell.

'Ben was a catastrophe. Have you never married?'

'No. I was in love with the wrong person for a long time, love unrequited, and wasted more time with silly affairs.'

'Is that habitual, having silly affairs? Did the women with whom you were having them take them so lightly too?' Rosie's voice was anxiously sharp. It made him sit up and think.

'No, it isn't habitual, and perhaps some of them took them seriously. I always did, at the start.'

'Oh. Good. Are you still flat-hunting?'

'I saw one this morning, before going to work. I'm not too fussed about where I live, but there was something architecturally inarticulate about the place. You had to climb into the sink to open the kitchen window and a fitted wardrobe in the bedroom blocked the view. It was large enough to house the ball-gowns of a complete formation dancing team. Everything was smothered in pale mock wood, even the lavatory seat, and the walls were covered with pale, fake woodgrain paper. The estate agent was pale and fake as well.'

'From your description it sounds as if you mind very much indeed where you live. So you didn't whip out your cheque book?'

'Well, I haven't time to be too picky. It would only be a temporary base, till something better turned up. Getting out of Tunbridge Wells fast is an imperative.'

A sudden breeze tickled the poplars and sent the last few pale petals from the apple trees fluttering down to the sun-blotched grass. Rosie suddenly asked if he would care to rent their guest room instead, which totally flummoxed Ollie.

'I could let you have a very reduced rate and still be making more than from the occasional B and B guest. We don't exactly have one hundred percent occupancy. You could rent it weekly and then, if you couldn't stand us and needed more privacy, you could clear off if you wanted to with no questions asked. And vice-versa.'

She leant forward, out of the curving shelter of his arm, and calmly poured more tea, not looking at him as she offered this, as if quite unaware of any ambiguous possibilities. Was the proposal for more than just the room? She left him to wonder for a few seconds before clarifying the situation, looking up, eyes large and apparently quite innocent, but pursing her lips in an attempt to suppress a wild giggle.

'That is *all* that's on offer for now, Ollie. Just the room and breakfast, and supper if you want it. I've got bookings till after the Bank Holiday, till after the Games. Then there's nothing till July. We could see how we all got on and reassess the situation then?' She meticulously fished a greenfly out of his tea before passing it to him with a smile that promised much.

Ollie decided to take what was offered thankfully, although he was unsure if he could cope with living in the bosom of such an idiosyncratic group of people. And would they be able to cope with him?

'Would your family accept the idea? I mean, I'd love it, but . . .'

'Aylwin would growl a little, but he'd soon get used to it. We now find it quite normal to breakfast with strangers, and you wouldn't be a stranger to them for long. Elvira, the Elfin Sempstress, wouldn't mind at all. She'll pounce on your shirts and turn the collars and cuffs, should any of them be threadbare and in need of it. She's probably the only person of her age in England who knows how to do it or would consider it worth doing. And dear Janice would be delirious. She's convinced you are the mysterious keeper of a Sad Secret, something Arthurian and romantic, and is determined to winkle it out!'

Ollie blenched. He'd have to keep an eye on Janice. But it all seemed apt, immediate. There was not much more he wanted out of life now than to be near Rosie. That problem was solved and there only remained the more pressing one of how to tell her . . .

'Yes, I'd like to take you up on it. It's obviously the only way I'll get to see enough of you.'

'You won't see me for dust till after the Games and . . .' she stopped, tantalisingly, and continued briskly '. . . I really must get a bit more phoning done now. It's looming horribly near and someone's coming in half an hour to go over the route of the Over-Seventies Cross Country Run.'

'Good Lord! Will they actually be running?'

'It doesn't matter if they run or crawl. Some will undoubtedly scamper, since the prize is a bottle of malt whisky. We're spending most of Friday and Saturday setting up the show. Do you know, there are thirty people working on this in some capacity or another? You will come to the Games, won't you? On Sunday, when they open?'

'I'd not miss it for the world. What time does it start?'

'Midday, but the heats of one or two events are earlier as we have so many would-be competitors. We're praying the weather will hold. Elvira and Janice went out yesterday evening to propitiate the weather gods with a pint of Green & Croswell's bitter, but there was a heavy shower immediately afterwards, diluting it even further, so perhaps the gods weren't too impressed.'

Ollie could feel the bodily warmth emanating from her, desired her deeply and incoherently seized the moment.

Janice had been watching with a proprietorial eye from the kitchen window. She had perceived Ollie's strangled, pavane-like courtship, the heads retreating and advancing as they sat with their backs to her on the bench, and found the tension quite unbearable. She washed up the same cup at least three times but was at last rewarded, felt a sudden rush of blood to the head when she looked up again and saw that Ollie had engulfed Rosie and appeared to be kissing her goodbye rather passionately. Most people find it easier to share other people's despair rather than their happiness. Janice was not one of them, and she was unaware of the prosaic nature of their conversation.

'If I gave you some Games posters ...' Rosie was saying, disentangling herself and shaking both with helpless laughter and an urgent and complicated desire both to enjoy and postpone '... and some drawing pins, would you be able to cover a few telegraph poles on your way home?'


The weather gods must have been appreciative of the libation after all since the sun rapidly burned through the early-morning mist on Sunday morning and all was fair. Elvira was trying to memorise her schedule whilst helping Nest and Lucinda set up the plant stall. Twelve till one, on the main gate with Sam Dicken; one till three, participating in the Ladies' Dyke Vaulting; three till five, helping, or rather supervising, Ossie with the Children's Dinosaur Hunt.

Aylwin was testing the public address system with Rush and the last of the vans and lorries were arriving. Rosie had been lent a classic Lambretta scooter and after decorating it with a couple of bunches of pink tulips from the pink tulip mine, put-putted backwards and forwards between the two fields, trouble-shooting, yelling instructions and thoroughly enjoying herself. In half an hour the public would start to arrive.

'Rosie, Rosie! Stop!' Sam Dicken panted, waylaying her. 'We've got a major problem! A truck's just driven up with a caravan — a dirty old trailer on its last legs — and parked it right across the entrance!'

'Well, get him to move, then.'

'He's uncoupled and driven off, leaving it there. And another one's done the same at the exit, further up the lane.'

'Forget the exit for the moment. We're trying to get people in, not out. Where's your tractor?'

'In the main field.'

'Quick! Off you go and get it — barge through a hedge if you have to. We can tow it away ourselves.' That it was deliberate sabotage, Rosie had no doubt.

✳      ✳      ✳

Vicky parked her car by Middhaze churchyard and marched through the grazing sheep and flax fields bordering the lane till she found a place from which she could view the pretty summer scene at a discreet distance, sheltered behind a hawthorn bush. Unmoved by the little pennants flapping gaily on the tents and the frenetic activity of the organizers, she peered through Paddy's racing binoculars and gloated as the sun glinted on the windscreens of the cars starting to pile up in the lane. The jam was threatening to tail back out on to the main road.

She picked out Rosie Hooke on a flower-bedecked scooter, riding slowly down the line of traffic, stopping and speaking to each driver. She watched, quivering with excitement as cars began to turn about in an adjacent gateway and leave. She couldn't quite see the actual blockage from that point, because of the angle of the hedge and the poplar trees, but was hopeful of its taking at least an hour or so to unravel, by which time a great many of the public would have become bored and driven away. There was a tractor, followed by a police car, squeezing their way past the line of cars; a lot of waving and to and fro-ing. Beside herself with glee, Vicky congratulated herself on her expertise in causing havoc.

Paddy would never admit that she had confessed, she thought smugly, should anyone try to point the legal finger at her, and Ollie wouldn't dare stoop so low as to implicate her, being implicated himself. In any case, there was no proof whatsoever. The police should by now be getting thoroughly miffed with their repeated visits to the Jack Cade. Its name would be mud. What a shame it wasn't raining.

'Hello, Vicky.'

The voice was quiet and familiar but she leapt about two feet in the air.

Ollie stood there, hands in his pockets, hostile.

'You're quite visible from the lane, you know. I saw the sun flashing on your bins as I drove up it. Are you watching a race? A shooting stick, I do believe! How comfortable you've made yourself. Have you brought a picnic as well?'

'Turncoat!' she spat out at him, accurately.

'You just couldn't keep away, could you? I think you would be wise to leave. Rosie has called the police, local reporters are about and they just may accept her version of events if she doesn't receive some sort of explanation from you soon. You've gone a bit too far, don't you think? Your dangerous-looking henchmen are parked up beside your car at the churchyard. I expect they're waiting for the pay-off.'

He turned on his heel.

'You know all about pay-offs, don't you?' she screeched after him. 'If you shop me, I'll pull you into it as well!'

He didn't turn but flapped a hand dismissively in the air at her, to signify that he couldn't care less, and went on his way. She watched him striding away, regretted the beautiful hair, the well-shaped body and the old friendship, almost hated herself for an instant before packing up and returning to face the two gypsies she had hired, sitting heavily on the bonnet of her car in the sunshine, smoking.

Earlier Ollie had approached the Jack Cade from the other end of the lane and had driven past Vicky's empty car. On arriving at the inn and seeing the tractor preparing to remove the first of the trailers, he'd found Janice and given her a message for Rosie. Rush was now ringing round likely relatives in an effort to obtain George Croswell's private telephone number. Janice was walking self-consciously back down the line of traffic with a large basket on her arm, explaining and apologizing to the waiting drivers and handing them each a free tulip and the injunction to 'Remember, flower power moves mountains'. The cars moved forward at last but it hadn't been an auspicious start to the Games.

*     *     *

Fiammetta squeaked instructions through a megaphone to the tug-of-war team from Fingle and then repeated them in French to the mighty team from Calais, both of whom were somewhat distracted by large blonde Maria bouncing up and down at the front of the crowd, waving her knickers in the air. Fiammetta ordered them to start pulling as soon as Rush's hand went down.

'*Tirez!*' she shrieked, and suddenly opposite her, through the horizontally straining bodies of the sweating teams, their boot heels digging desperately into the green turf as their coaches exhorted them to further and further effort, she caught sight of Ollie with Rosie. He was a striking-looking man in any case, and she hadn't forgotten his face since that dinner party, nor how noticeably chummy he had seemed to be with Vicky Croswell. Now he had an arm around Rosie and Fiammetta was instantly suspicious. Between bouts of shrieking and tugging, she grabbed Rush, busily fitting his Frog-hoppers into little yellow life jackets, and told him that she thought Rosie ought to be warned.

Rosie, ambushed on her own behind the beer tent, breezily admitted she already knew of their acquaintance but was shaken by Fiammetta's insistence that there had appeared to be rather more between Vicky and Ollie than that. Confronted with these suspicions, Rosie desperately pointed out that it was Ollie who'd warned them of Vicky's snooping that morning, and he who had undertaken the valuing and auctioning of the statue, and he would hardly be doing all that if he were in cahoots with Vicky, would he?

And it was Ollie of whom she was growing increasingly fond, she thought, near to tears, as she set out again to find him again amongst the ambling spectators, searching frantically up and down. She heard the cheers as the middle-aged vicar in red braces embroidered with 'Glory Be To God' in emerald green, in a triumph of faith over brawn, again out-manoeuvred younger and more powerful men in the hay-bale tossing competition.

She was held up by the necessity of uniting a lost child with its father before at last unearthing Ollie, at his ease in the shady tea tent.

He took one look at her face, white, angrily desperate, and was alarmed enough to drop his slice of walnut cake. He knew that whatever was distressing her, it concerned him. She sat down untidily, jogging the table and splashing his coffee.

'Why didn't you tell me you were Vicky's lover?'

'That was before she married.'

'You aren't now, then?'

'No.'

'But she's the person you were talking about, when you said you'd been in love with someone for a long time? Why didn't you tell me?'

'I thought you'd imagine I was on the rebound and not take me seriously.'

'And you *did* have something to do with all these annoyances we've been subjected to?'

'Only the very first, the men who turned out the electricity and made a mess of the party. After that I realized the whole thing was quite out of order and broke off diplomatic relations. I can't explain how she gets people under her thumb so easily without making myself look more ridiculous than I do already, and you wouldn't believe me. I'm very ashamed and very sorry. I've been trying to make it up to you since then, and wanting to tell you about it, but I was scared you wouldn't have anything more to do with me. I've had *nothing* to do with her since. Nothing to do with the dead chicken, or the farce at the gates this morning. I promise you, Rosie. Please, you must believe me?'

Rosie, her face taut and throat gritty with vexation, suddenly stamped her foot in annoyance. 'I'm *trying* to believe you, but I can't, quite. It all seems so childish. I want some time to think about it.'

'Rosie, please ...'

'I must get on. Prizes to present. Shoulders to pat. Boots

to lick.' She was distant, not at all reassured. 'I'm doing this because I can't imagine ever living anywhere else. I'm doing it because I *have* to pay that money back before they call in the loan. I want something to leave Aylwin, who's missed out on real parents . . .'

'Rosie, if I could find Michael Godley, try to recoup the money you should have had . . .'

'What difference do you suppose that would make?'

'Proof that I didn't want to deceive you, that I want to help you stay in the Jack Cade.'

'Oh, do what you like! I can't cope with this now.'

She left him sitting there miserably. He retrieved the uneaten walnut cake from the ground, but it had lost its half-walnut and was now redecorated with blades of dried grass.

# Chapter Twelve

Late on Monday morning, just as the smell of roast lamb with garlic and rosemary was beginning to circulate around the house of Mr and Mrs George Croswell, the phone rang. His wife, Mary, was out in the garden picking mint so George reluctantly answered it; it was a relative of Vicky's, an angry but controlled Kadely. It being a Bank Holiday, George was almost tempted to leave the troublesome matter till the next day; however, the import of the call was most disturbing and spoiled his lunch.

It was the second call that caused him to make the decision to visit the Jack Cade immediately. It came as he sat in the drawing-room with his feet up, gently digesting the lamb and the soggy *tarte tatin* which had followed it, and worrying about Paddy and Vicky whilst trying to finish the Saturday prize crossword in the *Telegraph*.

The second caller had been unknown to him, a polite young chap called Potter who had instantly caused further digestive disturbances by mentioning Sally Craddock. Mercifully Mary was again out in the garden and George swung his feet to the floor, abandoned number 23 across and sat stiff with apprehension, making tooth marks in his gold pen whilst fighting to recall events which had occurred more than twenty years before.

Half an hour later, after trudging round the sizeable gardens calling for Mary and finding her at last, silently throwing food to the carp in the pond quite close to the house, he explained he was going out for a drive. She was in one of her moods, merely nodded uninterestedly and went on carefully aiming chunks of greasy grey crumpet at the great bronze fish. He drove to the silent brewery, re-acquainted himself with the Jack Cade file and rang first Paddy, then the inn. Mrs Hooke wasn't available to be spoken to at that moment, since she was 'out in the field, coracle racing'.

A series of possible options bleated through his brain like sheep as he walked back to the Rover. He clearly remembered the area manager and accounts department bringing the Hookes' erratic mortgage repayments to his notice and the untoward nostalgia which had swept over him, causing him to insist that the Jack Cade should be given a certain amount of leeway.

A car behind hooted impatiently as he day-dreamed at the traffic lights in Bellhurst and he jumped nervously and drove on through the heavy holiday traffic towards Romney Marsh, his emotional turbulence steadily increasing.

He was dismayed by the large makeshift signs strung out along the new road advertising 'The Games at the Jack Cade – First Turning Left' and, on taking the first turning, to find No Parking cones along the lane and some sort of one-way system in force. He was assured by a young official that the inn was closed and its car park full. It was only after parting with a fiver in exchange for a map and a schedule of events that he was allowed into the overflowing car park in the field. How to find Rosie Hooke?

He carefully scrutinised the map but couldn't make head or tail of it and plodded off, asking along the way if anyone had seen Rosie. There was a friendly, carnival atmosphere amongst the drifting crowds and he could detect careful organisation beneath the colourful chaos but he wished he'd brought his panama, since the sun was frying his scalp through his thinning hair. Lost, he wandered towards a small group that had congregated near a white tape, pointing and applauding. A quick glance over his shoulder satisfied him that he wasn't in the way of an obstacle race, but as he ambled up to them, his hand was seized and pumped up and down and there was polite clapping.

'Well *done*, sir. That's a magnificent time!'

'What? I'm so sorry, what time?'

'The Over-Seventies Cross Country. You're first in!'

'No! I'm not racing. I'm not even over seventy. I'm just trying to find Mrs Hooke.'

There was general disappointment and the applause petered out. He was redirected to where a gathering of wild-haired young people in life jackets were jumping up and down on the edge of a dyke and cheering, and a pretty little dark girl with a clipboard and long wet hair stared flatteringly hard at him. Hot and very bothered, he asked again where he might discover Rosie.

'Sarah's just fishing her out now,' said the dark girl. 'Her coracle sank. Some of the contestants decided to fight dirty in the last race.'

She took an already sopping towel from the trestle table beside her and hurried forward as a lightly built woman in red, soaked and laughing, was hauled up the bank.

'Canute holed me below the waterline with a penknife! Bloody Vikings! Can't behave anywhere!'

'Rosie Hooke?' George stepped towards her and croaked: 'Rosie, I know this is an inopportune moment, but I have to speak to you. I'm George Croswell.' Was that a venomous hiss, or merely an intake of breath from the girl behind him?

Rosie carried on drying her face whilst staring at him with Sally's darkly intense, interested eyes. Muddy water streamed from her elbows and trickled from her trouser bottoms, but she seemed not at all abashed by her appearance.

'Good afternoon, George,' she said, holding out a wet hand. 'It's not inopportune but I have to go and change. I'd been expecting you to get in touch in any case. Come back to the house.' The voice was cool, but then he could hardly expect favour after what had taken place.

'How do you mend those things?' he asked as they crossed the plank bridge into the garden, the one where he had sat years before, entranced and besotted with her sister Sally.

'The coracles? They're easy to patch, I'm told by the experts. All you need is some canvas and pitch.'

He sat on a bench beneath the shady mulberry and waited for her, wishing that affairs between the brewery and Rosie might be so easily healed. A tall young man with spectacles and curly blond hair ducked out of the back door, carrying a tray full of bright little trophies, the cheap and cheerful kind acquired by the winners of darts or quiz matches. George's feet grew heavy, rooted themselves in the ground, and his stomach fluttered unbearably but he swallowed and said nothing. Then Rosie returned, swiftly showered down and freshly dressed in another red top and a long green skirt.

The next ten minutes were very, very difficult for George. He was unused to apologizing, particularly for the behaviour of a member of his own family, but he managed, since he knew that the apologies were the easier part and what was to come was worse.

Rosie sat rigidly still as he spoke, concentrating on his wavering words.

'I hope you didn't think, at any time, that Green & Croswell had anything to do with it?'

'It crossed my mind, but I'm sure now that Vicky was operating on her own because she wanted to buy the place on the cheap.'

Now began the painful part. The Potter fellow, in a chatty sort of way and without the hint of a threat, had informed George of past happenings concerning the delicious but troublesome Miss Sally Craddock. He had also informed him that Rosie, now widowed herself, had no idea who Aylwin's father was and that he would leave it to George to tell her; but George had been left in little doubt that she *would* be told anyway, should he fail to do so.

George now slowly explained that Sally's marriage, her death, the fact that her husband had walked off with the five thousand pounds with which he himself had so generously provided Sally for the child's upbringing, had all been unknown to him. Sally had never got in touch with him again for which he had been profoundly, and selfishly, grateful and although he had never forgotten her enchanting little face, he had never dared visit the Jack Cade again. He had expunged as far as he was able all thoughts of his baby, which he had only visited that one time, in Poole, when Sally had conveniently forgotten to tell him she now had a husband.

Rosie appeared to swallow all this and still sat quietly, as if awaiting further revelations.

George had been following the line of thought that as the boy still lived with her (there was no doubt in his mind that it was his own son he had seen walking across the garden) there was no possible way now that the brewery could turf them out of the place, but neither could he scrub out the loan without the most embarrassing questions being asked. There would be whispering amongst the staff. Paddy would obviously have to know and then probably Mary would find out too. But perhaps it would be best if they did, and perhaps it could be kept within the family.

Now that Vicky had made such a pig's ear of the whole business, he could, as Chairman, suggest that Green & Croswell should recompense the Jack Cade for the trouble caused, perhaps by extending the deadline of the loan as long as was necessary?

He outlined the offer to Rosie, who was still struggling to assimilate the implications of this new thread to the story. She rapidly came to the conclusion that, as far as the Jack Cade was concerned, the implications of Aylwin's parentage were all beneficial but George wasn't going to get away so lightly. She gazed at the aged version of Aylwin sitting opposite her, his eyes tight shut, and was highly amused.

'The resemblance between you is striking enough, I agree. Shall I tell you what would really help us?'

'Please do.'

'I want the tie removed now, the barrelage tie. It goes anyway, once the money is paid back.'

'That's business, I am afraid, dear girl.'

'It's my business too, and Aylwin's. If you remove it now, and I imagine it is within your power, as part of your compensation to us for stress and lost business through your daughter-in-law's interference, and with the extended deadline, we could pay it back within eight months, without having to wear ourselves into the ground organising events like this.'

George folded immediately.

'Right. I get your point. I'll see to it. Now, how shall we approach Aylwin?' He looked doubtfully at her, and she felt just a little sorry for him. 'After what's happened I don't expect he will be too pleased to find he's a Croswell? Even if he's upset, I'd like to make sure he's all right financially.'

'Leave it to me. Then he can make up his own mind. You could probably make a start by paying off a portion of the horrendous student loan he built up while at university, but we'll have to discuss it later in the week. It's four-thirty and I have to go and present prizes with Fiammetta.'

'I would, of course, appreciate it if none of this came out publicly.'

'I bet you would. But unlike your daughter-in-law, we're not vindictive. We won't tell. I can see it wouldn't be any good for Aylwin if we were at daggers drawn.'

'Thank you, Rosie. I'm getting old and need to tie up all the loose ends.'

So Aylwin was a mere loose end, was he? Tying up loose ends was a luxury most of them could not afford. Even so, as George left, Rosie had a satisfying mental picture of the whizzing balls in a pinball machine dropping into one high-scoring pocket after another.

George Croswell poked his head, which was full of disturbing

visions, tentatively round the greenhouse door. His legs felt
strangely shaky inside the dark and musty folds of his corduroy
trousers. He put a hand out to touch a large earthenware pot of
lemon verbena, as if to earth himself. It was very humid inside and
smelt strongly of tobacco as well as tomato plants. It was not the
kind of peaceful Bank Holiday weekend he had hoped for.

His wife was not potting up plants but sitting on a bench
in the lotus position, smoking and reading a tatty green Virago
paperback.

'George,' she said, looking up absently and speaking more
as if she were reminding herself of his name than replying. She
was not allowed to smoke in the house. The greenhouse was her
hiding place. He was intruding. Her grey hair was untidy and her
round brown eyes looked reproachful and, as so often these days,
slightly dotty.

'Mary.' He gave a little dry cough. 'There's something I've
been meaning to tell you . . .'

She stubbed the cigarette out in a yellow plastic mini-growbag
full of little hot red-pepper seedlings and with a sigh laid the book
down. The two diamond rings sparkled warningly on her rough
and extensively earthy hands.

'You've been caught speeding? You've lost money on the
horses? You've been unfaithful again? Which is it? This is an
awfully good book and I'd like to get back to it.'

'Twenty-two . . . no, twenty-three years ago . . .'

'Oh, for God's sake, Georgie! Who cares what happened
twenty-three years ago? You can't have been "meaning" to tell
me something for all that time?'

'No, perhaps not. But now I have to, I think. Oh, hell! It's so
hot in here, and smoky, it makes me feel sick. Can't we go back to
the house or walk round the garden?'

'No, I like it here. I expect it's guilt-sick not smoke-sick. The
plants don't mind the smoke; it keeps away the whitefly.'

'I was unfaithful to you.'

'On numerous occasions. I know, and I'm not interested.'

'There's a child,' he said, stumblingly, still clinging to the rim of the verbena pot to retain his balance and closing his eyes tight. 'A boy ... I mean, no, not a boy now, a young man.' He blurted it out. 'He's called Aylwin.'

'What a ghastly name! I hope you didn't have anything to do with that? Does Paddy know?'

'No, of course not. Not yet.'

'What fun for you!' The voice was harshly jolly, the eyes deeply hurt. He looked at the ground, nudging a trowel under the bench with his foot.

'Are you being hounded for money?' she continued, brightly. 'Have you been blackmailed? Is that why you've suddenly decided to sick up?'

'No, nothing like that. But I am guilty of something else by implication and a certain sum of money might be considered proper recompense for trouble caused. It seems Vicky ...'

'I think you'd better start, after all, twenty-three years ago. It's obviously something I don't want to hear, particularly if our daughter-in-law is involved. I'm going to light another cigarette and this is my greenhouse, so I don't want any moans. Open the door again if you're so fussy.'

Having expected hysteria, he was relieved that Mary had taken it so phlegmatically, but one could never tell how she was going to react ... A few minutes later there was the sound of breaking glass from that overheated haven at the bottom of the garden.

'Where is it? Where ... ah, here we are.' Rosie discovered the receipt which Ollie had given her for the statuette, and phoned the number. The bar was empty. It was past eleven in the evening and he sounded sleepy.

'You found Michael Godley. How? How did you do it?

'He's been in touch then, George Croswell?'

'He shuffled over this afternoon. He's really rather a nice old boy, if a bit on the sly side. He kept sizing me up, testing to see how much he might get away with. It was the combination of the guilt over Aylwin together with fear, I think, of possible legal action and bad publicity, that finally made the old goat so amenable, although I didn't have to mention them. He's coughing up. We're nearly home.'

'What's that music? Are you having a post-Games party?'

'I'm not having it, but the others don't seem so exhausted. They're all outside, dancing in the garden. Ollie, I'm sorry I doubted you. Very abject indeed. We wouldn't have stood a chance if you hadn't poked him out of his hole with a sharp stick. How *did* you find out?'

'I'll tell you later. I'm fairly tired too. I couldn't sleep last night and Bournemouth was further than I thought.'

'Bournemouth? Oh, Ollie! Would you come on Wednesday after work, to have supper with us? You could move in then, if you still want to?' There was quaver in her voice, quickly overcome. 'Aylwin could come over to you, with the van, and help with your things. We've still got an immense amount of clearing up to do, and there are B and B people staying tonight. Tomorrow morning I'm visiting the brewery, to get our affairs sorted out. Ollie, I *am* sorry.'

'Of course I'll come! You've got nothing to be sorry about and I can't wait to see you. I'll ring you tomorrow to find out how the brewery imbroglio brogled out. Goodnight, my love.'

Rosie walked out across the dark and dewy grass and sat on the corner of a table amongst the guttering candles in jam jars where a surreal café-concert was taking place. Sarah and Rollo had staggered home but Geoff Pocket was still playing a melodeon while Tiger Bright lay across a bench, snoring. Amongst the twirling figures, a giggling Janice waltzed clumsily at arm's length with Ossie, enraptured by his long curls. The rusty black Brian sported a large cardboard gold medal specially made for him by Rosie, in recognition of his having been the originator of the Games. He had Amber raunchily clasped by the buttocks to his narrow loins and whispered in her ear as they shuffled round the mulberry in the semi-dark. Up in its branches, Elvira and Aylwin sat with a bottle of wine, their legs dangling, Elvira's bare and filthy feet lovingly rubbing Aylwin's.

Rosie remembered Ollie's feet and shivered. This, the Jack Cade, was just a place. An enchanted place maybe, but just a place.

I'm not a tree, she thought, hugging herself. I've got feet too, can get up and go. There are other places. The thought came to her that after all their efforts to help her stay, she knew now that it was possible to leave if she wanted to. She had been imprisoning herself in the past and it was Sally who'd finally unlocked her. I've snared myself again, by becoming beholden to so many people but perhaps, subconsciously, that was what I wanted?

A mobile phone whinged through the jigging music and the maudlin, treacherous thoughts. Rush, lying entwined with Fiammetta in the lush orchard grass, sat up abruptly and cursed in the dark.

'Turn it off, for God's sake,' said Fiammetta. 'It's probably Peregrine again.'


'Megan, Megan? Is that you, darling? I can't speak for long. I'm virtually under house arrest! I've been sitting in my father-in-law's stuffy office for the past hour, being shouted at. It's all too silly and Paddy's supporting him. All about this Jack Cade thing. I'm grieving deeply, not allowed to have it, and that friend of Janie's, who's so clever with gardens and helped draw up plans in advance, has just sent in her bill.

'George has given in to the awful Hooke woman, he says to compensate for my intimidation, and there's something else afoot which he won't tell me about. I mean, it was hardly harassment, was it? I never asked anyone to murder her effing chicken. It's all quite out of proportion and now I'm under lock and key with nothing to look forward to. No, of course not, you dope. I'm not *literally* locked in. But George had the brewery's pompous old solicitor sitting there this morning, waiting to explain what a naughty girl I'd been and how I could have brought the good name of the brewery into disrepute, and that it was only thanks to Rosie Hooke that no action was being taken. The only thing one can do at times like that is imagine them sitting there without their trousers. It takes the mind off what they're saying wonderfully. And the worst thing, by far the worst, was that the Hooke woman was waiting downstairs to visit George as I left. She saw me and smiled, just like a smug tortoiseshell cat. Bloody Rush Kadely is in the thick of it somewhere. How I loathe them all!

'Have you seen Peregrine recently? No? Paddy's taking a couple of weeks' holiday early and we're going to Scotland on Friday so as, he says, I can't "interfere with the Jack Cade while the legal work's being sorted out". Paddy's in trouble too, for not telling his papa what I was allegedly up to. I mean, he's a grown man. He's sulking too. It'll be utterly mizz. And, trouble upon trouble, Cressie's here. Paddy had to go and fetch her from school after the row at the brewery. She's been sent home for sniffing deodorant. I thought she was old enough to know one sprays it under one's arms, not up one's nose. Yes, we'll have to take her with us and tramp about the hills. As Paddy's not speaking to me it'll be company of a sort. Ollie still isn't speaking to me either. He's gone to ground. Oh, Megan! I miss him dreadfully. Well, there's house hunting to look forward to again when we get back . . . Oh, must you go? Right. If you should see Ollie while I'm away . . . 'Bye, Megan.'

Vicky put the receiver down and started to cry.


On Wednesday evening Ollie and Rosie sat in the vegetable patch, between the ranks of onions and the fresh green spinach, catching the last rays of the sun in that part of the garden. The legs of the blue chairs brought out from the kitchen sank into the soft earth as they talked, a bottle of wine on a tray at their feet.

Ollie sat astride his chair facing Rosie, his arms resting

along its back as he told her the tale. He had foolishly driven directly from the Games on Sunday afternoon to Poole, with little clear idea of how he would proceed when he arrived and only remembering as he booked into a small hotel that the next day was a bank holiday.

'I realized that the places which would be most useful for tracing a previous inhabitant, libraries and town halls, would be shut. I spent a miserable night sweating between nylon sheets in a room with an unopenable window and drove around rather hopelessly next morning, unable to think straight, then sensibly turned and headed back to Kent. I thought if you and your parents had been unable to track him down so soon after the event, what hope did I have twenty-two years later?'

'We didn't try so very hard. We were mourning Sally, and it would have been difficult, you see, to follow up about the money without letting my parents know all the facts . . . I never told them that Aylwin wasn't Michael's.'

'Of course. Anyway, it's tempting to make out how arduous the quest was, the swinging across bottomless chasms on lianas and the swimming through raging torrents chased by wallabies, but I found him quite accidentally. I pulled up at a petrol station this side of Bournemouth to refuel, paid at the desk and asked for a receipt. There it was, printed across the top in large red letters: Michael Godley Garages. I let out such a howl of delight that I terrified the cashier witless but after some cajoling, she rang him and delivered my message. He agreed to meet me at midday at a pub a mile or so away.'

'He must have been completely astounded. It's difficult to remember his face. What's he like?'

'Big, gingery and prosperous, very prosperous, and also amiable. We got on rather well. He admitted to using the money Sally had had from Croswell Senior to buy into a small partnership in a garage. He's obviously done very well since then. He drinks Pernod and drives the latest Jag. He's married again, but although his wife knew he was a widower, she doesn't know anything else and he would rather keep it that way. So he told me what I wanted to know: that Aylwin's father was the managing director of the brewery that then owned the Jack Cade. Randy old George! I was so stunned I nearly fell off the stool.'

Ollie drained his glass and carefully put it down on the tray. He looked at Rosie and held out his hands.

'The best bit – shall I tell you the best bit now?'

'If you don't,' said Rosie, her glorious voice quite throaty with fondness, 'I'll roll you in the onions.'

'Michael Godley has an extremely guilty conscience, which is not something one usually associates with car dealers, is it? He asked me to let you know that he'll pay back the money. Don't expect any interest on it, but I'm quite certain he'll do as he says. I rather over-egged the pudding, telling him what poverty-stricken years you'd suffered and how valiantly you've been fighting to save your livelihood and how Aylwin's turned out a credit to you. He wants to come over one day and show off his flash car.'

Rosie got up and indicated she wanted to sit on Ollie's knee, which pleased him mightily, although the chair sank further into the ground.

'Do you lock your bedroom door? I don't want to make any more of a fool of myself by crashing about in the night.'

'Like Tom Jones in the inn at Upton? I've got a very old copy of *Tom Jones*. I'll find it for you when we go indoors, which we'll have to soon since Elvira and Aylwin will need help. Any more wailful choirs of small gnats and we'll have to make a run for it.'

'Aha! Keats, *To Autumn*. What a literary innkeeper! You didn't say about your door? I'm a bit older than Tom Jones and don't want to have to resort to an axe.'

'I don't lock it, not any more.'

'Did you tell the family about my involvement with Vicky?'

'No, and I won't. I don't want to undermine your authority.'

'What authority is that?'

'The authority I'm leaving you with, when I go sailing.'

'What! Leaving? Sailing? When?' Ollie sat up straight and she almost slipped off his knee, clutching him around the neck. The dozy grey eyes suddenly snapped awake, startled and anxious, even jealous.

'Next weekend. Canute has invited me, as he always promised. I'm joking about the authority. Everything is taken care of. It's only for a week. I'm very fond of Canute; he's an old man and not in good health; perhaps it'll be his last trip to France. He's taking two others with him as well, Ruthless Rush and Fiammetta the Suspicious. They're taking a break to get away from Peregrine the Persistent. Canute needs me to go, and although the timing's poor from our point of view, I want to go too. The inn is virtually safe and there's some considering to be done about its future. Could you hold on a little tighter? I'm sliding off again. I want to return with a clear head and make decisions. The auction will have taken place then and we'll find out if our gilded saint has helped us.' She breathed softly into his ear. 'It's strange, but after these few weeks, I'm in the mood for something more challenging.'

'I wouldn't dream of trying to stop you. You deserve a holiday.' Ollie considered her closely, his head on one side, eyes narrowing. 'How old did you say Canute was?'

'I didn't say anything about his age, but you really don't need to worry, since he's a very ancient mariner.'

'How do I know you'll come back? Will you hate to leave me?'

'I haven't been to bed with you yet.' Rosie's eyes positively glittered with amusement and expectation. 'I'll tell you in the morning.'

'You're appalling!'

'You deserve it. Pass the wine.'


Through the open back parlour window came the sound of a crash and a minute later Aylwin rushed out, calling for them to come. Janice had at last seen the child, and fainted.